JA...

# WALK

HODDER

First published in Great Britain in 2022 by Hodder & Stoughton
An Hachette UK company

This paperback edition published in 2023

2

A CIP catalogue record for this title is available from the British Library

Paperback ISBN 9781444790177
eBook ISBN 9781444790160

Typeset in Plantin Light by Palimpsest Book Production Ltd, Falkirk, Stirlingshire

Printed and bound in Great Britain by Clays Ltd, Elcograf S.p.A.

Hodder & Stoughton policy is to use papers that are natural, renewable
and recyclable products and made from wood grown in sustainable forests.
The logging and manufacturing processes are expected to conform
to the environmental regulations of the country of origin.

Hodder & Stoughton Ltd
Carmelite House
50 Victoria Embankment
London EC4Y 0DZ

www.hodder.co.uk

*For Schulze*

*Against the arduous march of time,*
*we walk*
*we run*
*we dance*
*we die*

> from 'Untitled' by Robert Crowther, as discovered in the opening cover of *Offa's Dyke Path: National Trail Guide*, in a box labelled: 'WALK'

# WALK

# I

*Prestatyn – The beach – Tourist art – Holiday
snaps – Stones – Rain – Shit Guinness – Uphill
struggles – Spare change – 'Fail to prepare . . .' –
Roman helmet – More uphill struggles –
The view – The Countryside Code.*

It's a bright morning when they first set off but by the time their train pulls in, the sky has dulled and there are dark clouds over the mountains. Benny checks his phone – already one o'clock. No new messages. He switches it off. He sips from his flask. He watches the station approach and braces himself for its final jolt. Stephen is sleeping opposite, his face against the glass. He doesn't appear to even feel the jolt. Benny has to shake at his knee to wake him.

They retrieve their packs from the luggage rack and step out onto the platform. There are a few old ladies still departing so Benny leads Stephen over to the benches, out of the way. They hoist the packs onto their shoulders, bind themselves in the various straps – fastening clips, tightening buckles. There's a slight breeze. It isn't raining yet, but it will soon, and Benny can't help but glance at the sky. They'd better hurry down to the beach, he says. They have to start at the beach because they have to collect a stone from there, which does mean walking a mile from the mountains and doubling back, but Benny says it's worth it. There's no point in doing something like this unless they're willing to do it right.

They set off down the road towards the beach. It's mostly semi-detached houses here, although there are also a couple of shops, fronts cluttered with buckets, spades, half-inflated rubber rings. Further down there's a children's play area, a crazy golf course. There aren't many people about, just the occasional dog walker. Stephen coughs. At one point he spits on the ground.

3

He's pale. It's possible he's hung-over. He often stays up late working on his art and this usually involves alcohol. Benny asks if he's OK and Stephen nods and they leave the conversation at that for now, concentrate on walking.

The wind is stronger down at the beach, the sky brooding. There's a hut signposted with a blue plastic '*i*'; two larger buildings with the words 'CAFÉ' and 'AMUSEMENTS' on the side in huge black letters, as if to be read from out at sea. Waves lick the sand. There's a thin band of fog on the horizon. Benny says he can't think of a word to describe this, the view. Stephen says the word is *grim*.

To the right of the buildings there's a patch of concrete with a sculpture in the centre. It's approximately fifteen feet tall and consists of three silver pillars supporting a silver disk, glittering through the grimness. Benny knows it's a sculpture because of the photos and the brief description in the guidebook. According to the book the sculpture indicates the end of the walk, as most people take the path south to north, but they're walking north to south, so for them it's the very beginning. What the sculpture is supposed to *be*, Benny isn't entirely sure. According to the guidebook, the locals call it 'the Polo Mint'. Stephen says it's a bad sculpture. He describes it as 'tourist art'.

They let their packs slide. Stephen retrieves his camera and takes photos. *Click* and *wind, click* and *wind*. There's a sense of irony, he says, that's very powerful. Benny removes a pre-rolled cigarette from behind his ear, lights it. Stephen asks if he can have a cigarette too and Benny shrugs and gives him the one from behind his other ear and Stephen smokes whilst taking his photos, turning to blow over his shoulder, keep the smoke from drifting into shot. Stephen then tells Benny to come kneel in front of the sculpture for a photo. (Why not a few holiday snaps too?) *Click* and *wind*. Stephen flicks away what's left of his cigarette, gives Benny the camera and kneels in front of the sculpture whilst Benny takes a photo of him. Then they place the camera on a wall and Stephen sets the auto-time function and runs over to kneel beside Benny and the camera clicks a photo all by itself: the two of them together, kneeling in front of the statue, smiling.

4

They search for stones. The idea is they each pick a stone from the beach then, in a couple of weeks' time, when they're at the end of the trail in Chepstow, they throw the stones back into the sea. It's not just the guidebook that says to do this, Benny's dad had mentioned it too, back when Benny was first planning the trip. So did Uncle Ian, when Benny phoned to ask about stopping off for a few days at Nan's old house in Llangollen. It's starting to rain and neither fancies the trek down to the beach, but there are stones about, scattered on the pavement, and they each find one they deem suitable. Stephen finds a large one, pointed. He says it reminds him of the pumice stone his mum uses on her corns. Benny's stone is flat, like a coin. A skimmer.

They pocket their stones. Benny picks up their cigarette butts and pockets them too, as there aren't any bins nearby. The rain's patter rises to a steady hiss. Benny says they should take shelter, there's no point being drenched from the off.

They hurry across the car park to the building labelled 'CAFÉ', packs slumped in their arms like brides over a threshold.

'Just listen to that rain, man . . . what a start . . .'

'Rain's rain, Ste. We'll just put on our macs. As long as it stops by sunset, we'll be OK.'

'Why sunset?'

'Sunset's when we set up camp. We don't want to set up camp in the rain.'

'Why not?'

'Because of the tent.'

'The tent? What'll happen to the tent?'

'It'll get wet.'

*Pause.*

'This Guinness, man. Even *Cal* wouldn't drink this. It's like the stuff at the Miners. Toilet water. *Watered down* toilet water.'

'Drink it. Contains iron. Keeps you strong.'

'It's bad enough I've paid for it, never mind having to drink it.'

'Think *iron*.'

*Pause.*

'How far today then?'

5

'Fifteen miles. Hopefully. If we make it past Bodfari I'll be happy.'

'Where'll we camp?'

'Here, look, there's some forest.'

'Forest?'

'I always wanted to camp in a forest.'

'Sounds good, man.'

'We can light a fire. Cook. I brought flint.'

'Great photos in a forest. Shadows. Plenty of atmosphere if the light's right.'

'How are the pictures of the grimness?'

'Fantastic, I'm sure.'

'Can I see them?'

'Not until we're home. It's real film, so you need to wait for development. I don't buy into the whole digital thing.'

'*Real* film?'

'It's more organic.'

'Oh.'

'The development . . . it's an important part of the process. You can *feel* it, you know? Digital's so . . .'

'What?'

'*Clinical.*'

'Right.' *Pause.* 'Anyway, if we can make it to the forest I'll be happy.'

*Pause.*

'Was your mum OK this morning, Ben? In the car? She seemed quiet.'

'She's OK.'

'She didn't mind?'

'What?'

'Driving us to the station.'

'No, she didn't mind.'

'She still giving those Sunday school classes?'

'Yep.'

'Strange to think, isn't it? That that's how we first met, in those Sunday school classes . . .'

'I guess.'

'She'd probably get on with my mum. Not that my mum's *religious*, per se, but she's into all that spirituality stuff. Birth stones. Maybe we should set them up.'

'*Set them up?*'

'Yeah. Like, on a friendship date.'

*Pause.*

'We'll have to set off soon, rain or no rain. We'll just have to put on our macs.'

'I think I left mine.'

'What?'

'My mac. I think I left it in your mum's car.'

'You don't have your rain mac?'

'I did, but then I left it.'

'You left your rain mac?'

'I'll get another *en route*. There'll be camping shops, right? It's a shame, it was this old yellow raincoat from, like, *the nineties*. It was so dorky, man. It was amazing.' *Pause.* 'Has she been OK, your mum? You know, the past few months?'

'She's OK.'

'But even, you know . . .'

'She's fine.'

'It's weird how things have worked out, with us and our mums. They're in the same boat now, really. Maybe we really *should* set them up. I have a—'

'Wait. Listen.'

*Pause.*

'What?'

'You hear that?'

'What?'

'The rain.'

*Pause.*

'I can't hear any rain.'

'Exactly.'

They step out into the car park. The air is warm now, the clouds dispersing. A sunbeam breaks through, lighting the Polo Mint in a golden, almost heavenly glow. Benny checks his phone: still no signal. Even here, right on the coast. Shouldn't the signal be stronger here? Aren't those phone signal towers usually out at sea? No wait, that's wind turbines. There are a few of those, he notices now, rotating silently through the thin band of fog. Benny looks away. He has some associations with fog that he doesn't really want to fixate on. He's glad they're turning their backs on it, walking away from it.

Stephen has signal. He says his battery's low because he forgot to charge it last night, but apart from that his phone's working fine. Benny considers asking to borrow it, see if he can check his messages, but he decides against it. No social media, no contact with the outside world – that's the whole point, really, isn't it? To get away from all that. To be out here, in the world, *living* for a change, rather than scrolling through snapshots of other people's lives.

They head back uphill towards the station. There are more passers-by now: runners, mums with pushchairs, an old man on a mobility scooter. There are a couple more dog walkers, although Stephen avoids the dogs as best he can, at one point crossing to Benny's left-hand side when a German shepherd approaches on the right. They soon pass by the station again and continue up the main road through the centre of town. It's a small town and the buildings are low on the skyline and above them the mountains loom, adorned with patches of grass and forest and rock.

The shops are typical for a rural high street – charity shops, bookies, smaller versions of supermarket chains with 'local' or 'express' after their names. There aren't as many homeless as back in the city, but still Stephen spots a couple, slumped outside William Hill, and that's enough to start him off on one of his tirades about the government, managed decline, the systematic disenfranchise-ment of the working classes, etc., etc. He soon trails off. It must occur to him that ranting at Benny isn't going to be of much use. Benny's long used to blocking out Stephen's speeches, much in the same way he blocks out the homeless mantra of 'any spare change'.

They stop at a Tesco Express and Benny nips inside whilst Stephen waits with the packs. Everything is overpriced but he picks up a couple of small bottles of Evian, so they can refill their flasks. Water is a priority. They each have a 2-litre bottle of tap water stowed away but they need the flasks to keep hydrated along the way. A little further up they stop at a newsagent's. Stephen doesn't normally smoke but he says he will now because they're on holiday and this means Benny'll need more papers. But the newsagent's doesn't have papers, only packs of cigarettes or E-cig refills, and the process of rolling is just as addictive as the nicotine, so Benny buys a multi-pack of Mars bars instead. Chocolate = energy. Energy is a priority.

Benny keeps an eye out, but he doesn't see anywhere that might sell a rain mac. He doesn't mention it. The clouds have thinned now, the sun is glaring. The streets have that wet pavement smell, a smell Benny always associates with his childhood. His dad had a saying: *fail to prepare, prepare to fail,*\* although he'd have been the first to admit that fully preparing for a walk like this is almost impossible. British weather is insane, predictable only in its unpredictability.

At the top of the hill they cross a junction and continue up a residential street. There's no pavement here so they walk on the road and Benny has to keep checking over his shoulder, make sure no cars are approaching from behind. By now his stomach is churning. The Guinness has left a thick, metallic taste. He's got a slight headache, although that's nothing new (it seems like he's had the same slight headache for months). His shoulders are beginning to ache too, as are his calves and hamstrings. So far they've only carried the packs short distances – from their bedrooms to the doorway of their houses, or from the doorway of their houses to Benny's mum's car, or between the various trains at the various stations at which they've changed – and it's not until now, when they really *walk*, that they're forced to comprehend the awesome weight on their shoulders.

Benny glances up at the mountains. His gaze settles back on the laces of his boots.

Less than a mile from the beach and already they can hear each other's breathing.

———

---

\* I believe this is actually quite a common saying.

9

'I just think it's such a shame, man. To see them on the streets like that, y'know?'

'I know.'

'It's disgusting is what it is.'

'It's better than back home, though. There are only a few.'

'Still, you know. "A few" is a few too many.'

'I know.'

*Pause.*

'Can you *feel* that?'

'What?'

'That ache in the . . . what is that? The clavicle?'

'That's your shoulder, Ste.'

'Can you *feel* it though?'

'Don't know.'

'Can't you? It's like my arms are going to drop off.'

'It's good for you to ache.'

'I don't believe you.'

'Believe it or not, it's good.'

'It *kills*, man.'

'It'll make you a stronger person. Overall.'

*Pause.*

'Can we break soon?'*

They reach a bend at the top of the hill. There's a patch of grass ahead. Another sculpture: an enormous Roman helmet about the size of a small car, half buried in the grass. This sculpture isn't mentioned in the guidebook. Benny prefers it to the previous sculpture because he likes the thought of a giant Roman soldier wandering around the mountains searching for his helmet. He doesn't mention this because Stephen probably has a strong opinion about it one way or the other and Benny doesn't want

---

* The packs were heavy though. I think we were both shocked by the weight of them, especially that first day. We'd have had a whole different outlook without them. We would have felt so much . . . *freer*. I mean it, Ben, just imagine how differently things could have turned out if we weren't having to contend with such a sustained physical burden.

to get into a debate he will neither understand nor care about.

They sit. Benny eats a Mars bar. He offers one to Stephen, who refuses. (He's vegan.) Benny's sweating now, the chocolate is sticky in the heat. They each don their sunglasses. Stephen also puts on this green plastic sun visor he's brought, the kind old ladies or poker dealers wear in films. He says it's from Oxfam, two pounds, a steal. Almost every item of clothing Stephen owns has been purchased for reasons of irony. Benny's cargo pants are the type that zip off at the knees, but Stephen's wearing old school Adidas tracksuit bottoms and so he has to empty his pack to find his shorts – a pair of chequered golf shorts Benny's sure must have once belonged to an old man – and change right there in the open. Benny tells him it's something they'll have to get used to, getting changed outdoors, but he agrees to keep a look out for dog walkers.

Stephen crouches in the bushes behind the half-buried helmet. His default appearance is gaunt and pale but occasionally, in moments of embarrassment such as this, a burning redness blooms from the centre of his cheeks, spreading down his neck and the V of bare white chest his T-shirt fails to cover. Stephen's T-shirt is the same as he always wears: a white, baggy XXL with the sleeves hacked off, adorned with an iron-on transfer of a black and white photograph. Today's iron-on transfer is a human skeleton wearing a trilby hat. The transfers are always a variation on this theme, always involving the skeleton. He brought it back from university, one of those anatomical models that stand in the corner of science classes on TV shows. He uses it in all of his artworks. He spends more time with that skeleton than with any living human. Which, it occurs to Benny now, means he should probably know the difference between a shoulder blade and a clavicle.*

Once Stephen's changed, they take the steps to the right of the helmet, continue along a series of paths and lanes that lead them up the side of the cliff. Further up they arrive at a wooden staircase.

---

* Fair point.

Stairs are hard on their thighs; they have to lean forward into a slight squat to offset the weight of the packs. The stairs wind up through the trees to an opening: the cliffside path. There's an incline to their left and the town, far below, to their right. By this time the sun is blazing. The grass is steaming. Benny and Stephen are panting.

They let their packs slide to the ground and sit on them. They sip from their flasks. Benny eats another Mars bar. Benny used to stay at his nan's sometimes, as a child, and he'd sleep up in the spare room (his father's old bedroom), and that's where his uncle would usually have one of his model railways set up, and this is what the view from the cliffside reminds him of now – a model town complete with felt grass and tiny trees and perfectly constructed miniature houses; a train edging along its track.

The sun glistens over the flat grey bed of the sea.

'Wow, man. Check out that view.'

'I know.'

'Just check – it – *out*. So glad we decided to do this.'

'Yeah?'

'Yeah! Getting out here, in the wilderness. Back to nature.'

'Good, isn't it?'

'Yeah, man. Just nice to break the routine. You know, get out of the attic.'

'Yeah.'

'And the photos . . .'

'Right.'

'The *photos*, man. They're going to be awesome.'

'I can imagine.'

'I mean, just look at this *view*, man. Amazing.'

'I know.'

'It was a great plan. It's an adventure. That's what it is, an adventure.'

'I know.'

Stephen takes more photos. *Click* and *wind. Click* and *wind.* He says he's doing well, he's getting more shots than he thought he would. Hopefully they'll find a camera shop along the way and he can pick up some extra film.

Benny rolls a cigarette. Stephen asks if he can have one too, so Benny hands it over, then rolls himself another, and the two of them light up. Stephen never smokes a full cigarette, not all the way down to the filter. He never inhales either, just lets the smoke linger in his mouth a few seconds, then releases it into the air. Sure enough, after a few puffs he stubs what's left out on the grass, goes to flick it over the cliffside. Then he notices Benny glaring and apologises, asks what he should do with it. Benny says to just put it in his pocket until they find a bin. There's a set of rules called the Countryside Code, which they have to obey at all times. One of those rules is to leave no trace of your visit – i.e. no litter. Benny's brought plenty of plastic bags so there's no reason they can't carry their rubbish with them, dispose of it each time they spot a bin along the trail.

They lie back, still taking in the view. Stephen pulls the sun visor down over his face. Benny says not to get too comfortable. They can't stop for long. They need to make some real progress today to keep on schedule. Benny wants to be rid of the sight of the sea. He won't be happy until it's disappeared completely from the horizon.

# II

*Offa's Dyke – Signs – Changing views – Fields –
Stiles – Sheep shit – Uses for wool – Socks – An
overlooked erogenous zone – Greeting fellow
walkers – Fear of dogs – Stables – Horseshit –
Sunburn – Hangover – A desire for dullness – A
refusal to smoke – 'The Wall' – Initial walk plans
– Cal – Christine – Inviting Stephen – Dirt road
– Break – Sweaty back – A test of veganism
(failed) – Uncle Ian – Dad's protestations –
Noodle talk – A few more hours before sunset.*

The path they're following is Offa's Dyke, a man-made ditch
that once extended from one side of the Welsh coast to the other.
According to the guidebook, the dyke itself dates back to around
750 AD and is named after an Anglo-Saxon king. Its original
purpose is unknown, although it roughly follows the English-
Welsh border. Most walkers travel south to north, but Benny has
decided to go north to south. This is the direction his dad took
when he and Uncle Ian walked it all those years ago. Benny's
dad said that, aside from a few key landmarks (i.e. the Clywidian
Range and the tower up on Moel Famau), this stretch is by far
the most boring part, and so it's best to get it out of the way
first.

They continue along the side of the cliff for a mile before
veering off into the fields. There's a fair amount of hostile vegetation here – brambles, nettles, thorn bushes with branches
stretching out over the path – but Benny doesn't want to have
to stop and reattach the zippable bottoms to his trousers, best

to just grin and bear it. The grass is long and wet, squelching beneath their feet. Occasionally the path narrows and they're forced to slow, extra careful with their footing. Stephen keeps slipping in his Nikes, which have zero grip.

There are plenty of signposts: green plastic plaques with acorn symbols and arrows, pointing them in their desired direction. The acorn is the National Trails logo and as long as they look out for it and follow the signs then they're on the right path. Benny's dad brought back one of these plaques as a memento the first time he walked this trail. Benny found it in the loft, in the 'WALK' box. It seems unlikely his dad would have pried it from the signpost himself (he was a great believer in the Countryside Code). More likely he found it on the ground, deemed it litter, decided picking it up and taking it home was the best course of action. Either way, Benny has it with him, stowed in his pocket. Occasionally he reaches in to squeeze it, for luck.

They don't really need luck. Nor do they need signposts – Benny was reading the guidebook over breakfast and knows today's route off by heart. In fact, Benny's been reading the guidebook every day for the past few months and could probably recount the entire walk, each map and trail, coiled snake-like through the patches of fields and forests, rivers and mountains. In the guidebook white patches indicate fields and green patches forests. There are squiggly brown lines to signify the varying gradient of the terrain. The guidebook is a new edition; his dad bought it at the W H Smith in Liverpool on 19th September last year. Benny knows this because a few weeks ago he discovered the guidebook in the 'WALK' box and the receipt was still tucked away in the inside cover.

Stephen has no guidebook. Stephen's only preparations have been to buy and pack a cheap rucksack, and already he's managed to lose his rain mac. He doesn't even know which way south is. In fact, he hasn't even enquired as to the direction they're taking, or how Benny's been able to lead them so effortlessly. Benny can hear him now, his steady pants accompanying the squeak of his trainers.

Benny tries to concentrate on his own footsteps, his own breathing.

'Amazing, isn't it, Ben?' *Pant. Pant. Pant.*

'Huh?'

'The view.' *Pant. Pant. Pant.*

'Yep. Still amazing.'

*Pant. Pant. Pant.* 'You can see where we've walked from. Look.'

'Huh?'

*Pant. Pant.* 'Down there.' *Pant. Pant. Pant.*

'Yeah.'

'There's the station.' *Pant.*

'Yes.'

'And the beach.' *Pant. Pant.*

'Yep.'

*Pant. Pant. Pant.* 'Where do you reckon the café is, man?' *Pant. Pant.* 'The place with the shit Guinness?'

'I don't know.'

*Pant. Pant. Pant.* 'I think *that* might be it. That white building down there. Do you reckon that might be it?'

'I don't know, Ste.'

*Pant. Pant. Pant.*

'I might stop soon.' *Pant. Pant. Pant.* 'Take some photos.'

'You just took some, didn't you?'

'The view's changed.' *Pant. Pant.*

'I thought you wanted to preserve film?'

'Fuck it, man. The view's changed.' *Pant. Pant. Pant.*

'Well, why don't you wait till we reach the fields? We can stop for a bit then. The view'll be the same there. We need to get a few miles under our belt.'

'But the view's nice here.' *Pant. Pant.* 'The sun.' *Pant. Pant.* 'The clouds.' *Pant. Pant.* 'Very . . .' *pant*, 'photogenic.' *Pant. Pant. Pant.*

'We'll stop when we reach the fields. We're nearly there now. The view'll be the same when we reach the fields.'

—

Half an hour later they reach the fields. The view is not the same. There are now rows of hedges along the cliffside obscuring most of the town. Stephen insists on stopping to take photos anyway. From what Benny can tell these are simply pictures of a clear blue sky.

Benny leans against a tree, sips from his flask. He refuses to unfasten his pack. If he unfastens, he'll end up sitting and smoking and that will mean taking another break and they can't have a proper break again until they're on to the next page of the guide-book. They have to get some serious miles under their belt if they want to get past Bodfari to the woods before sunset.

After a few pictures, Stephen slips off his own pack and sits on it. His T-shirt is now soaked with sweat and the ink of the skeleton picture has started to bleed at the edges. Benny still remembers going to visit Stephen during second year uni, when he'd just acquired the skeleton from that friend of his, the guy with the mullet and that ridiculous golden tracksuit, the one Benny ended up having that argument with after a few too many beers.* (Garth, that was his name.) The skeleton seemed another wacky in-joke between Stephen and his new friends at the time, all of whom wore the same odd mismatch of clothing and talked in the same London accent and shared Stephen's new tendency of declaring everything to be 'problematic'.

Benny could never get on board with those people, could never quite figure out why they dressed the way they did or said the things they did (some of them he couldn't even figure out what *gender* they were). When Stephen had said then that he was going to use the skeleton in all future artworks a few of them had laughed – and Benny had assumed he was genuinely joking. He'd never have guessed Stephen would end up bringing the thing back home after uni. He'd never imagined he'd be spending all his time with it; wearing T-shirts adorned with its image, three years on. All Benny can think, each time he sees that skeletal face on Stephen's T-shirts, is that it must be a nightmare to store.†

---

* Garth?

† Wrong, Frank actually fit quite snugly in the attic room. I had a gap for

17

It's already three o'clock by the time they turn their backs on the sea and continue south across the fields. To get from one field to the next they have to use the stiles. Stephen's never heard of a stile before and so Benny explains it's essentially a set of wooden steps, either side of a fence, that'll allow them to climb over. It's easier to demonstrate when they arrive at one, although the execution is more difficult than it sounds, especially with the packs, especially considering the lack of flexibility in Stephen's scrawny, strangely hairless legs. It takes Stephen three attempts to get over his first stile. He tells Benny that scaling any sort of fence makes him nervous, has done since school, when Cal told them that story about a year seven mangling his ballsack trying to escape over the back of the science block. Benny says it's all about confidence. You need a certain self-assurance. Hold on to the belief that your balls will remain intact. And he's right, as they pass from one field to the next Stephen's confidence grows. His climbing becomes smoother, almost natural-looking.

No two fields are the same. Each stile leads to variations: the size, the gradient, the position of the path. One field the ground is yellow and balding, the next a thick green lawn, like AstroTurf. Sometimes there is an actual cobbled pathway, others it's just worn grass or a dirt track. In theory they're following the dyke, although most of it is now indefinable. The guidebook says at points they will be able to see it – a clear trench in the land – but this won't be until further along the trail.

---

him at the end of the bed. And sure, Mum wasn't happy when I brought him back from uni. She thought him macabre, kept insisting she wanted 'that thing' out of the house, but I was equally insistent that we keep him, that he was important to my work. And yes, I admit, some nights were tense. There was the odd occasion I'd catch sight of him out of the corner of my eye and suffer a split-second panic, thinking there was someone in my room. The odd incident of waking, screaming, every fibre of my being in a state of blood-curdling terror at the sight of him, looming over my bed. The attic room had a skylight, angled in such a way that between 1 and 2 a.m. the moonlight projected a huge shadowy outline of Frank's skull on the far wall. So yes, it was . . . *creepy*. But I got used to it. By the time of the walk, Frank had been there for over two years. He was part of the furniture. Part of the family.

The one constant is sheep, everywhere that incessant baaing. Stephen says he'd like a few photos of them too, but Benny says there'll be plenty of time for that later – if there's one thing Wales has plenty of, it's sheep. Of course, sheep = sheep shit; they try to avoid it but it's everywhere, the grass infested with hard black pellets that cling to the soles of their shoes. The sheep keep their distance. It's still lambing season and a lot of them are protective mothers with babies.

Benny can't figure out why Wales needs so many sheep. His mum told him once that they outnumber the people here three-to-one – is there really such a demand for lamb? Then again, maybe it's not the meat people are interested in, but the wool; they're always wearing thick woollen jumpers here, he remembers that from the walks he did as a child. His dad had one – dark grey with brown, leather patches on the elbows. Benny tried it on, that night before the funeral, when he was rummaging through his dad's study. It still smelt how his dad used to, a mixture of cigarette smoke, Right Guard, and earth. It brought about a certain amount of nostalgia, considering how much his dad's smell had changed near the end, overwhelmed by that toxic blend of chemicals and urine. Benny had only worn the jumper for a matter of minutes that night. He found it too itchy. His neck came out in hives.

Benny tries to think of a single item of clothing he owns that's made from wool. Now he thinks of it, everything he has is synthetic; in winter he tends to just wear his fleece, or else that grey hoodie Sam bought him that first Christmas they were together. Then he remembers the socks. He's wearing a new pair of thick walking socks he bought at the camping shop, especially for the trip. He's pretty sure they're woollen. Or at least, like, ninety per cent wool. The socks are great – although his feet are hot, as far as he can tell there is no chafing, no blistering, as of yet. He treated himself to two new pairs, the second still stowed away in his pack. He's saving them for later in the trip.

There are few pleasures like donning an unworn sock, the fibres breaking free to accommodate the naked skin of the foot. So many nerve endings in a foot, it's such an overlooked erogenous zone.

Benny was always pleading with Sam for foot rubs a few years back, when they were in uni, although it was always to no avail. It was usually when the two of them were in bed watching television, and she'd complain that his feet were gnarly and smelt, and anyway there was no comfortable way to do it; even if she were to stay where she was, the position in which Benny'd have to twist himself in order to offer his foot to her, hunched over on his side with his leg doubled over, *looked* so uncomfortable it *made her* uncomfortable. She only ever massaged his feet once as far as he can remember. She made him wash them first, then did it properly, kneeling at the foot of the bed with massage-oiled hands. The whole time Benny couldn't enjoy it. His mind was elsewhere, imagining how good it would feel if her hands were working his dick instead.

'Fuck's sake.'
   'What?'
'Fuckin' sheep shit, all over my Nikes.'
'It's Wales, Ste, what did you expect?'
'You said a path. I was expecting a path.'
'Across the whole country?'
'Well, I didn't know there'd be so much shit, did I? *Jesus*, man.'*

Occasionally the trail leads them out onto stretches of road, and they keep an eye out for acorn plaques – their signal to veer off into the fields again. A few of the plaques are attached to actual arrow-shaped signs, but mostly they're just screwed to stiles or fence posts, a small confirmation that they're heading in the right direction. Benny has the guidebook tucked in his back pocket. Every so often he checks the map inside. Not because he needs to – just to see the bigger picture, their position in the grand scheme of the walk.

---

* Look, I'm aware I said 'man' sometimes (it was one of those little verbal tics I picked up from Garth, back in uni), but did I really say it *this much*? You're making me sound like some sort of Californian surfer dude here . . .

The dyke is supposedly a popular trail, but they don't spot any other walkers, not until about four o'clock, just as they're climbing another stile. The approaching walker is tall, lean, bald except for a silver ponytail at the back. He's fully kitted in rain-coat and walking boots, even brandishing a couple of those spiked hiking sticks they use in documentaries to scale Everest.

The walker waits at a distance until Benny and Stephen are over the stile, before approaching. Benny offers a hello, raises his hand slightly in suggestion of a wave. This is something they would do on those walks with his father and Uncle Ian, greet fellow walkers along the trail, although this time the man keeps his head down. He has headphones in, Benny notices as he passes – a distant buzz of classical music. The man climbs the stile, then continues across the field behind them.

Beyond the stables lies a farmhouse, where a woman in a kaftan is ferrying shopping from a Land Rover. Benny offers a 'hello' to her too and she smiles back awkwardly, retrieves another handful of bags and disappears up the path. Stephen sighs, shakes his head. Benny's not sure if this sighing is aimed at him or the woman.

Just then barking sounds from inside the Land Rover. It's a pitiful bark but Stephen crosses to the other side of the path anyway, speeds to the next stile. Stephen has had a fear of dogs since back when he and Benny first met. Benny still remembers when Ste first came to the house, how jumpy he was around Samson, so much so that Benny's dad would usually end up taking him out for a walk.

A little further on they arrive at a stables, complete with hay-chomping horses. Benny stops for a piss. There's horseshit all over the path. Horseshit is much larger than sheep shit, much sloppier too – like mounds of black meatballs, bound with bits of grass and straw. Stephen asks if Benny's really going to piss right here, out in the open, and Benny says yes, of course, where else? They're in the countryside now – this is accepted. Stephen asks what about . . . you know . . . *the other*. He's staring at the horseshit. Benny nods, that too. He has tissues and wet wipes, and a trowel to bury it, if it comes to that. *When* it comes to that.

Stephen swallows, nods. He's still eyeing the horseshit. It's as if he thinks it might make a sudden move towards them.

Benny crosses to the hedge at the side, unzips.

The sun blazes for the rest of the afternoon. There's no coverage, no patches of shade, no respite from the baking heat. Benny feels the sunburn as a tightening-of-skin, mostly on his forehead and neck, although there is a burning on his forearms too, which he keeps raised, chicken-wing-like, thumbs hooked into the straps of his pack. He should have brought suntan lotion. If he'd remembered he'd have picked some up back at the Tesco in Prestatyn. But he didn't. And so now they must suffer.

Stephen keeps complaining about how bright it is. Even with his sunglasses and green plastic visor, this sunlight's too much for him. His sunglasses are the little round type, like John Lennon* used to wear – each lens the size of a two-pound coin – so it's likely they're letting in a fair amount of light. He says he has a headache. He says he's hung-over. It was wrong of him to drink last night, he knows that now. But he was working on his art, he says. The drinking, it helps. And what's done is done, right? But still, this – walking in this heat – this is the last thing he needs.

Benny agrees, it isn't good walking weather. They want clouds, *dullness*. They don't want extremes of either hot or cold, sun or rain – just a nice, overcast middle ground. Benny tries to make light of it, says at least it will look nice in the photos.

By this point Stephen's taking a lot of photos. He's asking to stop roughly every ten to fifteen minutes. Benny knows this is just an excuse, that Stephen is looking for any justification to remove his backpack, but the truth is there's no point in de-packing. It doesn't help. The longer they're free from the packs the more painful it is when the time comes to put them back on. Plus, Benny has the tent, so his pack is by far the heaviest. If he

---

* I was thinking more Warhol TBH.

can manage to keep going, then there's no reason Stephen shouldn't be able to.

But Benny doesn't mention any of this. He refuses to smoke. He hopes this sends a clear enough message, him not smoking – his way of not endorsing these little breaks. It's a kindness, throwing Stephen in at the deep end. The aches and pains, the overall feeling of exhaustion, it used to get to Benny too, on those walks with his dad and Uncle Ian. Benny's dad would always ignore any pleas to slow down and, although Uncle Ian would usually relent and hoist Benny up onto his shoulders where he could bob along above, there came a point when Benny was too big for his uncle to carry, when he had no choice but to power on, break through that wall of pain. And Benny found that, after a while, he could. His dad was right. It's just about sticking at it, allowing your body to numb to the experience.

Originally Benny had thought it would be him and his dad taking this trip together. That had been how he'd first pictured it, those winter nights he'd lain awake, researching the dyke. He imagined it to be just like the old days, him and his father together in the Welsh countryside, only this time both as grown men, both fit enough to handle the physical toll of such a long-distance trail. It soon became obvious such a thing wouldn't be possible. His father's health declined rapidly at the start of the year. Mostly this manifested in an uptake of the same grim routines, i.e. more trips to the clinic, more pills to dispense, more coughing and sleeplessness and a lack of appetite, all forced upon an increasingly emaciated body. The idea that his treatment plan could allow for a couple of weeks' hiking in Wales became more laughable with each passing day. Benny was forced to consider other options.

Cal would have made a good choice of walking companion. Cal was an old friend of Benny's from after-school rugby, although he'd started hanging out with Benny and Stephen a lot during sixth form. That was when they first started drinking in the Miners together – back then it was the only pub in town that would turn a blind eye to the fact they were underage. The three of them had drifted apart after school, what with Stephen down in London, and Benny and Cal with their girlfriends, but once Stephen was back they began to see each other again, and in some ways it felt like they were still teenagers, spending their Friday nights binging on cheap Guinness and discussing Cal's relationship problems.

Cal lived with his girlfriend, Christine. There was a lot of drama between the two of them. It was the usual stuff; she smoked too much, drank too much, she snuck money from his wallet to fund her nights out. Christine was unemployed and kept missing her meetings at the job centre and getting herself sanctioned. Sometimes she cheated on Cal, or else Cal got caught cheating on her, and then there'd be the fallout from that – the screaming matches, the Facebook statuses, the ceremonial destruction of each other's belongings. Cal had always gone for the dramatic types – *bad girls*, he called them. Back in school his relationships would last a matter of weeks, but Christine was the exception. She and Cal were together for a couple of years and during that time she had proved that there was a correlation between the amount of time spent with him and the amount of drama that would ensue.

Cal worked in a warehouse for an online retail company. They were long shifts and his home life was chaotic and the only time he ever broke the unrelenting routine were those nights at the pub with Benny and Stephen. Often he'd get drunk. Often he'd say he was going to walk out on Christine, quit his job, go off travelling to South America or something, and leave all this behind. Then he'd disappear to the bar for a while and once he arrived back they'd find out he'd been chatting up girls, usually old flames from his schooldays (quite a few of them still drank in the Miners). Somehow Christine would find out and the cycle would continue, on and on, breaking up and making up, sex and violence in a continuous loop. Until that night in February, that is, when Cal and Christine had the *big* fight, the one that took a nastier turn than the others; the one from which the fallout had been too great, the consequences too severe for them all to carry on as usual.

Benny hasn't spoken to Cal at all since then.* It was a mutual thing – Cal stopped showing up for their Friday night drinks, and Benny didn't bother calling to check up on him. They left it at that. By then Benny had abandoned the idea of doing the walk. It was a couple of months later, when they were planning his dad's funeral, that he'd got the idea to do the thing on his own. That would be *even better*, he thought. A lone walk. A pilgrimage in his father's honour. He could scatter some of the ashes. Plus, it was a chance for him to get away from everyone. He could think things over, get some perspective.

Stephen wasn't ever a part of any of these plans. Not until a few weeks ago when Benny had mentioned it outside the Miners, pint of Guinness in one hand and penis in the other, pissing into the hedge at the back of the car park. They'd just come to the end of one of their drinking sessions and were about to nip over to the chippy before the walk home when Benny had decided to relieve himself, and it was in that moment, when he'd found himself feeling oddly sentimental, that, without thinking, he'd ended up inviting Stephen along on the walk. He regretted it immediately.† Stephen seemed excited though, said the trip sounded amazing. He could take photographs, landscape shots for his portfolio. They could have a laugh, like the old days.

As the afternoon of that first day's walk wears on, Benny can't help but think of Cal. He imagines what it would be like if Cal were here instead of Stephen. Would Cal be this exhausted just a few hours in? Would Cal have forgotten his raincoat?

Would Cal be so pale and sweaty and *slow*?‡

—

* Are you really just going to skim over this, Ben? I mean, wasn't what happened with Cal and Christine actually a pretty big deal, in terms of our own personal history? You'll happily dedicate entire paragraphs to a foot massage, yet what Cal did only gets a brief reference?

† Nice to know.

‡ Maybe not, but he also has a track record of committing acts of physical violence against women – is this also an attribute you look for in a walking companion, Ben?

25

They come out onto a dirt road. They follow it for the next half an hour and it leads them up past fields and farms, over cattle grids and up into hills of fern bushes. The sun is getting low now. Stephen's sweating like crazy. His face is beaded with it – his fringe damp, curling from the elastic band of his sun visor. His panting has a rattle to it, as if there's something solid lodged in his throat.

Benny spots a tree ahead at the side of the road and suggests they could rest there. Stephen doesn't answer but it's obvious from his squeaking inhalations that he agrees.

'Come on, Ste. Here. There we go. Just here.'
*Pant. Pant. Pant. Pant.*

Stephen gasps as the weight slips from his shoulders, collapses on the grass. Benny sits beside him. His own back is wet now and there's a dark patch on his pack and when he presses into the sponge, sweat dribbles out. He wipes his finger on his trousers, rolls a cigarette.

Stephen asks how far they've come. Benny checks the guide-book. A mile is the equivalent to two inches of page. Benny approximates using his fingers: they've walked five miles. Stephen asks how much further till they reach Bodfari. Benny approximates again: another six miles. There's a smaller town between them and Bodfari, called Rhuallt. Benny says if they make it to Rhuallt he'll be happy. It's OK for them to slack a little on their first day. Benny booked a few extra days off work, just in case. Or else, they could only stay for one night at his uncle's. It's not a problem.

Benny checks his phone. No messages. No signal either, although at least his battery's holding up (95%). He retrieves another Mars bar, the packet hot and limp in his hand. He tears the plastic open and squeezes half into his mouth. He asks if Stephen's sure he wouldn't like the other half and Stephen stares at it for a few seconds and then nods submissively, takes the packet from him. Benny asks if he'd like a cigarette too and Stephen swallows some Mars bar and nods again, and so Benny rolls another.

They sip from their flasks. Benny thought the flasks were a good idea because they're lightweight and clip onto the sides of the packs for easy access, but they're made of aluminium and have absorbed the heat from the sun, and so now the water inside is hot. They drink it anyway. They smoke and sip and admire the view. The sea's still visible at the edge of the fields, spanning out into the distance.

'So, your uncle . . .'

'Ian.'

'When do we get to his?'

'Sunday. Maybe Monday.'

'And we can stop there?'

'For a day or two, yeah. I haven't seen him for years. We might want to play it by ear.'

'He wasn't at the funeral?'

'No.'

'Really?'

'I think I would have noticed.'

'Right.' *Pause.* 'Sorry. Just surprised is all.'

'And my mum doesn't know we're staying with him, so no photos please.'

'Right.' *Pause.* 'He used to go walking, right? With your dad?'

'Yeah.'

'And you went with them?'

'Sometimes.'

'You ever walk here? This route, I mean. The Offald—'

'Offa's Dyke. No, when I'd go it was just daytrips. Sometimes we'd camp, but usually it was just for one night.'

'But they did this walk, right?'

'Yeah, once.'

*Pause.*

'Strange to think, isn't it? They will have walked this exact same path.'

'Yep.'

'They could have sat in this exact spot.'

'Mmhmm.'

27

*Pause.*

'What about your mum? She never go with you?'

'She wasn't really into it.'

'She's not Welsh, is she?'

'You don't have to be Welsh to go walking, Ste.'

'No, I know. I mean . . . because your dad, he had the accent, but your mum . . .'

'He moved to England when he met my mum.'

'Right.' *Pause.* 'And your uncle, he stayed?'

'Well, he didn't marry my mum, did he?'

'No, but I mean he's still in Clang . . . what is it?'

'Llangollen.'

'Right.'

'He's still at my nan's old house, yeah. He never left that house. He loves it there in Llangollen. He likes trains and they're big on trains there. They have their own steam train in the town. Or something. I don't know, it's all very nerdy. He'll probably show us.'

'Right.'

'But my dad loved it here. The countryside, I mean. These hills and fields . . . this country was his life. He wanted Wales to be independent. He was very politically active, in his day.'

'I remember.'

'Hmm?'

'Back in school. He was always ranting in class. Slagging off the government.'

'Right, yeah.'

'We used to try and bate him in English. Get your dad to go off on one about politics. Meant we didn't have to do any work.'

'Yeah, I remember.'

'Must have been funny for you, that.'

'Not *funny*, so much. Just embarrassing.'

'Wasn't he protesting outside the job centre at one point too?'

'Yeah.'

'I remember seeing the pictures on Facebook. Was it first year uni, during the election?'

'I believe so, Ste, yeah.'

28

*Pause.*

'You heard from Sam recently?'

'No.'

'Does she know? You know, about your dad?'

'No idea.'

'Really?'

'Well, she knew he was ill, obviously.'

'Yeah but, you know . . .'

'No idea, Ste.'

'I was surprised she wasn't there. At the funeral.'

'I couldn't deal with her too. I already had Mum and Amy to contend with. It would have been too much.'

'It might have helped, having her with you.'

'It's complicated.'

'Right.' *Pause.* 'Sorry.' *Pause.* 'I'm not trying to pry. It's just . . . you've been *different* the past few months.'

'I'm fine.'

'You've been quiet. Even quieter than usual, I mean.'

'I'm fine, honestly.'

'All that stuff with Cal, and then your dad . . .'

'I'm fine.'

'Right.'

'I mean, I'm not *happy*, obviously. But I'm OK.'

'You're OK.'

'It's all OK.'

'Right.'

*Pause.*

'Anyway, tonight will be good. We'll camp in Rhuallt, make a fire, cook up a feast. It'll be good.'

'Yeah, man. That's the spirit. What's on the menu?'

'Noodles.'

'*Mmmm.* What flavour?'

'Whatever you desire. We have them all. Beef, chicken, *curried* chicken.'

'They vegan?'

'Yep.'

'You sure?'

'Don't worry, I checked. They've got the little green V. They're twenty-five pence a packet, Ste, you don't get meat for that price. It's just flavoured dust, like on crisps.'

'Cool.'

*Pause.*

'Come on, let's keep moving. I reckon we've got a few more hours before sunset.'

# III

*Campsite – The tent – Camping Shop Mike – The practice run – Tent erection – Noodles – Coffee – A welcome chill – Campfires – Ghost stories – Firewood – 'Alpha male Viking' – Flint – Matches – Smoke – A bye-law.*

They walk only half an hour longer. It's not yet sunset and they haven't yet reached Rhuallt but Stephen has slowed so much that Benny has to stop every thirty yards and wait for him. Stephen says he needs a good sleep. He was up late, that's all it is. He needs an early night. He'll be stronger tomorrow.

By this point the path is ascending through a knoll of ferns. Stephen stops, slumps amongst the ferns. He lies there like a fallen scarecrow, leaves sprouting between his arms and legs. Benny's mind flits back to this morning, to the Roman helmet half buried in the grass.* He tells Stephen they need to keep moving. They need to find an appropriate field to set up camp. This is a priority.

They have to veer from the path to find a campsite. This is a violation of the Countryside Code, but Benny knows if they keep following the trail then the chances are they won't see anywhere suitable between here and Rhuallt, and he doubts there'll be anywhere to pitch up there. His dad used to claim that locals would sometimes allow walkers to camp in their gardens on major trails such as this but Benny doesn't fancy knocking and asking, not on their first night.

A short detour through the ferns and they come upon a field, just off the path. A slight incline but clear at least. No sheep

---

* OK, Ben. Yes. For the record, that was a shit sculpture.

either, which means no sheep shit, although they can still hear a faint baaing in the distance.

'Over there?'
　'How about here?'
　'Here?'
　'Yeah, man. Sheltered.'

The tent belonged to Benny's dad. It's the same one they used to share back on those weekend camping trips with Uncle Ian. Benny found it in the loft, in the 'WALK' box, along with the mess tin, the gas heater, the sleeping bags and guidebook. Everything else he picked up from the camping shop in town last Saturday, during his final preparations. He had invited Stephen along to the camping shop too, but Stephen had declined, said he'd had a breakthrough with his art. And that was fine, Benny was happy to pick up the supplies himself. Stephen had been blessed with the meandering mind of an artist and if Benny was in charge of the supplies then at least he could ensure they had the right equipment. He'd told Stephen to just make sure he brought three things: a strong backpack, appropriate footwear, and a rain mac.

Benny had considered splashing out on a new tent, that afternoon in the camping shop. They had a whole range of them there – display models set up in a circle around a glowing, plastic campfire. The salesman had asked if Benny was walking Offa's Dyke alone and in that moment Benny had forgotten he'd invited Stephen along, had answered yes without thinking, and the next thing he knew he was being given the hard sell at the rows of nifty-looking one-man tents, each tucked away in a coloured sack not much larger than a bag of flour. Benny had thought about it. He could have admitted to Stephen that he hadn't meant to invite him, that he was drunk that night in the Miners. He could have explained that he really needed some time alone. But then the camping shop guy (Mike, he was called) had shown Benny their demonstration model, set it up next to the others on the patch of fake grass, and Benny had discovered that the one-mans were more like glorified sleeping bags than actual tents. He did as Mike suggested, tried it out 'for size', but as soon as he had he realised that *size* was exactly the problem. The thing was tiny, like being encased in some sort of waterproof, canvas coffin. Once inside, Benny had started to panic. He managed to make a complete idiot of himself, trying to claw his way back out again.

After that he decided to stick to the plan. Let Stephen come along, take his dad's tent for the two of them to share. Now he thinks maybe this was the wrong call. He and Stephen have agreed to share the load, carry the tent alternate days, but Benny's been stuck carrying it the first day and as he unbuckles his pack for the final time all he can think is that at least tomorrow will be easier.

'That tent looks *old*, man.'

'It'll do.'

'You sure? What are those . . . holes?'

'They're just stains. It's well loved, that's all.'

'Yikes.'

'It's a good tent, Ste. Solid. They don't make them like this any more.'

'If you say so.'

'Trust me, it's a good tent. It'll do the job.'

Benny hasn't thought much about the practicalities of him and Stephen sharing the tent. It's only now, as he's laying out the groundsheet, that he realises how small it is, despite its weight. It seemed huge, back on those weekends away. Uncle Ian would sleep in his own tent and Benny and his dad would share this one. Mind you, the last time Benny went on one of those trips he was half the size he is now.

The spot they've chosen is at the side of the field, beneath the branches of a large oak tree. Benny begins assembling the frame – unfurling the poles, slotting them together. The tent poles always remind him of wands from a child's magic set, only twice as long and joined end-on-end, nunchuck-like, with elasticated string. Once these are assembled, Benny sets about feeding them through the tunnels in the canvas. He did a practice run, setting up the tent. He pitched up last Saturday in the back garden, that patch of lawn near the flowerbeds where Samson is buried. He wanted to prepare, make sure all the parts were there, check there weren't any holes in the canvas, etc. His mum watched from the patio, wrapped in a blanket with a cigarette and a mug of hot wine. She loves hot wine now, has done since Christmas, when Amy's fiancé brought that bottle with the Dickensian street scene on the label. She hasn't been able to get the proper mulled stuff since, settles for adding a little Splenda to whatever red's on offer in the supermarket, then blasting it for a few minutes in the microwave.

Benny had found the tent poles fiddly during the practice run. He'd knelt there, trying to feed them through the slots in the canvas, whilst his mum watched from the doorstep, wincing, tutting, sipping from her steaming mug. She always used the same mug, the one Benny's father brought back from one of their trips; a faded picture of Jesus surrounded by a flock of sheep with the words 'Jesus Loves Ewe'. After a few minutes of watching Benny struggle, she placed the mug on the step, hobbled over to help. But Benny refused. He'd have to be able to do it alone on the day, wouldn't he? Then the pole snagged, and she reached over to try and guide it and Benny forced it and it split through the canvas. His mother gasped and Benny snapped at her, said something he shouldn't have, and she gathered her duvet, emptied her wine in the flowerbed and disappeared inside.

It's easier now, probably because the only audience is Stephen, who at first lingers by the groundsheet as if he's going to be of some assistance, but soon ends up leaning against the tree, fiddling with his camera, not even pretending to pay attention to the erection of the tent. The pole snags again at that same tear in the canvas but this time Benny is gentle, guides it through. He raises the roof. He raises the porch. He secures the ends of the tent poles into the eyelets in the groundsheet, crawls inside to hook the inner awning in place. The tent is bright red, which is unfortunate (he'd prefer green, less conspicuous for rough camping) but it's still in good condition, despite its age. He tips out pegs from their bag, fastens it to the ground. The tree roots cause a few problems impaling but he stamps away at them until the guy ropes are taut.

Stephen raises his camera, takes a couple of photos of Benny's efforts.

*Click.*
   *Wind, wind, wind.*
   'I thought you wanted landscape shots?'
   'I wanted landscapes, yeah, because I wanted to see if I'm any good at landscapes, but I also want to capture *everything*.'
   'Right.' *Pause.* 'Well, I think we're all set here . . .'
   'Just a couple more.'
   *Click.*
   *Wind, wind, wind.*
   *Click.*
   *Pause.*
   'Done?'
   'Done.'
   'Right. Food.'

They huddle outside the porch to cook dinner. Benny unpacks the cooking equipment; the mugs and sporks, and the mess tin and gas heater, as well as the bag of food supplies he picked up from the supermarket. He brought instant noodles mostly. Instant noodles he knows, instant noodles were pretty much all he and Sam lived on in their first year of uni, before she started with all the healthy lifestyle stuff.

Right now, the noodles aren't so instant. The process is simple enough: light the gas, a litre of water in the mess tin, wait for it to boil. And so, they wait. Forever passes and still, they wait. Birds sing. Sheep baa at each other. Thousands of tiny bugs crawl in the surrounding grass, and still not a bubble of hope from the water. And the sun is setting now. And they're hungry – they didn't realise the extent of their hunger. But now, huddled over the mess tin, surrounded by noodle packets with misleadingly delicious-looking meals on their covers, they can feel it, gnawing within.

And it's hard, waiting; Benny occasionally dipping his finger into the water, only to sigh at its tepidness. Even harder's figuring out how to sit – there's nothing substantial to lean on here except maybe the tree trunk, although they've pitched the tent facing away from it, which means the gas heater is nowhere near. Benny sits cross-legged. Stephen lies on his front. Then Benny's legs are dead, and Stephen says his elbows ache, and they have to keep shifting around, settling into different but equally uncomfortable positions. The heater is essentially a gas canister with a little burner spout screwed into the top, and the whole time Benny has to keep hold of the handle of the mess tin, so it doesn't slip from the heater and spill.

Eventually there's some movement in the water, one bubble and then the next, until there's enough of a simmer to add noodles and wait for three minutes like the pack suggests and then add the chicken flavouring and *eat*. The noodles taste like nothing – not chicken, not anything – but they're *hot* and for this Benny's grateful. It was him who provided the noodles, as well as a few packets of rice and a jar of instant coffee. He also brought the sporks and the mugs and the gas heater and mess tin. Stephen brought nothing. It seems it hadn't even occurred to him that they would need to eat. Maybe he thought they were going to hunt something. Butcher a sheep perhaps, eat it raw. Fuck veganism, a day in the wild and he'd suddenly emerge a carnivorous alpha male, tearing a lamb apart with his bare hands.★

Benny retrieves some baby wipes and scrubs the tin clean. Then he adds more water and begins the process of boiling all over again, this time adding coffee granules. Maybe he hasn't cleaned the tin enough, or maybe the noodle flavouring has a delayed effect on the taste buds, but either way the coffee has a distinct hint of chicken. Still, it's incredible after an afternoon of warm water and melted Mars bars. He wipes the tin a final time and discards it in the corner of the porch, along with the empty noodle wrappers.

---

★ For the record, I did not think this.

By now the sun is sinking behind the fields. There's a welcome chill to the air.

'I'm cold.'

Benny says he'll make a fire. This was always a highlight of those trips with his dad and Uncle Ian. Daytime mostly consisted of map-reading, arguing, trekking the trail in silence. Then evening would come and the whole atmosphere would change. Any bickering between his dad and uncle would die off and the two of them would lie back in the glow of the flames, feet up on their packs, sipping from their hipflasks. Sometimes they'd tell stories, a mixture of teenage reminiscences and urban legends. They'd start with memories of their childhood in Wales, old friends, girlfriends, adventures exploring the woods. Then, as the night wore on, they'd shift to the more macabre, campfire stuff – rumours of cannibals hiding in the mountains, or the spirits of lost ramblers that wander through the trees at night.

These stories were usually Benny's uncle's doing – owing a lot to those 70s horror films he loved – although he was always sure to retell them in a way that attributed them to real people (somebody's cousin, a friend-of-a-friend, etc.) which helped give them a certain amount of credibility. They enjoyed scaring themselves. Benny's dad was quite philosophical about it, said people liked ghost stories because they put forth a positive view of the world – after all, if there really were ghosts, then that would be proof of an afterlife, which was the ultimate sort of optimism. Benny's uncle insisted on a simpler motivation. He just thought ghost stories were *cool*. Either way, Benny understood the power of those stories. It was about creating an atmosphere: the safety of camp. The firelight an oasis in the dark unknown.

Benny's hoping a campfire will provide similar comfort for him and Stephen. But first he needs firewood. He rummages through his pack for his penknife. He briefly considers the hatchet – another purchase from the camping shop, still in its plastic packaging. It didn't seem as big when he bought it, but now, feeling the length of the handle, the weight of it, it seems at once menacing and embarrassing, and he knows he will feel silly holding it. Instead, he sticks with the penknife. He scours bushes for dry patches. He saws at them. They're only twigs, but they should do as kindling, just to get it going.

Benny's dad never looked silly holding a hatchet. He'd had the same one for years – a Helko with a slender, dark-stained handle – although it had been absent from the 'WALK' box when Benny brought it down from the loft, so God knows where it ended up. During the day, whilst they were walking, his dad would wear his axe with pride, hooked to his pack so it bounced at his hip with each step. When evening came, he'd collect the firewood, felling branches methodically, occasionally tossing the axe from one hand to the other. He suited it; his whole beard-and-long-hair look seemed less English teacher, more alpha-male-Viking when he was hacking away at a tree branch. Uncle Ian worked the flint, got the kindling going. They assumed these roles without question. It had always been this way. Benny's role was collecting tinder; grass or leaves ideally, though if it had been raining (and it usually had) he'd seek out a dry piece of bark and whittle away at its insides.

Now Benny has all of these roles. Luckily there's plenty of potential firewood around the base of the tree. He gathers branches for kindling, finds a log he can strip for tinder. He works at the log with his knife, steady strokes, careful not to slice his thumb; crafts a sort of bird's nest out of the shavings, then rummages through his pack for flint. Mike had offered a demo of the flint (Benny was the only customer that morning in the camping shop), but Benny had said he'd seen this done enough times to remember. Assembling a bird's nest of tinder and kindling is step one . . . then what? Scrape the flint? Is that step two? Is that it, just those two steps? The flint is a long black tube with a flat plastic part at the end, with a hole so you can attach it to your keys. There's an iron file hooked to it, which Benny scrapes with. The sparks come pouring, showering the nest. He scrapes and scrapes for a good few minutes, but the tinder doesn't light.

He tries scraping with the penknife instead. That's how his uncle used to do it; hack at the flint with the edge of his knife-blade. Only, when Benny tries it, there are even fewer sparks, and still no flame. Maybe the twigs are damp, Stephen says. Maybe the flint's broken. Benny keeps trying. Stephen winces at each scrape. Stephen has this amazingly dramatic wince-face. His top lip rises so high that gum is visible. Cal used to do all sorts of disgusting things, back when they were in school – pick his nose, chew his tie, crack his knuckles – just so they could see Stephen wince.

Stephen asks if Benny doesn't maybe have any matches left. You know, the ones they used to light the gas burners? The ones they've been using to light their cigarettes all day? Benny says nothing. Mike said flint was easy, foolproof. Flint was an essential. Matches will get wet and let you down, but flint will always be there.

'What now?'

Benny fetches the matches. He should have brought more than one box, he realises that now. They'll soon run out, with the amount of cigarettes they're smoking. Benny always opts for matches over a lighter. Lighters feel cheap and flimsy and they always seem to fail on him. There's nothing like lighting a cigarette with a match – the flaring to life of the flame, the thin strand of curling smoke, the woody flavour of that first inhalation.

By now there's a breeze. The leaves above them hiss, the branches rattle. The matches keep blowing out. Benny's wasted half the pack before the nest catches. They'll need more, he says. They'll pick some up tomorrow in Rhuallt. This is a new priority.

Then suddenly: smoke. Not much in the way of a flame, as far as he can see, but a lot of smoke. The wind changes and the smoke drifts towards them. Stephen coughs, pulls the green sun visor down over his eyes. He asks if maybe this is a bad idea. Isn't this someone's land? What if someone shows up, tells them to put it out? What if someone asks them to move?

Smoke billows.

Benny turns from the fire, takes a breath of clean air. His headache is getting worse and this isn't helping. Stephen's right of course, Benny knows he's right. Benny should have thought of this, the whole wild camping issue. In Scotland you can camp anywhere you like, it's written into the law. England and Wales are different though, rightly speaking they should have asked permission. This was a bye-law they tended to ignore when he went camping as a child, his father's logic being that, as long as they were respectful, followed the Countryside Code, then they weren't causing any harm. But now there's smoke and with this the chance some farmer will show up and force them to move on.

After a few minutes Benny stamps out the fire. The smoke just keeps on coming. He douses it in half a litre of water, but this seems to cause even more smoke. He keeps kicking and stamping at it until the twigs are scattered and the smoke is dispersed. By this point the sun has sunk into the horizon. The light has faded. Stephen's donned this baggy, green Christmas jumper. On the front is a snowman, an orange-wool carrot jutting three-dimensionally from its face.

He's shivering.

'Maybe we should just, like, get inside the tent, man?'

# IV

Benny didn't actually sleep in the tent, that night of the practice run. He was planning on it – even brought out a flask of coffee and a ham sandwich, in case he was peckish in the night – but after his mum had disappeared inside, he began to feel guilty. He shouldn't have snapped at her when the pole snagged. And he didn't like the thought of her sleeping alone in that empty house. So he dismantled the tent, packed it away. He scattered the sandwich on the grass for the birds and went inside.

Which means the last time Benny actually slept in the tent must have been more than a decade ago, one of his walks with his dad. It's a lot smaller than he remembers, especially with the packs (which they stash near the entrance and which take up as much room as a whole other person). Benny and Stephen sit opposite each other, cross-legged on the groundsheet. It's just as cold in here as it was out in the field although at least there's some light, courtesy of the wind-up torch. Benny ties it to a loop of fabric in the ceiling. Stephen takes off his sunglasses, slips off his sun visor, tosses them on top of his pack. The visor has left a pale patch of un-sunburnt skin across his forehead. Just then Benny realises his and Stephen's knees are touching. He tries to back up a little, but his elbows are already pressed into the back of the tent. He soon gives up. What does it matter, really, if their knees are touching?

Stephen retrieves a tissue from his pocket, blows his nose. He snorts phlegm down the back of his throat. It makes this sound as he snorts: *hoik*. He does so twice more. Benny asks if everything's OK and Stephen nods. He has a problem with his sinuses, he says. Mucus builds. It's something he's been struggling with for years. He tells Benny that usually he disappears to the toilet to empty his nasal passages in private. But, he says, if he's going to be out here with Benny for two full weeks, then he has no choice, at some point he's going to have to unblock his nasal passages in front of him, and so it may as well be right now. This is an evolution in their friendship. He tells Benny that, as far as he remembers, nobody else has ever seen him unblocking his nasal passages like this.

After a few more *hoik*s Stephen drags his pack over, rummages for his camera bag. It's brown leather, with an orange felt interior and several different pouches for the flash and film. There's a separate padded case within for his lenses and it's from here that he retrieves a small, clear bag containing a furred green substance, wags it suggestively in the torchlight. Benny asks if that's what he thinks it is and Stephen says it isn't basil, if that what he's thinking, and the two of them laugh.* Benny asks if it's a good idea, to be smoking weed, what with Stephen's sinus problems – maybe he should give the ciggies a rest too? Stephen says the odd smoke doesn't hurt. And anyway, a quick spliff before bed might be just the thing to settle them.

---

* Which of course is another Cal reference, isn't it? His faux-weed dealing enterprise back in sixth form. Interesting that we can laugh about the old, schoolday-era Cal without having to contemplate the horror of what happened with him and Christine. It's almost as if they're two separate people; childhood Cal is excused his violence and misogyny due to the fact that we had fun getting drunk with him, whereas the late-era Cal of those nights in the Miners was always a bit of a downer, so it's easy to allow any bad feeling to drift his way. Really, we should have been taking a bit more responsibility. What had we done to encourage this sort of behaviour? Should we have challenged him more often regarding the problematic nature of his thinking? (I guess it's easy to reconsider these things after the event, isn't it?)

But Benny says no. They need to keep clear heads for tomorrow. They need to feel refreshed. Maybe later, when they get to Llangollen. His uncle won't mind, he used to be a bit of a stoner himself back in the day. Benny remembers his uncle's bedroom always having that distinctive weed smell, although back then Benny was too young to know what it was.

Stephen stashes the weed again. He takes the camera from round his neck, makes as if to put it away, but instead he aims it. Before Benny can even raise his hand in protest, he is blinded by the flash.

*Click* and *wind*.

Benny rubs his eyes. There are many, swirling, brightly coloured blotches. He rubs again. By the time he can make out Stephen's face again the camera is away in its case.

'Thanks.'

'You're welcome.'

'I love the constant photos. Especially with the flash. It's not at all annoying.'

'It'll be good, that. The surprise in your face. *The horror, the horror.*'

'Right. Great.' *Pause.* 'Successful day, photo-wise?'

'Impossible to say, man.'

'Because it's not digital, you mean? You can't look back at them?'

'Not just that. I mean you're right, I can't, but that's *good,* I think. You need time for reflection. You need hindsight for this sort of artistic process.'

'Right.'

'That's why digital's so . . .'

'Problematic? Clinical?'

'. . . *shit.*'

'Oh.'

'In my opinion anyway. For me the wait is important. The wait is as much a part of it as anything. *The patience of development.* You have to give it a few days before you can see what you've got. It's surprising actually. Often it's the most obscure photo, the one you don't even remember taking, that turns out to be art.'

'Right.' *Pause.* 'And how do you know? You know, which ones are art?'

'Well, it's hard to define. Actually it's impossible, there is no real definition for art. Art is whatever an artist perceives it to be.'

'You think that photo of *me* will be art?'

'Who knows? A lot of these will be a waste of film. Some will be holiday photos. Hopefully a few will be art. Some of the landscapes maybe. I'm focusing on landscapes because they're the polar opposite of what I've been working on for the last few years. The whole *Doomed Youth* project, I mean. Sometimes it's good to get outside your comfort zone, try something different, you know?'

'Right.'

'It's hard because what I do isn't photography, per se. I try to blank out any eye for the aesthetic, create something *new*. That's what art is all about, finding something original. A piece of art isn't a photograph, it transcends that. Photography is a way of capturing life, whereas art is *life itself*.'

'Right.'

'Or death itself, in my case.'

*Pause.*

'Right.'

*Pause.*

'This is my . . . you know . . . *method*. I'm not saying it's the only way, or even the best way. Just *my* way.'

'But at home you set up scenes, right? With the skeleton?'

'I create sculptures, yeah. Or "scenes", if that's how you want to put it. I use Frank for those. I actually started all that in uni, experimenting with alternative visual forms, but the sculptures never really worked on their own. Not until I started photographing them. At first it was just a way to document, an image of the sculpture for my portfolio. But the more I got into it the more I realised that the sculptures . . . I'm trying not to say *came to life* because I can't deal with the clichéd sentiment of that, or the possibility of making some sort of horrible pun regarding Frank's skeletal nature. You know what I mean. They weren't *art*, so to

44

speak, until they were photographs. And not all, just *some* photographs. Like, roughly one in every thirty pictures. I think it's to do with the concept as a whole. I mean, it's not just mortality itself that I'm trying to grapple with, but rather how governmental systematic dehumanisation is essentially writing off a large demographic of an entire generation. And it can be hard, capturing that.'

'I can imagine.' *Pause.* 'And then . . . the T-shirts?'

'The T-shirt thing is . . . something else. That's another angle I'm experimenting with.'

'Right.'

'I don't really want to get into that now.'

'Sure.' *Pause.* 'What about the others though? I mean, the photos that *aren't* art?'

'I burn them.'

'Really?'

'I have to, Ben. Can you imagine if someone found them? Say in like a hundred years, after I'm dead. They wouldn't know which is which, art and photography. All photography has to be destroyed. Only the art can stay.'

'So you'll burn *all* the non-art pictures? Even the holiday photos?'

'Well, we can keep those if you like. You can have those.'

'Thanks.'

'Anyway, like I said, now I'm trying something different. A new direction. Hence the landscapes. It would have been good to have got to some forest shots today . . .'

'It would have been nice if we'd been able to reach the forest, yes.'

*Pause.*

'How about you, Ben?'

'What?'

'You asked if my day was successful . . . how about yours? Did you enjoy it?'

'*Enjoy* it?'

'Well, you wanted to get away from it all, you said. Do you feel . . . *away*?'

'Erm . . .'

'I know it's only the first day, but *I* certainly feel better. Out here, away from the attic. I mean it was a shock to the system, all that walking, but sat here now I feel less . . . trapped.'

'Trapped?'

'Claustrophobic.'

'You mean the tent?'

'I mean *life*, Ben. *Metaphorically* trapped.'

'Right.'

'I mean, living in the attic isn't ideal. And who wants to live with their mum their whole life? And then there's all the bullshit with the job centre . . .'

'You need a job, Ste.'

'I'm an artist, man. I *have* a job. I just don't make any money from it.'

'But you need an income. Paid employment.'

'Ha.'

'I mean it, Ste.'

'I've looked, there's nothing.'

'Look harder.'

'I'm an *artist*, man.'

'But you need something. You can't just live in the attic the whole time.'

'Why not?'

'Because the government can't fund you to take photos of a skeleton.'

'They hardly *fund me*, Ben. What they give me barely covers the cost of the film.'

'So, you need paid employment.'

'We're going around in circles here.'

'You don't want a life on benefits, Ste. Trust me. You don't know what it's like. I have to speak to these people every day. It's not a life.'

'So, what? I should pack in the art and work at the call centre, like you?'

'Not necessarily . . .'

'Well, where else would I go?'

'Anywhere! You're an intelligent guy. You've got a degree.'

'Yeah, yeah.'

'Surely you can find *something*.'

'You sound like my mum. She's always going on about my degree.'

'Well, that's understandable. Didn't you say you were the first person in your family to go to uni?'

'And?'

'And so that's a big deal for her.'

'It means nothing though. An art degree. It's all about what you learn, not the piece of paper you get at the end.'

'It's still a qualification, Ste. You have to think about these things. You're building up a bigger and bigger gap in your employment history and that'll just make it harder in the long run. You'll have to find work eventually.'

'So you've said.'

'I mean it.'

'Let's just leave it, Ben, yeah?'

Stephen crawls over to the porch. He says he needs to nip outside for a minute. He asks if Benny has that toilet roll he mentioned earlier, and Benny retrieves the little drawstring bag he's nicknamed his 'shit-kit', complete with trowel and biodegradable wet wipes. He tells Stephen to dig a hole, make sure his shit's well buried.

Benny sits alone in the tent. He's been cross-legged for about twenty minutes now and his right foot is numb and as he raises his left knee he feels the blood rushing back, the swarming pulse of it. His head is still aching. He gets out the first-aid kit, finds the ibuprofen, washes a couple down with water from his flask.

Stephen's pack is still open, one of his T-shirts bunched at the top. Benny can just make out the iron transfer of the skeleton grinning at him. Benny tries to imagine how he'll look in the photo Stephen just took – a bit skull-like himself, probably, given how thin his hair's been looking recently. He tries to avoid bright lights these days due to the fact that in bright lights he can see right through his fringe to his scalp, a premonition of his future-bald self. Sometimes it seems to Benny as if his fringe is composed of a sort of *ghost hair*. It's as if he's already bald, and this wispy residue is just haunting his forehead. He dreads to think how it'll look under the glare of Stephen's camera flash.

Suddenly Benny has a thought. He can't help but wonder what Cal would do right now, if he was here with them. If that whole incident with Christine had never happened, and Benny had invited both Stephen *and* Cal along, and so instead it had been the three of them taking this trip together. There's no way Cal would have let an opportunity like this slip by – being left alone in the tent with all Stephen's possessions. There's no way Cal wouldn't have pulled some kind of prank on Stephen. He'd have probably opted for something cruel, like emptying Stephen's gas burner, or setting fire to all of his clothing, but Benny tries to think of something with less potential for compromising the success of the walk.

Then he spots the camera bag. He crawls over to Stephen's pack, slides the camera from its case. It's a relic: a genuine Canon EOS from the 90s. Benny still remembers the story; how Stephen had spotted it in a flea market on the way to one of his lectures and that Garth guy had treated him to it. The camera cost over a hundred pounds, yet apparently Ste's posh mate had just handed over the cash like it was nothing.

The camera is surprisingly heavy, especially the lens, which Benny has to cradle with his other hand. The functionality is simple enough – not all the complicated settings digital cameras have, just a shutter and a focus and a large black button to take the photos. Benny balances the camera on his stomach, edges his trousers down. He lifts his penis over the lip of his boxers. After a couple of flashes, he realises he's left the lens cap on and unclips it, takes a couple more. He's chuckling now, he can't help it – he's imagining Stephen in the attic, developing them in his makeshift darkroom, trying to figure out what it is. Benny stifles his laughter. He slots the camera back in its case. A little 'art' for Stephen, he thinks. A little reward for the 'patience of development'.★

---

★ Mature, Ben. Very mature. (I'm sure Cal would be proud.) Also, as if I didn't know you were up to something! I'd have been able to see that flash going off a mile away, man! Although, amazing story: this photo actually

Once Stephen has returned, Benny decides it's time to get some sleep. They unfurl their mats, lay out their sleeping bags, inflate their pillows. There's no room for any gap between the mats and it's impossible to deny that what they've laid out looks more like a double bed, rather than two singles. Benny nearly makes a joke about it – how the two of them can snuggle for warmth – but he decides against it.

He crawls into his sleeping bag, wriggles out of his T-shirt and trousers, folds them in the corner of the tent. Stephen undresses right in front of him. He still wears those tight white briefs, the ones he was so harshly ridiculed for back in high school when he'd undress for PE, although now he's more than likely wearing them ironically. Benny's given Stephen the sleeping bag with the broken zip, which makes it more of a blanket really. He tells Stephen to wrap himself up, bind tightly for optimum insulation.

Stephen says goodnight. Benny grunts in response. He reaches for the torch, still hanging from the fabric loop in the ceiling, and turns out the light.

---

ended up at the funeral, as part of the display. Did you notice? Top-right, with the more abstract stuff. Typical for Mum to arrange the photos by how much she recognised of their content. By the way, you were right about the new films – she shouldn't have used anything from any of them. Mum was hopelessly out of her depth when it came to choosing which were display-worthy. I wish you'd gone ahead and burnt them all, really. But still, I understand why you wanted to keep them. Why you felt you didn't have the right to destroy them.

Whatever. What's done is done. And it *was* funny, her choosing this one. Mum mustn't have had a clue, otherwise there's no way she would have knowingly exhibited it to all our family and friends on such an occasion. I guess it is hard to make it out if you don't know what you're looking at. Especially with the blurriness and the fact that it's shot on black & white film. Still, it's amazing nobody spotted it. I mean, the balls are right there! Once you've seen it you can't unsee it! I'm especially surprised at the guys from uni – they have the trained eye of the artist and therefore see phallic imagery everywhere, but show them a photo of a genuine set of cock and bollocks and they don't know what to make of it. Or maybe they did, and just didn't want to say anything. It wasn't really the time or place to point it out, I guess.

Benny lies there in the darkness. The ground is hard against his back. He brought the lightweight sleeping mats because of how heavy the pack was getting and now he realises this was a mistake, a failure on his part; he should have brought the heavy-duty ones. Another mistake was allowing Stephen to choose their camping spot – it feels like each time Benny moves there's another root there, nuzzling. He wants to roll over on his front but by now there's a near perfect stillness and such a substantial movement would feel like a violation of this.

Benny wonders if anyone in the history of humanity has ever been able to get to sleep lying on their back. Just then Stephen's breathing grows heavier. He's on his back, exhaling through his nose, his congested nasal passages emitting a high-pitched whistle. He breathes slightly too fast, an almost-pant, and Benny catches his own breath falling into the same rhythm, has to force himself to slow down. Maybe he should have suggested they lie top-and-tail. Although, thinking about it, that would have meant his face was right next to Stephen's recently-Nike-encased feet, which he can already smell from the other end of the tent – a mixture of sweat, rubber and sheep shit. Plus, as Sam was fond of saying each time they'd argue, and Benny would insist on this sleeping arrangement: *the good stuff stays in the middle either way.*

Recently Benny's been resorting to masturbation as a means of coping with his insomnia. He's found that focusing on sex is the best way to keep his mind from wandering to anything he doesn't want to think about. These are the only occasions when he allows himself to think about Sam, although he imagines her wholly as an object* (the softness of skin, the tang of sweat, the sound of hot slapping flesh, etc., etc.). It's a reliable method – even if he doesn't manage to drift off after the first orgasm he can just keep trying, again and again, and by the third or fourth he's so drained he can usually manage to get to sleep. Right now, this method doesn't seem so appealing.† Instead Benny empties his mind as best he can. He tries to forget today, their lateness, their lack of

---

* OK, now *this* is problematic . . .
† THANK GOD.

miles. He tries to forget his failure with the fire. He concentrates on breathing. This is a technique his dad taught him, those nights camping, when he was too excited to sleep. Each time he inhales he pictures a large white screen, the word **IN** printed in huge black letters. Each time he exhales, he thinks: **OUT**.

Benny's not sure why he finds it so difficult to sleep right now. The truth is he's exhausted, has been for months, although he's certain this exhaustion is less to do with a lack of sleep, and more a result of the detachment he's been feeling, the general state of numbness he's come to think of as 'The Fog'. For a while now everything inside him seems to have settled into one long, pervading stillness. Sometimes he imagines this as an actual physical entity – a white mist that amasses in the air around him – although other times it's more like a filter through which everything else is diluted. Except for that unfortunate incident in the camping shop, Benny's managed to keep The Fog at bay the past few weeks. Since he decided to go ahead with the walk he's been able to fill his thoughts with maps and schedules, lists of equipment and supplies. But the truth is The Fog has never really left him. It's always there, lingering.

But he's *here* now. *They're* here. And they're doing it: crossing a country by foot. Benny often associates The Fog with the routine he's got himself into, answering calls at work, scrolling through Facebook and Instagram on his breaks, watching the quiz channel with Mum of an evening, or else meeting Stephen at the Miners once a fortnight for a few pints of watery Guinness. Now Benny's broken that routine. Now they're out here in the wilderness *doing something*. And sure, they haven't got that many miles under their belt yet, but tomorrow will be better. He knows the guidebook cover to cover now, can even picture the maps, if necessary. Tomorrow's flatland mostly. Farmland, fields, towns. A chance to eat up some miles before they get up into the mountains. He tries to focus on that.

Benny found the guidebook in the loft. Which was odd, considering it's a new edition. Still, no matter what it was doing up there, the fact that his dad had gone out and bought a brand-new copy meant he'd been taking Benny's suggestion seriously; he was at least considering the prospect of them undertaking this trip together. Perhaps he'd been up in the loft taking stock of the inventory, had left the guidebook up there by mistake. (It's a possibility.) Perhaps if the chemo hadn't taken such a toll in the weeks that followed, he'd have brought the 'WALK' box down himself, and he and Benny could have begun to plan this thing together.

And his dad keeping the receipt – that didn't mean he was necessarily going to *return* the guidebook. On the contrary, this was something Benny's dad did with all his best-loved books – a receipt, a bus ticket, anything with the date on, a little reminder of when it was bought and read. Benny only observed him doing this during those final months, although according to Benny's mum he'd done it all his life. The more Benny thinks about it now, the more out of character it seems. A bit like his poetry, in that respect: a rare and uncharacteristic act of sentimentality. Although it didn't work – a fact Benny discovered that day he was looking for something to read at the funeral, when he began picking books at random from the shelves in his father's study. Most of the receipts and tickets had long since faded, his father's books now containing only blank slips of paper.

But no, Benny doesn't want this. He doesn't want to think about his dad. Because these memories, they carry others – images of him asleep on the sofa bed in the living room, or in that armchair in the chemo ward, doing Sudoku whilst he waited for the IV to empty, or in the hospice those final days, drifting in and out of consciousness whilst Benny and his mum sat either side of him, watching the quiz channel. These memories are fleeting – nothing concrete, just snapshots. The only fully depicted image is from Benny's first proper day at the call centre; that night he went to the Miners after his first shift, then arrived home to find his father sitting there at the kitchen table, frowning over the top of his glasses. More and more this is becoming Benny's go-to image of his dad: cheeks gaunt, eyes reddened, a cigarette lodged between his skinny white fingers. And that face he pulled as Benny walked in, that look of utter disdain.

Benny wishes he could stop thinking altogether, plug the flow somehow. He's managed to keep his father from his mind all day, but here, at night, alone with his thoughts, it's so much harder to maintain control. He wishes he'd brought earplugs, a defence against Stephen's snoring. He wishes he had a pillow or a proper sleeping mat – these roots are a nightmare on his back.

Suddenly Benny thinks back to earlier, when Stephen nipped out for a shit. Those photos he took of his own dick. He cringes. (How childish! How stupid!) He wonders if there's a way to delete them, but of course it's not so easy with these old cameras. He could open the back, spoil the negative, but then Stephen would lose all of the other pictures he took today along with them.

But again, why focus on this stuff? What good will it do?

Best not to think about it. Best to let it go, let it linger above him. Let it become another component of the vague mass of The Fog.

Best to just concentrate on breathing:

**IN** and **OUT**.
**IN** and **OUT**.
**IN** and **OUT**.

And this method must work eventually; Benny does achieve sleep. He must do, because next thing he knows he's waking in the night, one of those abrupt, sitting-up-in-horror awakenings, as if he's been having a nightmare. Whether he *has* in fact been having a nightmare, it's impossible to know. He hasn't remembered his dreams for months now.

The air is icy. Even in the near-pitch dark he can still see the clouds of his breath, billowing. He's shivering too, his teeth rattling (never before in his life have his teeth actually *rattled*). He reaches over, rummages through his pack, dons every last piece of clothing – T-shirts, fleece, coat and hat. He binds himself in his sleeping bag, drags it up over his head: huddled, foetal. The tent shudders. Branches scratch at the roof like some giant creature, trying to claw its way inside.

Benny rolls onto his front, clenches his jaw to stop the chattering. There's a steady hiss of rain. The walls of the tent flap in the wind. He can smell the earth, the rain. There's still a hint of his father's scent in the groundsheet, that same combination of

Right Guard and cigarette smoke that the old jumper had. Benny ignores the trembling, ignores the cold.

Soon the rattle of the rain dies down. Soon Benny relaxes, lets his mind numb, lets go of the memories that linger in The Fog.

He ignores them, like he ignores the tree roots beneath him. Like he ignores Stephen's whistling snores and gurgling stomach. Like he ignores the sheep, ever baaing in the distance.*

---

* OK, I get that the breathing thing can be annoying, Ben, I really do, but my sinuses were blocked (I mean, I can't be held accountable for *that*, surely?). As for my gurgling belly, well, I'll admit now, I never did manage to squeeze out a shit that first night, nor for the next few days; not until that fateful morning at World's End were my bowels finally voided. TBH, I can't quite fathom how you were able to do it so easily, squatting there with your pants round your ankles. There was no way I'd ever reach the requisite level of relaxation to achieve a decent bowel movement in such a position. It seemed to go against all primal instinct: to bare one's arsehole in nature.

Still, I'm sorry I kept you up. I apologise. I mean, let's be honest here, it sounds like I wasn't the root cause of your insomnia (it actually sounds like my snoring was the *least* of your problems), but still, you had a lot on your plate, I didn't mean to add to it. I have to say though, when it comes to how you're choosing to portray this, I can't help but note that some aspects are . . . (and I'm sorry to use this word again) *problematic*. I understand a lot of your frustrations here, Ben, I really do. These little niggles – these idiosyncrasies and petty annoyances – they can start to grind after a certain amount of time in each other's company. (I mean, let's be honest, if you think *you* were a pleasure to be around those four days then I've got some news for you . . .)

But still, I've got this sneaking suspicion that you might be focusing on this stuff as a way of somehow trying to justify what happened at World's End. And, if so, you're way off the mark, man. I mean seriously. What you did that day isn't something you can excuse yourself from, no matter how much work you put into painting me somehow worthy of your disdain. It's something that, sooner or later, you're just going to have to go ahead and face up to.

Whether by that point you'll still be portraying yourself as the victim, well I guess we'll just have to wait and see, won't we?

# RUN

# V

*Heat – Aches and pains – Message to Sam –*
*Alarm – The usual routine – Call centre – Human*
*stress ball – Background image – Breakfast –*
*Mucus slug – Back on the path – Carrying the*
*tent – Inhaler – Rhuallt – No one's home – Fields*
*– Tastes like chicken – Ramblers – Thirst –*
*Puddles – Poor Nikes – A fall.*

The sun rises. The walls of the tent glow a bright burning red. The air inside gets hotter and hotter and hotter. Until it's unbearable.

Benny kicks back his sleeping bag. He tears off his hat, wriggles from his coat and fleece. He unzips the door flap and stumbles out through the porch, squinting, stealing gasps of cool morning air. His muscles are aching, especially his thighs and calves, and with each movement comes a series of tearing pains. He's sweating. He can feel yesterday's sunburn, a heat radiating from his face and forearms. He can feel the dull throb of the headache, now settled at the front of his skull.

He retrieves his sunglasses from his pack, as well as his tobacco pouch, then sits in the porch, feet in the icy wet grass, rolling a cigarette. He listens to the birds, the sheep in the distance. He watches bugs, so many unidentifiable black flecks with legs and antennae and lives of their own, infesting the grass beneath him.

He breathes – **IN** and **OUT**, **IN** and **OUT** – whilst Stephen snores in the tent behind.

There's a throbbing pain in his thigh. He hadn't noticed at first, what with all his other aches and pains, but he realises it's due to his pocket having flipped over, the contents balled tight. He works his fingers inside, retrieves the little Offa's Dyke plaque with the acorn symbol. But no, not just that, also the stone, the skimmer from Prestatyn beach. But not just that, also his phone, its screen black and mirror-like in the sunlight. He lays them out, one by one, on the groundsheet of the porch. He picks up the phone again, takes a second to examine his hairline in the reflection before holding down the power button. '**HELLO**', it reads as it loads.

He'd messaged Sam yesterday morning. It was the first time in months, the first time since she went back to Ireland. He had told her everything, about his dad, the trip to Wales, about how much he'd regretted what he'd said the last time they'd spoken. It was a message he'd been constructing in his head for weeks, yet it still took nearly the whole train ride to type it out. He doesn't know what he's hoping to get in the way of a response. Once he'd sent the message he deleted it from his phone, knowing that otherwise he would obsess over it, reread it again and again. He can't remember now whether he finished on a note that would warrant a reply. He can't remember if he'd mentioned that the trail they were taking would likely leave them without phone signal for days on end. He can't remember if he took out the part where he said he was still in love with her.

The phone loads up. A background image appears: a photo of Sam's cat, Maggie. He should have changed that by now, should have deleted it when she moved back to Ireland, that way he wouldn't have to feel that jolt of regret each time he switched on his phone, the memory of Sam pouring forth from that cat's slightly riled glare. His phone is now on 72% battery, which is odd – he's sure it was in the 90s yesterday (how can the battery drain even when it's switched off?). There are no new messages. Then again, still no signal, so she's not necessarily ignoring him. He checks his hairline again. He briefly considers examining it more thoroughly in the forward-facing camera but decides against it. He holds down the power button. ('**GOODBYE**'.)

Benny retrieves the packet of ibuprofen, swallows down a couple of pills. He remembers his father once telling him that the pain in his muscles was a good thing, a result of the tissue rebuilding, an indication that his body is getting stronger. He traces the soles of his feet with his fingertips, still raw, the under-side of his toes reddened, ready to blister. His shins are tender too, the combination of nettles and brambles and the rubbing of his boots – and there's sunburn on his neck and forehead. But still, he's not too irked by these pains. He thinks of them as *ailments*. This was one of his mum's words. She used it often when he and Amy were little, a way to make them reassess the seriousness of childhood cuts and knee-scrapes. And it works, attaching this term to his various aches and pains. *Ailments*. It reduces them somehow.

Suddenly his phone lights up again, this time of its own initia-tive. A little bell symbol appears and the alarm sounds with two options: '**Snooze**' or '**Cancel**'. The alarm is the intro to a song, the only song on his phone's internal storage: 'Dancing in the Moonlight' by Thin Lizzy. It's a song Benny loved back in univer-sity and at one point associated with Sam (with whom he literally danced in the moonlight on their first date) but now only asso-ciates with early mornings. He hasn't listened to more than the first two lines for years. He should change it. He will change it, at some point. Just not today.

He listens to the opening two lines, then selects '**Cancel**'. Usually he'd have snoozed a couple of times before climbing out of bed, showering and getting dressed, driving down to the call centre. Usually he'd be contemplating a day of sitting alongside rows of other bored twenty-somethings, navigating the intricacies of the UK benefits system. The callers are Universal Credit claimants, although they've often got a whole host of other prob-lems they want to offload on their call handler – stuff about landlords or loan sharks, bad bosses and zero-hour contracts – none of which Benny has any control over. Nor does he have much control over their benefit payments; there's usually some issue there too, a shortfall or a sanction or a problem with their claim date, although all Benny can really do is talk them through the reality of their situation. Sometimes it's just that they want someone to moan at. Sometimes they cry, beg. Still, Benny just browses their claim, advises them as best he can, all while trying to keep down his call time averages. He's not a manager; he's not a decision maker. So, mostly, this is Benny's job; to take the blame for things he hasn't done. To be a human stress ball. And to nod, always nodding along, faux-sympathetically, only to realise that he's speaking to them over the phone, that nobody can even see him nodding.

But still, he needs the money. There's no way his mum could afford the mortgage without him. And, like his employment advisor said back when he first applied, the DWP is the only organisation in the area with jobs right now. It's a good stopgap, a place to work whilst he searches for an entry into his chosen career path. And sure, there's a certain irony that the only place he can find work is answering calls for Universal Credit, but that's true for a lot of people – especially other recent graduates. Unemployment levels meant record numbers of applications, which in turn meant a brand-new call centre, just down the road from where Benny grew up, and so loads of people from school now work there. There are people at the call centre with Biology degrees, Psychology degrees. There are people with Engineering degrees, like Benny, and many with Arts and Humanities degrees, all sitting together in rows of polystyrene cubicles, with headsets, answering: *Hi, you're through to Universal Credit, INSERT NAME speaking . . .*

Stephen could get a job there too. Benny's forwarded him links to positions on three separate occasions, but whenever he mentions it Stephen swiftly changes the subject. Benny always assumed Stephen was unlucky in the application process or maybe felt unsure about applying, seems a lot of their old class-mates are there, but it turns out Stephen's been avoiding it for reasons of moral superiority.* Benny's aware Stephen isn't a fan of the government (Benny isn't either) but sometimes you have to make the best of a bad situation.† It's an employer's market out there. Benny's reasoning is that, if he didn't take the job, they'd just be giving the salary to someone else. It was better to be on the inside, working for them, than having to attend those soul-destroying meetings every week at the job centre.

---

* Or 'human decency'?

† How very capitalist of you, Ben.

Benny closes his eyes. For a moment he imagines he's back in the call centre, about to accept his first caller of the day. He summons the feeling of his office chair pressing into his back. The tightness of his headset. The smell of dust burning in computer fans.

Then he opens his eyes, takes in the valleys. He sighs.

He switches his phone on again and takes a photo. The tree, the remnants of last night's attempt at a fire – the fields, the path ahead. It's a good photo, he thinks. Maybe not 'art', maybe not T-shirt-worthy, but the sky's blue and there's a nice view and the branches of the tree frame it all in a way that's pleasing to the eye. He deletes the picture of Sam's cat, sets this as his new background. His battery has now dropped to 68%, but it's worth it.

Then he switches off his phone again. He slips it back in his pocket, along with the plaque and the stone. He takes one final drag of his cigarette and stubs it out in the grass, then pockets that too.

He reaches into the tent, holding his breath against the tang of sweat and sleeping, and shakes Stephen's ankle.

'Come on, Ste.'

'Hmm?'

'We've got to get going. Need to get back on the road. A.S.A.P.'

'*Urgh.*'

They cook more noodles for breakfast, then bag up their rubbish. Benny nips behind the bushes, finds a private spot to take a shit. He digs a hole with the trowel and squats there for a minute, allowing gravity to do its work – then stands and fastens his trousers. Human shit is somehow more disgusting than that of any other animal, which is probably why his father was always insistent they bury it as deeply as possible back on their camping trips. It smells worse too – a stench that (thankfully) fades as soon as he refills the hole.

Benny returns to find Stephen sitting on the grass. He offers him the trowel and toilet paper, but Ste takes one look at them and winces. He says he's fine thanks, he doesn't need them. He says he feels refreshed today, although he looks just as worn out as last night – his breathing forced, a small but very green slug of mucus edging from his left nostril. There are patches of sunburn on his cheeks and neck and his arms are mottled pink. His fringe has continued to curl in the night and he keeps pawing at it, trying to secure it beneath the white elastic of his sun visor. He snorts a few times but never manages to retract the mucus slug. It remains wedged there in his nostril, like a pea.

It's Stephen's turn to carry the tent today. Benny promises himself he'll make Stephen do it, no matter how tired he appears. After all, it's Benny who has to dismantle the thing; has to fold up the frame, roll the ground sheet, slot everything into that unnecessarily tight canvas bag. Stephen makes the minimal effort of collecting the pegs before slumping against the tree trunk, staring at his trainers, playing with his fringe. Once the tent is packed away Benny carries it over, drops it at Stephen's feet, waits. But Stephen says nothing. He keeps his head down, trying to drag his hair in place over his left eyebrow, muttering each time it springs back into its former curl. So it's Benny who ends up hoisting the tent-bag and fastening it to the top of his pack, and it's Benny who then struggles under its weight as they continue through the ferns, down the path into Rhuallt.*

The ground here is rocky. Benny's feet are aching. Even through his walking boots, the rocks nuzzle his still-tender soles. He can't imagine how Stephen's feet must feel. Stephen's tracksuit finishes a good six inches above his ankle and he appears not to be wearing any socks, which means the soles of his feet are protected only by his flimsy Nikes.† Soon they come out on a country road, follow it south-east into the town. Benny sips from his flask. They didn't add any flavour-packets to their breakfast noodles because they weren't sure the chicken flavouring

---

* You could have just *asked*, you know?

† Wrong. I was in fact wearing ankle socks. (Also, for the record, I don't remember you once mentioning I should buy boots. A backpack, yes – a rain mac – but never *boots*.)

would make for a particularly pleasant first meal of the day. Plus, they needed to save the water, as it's the only water they have left. And so, this is what Benny sips: thick, frothy noodle water. They didn't wash this morning either, just made do with wet wipes and deodorant. They didn't brush their teeth or brew coffee; made do with chewing gum instead. They must find more water soon. This is a priority.

Benny thought he'd get used to the weight of the pack – that today would be easier – but the truth is it somehow feels even heavier than yesterday. It's not just the tent, he's also carrying all of the cooking equipment, food, water, etc. Plus, there's the bag of rubbish (which he's tied to one of the shoulder straps, and which bounces at his elbow with each step). Then there's the clothes, the toiletries, the hatchet, the trowel, the flint, the penknife, not to mention the plastic tub containing a portion of his dad's ashes. The weight reminds him of Sam. Sometimes Benny used to give her piggybacks. Only short distances, like through the kitchen in winter when the tiles were cold, or across the communal garden on summer mornings when the grass was dewy. As they continue their descent into Rhuallt, Benny can't help but consider whether he'd have agreed to give Sam a piggyback across an entire country.

By this point Stephen's straggling a little so Benny stops and waits at the bottom of the hill. Stephen *hoik*s a wad of phlegm into the ferns to his left. He's clutching a small plastic object that he rattles and holds to his mouth. He breathes in, and as he does so it makes this sound: *hiccchhht*.

'You OK?'
   'Yeah, man. Great.'
'What is that, an inhaler?'
   'Yeah.'
'I didn't know you had asthma.'
   'It's just allergies. They think that's what causes the mucus.'
'Allergic to what?'
   'They don't know.' *Hiccchhht*. 'They think it might be animal hair. Although, sometimes I get it when I drink too.'

63

'Animal hair?'

'Yeah, like pet hair.'

'Do you have any pets?'

'No.'

'Well, there aren't any animals out here . . . Except sheep. Maybe you're allergic to sheep.'

'I think I'm allergic to life.'

*Hoik.*

'Nose still blocked too, eh?'

'It gets this way sometimes, man. The mucus. Some days it's like I'm drowning in the stuff.'

*Hoik.*

*Hiccchhht.*

They continue through Rhuallt. It's not so much a town, more a collection of country lanes, hedges obscuring the occasional house. Benny can't see anywhere to fill up their water bottles. Stephen says maybe they should knock at one of the houses, ask to use their tap.

Benny knocks at four different houses but there's no answer. Maybe no one's home. Maybe they're still in bed. Or maybe it's because each time Benny knocks, Stephen slides off his pack and sits there at the end of the driveway, sipping what's left of their noodle water, playing with his corkscrewing curls of hair. Anyone in their right mind who hears knocking and peers out the window to see *that* at the end of their path isn't likely to come and answer the door.

Benny glances round the side of a couple of houses to see if there's an outside tap they can help themselves to. There isn't.

Their departure from Rhuallt is as uneventful as their arrival. The lack of water's still an issue but Benny's glad, really, to be out of the town. They're making progress; soon they'll reach the next page. They'll pass through Bodfari (where they're bound to find water) and be up in the mountains. That's what Benny craves today: mountains. Occasionally he can make them out, a bank of grass and rock in the distance. In the guidebook it's three pages. Seventeen inches. Seven miles. All he keeps thinking is

64

that, once they're the other side of the mountains, they're sure to be rid of the sight of the sea.

'I'm sure I can taste chicken, man.'
　'That's impossible.'
　'Honestly. This water tastes like chicken. You sure this is vegan?'
　'We didn't add any flavouring, Ste. It's just noodle water.'
　'I'm still getting chicken.'
　'Well, I don't know how.'
　'It's not unpleasant, man. Just . . . *chickeny*.'
　*Hiccchhht.*

In the next field, they approach an elderly couple, the first people they've seen all morning. They're a young-looking old couple. Fit. It's obvious they're old, but hard to guess *how* old exactly because of how fit they look. Each is wearing a purple fleece and lycra shorts that show off their tanned, muscular legs. The man's hair is slicked back – slightly receding, but when he turns to glance at the path behind there's minimal thinning at the crown, so he's doing well for his age, follicularly speaking. The old lady has a sun visor, not unlike Stephen's. Neither has a pack, just a minuscule, drawstring bag.

　Benny prepares to give the usual nod-and-smile reserved for these passings but the old couple stop right in front of them, and so Benny and Stephen have no choice but to also stop and make small talk. It turns out the old couple are walking the dyke too, only south to north, which means they'll most likely finish this afternoon. The woman asks if Benny and Stephen set off that morning. Benny's about to lie, pretend this is their first day, when Stephen says no, they started yesterday. The old couple smile at each other: two sets of small white teeth, faces lined like cracked clay. Stephen smiles back, takes another hit from his inhaler.

　They endure the conversation for a few more minutes. The man points to the tent on Benny's back, says they're brave, carrying a load like that and Benny nods, unsure of how to respond. The woman asks if they're seasoned ramblers and Benny winces slightly at that term. He doesn't want to think of him and

Stephen as *ramblers* – prefers the term *explorers* or *adventurers*. The old couple however *are* ramblers, that much is clear, and there's something in the dorkiness of this that allows Benny to internally sneer; something about this rambler status that allows him to overlook the fact that, in spite of their age, the old couple are clearly fitter and more prepared than him and Stephen, and instead let all sorts of subversive thoughts flood forth, e.g. that they're probably retired geography teachers who go everywhere in those matching fleeces and bore people to death at dinner parties discussing their many walking holidays and that they probably haven't had sex once in the last thirty years. Benny was going to ask how far it is to Bodfari, or if they know of a place to obtain some water nearby, or maybe just enquire as to where the hell all of *their* camping gear is, seems him and Stephen are stooped, panting from the weight on their backs, yet somehow this elderly couple are surviving a cross-country walk with just two drawstring bags and a sun visor. But these people are *ramblers* and Benny doesn't want to ask them anything.

Benny says he and Stephen had best be leaving. The old woman says yes, they've still got a long way to go. They bid each other farewell, the old couple heading north, Benny and Stephen continuing south.

Before long they've lost sight of them along the road.*

----

* It's interesting that you make these distinctions about who you consider to be 'ramblers'. I mean, why did your dad not fit this definition? Didn't he also buy into that whole lifestyle? Haven't *you*, for that matter, what with all the equipment and walking gear and the 'Countryside Code'? (Also, is there really that much of a difference, in terms of levels of dorkiness, between Geography and English teachers?)

In saying that, I suppose a glamorised version of a recently deceased father is a fairly common trait, psychologically speaking. I had a similar thing with Garth from uni. Not that I saw Garth as a *father figure* or anything (please don't read too much into potential Freudian connotations there), but when I think back, I definitely remember our relationship with a certain amount of rose-tintedness. By the time of the walk I hadn't seen Garth for over a year, although he was prolific on social media, and had recently posted pictures of his London gallery work – his latest *Unstill Life* pieces – which were truly shocking, in the best possible way. I still thought

'They were nice.'

'Yeah?'

'Yeah, man.' *Pause.* 'Although, like . . . maybe we should have asked for water.'

'You see the size of their packs? Did it look like they had water to spare?'

'They might have known of somewhere though. A tap. Or a fountain. Or, like, a *mountain spring*.'

'We'll find some, Ste. Don't worry.'

'I think this noodle water's just making it worse. It seems to be coating my throat. You sure you can't taste that? Like a thick, chicken taste?'

'Don't drink it then.'

'It just seems to be making me thirstier. We should have asked them, man.'

'You could always run after them.'

'We should have asked where to get a decent breakfast too. Those noodles did nothing, I'm starving.'

They arrive at a bridge that passes over a main road. Traffic speeds by below. It's a shock, what with how quiet their morning's been. All they've heard so far is baaing and birdsong and now this: the roar of the motorway. For everyone else this is just a normal day. The rush-hour commute.

---

about Garth pretty much every day – how could I not? He gave me the camera. He gave me Frank. He fostered within me a political conscience, as well as a genuine artistic purpose. He was a bigger influence on me than anyone else I'd ever come across in my life. There was just something about that whole experience – the house with him and Olga, the artistic journey, the copious amounts of drinking and fucking and drug taking. It didn't seem like anything could ever live up to it. I remember when it was all over, when I came home, how I'd lie there in bed in the attic room, wishing I could go back, even just for one night. Even just to attend one of those legendary 'ARTies' again. I didn't give much thought to the flip-side of that lifestyle: the hangovers / the mess / the more volatile sides to Garth's personality. Nor did I fixate on how difficult things became, finan-cially. I just remembered the good times.

They head west, continue parallel to the main road for a few hundred yards, then follow the signs across more fields. The first few are relatively dry, but as they descend the grass gets boggy. It's possible this is a result of last night's downpour, although there are also strips of hose on the ground, so it could be some sort of botched irrigation system. Soon they come to a field that's entirely waterlogged – brown puddles the size of garden ponds. There's a large oak tree in the middle. At the far side is a stile, leading to a patch of trees.

Benny leads the way, avoiding the larger puddles as best he can.

'Ick.'
    'Just try to follow my lead, Ste.'
    'My poor Nikes, man. Jesus.'

Benny's boots squelch in the grass. Mud bubbles. There's a gutter-stench of stagnant water.

His boots are still relatively unsoiled; yesterday they remained quite clean (except for the sheep shit, clogging the soles), but here, in the muddied field just outside of Rhuallt, they are finally *dirty*. Each step the waterline rises, discolours them, dying the brown leather black. Camping Shop Mike said the boots were an investment, that they will last for years, that real leather never spoils, but Benny has been secretly hoping that they'd dirty a bit. That it wouldn't take long for them to get that worn look.

A few more steps and Benny arrives at the tree. He uses the branches to steady himself.

'It's quite dry up here, Ste.'
    *[Distant.]* 'What?'
    'It's better here by the tree. Not quite so muddy.'
    *Pause. [Distant.]* 'Right.'

Benny continues until he reaches the fence at the back of the field. He leans against the stile, scrapes some of the mud from his boots on the wooden step. He turns back.

Stephen's still only halfway across. He hasn't even reached the tree yet. He shouts over that one of his Nikes is stuck. He's sinking. Then his foot pops out: trainerless, white and flailing. All of his weight's now on the other foot, the muddied water rising to his shin. He reaches to retrieve his trainer and there's a loud sucking sound as he pulls it from the ground, and then he loses his balance, topples, splatters in the mud.

He moans.

Benny takes a cigarette from behind his ear, lights it.


'I think it's sprained, man.'

'If it was sprained, you'd feel it.'

'I *can* feel it.'

'*Really* feel it. You'd *know* if it was sprained.'

'Isn't that when you break something? Isn't it, "You'd know if it was *broken*"? I thought sprains varied, in terms of pain.'

'Let's see.'

'There, look.'

'It's too muddy, I can't—'

'Hang on.' *Pause.* 'Ick.'

'It's red, but I think that's just sunburn. It doesn't look sprained.'

'What does sprained look like?'

'I don't know. You'd just know, I think. There wouldn't be this doubt. Not if it was properly sprained.' *Pause.* 'We'll keep an eye on it, OK?'

'Keep an eye on it?'

'Yeah.'

'*Great.*'

*Pause.*

'What else can we do?'

# VI

*Road to Bodfari – Broken sunglasses – The thirst
returns – Running – Sam's water bottle – Mind
over matter – Chest buckle – A not very sophisticated pack – Stephen's invite – Depth perception
– Bench – Mental images of thick-cut chips.*

They descend through the trees to a country lane. Occasionally
the trail splits across a field or two, but mostly it's just road –
miles and miles of hedge-lined tarmac. How many miles, Benny
doesn't know. It'd be easy enough to find out, but he doesn't
want to stop to retrieve the guidebook. He keeps telling himself
that this is the boring part, that they're getting it out the way
first. That's what his father had said. There are some good views
tomorrow, up in the mountains, but aside from that the northern
leg is a bit dull. Benny just needs to wait it out, keep walking.

The sun's out now. Stephen insists on stopping to search for
his sunglasses, but once he puts them on, he finds one of the
lenses has popped out. He now looks less like John Lennon, more
like some sort of deranged pirate. He adds the sunglasses to the
contents of the rubbish bag, tied to Benny's pack; says it's a good
job he also brought the sun visor.

By this point the thirst aches. Benny tries to distance himself
from it, imagine it as another *ailment*, something he can tolerate,
but as the morning wears on it becomes all he can think about.
They should have knocked at more cottages back in Rhuallt.
Stephen should have knocked too. They could have found water
if they'd tried. If Stephen had even pretended to try. It was a
priority and they failed and now they're suffering.

It dawns on Benny that he hasn't known thirst like this for
years – not since back in uni, those mornings he used to go

running with Sam. Benny lived at home as a student, although he stayed over at Sam's more and more as time went on, and he could never quite get on board with all her healthy lifestyle stuff; the workouts, the Instagram photos, the tubs of chicken and couscous she'd prepare each night before bed. He did go running with her a few times – a lap of the campus that took them along Hankin Street and through University Square, finishing back at her accommodation building – and often by the end of those runs he'd find himself experiencing whole new levels of all-consuming thirst.

It was his own fault, really – he should have got one of those water bottles all the other runners seemed to have. Sam told him as much (at one point even offering to buy him one as a gift) but, at the time, such a purchase felt like a commitment to a new lifestyle that he wasn't willing to make. Sometimes on their runs Sam would slow a little, offer him sips from her own bottle, but Benny tended to refuse. Sam had this special water bottle with a 'natural filter', a stick of charcoal that bobbed around as she ran. The idea was that it purified the water, although each time Benny saw that floating black lump he couldn't help but think of an unflushable turd in a toilet bowl.

Sometimes it was nice though, in a way, to experience that thirst. It made it all the more satisfying when he got home and was finally able to pour himself that long-awaited glass of water. In fact, often it was this very thought that spurred him on. He'd spend his time running imagining it: the hiss of the tap . . . the shudder of the spout . . . the crashing torrent as the glass filled . . . the clink of the hard rim against his teeth and then . . . *ahh*, the ultimate satisfaction, that cool, soothing texture flooding his mouth. How can water, a drink widely acknowledged to have absolutely no taste, taste so *good*? Benny remembers how, some-times, on the final stretch of their morning runs, he'd deliberately torture himself; conjure up images of the water whilst maintaining an open mouth, in order to dry out his tongue as much as possible. It all built to that sweet moment when he was standing there in the flat's communal kitchen, pint of water on the work surface before him, sweating icy droplets. This was the moment he loved most – not the drinking of the water, but those few seconds *before* drinking it, when he'd think: *This is it, this is what I've been waiting for. I'm going to drink the water.* And then he'd drink the water.

Right now, there's no pint of water. Right now, there's not even any warm, noodle run-off left. And Benny's thirsty. And these thoughts, they spread like wildfire. He can't help but picture vast lakes or waterfalls. Trickling streams. He can't help but summon up the taste of other refreshments, long since consumed: the cool smoothness of the Guinness yesterday at that café in Prestatyn, or those Calippos Sam would buy on those sunny days at the start of term, as they walked back from their lectures. Benny's dad was expert at rationing. He was always in charge of the water on their walks and would monitor its usage, refilling their personal flasks only as and when he deemed fit. On all those walks with his dad and Uncle Ian, Benny doesn't once remember running out of water.

But Benny doesn't want to dwell on this stuff. This isn't the point. He's supposed to be clearing his mind, walking *away* from all this. Already he knows the plan is flawed. On a trip like this he's going to be pretty much alone with his thoughts for days on end. How's he supposed to not *think*?

*Mind over matter.* That's something people say, isn't it? Although what the fuck does that even mean? Because delving into his mind has made Benny even thirstier than before. By now he longs for rain. Fuck Stephen, fuck his lack of mac. Benny just wants to tilt his head back, welcome the deluge with an open mouth.

'Agh, my ankle, man. I really think I hurt it.'
*Hiccchhht.*

Benny sighs. The weight of the pack is beginning to wear on him. He fiddles with the two strips of elastic that hang from the shoulder straps. At the end of each strip is a fabric loop, holding alternate halves of a black, plastic, snap-fit buckle – the left strip home to the actual buckle-part, the right the three-pronged fork.

Once joined (with a satisfying click) the buckle holds the elastic tightly across his chest. It's designed to redistribute some of the weight from his shoulders, but Benny clips and unclips and can't decide whether the pressure is eased or not. In the end he decides it makes little difference, certainly not enough to justify the rubbing of the buckle on his chest, which soon starts to itch.

Stephen's pack doesn't have a chest buckle. It isn't a very sophisticated pack. Ste picked it up at Oxfam, along with the sun visor. They had plenty of proper packs at the camping shop, but Stephen had chosen not to come along. It would have been a nice gesture on his part – to join Benny on that trip to the camping shop. If Stephen had been there then maybe Mike wouldn't have been giving such a hard sell on the one-man tents, and Benny wouldn't have felt compelled to test one of them out, which would have saved him from that whole embarrassing incident.

Stephen had seemed enthusiastic about the walk, when Benny first invited him. Ste kept going on about how amazing it'd be, the two of them out in the wilderness – the landscape shots, the pubs, etc., etc. Benny didn't interrupt this stream of enthusiasm. They were in the car park of the Miners, and Benny was too busy concentrating on his own stream of piss – trying his best to avoid dousing his shoes – as, in his drunken state, this took up most of his mental capacity. Walking home he changed the subject, pushed the trip to the back of his mind. He didn't think about it at all until the next morning, when the memory rode back on the wave of familiar white horror: The Fog. When he remembered inviting Stephen, Benny laughed out loud – a single *ha* – then spent three minutes silent-screaming into his pillow.

But no, enough of this. Benny licks his lips. He closes his eyes. Various sounds merge: the breathing, the clomping of his boots, the stamp-then-scrape of Stephen's limping. The sheep, unseen but ever-baaing in the distance. There's a rhythmic quality to it all.

'I mean it, man. This ankle. Jesus.'
*Hiccchhht. Hoik.*

—

Benny devises a way to make time pass; a method to occupy his mind for that last stretch to Bodfari. It goes something like this:

First, he picks an object on the horizon – a tree, a rock, a sheep. He then fixates on this one object, clears his mind of everything else. He concentrates on the appearance of the object in that present moment – its size, shape, colour. He closes his eyes, holds the image of it in his mind, waits for second after second to pass. Then he opens his eyes, evaluates how much the object has grown, how much nearer it is, how this passage of time has brought some sort of bounty, an edging-towards-a-final-destination, however slight. It's not the most engrossing activity but it stops his thoughts straying to his thirst. Or his dad. Or Sam. Or his hairline.

And it works. Inevitably each object grows, reaches its literal size, passes them, then recedes along the road behind. Time is passing. Inches of map. One step and then the next step. One mile and then the next.

Still, each time he turns to watch the object shrink behind, Benny can't help but imagine the flat bed of the sea – never shifting, never shrinking.

'Urgnflk. This fuckin' ankle, man. I'm telling you. Grdfgdf. *Agghh.*'

Suddenly: a bench. It appears on the horizon, grows to its literal size and Benny and Stephen stop and sit. Neither removes his pack. Instead they perch at the edge, heads hung, panting. Benny's head is hurting. He wants more ibuprofen. He wants to smoke, too (*needs* to smoke) but is aware that smoking will only increase the thirst.

Stephen asks how far now. Benny shrugs. No landmarks means no way of knowing. They're somewhere in the few inches of map between Rhuallt and Bodfari. That's all he can be sure of. Eventually a forest should appear. Just beyond that will be Bodfari. As soon as they see forest, they'll know they've nearly reached the town.

There's a pub in Bodfari. Benny spotted it in the guidebook yesterday, a tiny blue pint symbol. Maybe they could have a beer?

Maybe they could get a cooked meal? As soon as Benny mentions it, he knows it was a bad idea – the wrong moment. What follows is a silence filled with images of cold pints of Guinness and thick-cut chips.

Soon they set off again. The clouds disperse. The sun glares down. No matter how much they squint, there's no sign of any forest on the horizon.

Benny tries his best to ignore Stephen, concentrate on his walking.

One step and then the next step.

One mile and then the next mile.★

---

★ I'm genuinely sorry that I was such a liability to you, Ben – but I have to disagree with some of the stuff you've said here, especially with regards to my position as your walking companion. Not so much the stuff about my helplessness (I'm aware how out of my depth I was with regard to the physical demands of the trip) but rather your assumptions that I didn't *care*. I get that this was a big deal for you, but you're making out like I agreed to come along on a whim, which simply is not true. For one thing, I was aware of the walk long before that night in the Miners. You mentioned it one night the year before, back when Cal was still on the scene, remember? Cal was excited about the idea, said we should all go, but you insisted you wanted to go with your dad. Still, even back then I was hoping you'd change your mind, that we could all go. It sounded like an adventure.

I mean, just consider where I was at that point, Ben, in terms of my mental and spiritual wellbeing. I'd come home from university a failure. Granted, you weren't yet aware of the extent of my failings (you didn't know about my dropping out of the course) but at the very least you must have realised how lacking I was, from a financial perspective. I was hopeless; bereft in a world that appeared to not only be questioning the value of the arts, but the value of humanity itself. And then that whole thing with Cal, that affected me too, you know. Our already diminished friendship group cut down even further. I was spending the vast majority of time in my room by that point, concentrating on *Doomed Youth Pt.7*. An occasional trip to the pub with you was the only time I left the house, the only time I left the attic really. My room had everything I needed. I'd set up my studio there. I had my own mini-fridge full of beers. I had that 2l cider bottle with the top cut off I'd piss into. Each morning I'd pour the piss out the window. I mean *Jesus*, man, this was my life.

So when you mentioned the walk again, asked if I'd like to come along,

75

it felt exciting; a chance to get away from the routine. But you're right about one thing, I didn't get involved with the planning of the trip, not as much as I'd have liked to, and this did have a massive effect on my overall preparedness. But it's not just that I couldn't be bothered, I made a *conscious decision* to distance myself from you during those few weeks. I could tell that you regretted inviting me. I knew as much that night in the Miners car park (FYI you're terrible at hiding that kind of stuff, especially when you've had a few drinks). Then, the next time we met up, when I asked about arrangements, I saw that look in your eyes, that fraction-of-a-second glance of horror before the shutters went down, before you tried to act all nonchalant about it. So I didn't mention it again. Not until the week before, when I messaged you to ask what the plans were. And I can see now, how that looked bad on my part, uncaring, but I felt as if I had no choice. I knew that my position as your walking companion was temperamental at best and I didn't want to give you any opportunity to uninvite me. I needed this as much as you did.

So I'm sorry you felt this way. And I'm sorry to keep interrupting. But I think it's important to set the record straight. I mean, isn't that what this is all about, Ben? Explaining how things played out on that trip? Setting the record straight?

# VII

*Forest – Pub – Two Welshmen – Drinks order –*
*Snacks order – 'The Royal Shitannia' – Money*
*– 'Grim is good' – Filling bottles – Eyed with*
*suspicion – Inquisition – A bet – Departure.*

They continue along country roads for another hour. Eventually
they arrive at the small patch of forest. This is the same forest they'd
planned to camp in yesterday, although it's now obvious how
unrealistic this plan was. There's hardly any floor space for the
tent and pegging would have been impossible due to the density
of the roots. Through the gaps in the trees they can just about
make out fields and a town below.

The trail curves south. They descend a hedge-lined road. At
the bottom is a building – black and white, Tudor-style, rows of
picnic tables out front. The pub.

They take a seat at one of the tables, catch their breath. They
unbuckle their packs, let them slide to the pavement. They feel
so much lighter without them, as if they could float away. Benny
rubs at his shoulders where the straps have left deep red inden-
tations, chafed skin. His sunburn tingles in the breeze. Stephen
takes a few shots from his inhaler then unties his trainers, peels
off his socks, wrings the muddied water from them and lays them
on the table to dry. He lifts his leg, guides it up onto the bench,
wincing at the pain in his ankle.

He slouches back against the wall, sighs.

'I'll get the drinks then, shall I?'

Benny steps inside the pub. The interior is dark, the walls papered
florally, lined with shelves displaying what Benny's dad would

have described as *tat* – an assortment of teapots, Toby Jugs, porcelain figurines and decorative dinner plates. There's an excessive amount of side tables and mismatching armchairs between the doorway and the bar at the far side of the room, where a single punter is propped, chatting with the barman. Both are old, rotund Welshmen – flat caps, beards, those thick woollen jumpers with dark leather elbow patches. They're speaking their native tongue. Which should be no surprise, really, that there are Welsh-speakers here in Bodfari, but for a moment it stops Benny in his tracks.

Suddenly they cease talking and turn to Benny. The punter shifts in his stool, leans back against the bar. The barman calls over in Welsh, something with an inflection at the end, a question. Benny just smiles, tries to appear casual as he edges through the furniture towards the bar. He tells the barman he's sorry, he's English, he doesn't understand. He stops at the bar, raises two fingers like a peace sign, explains that he'd just like two pints of tap water and two Guinnesses, please. The barman nods. He turns to the Guinness tap, pours each drink slowly, waiting for the obligatory settling period, never once allowing his face to break into a smile. Benny turns to the man beside him – his fellow punter – but finds him avoiding eye contact, staring straight down into his pint. Benny doesn't take offence. He is, after all, a young English walker, a type they probably see a lot of and judge accordingly. Plus, he hasn't washed for over twenty-four hours now, so there's a good chance he's stinking the place out. Instead he stares ahead at the paintings on the wall behind the bar. They are watercolours mostly, blurred approximations of farms and fields.

Benny asks if they're still serving food. The barman shakes his head – no, it's past lunchtime – hands Benny his change. What about dinner? It's not dinnertime for a good few hours yet. Benny asks if they sell crisps and the barman nods and so Benny orders a selection, every flavour the pub has to offer. It turns out all they have are variants of beef – Walkers Beef & Onion, McCoy's Flame Grilled Steak, BBQ Beef Hula Hoops. Benny asks if they're vegan and the barman shrugs and so Benny says it's OK, he'll take one of each, as well as two packets of peanuts. He pays with another twenty (the last of his physical cash) then carries everything out together, all four glasses cupped between his two hands, crisps and nuts stuffed in pockets or tucked under his arms. He loses his grip on one of the packets of nuts, watches it bounce on a chair and disappear under the table. He decides to leave it. The whole time he can feel the barman watching.

He manages to transport the drinks outside without any serious spills. By this point Stephen is slumped across the table but the thud of glass against the hard surface rouses him and he sits up, joins Benny in gaping awestruck at the drinks. Benny wants to pause, to take in this moment, appreciate the sacredness of it, these final pre-drinking seconds of his soon-to-be-eradicated thirst – but Stephen pays no attention. He grabs his water without a thought, glugs it in great gasping swallows. Benny shrugs, joins in. The water is cold. He can feel the chill of it spread through every cell in his body. It feels incredible. Once the water's gone, the two of them move on to their Guinnesses, steady sips of black liquid velvet. So rich, so thick; it was yesterday – only yesterday! – that they last drank Guinness and yet it feels like weeks ago. This is good Guinness too; this isn't like that swill at the café yesterday or the watered-down stuff at the Miners. This is cold, creamy, hints of chocolate and coffee and a chalky other-ness Benny can't put his finger on. It was something he and Sam used to argue about, the taste of the Guinness in certain pubs. That was before her healthy lifestyle stuff started, when she gave up alcohol and weed and anything else that could be considered fun. Benny would always insist that Guinness was the same in every pub, but Sam was Irish, which made her the expert. It's only recently that Benny's begun to realise she was right; there is such a thing as quality Guinness – and this is it.

Stephen examines the crisps. Before he can complain about the overwhelming beefiness of the selection, Benny holds up a pack, searches out the little green *suitable for vegetarians* logo on the back (they all have it). Stephen nods. He checks the list of ingredients himself and can't help but point out that some of the crisps contain a small amount of dried milk extract, which he

79

would usually refuse to eat, although today he'll make an exception.

They peel open each packet, lay them flat on the wooden table – a picnic, Stephen calls it, a *feast* – then gobble them down in great greedy handfuls. They eat until their mouths are shredded, until all that remains on the table are the foil insides, glistening salty in the sun – Stephen's socks hardening on the table beside them.

Benny rolls a cigarette. Stephen asks if he can have one too and Benny asks if that's wise, given that he keeps having to puff on that inhaler of his. But Stephen says it's fine – he can still smoke, his breathing isn't *that* bad – so Benny rolls him one as well. The picnic bench isn't particularly comfortable – there's nothing to lean back on – and so instead Benny stoops forward, allows his elbows to take the weight. Stephen does the same.

They sit, hunched like that. Sip their Guinnesses. Smoke.

'They were speaking Welsh in there.'

'Really?'

'Yeah.'

'Weird, isn't it? You don't really think of it as a different country. With, you know . . . a different language.'

'Yeah.'

'I mean, it looks just like the English countryside, doesn't it? The weather's just as shit. And they have the same laws here, the same government, right?'

'The very same.'

'Just as bad as England then, really, isn't it?'

'I guess.'

'Looks like your dad was onto something. Should have become independent, man. Save sinking with the Royal Shitannia.'

'Probably.'

*Pause.*

'Weird to think, though, isn't it? If your dad's political aspirations had come true – I mean, if they'd become independent and that – he'd have probably never left here, would he? You'd be speaking Welsh too.'

'I doubt it. I think it's only old farmers and pub landlords that still actually speak the language.'

'Right, yeah.'

'Can't imagine anyone our age doing it.'

'Right.' *Pause.* 'Did he speak it though? Your dad, I mean.'

'Sometimes, with my nan or Uncle Ian. Although I think it was only when he didn't want me to know what they were saying.'

'Right.'

*Pause.*

'I've been thinking, Ste. We need to be conscious of money.'

'I thought we had plenty of money?'

'We had *some*. I just spent most of it.'

'I don't think there's much left of my overdraft, man. Maybe a bit, like . . .'

'*Cash*, I mean. Nowhere takes cards out here, Ste. Money in the bank means nothing. We should have got more out at the start.'

'I thought we didn't need money. I thought we were *surviving in the wilderness*?'

'And how do you plan to pay for your rain mac?'

*Pause.*

'How far then? Today, I mean?'

'Nearly five miles.'

'Wow. And what time is it?'

'Nearly three.'

'That's not bad then?'

'It's OK. Better than yesterday.'

'So how far overall, do you think? You know, if we keep it up?'

'We need to get over this first mountain range. Hang on.' *Pause.* 'See here . . .? All the brown circles . . .? We make it past there I'll be happy. Then we'll have made a dent.'

'Any more pubs along the way?'

'There's a restaurant somewhere beyond the mountains. Maybe we can get something there. Hopefully we'll find a cashpoint or something.'

'When'll that be?'

'Tomorrow probably.'

'So, one pub a day?'

'If we're lucky.'

'Jesus, man. Talk about all work no play. What about when we stop? At your uncle's?'

'Well yeah, we can drink then. There'll be a few pubs in Llangollen. And cashpoints. It's a proper town.'

'We'll have a few days off though, right? Like a little holiday?'

'Depending how long it takes us to get there.'

'What's that mean?'

'Well, we have to stick to the schedule, Ste. I only have so long off work. We want to complete this thing.'

'Right.'

'That's the whole point.'

'Right. Of course. Yeah.'

'We need to get to Chepstow. Throw our stones in the sea.'

'Right.'

'You still have your stone, right? From the beach?'

'Er . . . yeah. Somewhere. In my pack, probably.'

'I hope so.' *Pause.* 'No photos today?'

'Nothing's grabbed me.'

'*Nothing?*'

'Well, it's all very samey, isn't it, really? Roads. Trees. Fields.'

'Didn't stop you yesterday.'

'No . . .'

'Plus, the weather's better today.'

'Nah, yesterday was more interesting. Well, the morning was.'

'Interesting?'

'More variety. Sun's boring.'

'Really?'

'Yeah, man. Grim is good.'

'Grim is good?'

'Anything atmospheric. Or dramatic. A storm would be good.'

'A storm would not be good, Ste.'

'Oh, right.' *Pause.* 'Yeah.'

*Pause.*

'How's the ankle?'

'Swollen as fuck, man. Hang on . . .' *Pause.* 'See?'

'I can't tell.'
'Compare it to the other one, though. See? It's bulging.'
*Pause.*
'I really can't tell.'

They finish their cigarettes, swallow what's left of their Guinness, and Benny suggests they fill up the water bottles and leave. Stephen nods, says that's a good idea. He's sitting back, massaging his ankle with his thumbs. Benny doesn't relish the thought of venturing back into the pub, but he knows he can't afford the luxury of worrying about the opinions of the locals. They're trying to survive here, they have priorities. Water is one of them.

Benny steps back inside. It's only now that he notices the smell – a mixture of stale beer and furniture polish. It reminds him of the Miners, which (as Stephen is always sure to point out) is really nothing more than a glorified old man pub itself, the only difference being that the smell of the Miners has that additional sickening blend of generously applied perfume and aftershave; the pub's main function being as a place to meet for cheap pre-town drinks. This time the barman and punter are silent the moment Benny steps through the door. It's as if they've been waiting for him. Benny considers asking the barman if he'd fill the 2-litre bottles, but then he spots the gents' over to the right, decides it's easier to just do it himself.

The gents' consists of a cubicle, a single toilet and a small, yellowed sink – a room so cramped you could shit and wash your hands at the same time. The water pressure is virtually non-existent and so Benny's in there for a while, bending the bottles to angle them in a way that catches the trickle from the tap. He ends up sitting on the toilet whilst he waits. He considers taking a shit (why not, whilst the luxury presents itself?) but isn't sure he can manage to squeeze out a second one today, especially knowing the barman and punter are waiting just outside the door. There's a mirror above the sink but he avoids his reflection. He knows he'll only fixate on his hairline.

Once the bottles are filled, Benny slots them into a plastic bag and steps back out into the pub. The Welshmen are still staring.

Benny nods to them and makes for the exit when one of them calls out. What he actually *says*, Benny's not entirely sure. It echoes in his mind as a guttural bark, lacking any sort of linguistic definition (probably it's Welsh). When Benny turns back, the barman and punter are still in their previous positions – barman stooped forwards against the bar, whilst the punter leans back, hands on his belly. For a moment Benny wonders if maybe he'd imagined the noise.

Then the barman speaks again.

He asks what Benny's up to. Benny shrugs, says he was just using the toilet. The barman glances to his punter, then back to Benny. He shakes his head. He doesn't mean that, he says. He means what's Benny doing *here*. As in *Wales*.

Benny shrugs again. He says they're walkers. (Isn't that obvious?) That's why they're here. They're walking.

The barman glances at the punter, who smiles down into his pint. There's something about the barman that reminds Benny of his father. Maybe it's the beard. Maybe it's the sheepskin jumper. Maybe it's the look of sheer contempt that's settled over his face.

He shakes his head again.

'I mean *what walk is it you're doing*? Is it the dyke, or what?'

Benny laughs. He's not quite sure why (maybe it's a sense of relief at finally understanding the barman's line of questioning). He says yes, they're walking the dyke. *Offa's* Dyke, he clarifies, as if there's the possibility of several other dyke-based trails in the area. Then, as if to prove it, he reaches into his pocket, searches for the stone from Prestatyn beach, holds it out to them. There's a pause then. All three of them staring at the stone in his hand.

Suddenly Benny finds himself talking again. He's explaining how it works, how you're supposed to take a stone from the beach at one end of the trail, then toss it into the sea at the other, in Chepstow. The barman interrupts. He says yes, he's aware of the tradition with the stones. He asks if they just started the walk today.

No, Benny says. They started yesterday.

And then the barman's head is in his hands. And suddenly the punter is laughing – this hacking cough of a laugh – and saying *I told you so*, again and again. (*I told you so! I told you!*)

After a few seconds the barman looks up again and apologises. He explains that they'd had a bet, based on the direction Benny and Stephen were taking the trail. The barman had been sure they were coming to the end of the dyke, whereas the punter had guessed they'd only just begun, and now it means the barman has to give the punter a free whiskey, as payment.

The punter interrupts, still laughing. He says he can tell by the boots. (*Look at the boots!*) Benny finds himself looking down at his own boots. He'd thought they were muddy by now – given their earlier trek through the water-logged field – but when he looks the mud is only really an inch or so above each sole, the laces still bright and clean.

The barman says he can't believe it. He says he was sure they must have been nearing the end. He's staring outside now, and Benny realises that from here he can make out their table. Stephen sits there, nursing his ankle.

The barman shakes his head.

'I mean, look at the state of your friend there . . .'

Benny shrugs. He's not sure what he's shrugging at. The barman and the punter are both laughing now. He waits a moment longer, meeting their stares (back and forth: barman, then punter, then barman again). He wants to stand his ground, prove a point, though what point he's proving, he has no idea. The barman says something in Welsh and the punter wipes his eyes and replies, also in Welsh. The punter removes his cap to reveal a large, bald head, covered with pink scabs. He runs his fingers over them.

Benny turns to leave. The stone from Prestatyn feels hot in his hand. He pockets it.

He can still feel their eyes on him as he steps back outside.

—

'You OK, man?'

'Let's go.'

'You get the water?'

'Yeah, let's go.'

'OK, just let me get . . . just need to put my socks on . . .'

'OK, just hurry up. We can't waste any more time here. We need to keep moving.'

# VIII

*Proper roads – Closed shop – Aching feet – Cows
– Manic mooing – Laughter – A diversion – 'Run'
– Sam the cat – Talk of old classmates – Cal
stories – Mountaintop – Cairn – Ram skull –
Stormy weather – More running – Exposure
– 'NO CAMPING' – A wet and frenzied erection.*

They pass through Bodfari. It's bigger, more of an actual town
than Rhuallt; proper residential roads with

## ARAF
## SLOW

written in huge white letters, and so Benny thinks maybe there's
a chance they'll find a cashpoint, or somewhere to buy more
matches or cigarettes, maybe even a rain mac, but they find
nothing. Just a corner shop that's boarded up with a sign on the
front saying **'Blame Tory Cuts'**. Someone's drawn a little **'n'**
above **'Cuts'**, with an arrow, placing it between the **'u'** and the
**'t'**. Stephen finds this amusing enough to take a photo. There
are no other residents, no fellow walkers.

It hurts, walking on tarmac. By now they're used to mud and
grass and the hard road pains the balls of their feet. Benny can
feel something patting against the back of his thigh, remembers
it's the bag of rubbish from this morning. He'd meant to dispose
of it back in the pub, but never mind, they're bound to pass a
bin at some point. They spot an acorn plaque on a fence at a
gap in the hedges – the turnoff for the trail. They head west,
across a small river and along some country roads. Eventually

they reach fields again, more sheep and sheep shit and that ever-present chorus of baaing. Each time they climb a stile there seems to be more of them, scattered over the hillside. They chew mindlessly, paying no interest to the two walkers passing by.

Soon they arrive at a field of cows. Cows are more curious than sheep and there are already a few at the stile, waiting as they approach. Cows are also much larger than sheep, surprisingly large to Benny, who hasn't really considered the prospect of encountering cows until this very moment, when he's literally face to face with them. There are several varieties: brown cows, black cows, cows with that standard black-and-white camo pattern. All are freakily muscular and have these plastic, yellow tags on their ears, which make a flapping sound when they shake their heads to rid themselves of flies. It isn't working, there are flies all over them, probably because of how much they smell like shit. Stephen wants to stop and take photos of the cows, and as he does more and more approach, so many they're blocking the other side of the stile. They show no sign of losing interest and dispersing, even when he puts the camera away. With each passing second more of them wander across from the far side of the field.

Stephen asks what they should do. Benny doesn't know. Stephen asks if they could detour and Benny points out there's a fence right the way across that's too high to climb and the only place they can get over is here at the stile. One of the cows strains to sniff at them. It moos. Of course it moos – the fact that cows moo was one of the first things they learnt as children, a cornerstone of their nursery school education – but for some reason that noise, so recognisable and yet so ridiculous, takes them by surprise. It sets off something inside them and they have to laugh. It's the face too, those wide eyes and flaring nostrils. They can't stop laughing. Stephen leans against the fence, he's laughing so much.

Benny mounts the stile. The cows back away, unsure at first. He hoists a leg over and they shuffle forwards, strain to sniff at his boot. He tries to kick his way through, but the barrage of heads is unflinching. One lurches. A mouth opens and a tongue is extended, long and pink, curling up into Benny's shorts. Benny squeals, falling backwards against Stephen and the two of them hit the ground hard, weighed down by their packs. They lie there on the wet grass, laughing, the cows glaring down at them with ever more manic mooing.

*Laughter.*
  *Mooooo.*
  'Did you see its . . .' *Laughter.* '. . . its fucking . . .' *Laughter.* '. . . did you see its fucking *face*?!'
  *Laughter.*
  *Mooooo.*
  *Laughter.*
  *Mooooo. Mooooooooooooooo.*

Their new plan goes like this: Benny walks down to the far end of the field, rattles the fence, calling out to the cows to come see him, he's got some treats for them, some . . . erm . . . milk . . . Grown cows have no particular interest in milk, a fact that occurs to Benny as soon as he's said it. Luckily cows also have little or no understanding of the human language and instead are attracted to sound and movement and so the plan works; they soon forget about Stephen and file off down the field to moo at Benny instead.
  Once most of the cows have made their way over, Benny gives a thumbs up, watches as Stephen climbs the stile, hobbles out across the field. It's then Stephen's turn to distract the cows, and he does so by waving his arms and mooing at them. Eventually the herd turns back, focuses on this new distraction, and Benny can retreat to the stile, climb over. He makes a beeline for Stephen, flanking the cows from a distance, and the two of them hurry to the other side of the field where the next stile is waiting.
  And the cows follow.

'Don't run.'
  'I'm not.'
  'Just walk. Quickly.'
  'I am. And it fucking hurts by the way. My ankle . . .'

'They're just curious, is all. They think we're going to feed them or something.'

'Oh God, they're gaining on us, man. We could get trampled here. We could die. We could actually die. Can you imagine?'

'Just keep walking.'

'Fuck me, man, there's so many of them!'

'Don't look. Just *walk*.'

*Pause.*

'Wait . . . what if it's the crisps, man? Remember the crisps? They were beef. They can smell the beef on us.'

'Don't be stupid.'

'I'm telling you, they can smell it.'

'They were vegan. We checked, remember?'

'Nah, the milk. The powdered milk.'

'Don't be stupid.'

'Plus, you know, the residue. The beefiness.'

'They're just cows, Ste. How dangerous can they be?'

'They're *fast*, man.'

'How dangerous can any barnyard animal be?'

*Pause.*

'They're closing in!'

'Don't shout. Just walk, OK? Just head for the stile.'

'I am.' *Pause.* 'Oh God, it's licking my back, man. Fucking hell, Ben, it's *licking* me!'

They run as fast as they can. Benny can feel the pack, bouncing with every stride – rubbing at his sunburnt shoulders, butting at the base of his spine. His calves ache. There are sharp pains in his toes and heels where blisters have formed. He's trying his best to avoid the cow shit, which he knows from past experience can be a serious slip-hazard. Cow shit is much wetter than that of sheep or horses, and even more offensive on the nostrils. It's everywhere here; fly-infested mud-puddles, obscured like land-mines amongst the long grass.

Already Benny is out of breath. He always hated running – he never understood Sam's obsession with it. The morning runs, the evening runs, the occasional lunchtime run in-between. He can hear Stephen beside him, gasping at the pain in his ankle. And then there's the cows; their mass trot, their mooing. Benny turns and one of them is right there with that tongue, that pink snake-of-a-tongue, curling out towards him.

Soon they're at the stile and Benny's the first to mount it. His foot slips; his shin scrapes against the splintering wood. He cries out, grabs at the fence and hoists himself up. A second later and he's over, kneeling there in the mud, reaching up and dragging Stephen across with him. The two of them are on the ground, gazing up, gasping at the bulbous cow heads, straining over the stile to glare at them. Benny gives them the finger, tells them better luck next time, calls them wankers. Stephen pants, smiles at Benny.

The cows just stand there, mooing.

*Moooo. Moooo. Mooooo.*
    '*Fuck*, man.'
    *Moooo. Moooo. Mooooo.*
    'Don't fucking shut up, do they?'
    *Mooooo. Mooooo. Moooooooooooooooooooooooooo.*

Once they've sat and caught their breath for a minute they turn their backs on the cows and continue south. The sky has clouded over now and the shade it provides allows them a slight relief. The path is just a dirt road here, rising through farmland and patches of ferns. After a while Benny realises they're skirting a hillside. There's an incline to their left; a fence between them and the sloping fields to their right.

They're still wet from the grass and splintered from the stiles and their feet hurt more than ever but spirits are high and every so often one of them laughs. It's the memory of those cows, their mooing faces. Each time they think of it they can't keep from sniggering. This is a stage they'd sometimes reach back in school – a state of delirium that took hold after spending too long in each other's company. They'd spend pretty much all of their free time together back then, would usually end up at Stephen's after school, drinking beer in the attic room, or playing Xbox, or else, later, when they realised they could get served in the Miners, sitting in that booth at the back of the pub. Benny and Cal would talk about girls and scoring weed whilst Stephen nodded along (pretending to also like weed, pretending to also like girls). They were still teenagers then, so maybe it was just the thrill of talking about sex, or the initial buzz of first experimenting with mind-altering substances, or maybe it was just being there together at that time in their lives, but sometimes they'd reach a stage where one of them would suddenly start laughing at something (usually something stupid Stephen had said or some needlessly offensive comment of Cal's) and the others wouldn't be able to keep from laughing too. This would go on for a while, until they were in tears, barely able to breathe. They'd lose track of the initial cause of laughter altogether, end up just laughing at one another's ludicrous laughing faces.

Today their delirium is not so prolonged. They laugh less and less as the monotony of walking kicks in. The struggle, the steepness of the hill. The sky is overcast. There's a warm breeze. There are no more cows, just sheep, which they can faintly hear baaing from the surrounding fields. The path grows steeper. The expanse of fields to their right fades into the grey sky. Benny checks his phone again. 64% battery now and still no signal, no new messages from Sam. He tries to imagine the moment she received his message yesterday, her reaction to the words he wrote. He has no idea what this would be. He has no idea if Sam still has any feelings towards him. In fact, it's highly possible that by now she's in a relationship with somebody else.

Sam has this habit of slinking inside his thoughts and just sitting there, staring him out. It can be unnerving – there's something savage in those eyes. He often imagines Sam as a cat. She moves a bit like a cat and her hair is silky black and there's a certain sleekness to her movements sometimes, something panther-like (she was especially sleek during those early morning runs). Also, her eyes had a feline quality, something to do with how she did her eyeliner. Plus, Sam *has* a cat: Maggie, her perfect spirit animal. That way Maggie would rub against Benny's legs when he entered the flat, raising her rear each time he stroked her. The way she'd suddenly turn, hiss, show her teeth. That was Sam all over.

But Benny doesn't want to think about this – any of it. He wants to just empty his mind and *walk*. The path grows steadily steeper, but by now his thighs are numb to it. Stephen seems more comfortable too. He's still limping on his bad ankle but at least he's finally managed to get his breathing under control.

'It would be quicker if we talked, man.'
 'What do you mean?'
 'Time passes more quickly when we talk.'
 *Pause.*
 'What do you want to talk about?'

Of course, Benny knows what 'talking' means. It'll be like those Friday nights he and Stephen meet at the Miners – they always end up going over the same old stuff. The conversation tends to go one of two ways: either they'll reminisce about their school-days, or else Stephen will try and get Benny to gossip about their old classmates, a lot of whom are now Benny's colleagues (and are often there in the pub with them on these nights out, what with the Miners being just up the road from the call centre). Benny doesn't want this though, not now. He's in no mood to reminisce or gossip. He's trying to look forwards. That's what this trip is all about. He wants to *do* something. Just for once he wants to live *in the moment*.

But Stephen's right, talking will make the time pass. And with time comes miles. Pages. Inch after inch of unending map.

Plus, Benny figures anything is better than being alone with his thoughts right now.

So they talk. Their conversation adheres to its usual pattern. Stephen takes the lead, brings up people from school, enquires after them. Benny surrenders what he knows from the rumours he's heard at work. Stephen has a basic understanding of the goings-on amongst Benny's colleagues because he follows a lot of their old classmates on social media, but he's usually keen to attend the meet-ups at the Miners so he can witness the subjects of his contempt first-hand. He never goes as far as actually *talking* to any of them; instead he and Benny stick to their regular table in the corner, out of sight, where they can observe Benny's colleagues with an Attenborough-like sense of detachment. Usually Benny's nursing a watery Guinness, sipping more and more frequently as Stephen gets himself riled up at the familiar faces he spots at the bar.

Out here in the Welsh countryside, they don't have the luxury of studying their subjects first-hand, but Stephen's still able to think up a few popular candidates. For example, there's this one guy that works with Benny who used to be the biggest nerd in their maths class. He was actually a friend of Stephen's, back in primary school, but has since become popular and gym-obsessed and is now built like a wrestler and doesn't even bother to acknowledge Stephen when he passes him on the way to the toilets, and he constantly posts updates on social media about his muscle gains with hashtags like **#gymlife** and **#legday** and photos of his high-protein meal plans and workout routines and biceps, and this deeply offends Stephen because of how totally self-obsessed it is. Stephen can't stand it. He says (in words that show a surprising lack of self-awareness, considering his friends from uni) that this sort of narcissistic fakery is everything that's wrong with their generation. Or there's this girl who used to be in their English class who went to Ibiza last month and never shut up about it, posting a countdown of statuses each day for two weeks beforehand, along with photos and the caption **#holidaygear**. And then, when she was actually there, followed it up with a continuous barrage of selfies, each one with **#bestdayever**, even though she was there for fourteen days in total and, like, how can every day be the *best day ever*? She uploaded forty-three photos of her trip in total, most of which were pretty much the same image – her in front of the mirror, pouting – and this infuriated Stephen, made his skin crawl, made him sick to his stomach. How self-centred? How narcissistic? etc., etc., etc.

Recently there's this one ex-classmate who's been repeatedly changing her relationship status online, as well as posting updates with detailed accounts of her thoughts and feelings regarding her boyfriend. One day it's how perfect and thoughtful he is, the next how much of a scummy love rat he is. One day it's how he's going to make a wonderful father, the next that he's not getting anywhere near the baby and if he even tries she'll get her brothers to put him in the hospital. A few weeks ago, she uploaded a photo of his penis, which was apparently tiny. She was suspended from work (her boyfriend is also a DWP call handler and this was considered a form of sexual harassment in the workplace). But the next week she was back in the call centre and they were back together again, and their relationship status was set to 'engaged'.

'I mean, how tacky, right?'

'Yeah.'

'Like, aren't they devaluing it? The whole *concept* of love?'

'Yeah.'

'Aren't they worried about their child? I mean, don't they realise this stuff *stays* there? That one day they'll scroll back and *find* all this shit?'

'Yeah.'

Neither mentions that they've already had these same conversations. That Stephen has complained about his old friend's gym updates many times before. That the barrage of holiday selfies ended weeks ago now. That Benny messaged Stephen the details of the dick-pic-uploader's suspension in real time and Stephen shared these same opinions on it that very day. Instead they just keep walking and talking, the path ever-steeper as the afternoon wears on. Sometimes Benny feels like all they ever do is have the same conversations over and over. Like his twenties are wasting away, year by year, with only his Friday nights at the Miners to remember them by. Because what are *they* doing with their lives, him and Stephen? They aren't getting fit, or going to Ibiza – they aren't getting married, or having kids. Most Friday nights they're just sitting in the corner of a grimy pub, like a couple of old crones, *whinging*.

It becomes less and less enjoyable, this kind of talk. There's an initial buzz to it because it's like they're back in sixth form – their bitchy gossiping heyday – and there's nostalgia to that. They were teenagers then. The sex, the heartache, the drama; it was new and exciting, adult life just beginning. But nostalgia soon fades, becomes just a reminder of how much worse things are now. Sure, in sixth form they were anxious and shy and fearful and virginal, but they were happy.* As a teenager Benny thought leaving school would make him feel more like an adult. He thought the same when he graduated, when he found a job. But he still feels the same as always: a child, alone. It's as if his body is growing older whilst his terrified teenage mind remains trapped inside. And now he's well into his twenties. His dad is gone. Sam is gone. Cal is gone. Even his *hair* is going. And all the excitement about the possibilities of adulthood have faded: the time has come for him to be a man. And so every day he goes and sits in one of the cubicles at the call centre, rushes through the same default answers with benefits claimants to try to bring down his call time averages. And it's as if the best years of his life are slipping away, one day at a time.

But at least he has a job. At least he's not one of those unemployed people on the other end of the line, with nowhere left to turn. And at least now they're out here, actually doing something. They're walking across a country – that's got to be some sort of life-changing event, right? That's got to count for something? Maybe he should upload some pictures too, him and Stephen out on this adventure together. He has considered it before now (although his lack of phone signal might be an issue). He had thought maybe they could sort through some of Stephen's pictures, select a few to upload once the walk was finished, but he hadn't realised Ste would be using such outdated equipment as 'real' film.

And anyway, it's understandable, really, Stephen's need to berate Benny's colleagues. A lot of them are people who gave Stephen a bad time at school. Benny was Stephen's only real friend back then. Cal was more Benny's friend (his relationship

---

* Speak for yourself, Ben.

to Stephen was mostly built on a desire to constantly berate him). Stephen was effeminate, skinny. Plus, he had the glasses, those dorky clothes, the bowl haircut. It couldn't have been easy, being Ste.

But things changed when he went to uni. Suddenly Stephen made all these friends of his own, came back with this newfound confidence. Stephen got to spend three years as a trendy art student, three years with that Garth guy and his eccentric entourage, placing himself on some sort of moral high ground and claiming there was something 'problematic' about anything Benny or Cal said. Stephen probably thought his new life would last forever, that his new friendships would continue to evolve, that he'd be this cool, pompous artist-type for the rest of his life. But then his course ended and he had to come home to his mum and everything back here was the same – the same cliques, the same hierarchy, his position unchanged. Now he spends most of his time up in his attic room, with that skeleton (a room Cal once nicknamed 'The Problem-Attic'*). And everyone from school still thinks him a loser – it's clear from the way they snub him in the Miners – although according to him *they're* the pathetic ones, so obvious in their tastes, their desires, their petty dramas. Not to mention that they've sold their souls . . . that they all now work at the call centre, taking blood money from the DWP.†

---

* That is pretty good, to be fair.

† OK, I concede here, Ben, I genuinely have no idea why I was so preoccupied with these people and their petty drama. I would have sworn, by this point, that I couldn't give two shits about them. I told myself again and again that I'd moved on from all that. That, after my experience with Garth and Olga and the London art scene, I'd, like, *evolved* or something. And yet, you're right, I still followed all our old classmates on social media, didn't I? And I always insisted on meeting at the Miners (which obviously wasn't due to the quality of their Guinness . . .). I don't know, I guess it's hard to escape the people you went to school with. Maybe that childhood social order is such a fundamental part of our development that it's destined to haunt us for the rest of our lives. It was about being *witnessed* by them, I think. Going to the Miners, I mean. I wanted them to *see me*, existing. The *new* me – whether they recognised the change or not. I wanted them to know that I had survived all their nastiness and come out of it a stronger person.

But whatever. It doesn't matter. None of this matters. Because all this talk of old classmates is just a precursor, a warm-up before the conversation takes its inevitable turn to the king of old classmates: Cal. Not what happened with Christine, not right away. First they remember happier times; sixth form, the years their friendship peaked. Today it's Benny who brings Cal into the conversation, although it's entirely by accident. He mentions Danni Wilber, and Stephen asks if she's the girl Cal used to meet in the park after school for hand jobs, and Benny laughs and says yes, he forgot about that, what exactly did she get out of that weird arrangement anyway? Six months it went on for and she never got anything in return. After that, the Cal stories keep coming. There's the time in PE when he wore one of the girls' sports bras with two socks stuffed inside; or the time in English when he put a condom on a baguette and hid in the teacher's cupboard; or when he first got that job in the warehouse and would steal them all kinds of useless things (rubber gloves, golf balls, boxes of bladder-leak underwear).

And then the mention of the warehouse leads Benny to remember the time Cal arrived at the pub with those rolls of Christmas wrapping paper he'd stolen, and they decided to pull a practical joke on Ste's art teacher, Mr Watt. How the three of them stumbled over in the early hours of the morning, drunk, and set about gift-wrapping Mr Watt's car; the drunken giggling,

---

Looking back, I don't think it ever worked. I don't think any of them really noticed me. I mean sure, a lot of them came to the funeral, but I think we can put that down to novelty value alone; as far as I'm aware, it was the first time someone from our school had died (and in such a dramatic way!) and so their attendance isn't proof any of them really gave a shit about me, one way or the other. It was just about them playing a role: my grief-stricken classmates. *You* were the only one I saw showing genuine emotion that afternoon, Ben. At the funeral, I mean. I can still picture you, hunched there in front of the display. I can still hear that primal wailing you gave out as that wave of emotion came over you. And sure, maybe it could be argued that was just guilt or whatever, but still, I appreciated it. To me it felt like genuine *grief*, you know? TBH, I felt closer to you right then than at any moment in my entire life.

and creaking of Sellotape, the crinkling of the paper as they unravelled it over the bonnet, the squeaking of their teeth on the cellophane as they tore it from the roll. And the shushing, all the time shushing each other, their shushing loudest of all. And those Santas, those little Santa faces grinning up at them from the paper. And the photo they took of themselves, thumbs up and grinning around the red-wrapped car, lighting them in its flash for a second before they scattered and fled.

And now, years later, climbing a hill in Wales, Benny and Stephen laugh about it. Laugh so hard they have to stop and sit on the ground for a few minutes, just to try and contain themselves.

'It was probably quite useful, actually, wasn't it? The next morning, he wouldn't have had to de-ice the windows . . .'
*Pause.*
'Why did he do it, man?'
'Who?'
'Cal.'
'Because it was funny!'
'Not the car, Ben. The other thing.'
'Oh.'
'What was he *thinking*?'
'He wasn't. He wasn't thinking.'
'I know she drove him crazy. She drove us crazy too, just from the stories. But what he did? *Jesus*, man.'
'I just . . . I don't know, Ste. I just don't know.'

And here they go again. This is what they've been skirting around, what the whole conversation has been building towards – the big fight between Cal and Christine. They start with various details from that night. Benny remembers how dishevelled Cal looked when he first arrived, how his hair was wet and only half his face had stubble, due to the fact he'd been in the middle of shaving when the fight occurred. Then Stephen recalls how Cal had been shaking when he got there – his legs bouncing under the table, his hands trembling in his lap – and at first they thought it was due to the cold. Cal didn't have a coat, had walked all the way to the pub in just a T-shirt and jeans, and his skin felt like ice when Benny had guided him past the pool tables to their usual space in the corner. Which was why Benny had immediately gone to fetch a whiskey from the bar, had left Stephen alone with him for a few minutes, and it was at that point Ste had noticed the bruising on his neck, the crescents of dried blood beneath each of his fingernails.

Cal had been quiet for the first half-hour, but after working his way through two whiskies and the best part of a pint of Guinness, he began to elaborate on the cause of the night's argument. It turned out Christine had left her phone unlocked and Cal had taken the opportunity to scan through her messages, and (predictably) he'd caught her cheating again. But not just cheating, this time it was worse than that – she'd been doing it for *money*. She'd been sanctioned by the job centre again – six months without pay this time – and instead of telling Cal, she'd been getting handouts off some guy she knew from her old job, some balding, middle-aged coke dealer Cal recognised from her Facebook profile. Cal knew she'd done camgirl stuff in the past, he didn't mind that too much. But *this* – literally prostituting herself for the odd twenty quid here and there – *this* was a step too far. Apparently it was when Cal communicated this to her that Christine went nuts and started attacking him. According to Cal, all he'd really done was fight back. It's not like it was him who started it or anything. It was not like he'd had any prior intention to hurt her.

Benny and Stephen go through their usual analysis of these events. They make the same old points and counterpoints. Like how yes, it was wrong for Cal to invade Christine's privacy, but also wrong of her to embark upon such a venture in the first place without telling him. After that Stephen's always sure to point out that sex work isn't necessarily immoral *in and of itself*, because, sure, it may historically be a deeply misogynistic by-product of a corrupt patriarchal society, but nowadays it could be seen as empowering for women, under certain circumstances. They both agree on domestic violence being inexcusable under *any* circumstances, although then Benny always feels the need to try and excuse just a little bit by pointing out that, to be fair to Cal, it did sound as though he was in some part defending himself. And with that comes Stephen's rant on the inherent problematic nature of this train of thought, the prevalence of victim blaming as a foundation of the patriarchy, etc., etc., etc.

Neither mentions how repetitive all of this is. How this is the same conversation they've had time and time again. How, each time they discuss it, Stephen uses that same phrase: *the prevalence of victim blaming as a foundation of the patriarchy*. Because it was *dramatic*, what happened with Cal and Christine. The fact that Benny and Stephen were with him that night, just after it happened. The fact they went back to the flat and witnessed for themselves the carnage there (the smashed bottles, the broken mirror, the splatters of blood on the floor). Talking about it makes Benny's stomach lurch, but it's also thrilling, in a way. Like those campfire ghost stories Uncle Ian used to tell. It has that same sort of thrill to it.

They don't really talk about Christine much – just the incident as they saw it, from their side. They try not to mention her by name. They never discuss the picture she uploaded either (**#scumbag #abuser #lookwhathedidtomyface**). Benny has never told Stephen about the time she phoned the call centre. This was a few weeks later, during his first shift as a DWP call handler – that same day he got home to find his dad waiting up for him at the kitchen table. After a brief training period, they'd finally been trusted to receive their first calls from claimants, and who should just happen to call that afternoon but *her*. All of Benny's fellow new starters had gone to the Miners after work to celebrate the completion of their first proper shift and Benny had had to go along with them, although he wasn't particularly in the mood for socialising. All he could think about was Christine; how fragile she sounded on the other end of the line; how he'd disconnected the call not long after she'd recognised his voice. He couldn't believe she'd got through to him, of all the available call handlers. The more he considered it, the more it felt like something too significant to ignore.

And yet he ignored it, didn't he? He supped beer with his new colleagues. He felt the memory of Christine rise from his mind and join that body of ill feeling that now hung above him at all times, that vast entity he'd begun to think of as 'The Fog'.

'Have you seen him, recently? Cal, I mean.'
  'Not recently, no.'
  'Didn't you see him one time, though? At the bus stop?'
  'I drove past him at a bus stop, yeah.'
  'And he was all suited-up?'
  'Yeah, like he was going to a job interview.'
  'Or to court . . .'

By this point the sky has clouded. The wind is getting stronger. Everything's flapping – their clothes, their hair, the bag of rubbish still tied to Benny's pack. Benny removes his sunglasses, hooks them in the collar of his shirt. A little further up they stop so that Stephen can retrieve his jumper and change back into his track pants again. Benny dons his coat. He switches his phone on to check the time. (59% battery.) It's only half six, too early to be getting so dark. Rain is starting to spit. They need to find somewhere to camp, and soon. This is a priority.

They keep walking. Benny has spent the last couple of hours focused on the path ahead and it's only now he notices there's a steep drop to the fields on both sides.

A few minutes later the hill plateaus. The strain on their legs eases into comfortable walking again. They approach a knee-high pile of rocks.

It's only then that Benny realises they're at the summit of a mountain.

'No way.'
  'It's the top, Ste! That's what the stones mean!'
  'We can't be . . .'
  'We are!'
  'Shit, you're right! Look at the view, man! The fucking view! Of course we are! We climbed a mountain! We climbed a mountain without even knowing it!'

'I know!'
'We climbed a fucking *mountain*!'

They embrace. Both are laughing, tears in their eyes from the wind. There's a huge bank of grey cloud above them now, but there are spots on the horizon where the sun is breaking through – vast golden columns, connecting the sky to the fields and forest below. There are tiny houses, speckles of sheep. Puddled lakes shimmering. Benny can barely even make out the sea any more, it's so far in the distance.

'This *view*, man. It's like a painting!'
'I know.'
'It's like it isn't even *real*.'
'I know!' *Pause.* 'Shouldn't you be taking photos?'

Stephen rummages for his camera. Meanwhile, Benny gets out the guidebook. The pages flap wildly. He hunches, just about managing to shelter it enough to find their current page and decipher their location. They've reached Moel Arthur, the Clwydian Range. It seems impossible but they must have – this is the first mountaintop they cross on the trail. Stephen's idea worked. They talked and time passed. They climbed a mountain.

Benny pockets the guidebook. He retrieves his tobacco pouch and peels it open. He knows it's a stupid idea but a small part of him believes that, if he's careful, maybe he can roll a celebratory cigarette without the wind being too much of a problem. He's wrong: a swarm of papers bursts forth, fluttering into the air. He grabs at them – not only to save from littering, but also because of how low his rations are getting. He manages to snatch a few from the wind before they're carried off and stashes them in his coat pockets. He kneels and tries to roll but the tobacco's blowing everywhere too, a huge ball of it escapes and skitters along the mountaintop like a tiny tumbleweed. Benny laughs. All he wants is to sit and smoke, but it seems the elements are against him.

He crosses to the pile of stones, the marker that indicates a mountaintop. A *cairn*, that's what it's called. That's what his dad used to call them. He thinks, if he kneels at it, that maybe it'll provide a little shelter.

That's when he spots it: a white object resting on the stones.

'Ste?'
  'Yeah?'
  'Ste, look, what's this?'
  'Hmm?'
  'On the cairn, Ste.'
  'The *what*?'
  'On the stones. There's something on the stones.'

At first Benny's not sure what to make of it. He's certain it wasn't there a few seconds earlier, although maybe they were just too excited to notice, too enthralled in their celebrations at reaching the summit. Possibly it was camouflaged by the stones (although that seems unlikely, given that it's such a dazzling white).

Stephen asks what it is. Benny doesn't answer. It's obvious what it is. Stephen waits a second, then asks what it *was* – a dog? Benny says it was probably a sheep. Stephen nods – that makes sense.

Benny kneels to examine it. The cairn's about knee-height and the skull has been placed right on top. For what purpose he doesn't know, will never know. It's roughly the size and shape of a rugby ball; teeth, snout, gaping eyeholes. Everything else has rotted away, not a scrap of flesh or even dirt, just thin white bone, bleached by the sun. A grinning reminder of what was once life. It's only then he notices the horns – two nubs at the temples, darker than the rest of it.

It's a ram, he tells Stephen. A small ram. Maybe a baby.

Benny hears a click. He turns to see Stephen's camera, a tiny image of the skull reflected within the lens. Stephen winds it, then clicks another picture. He kneels beside Benny, nudges the skull, angles it, then raises the camera again.

—

'I don't think you should do that.'

'Why?'

*Click. Wind.*

'It just doesn't seem right, taking photos of it.'

'It's just a sheep.'

'It's a ram.'

'A ram, whatever.' *Click. Wind.* 'It's cool, man. I'm getting Damien Hirst vibes. Or, like, Georgia O'Keefe, you know?'

*Click. Wind.*

'I just . . . I don't know. I just think you should leave it alone, yeah?'

Stephen drags out his camera bag. He slips out the felt-lined lens case, unscrews the lens on the camera and swaps it for another, slightly smaller lens. He raises the camera, carries on taking photos.

'Come on now, Ste. That's enough.'

'Just a few more, man. I've got a good feeling about this.'

*Click. Wind.*

'It was an animal, a living thing. Doesn't it deserve some respect? I mean, isn't that your whole vegan philosophy?'

'No.'

*Click. Wind.*

'I just think we should, you know, *show some respect.*'

'Are you joking? I can't tell if you're joking.'

*Click. Wind.*

'Just stop it, OK? Stop taking photos.'

'Why, man?'

'Just stop it, all right?'

'Why?'

*Click. Wind.*

'Just fucking *stop it!*'

Stephen topples back. He lands on his shoulder, camera clutched to his chest. He glares up at Benny, mouth agape.

Benny's not sure what he was hoping to achieve, making a grab for the camera. What would he have done if he'd got it? Pitched it off the edge of the mountain? Shattered it against the cairn?

He turns back to the skull.

'I just think it deserves some respect. That's all.'

Stephen climbs to his feet, hobbles back to the edge of the plateau. Benny keeps his eyes on the skull. He shivers. Each time he looks away he can still feel those empty eye sockets, that dead stare boring into him. He notices a few cigarette papers, fluttering at the foot of the cairn, but for some reason he doesn't want to reach down and pick them up.

After a minute or two Benny forces himself to turn. Stephen is standing a good distance away. He's donned his jumper. He's aiming his camera for a few more landscape pictures, struggling to keep his fringe from blowing into shot.

The wind is roaring now. The sky rumbles.

'Ste!' *Pause.* 'STE!'
    'What?'
    'I think we should leave now.'
    'What?'
    'We should leave! We've got to get down the mountain!'
    'I can't hear you!'
    'IT'S GETTING DARK, STE. WE'VE GOT TO GET DOWN BEFORE NIGHTFALL. WE'VE GOT TO FIND SOMEWHERE TO CAMP!'

Stephen nods to Benny, takes one final shot of the sky before slotting his camera away in its case. Benny gets out the guidebook again, kneels, tries his best to shelter it. He flips through the pages to their current map. They need a plan, that's all. They just need somewhere sheltered from the wind where they can set up camp. In half a mile the path runs alongside woodland. Benny remembers the patch of forest they passed this morning – the mass of roots, the lack of available tent space. Still, woodland seems to be all there is, so they'll have to make it work.

Stephen approaches. Benny slips the guidebook back into his pocket, hoists his pack onto his shoulders. He tells Stephen that they'd better get moving. Stephen fetches his own pack, asks where they're going to camp. Benny tells him not to worry, it's all in hand, then leads them down the hill, away from the cairn. They're against the wind now, its torrent unrelenting. It claws under Benny's coat, icy on the sweat that lingers at his lower back. His hair flaps in disarray. He wishes he had his hat, but stopping to rummage through his pack right now would be idiotic.

Suddenly Stephen drops behind. He unbuckles his pack, begins searching through it. He gets out his camera case, shouting for Benny to stop, not realising that Benny has already stopped, that he's watching everything he's doing.

Stephen says he's left something up at the cairn. It's one of his camera lenses. He needs to go back.

Stephen struggles back up the hill to the cairn. He kneels there, rummaging through his pack. Benny turns away, his eyes watering in the wind. There's lightning – a fraction of a second, a blink-and-you-miss-it flash, followed by a murmur of thunder. Benny turns back, yells for Stephen to hurry. Stephen kneels there, making no sign of having heard.

Eventually he stands, hobbles back down, panting, struggling to keep the weight on his good ankle. He says he's sorry, it's just that lenses are so expensive. Benny tells him it's fine, but right now they need to keep moving. They need shelter. They need to get to the trees. This is a priority.

Benny's dad had a saying. Well, actually it was quite a common saying, but his dad used it enough to assert ownership. He said it on their walking trips. He said it when he was marking school-work. He said it when Benny's sister discovered she didn't have enough for a deposit that first week she was in Austria, when Benny complained about struggling to find a job in the engineering sector after university.

The saying was this: 'Fail to prepare, prepare to fail.'

Benny had kept that saying at the forefront of his mind throughout the planning of the walk. It was also a rule in the

Countryside Code (or a variation of it was): 'Plan ahead and be prepared,' it said. And Benny *had* planned. He *had* prepared. He went to the camping shop. He practised erecting the tent. He even memorised the maps in the guidebook. He's more prepared for this walk than anything he's ever done in his life.

Which is why, fifteen minutes later, when they reach the woodland and find the trees too dense to camp in, the ground too steep to pitch their tent on, Benny refuses to let it get to him. They'll find a way, he's sure of it. He has prepared for every eventuality. He just needs to focus.

What would his dad do?

By now Benny really wants a cigarette. He wishes he'd picked up a pack of them at that Tesco in Prestatyn – that way he wouldn't have to attempt rolling in this wind. He gets out the guidebook again, searches for their current position on the map. The sky is almost black now. Raindrops dot the pages. There's an electric feel to the air.

'WHAT NOW?'

'HUH?'

'I SAID, WHAT NOW?'

'I'M LOOKING.'

*Pause.*

'IS THERE ANYWHERE ELSE AROUND HERE WE COULD SET UP?'

'LIKE WHERE?'

'ANYWHERE!'

'IT'S TOO EXPOSED, STE. WE NEED SOMEWHERE THAT'S NOT SO EXPOSED.'

'LIKE WHERE, THOUGH?!'

'JUST GIVE ME A MINUTE, STE! I'M LOOKING!'

There's a car park up ahead. What this 'car park' will actually consist of, Benny doesn't know. A small blue 'P' in the guidebook: this is all he knows. Maybe there's a bunk house there. Maybe there's a toilet they can shelter in. Whatever it is, it's something to aim for.

They break into a run. Running hurts, especially as they're now going downhill. Uphill may have ached, but downhill is hell on the ankles. All the balancing, the amount of concentration it requires just to keep from slipping. Stephen winces at every step. The wind is behind them now; ahead, the jagged peaks of the mountain range. The darkening clouds above. Benny can hear the sea. It's impossible, but he swears he can hear it on the wind – that slow roll and crashing of waves.

And each time he shuts his eyes he sees that skull. Its blackened eyeholes. Its white-toothed grin.

'HURRY. DON'T STOP.'

'IT'S MY ANKLE, BEN! MY FUCKING ANKLE! I TOLD YOU IT WAS SPRAINED!'

'WE CAN'T STOP!'

They arrive at the car park. There's nothing here: just tarmac. Surrounding it are overgrown bushes and trees; there's no grass, nowhere to pitch a tent. It's starting to rain now. Benny dons his mac. He unzips the top of his pack, drags out the orange rain protector and fixes it in place. Stephen's pack doesn't have one. Stephen's pack isn't even a pack, really – it has no side pockets, no chest support, no tassels with which to bind a tent or sleeping mat. It's more of a schoolbag.

Benny retrieves a plastic bag from his own pack, tries wrapping it over Stephen's as a makeshift protector. But the wind soon catches it, carries it away. Stephen's jumper is absorbing a lot of water. It hangs heavy on him.

'THIS IS BAD. WE *NEED* SOMEWHERE. UNDERSTAND? *NEED!*'

'I KNOW, MAN!'

'SPLIT UP. FIND SOMEWHERE. OK? WE'LL LEAVE THE PACKS IN THESE BUSHES. YOU GO THAT WAY. MEET BACK HERE IN TEN MINUTES. OK?'

—

Benny jogs down a gravel pathway, descending from the car park. The surrounding area's all brambles and rock, not a single patch of grass to pitch up. With the amount of fields they've passed through today, Benny never thought he'd be actively seeking out *grass*. To his left the mountain falls in a sheer drop. The sky flashes again, brighter this time. Thunder follows.

They could die. Benny hasn't even considered this until now and suddenly it's a very real possibility. Exposure. Human beings cannot survive in the mountains all night with nowhere to sleep. This has been established. How many stupid hikers have died up on these mountains? The peaks are probably littered with human skeletons. Benny seems to remember someone on the news a few years ago . . . gone missing . . . found dead . . . where *was* that? His dad made a big deal of it, called them idiots, said people had to respect nature. (Fail to prepare . . .)

Why did they have to talk about Cal? Why did they have to bring up what happened? Because talking about it brings back the memory of Christine. The picture she uploaded. It was only there for a few hours (someone reported it, flagged it 'offensive', and it was quickly removed). But then there was the phone call in work, her voice at the other end of the line. It sounded broken. It was as if Cal had broken her. Not just her face, but something else. Her voice was missing something. He had broken something inside her.

And each time Benny blinks he sees a flash of that skull. That fucking sheep skull.

Benny stops when he realises how far he's gone. How far away Stephen is, alone with no tent and no mac. The gravel path just keeps going and going, curves right the way around the side of the mountain. Maybe he'd find somewhere – some patch of grass – if he had time to search more. But there is no time. He has to go back.

He turns.

And there's Stephen, limping up the path towards him.

—

'BEN!'
  'WHAT?'
  'BEN! HERE!'
  'WHAT!'
  'I'VE FOUND SOMEWHERE! QUICK!'
  'WHAT?'
  'I'VE FOUND SOMEWHERE TO CAMP!'

A park. Just a little further along the path. There are trees and fern bushes and grass – a whole *lawn* of grass – Benny never thought he'd be so glad to see it. There's a large sign that says, '**NO CAMPING**', a picture of a tent with a big red cross through it.

Benny slips off his pack, drags out the tent bag. He spreads the ground sheet right next to the sign. He figures this at least shows they're genuine – they're aware they're disobeying the rules, but this is an emergency, and to show this they'll pitch up right next to this massive '**NO CAMPING**' sign. It's only after they've started assembling the frame that he realises it could also be seen as an act of rebellion; a great big *fuck you* to the powers that be. But whatever. The rain's getting heavier, they need to set up. This is their priority.

Stephen helps today – slotting tent poles together, feeding them through the loops, pinning the groundsheet with his knees and elbows to keep it from flapping in the wind. Occasionally Benny shouts orders and Stephen nods and obeys and occasionally shouts back, but Benny can't hear anything now, just the rattle of the rain against the hood of his mac. Benny never accounted for this in the practice run, the possibility of having to set up in such extreme conditions. He finds he's quicker, more instinctive. He has this one purpose, this will to survive.

The rain attacks from all sides. It puddles on the flat roof of the tent, in the folds of the orange rain-protector on Benny's pack. It runs down Benny's waterproofs, gathers in his boots. His socks are sodden, squelching ice water with every step. It's worse for Stephen. At least Benny has his mac; Stephen's jumper has expanded to the point where the whole thing is sagging under its own weight, water streaming from the hem and cuffs and the end of the snowman's orange, woollen nose. Stephen's hair is stuck flat to his head like a helmet. He struggles with the final tent pole – that familiar tear in the lining. The canvas splits a little wider and Benny shouts for him to stop forcing it, and Stephen obeys. Benny kneels beside him, guides it through.

The sky flashes again. The thunder is a deep, steady rumble that persists for five seconds or more. As they raise the roof it occurs to Benny that clutching tent poles in a lightning storm isn't a good idea. Nor is pitching up so close to the '**NO CAMPING**' sign, which is held in place by a tall, metal post. They peg the tent as best they can, but the ground is already muddied by the rain. Benny has an image of the wind carrying them off in the night. He ties a couple of the guy ropes to the post of the '**NO CAMPING**' sign. It'll have to do.

Once the tent seems secure, they crawl inside, dragging their packs with them. Benny struggles to zip the porch shut. His fingers have long since numbed. Stephen reaches over to help, clutches the two halves of the canvas together, but a slither of fabric has bunched and caught in the mechanism of the zipper and no matter how hard Benny tries he can't close it.

He stops a moment, breathes. He tells himself that it's OK, they're safe now. He pinches at the fabric one last time, gives the zipper a final tug, gasps as it pops free and glides down with ease.

The roar of the rain is suddenly dulled to a hiss.

Everything is still.

# IX

*Close call – Wet clothes – Tighty whities – Wet
Sam – Emptying the packs – Dry clothes –
Ruined lenses – Pre-uni Stephen – Irony as
fashion – 'How do I look?' – Fire hazard –
Noodles – Park ranger – Split spliff – Plastic
tub – Charity – A rise in homelessness –
More on Stephen's art – Absent fathers.*

'That was close.'

'I know.'

'No, that was too close. That was scary-close. We need to be more careful.'

'I know, man.'

*Hiccchhht.*

'Look at you, you'll catch pneumonia.'

'I'm OK.'

'You need to get those clothes off.'

'Right.'

*Hiccchhht.*

'I mean it, Ste. We need to get you into something dry.'

Stephen peels off his jumper. He removes his T-shirt, his trainers, socks, jeans. He's still just as skinny as he was in school, still with the same pigeon chest and visible ribs and those unusually long nipple hairs that Cal was so fond of pointing out in the changing room during PE.* Everything is soaked, even his tight white briefs.

---

* And, on occasion, wrestling me to the ground to pluck out – much to the delight of the rest of the class.

They cling to his skin, leaving little to the imagination. He crawls over to the porch to wring out the rest of his clothes at the entrance and his hair has flattened now into its old familiar bowl-shape, and the combination of this and the briefs makes him look a bit like that boy from *The Jungle Book*.*

Benny unzips his coat, lays it in the porch next to Stephen's drenched clothing. He removes a small hand towel from his pack, dabs at his face and neck. He'd rather have brought something bigger – a proper bath towel so that he could have a decent wash each morning, instead of having to make do with the clammy smear of the wet wipes – but he knew carrying it would be impractical. This towel is tiny, more of a flannel really, but at least it's something dry he can pat himself down with.

Benny can't help but remember a time he and Sam were caught out in a storm, back when they were first going out. This was early on, those freakishly hot summer nights he'd meet Sam after her Friday afternoon lecture, and the two of them would stop at that Tesco on Hankin Street for a Calippo on the way home. One night there was a sudden downpour, and he can still remember them running back to the flat – the splashing, the squealing, the rain cascading the pavement, as if they were walking through a stream. He could think back on this as a romantic memory if he wanted to, imagine them arriving back at the flat, their undressing leading to sex – their wet bodies slapping together, etc., etc., (he sometimes imagines it this way whilst he's masturbating). But the truth is Sam spent the next hour examining herself in her phone camera, moaning about how frizzy her hair had got. She insisted on applying conditioner; had even worn a shower cap to bed so it could soak in overnight. Another way Sam was like a cat: she hated getting wet. Another: she loved to groom. Another: she always got her own way.

Benny realises Stephen is staring at him. No, not him, he's staring at the towel. Stephen is still naked except for his tighty whities and his nose and hair are dripping. Benny asks if he'd like to use the towel and Stephen nods and so Benny hands it

---

* Mowgli?

over, watches as Stephen plunges his face into it, then scrubs at his hair. Benny flattens down his own hair, combs it to the left with his fingers. Then he remembers, he's recently switched his parting to the right due to the fact it makes his hairline look less receded, and so he combs it that way instead.

Once Stephen's finished, he offers the towel back, but Benny says to toss it in the porch. Best to keep the wet stuff out there.

'Man, listen to that rain.'

'Crazy, isn't it?'

'It's like . . . *apocalyptic*, man. It's like the sky is falling.'

'I thought you wanted this. I thought you said a storm would be good for your photos.'

'Not like this, man. It sounds like the end of the world out there.'

Benny sets about emptying his pack. It's a difficult task considering the lack of available floor space. He drags out the food bag, the mess tin, the gas heater, the water bottles. A little rainwater has got inside the pack itself and everything is speckled with droplets. The corners of the guidebook have begun to curl, which is a shame. It's not that the guidebook has any sentimental value in and of itself, but it does contain his father's final poem.

Benny glances over to make sure Stephen's still busy wringing out his clothes at the porch, then takes a moment to retrieve the plastic tub from the bottom of his pack. He peels the lid off and checks the contents. He doesn't like looking at the ashes. They remind him of the contents of a vacuum cleaner, only with less hair and more bone fragments. He hated having to transfer a portion from the urn – the way the dust rose, then settled on his clothing (he was sure he must have breathed some of it in). It's less dusty now, more of a paste. The damp must have got in there, too. He sighs and seals the tub again, then slips it back into his pack.

He drags out his clothing. It's walk-wear mostly – hat, fleece, a couple of breathable, camo-print T-shirts (also BOGOF in the camping shop) and a bundle of old, black sports socks. He finds what he's after at the bottom, the pair of crisp, white walking socks, still folded in their cardboard sleeve. He slips off his boots, peels off the soiled socks, and flexes his wrinkled toes in the cold air. He knows he should wait, keep the new socks for some time further along the trail, but he also knows how good it'll feel; that snug new-sock sensation against his sodden, blistered feet. He can't resist. And he's right not to; the feeling is almost *orgasmic*.

Stephen empties his own pack. He's shivering now. He rummages for spare clothing but everything he pulls out is soaked – his T-shirts, his shorts, his briefs. He pulls out a handful of tiny socks that remind Benny of something a baby would wear.\*

Stephen unzips the entrance and for a moment the chill of the wind tears back inside the tent. He attempts to wring out his T-shirts on the grass outside, but each time they soak up more rain in the process. In the end Stephen dumps them, one by one, in the porch. Each is sleeveless and white, adorned with photos of his skeleton, Frank. There's Frank in a leotard; Frank with armbands and snorkel and rubber ring; Frank in a blond wig, lipstick, a strap-on dildo. Even clean and dry, these T-shirts look terrible.† Not just because of the transfers, but also their cheap quality – so thin that when Stephen wears them in direct sunlight his nipple hair is visible. Also, the fact they're sleeveless (Stephen hasn't exactly got the arms to complement a lack of sleeves). He doesn't buy them like this, rather he opts to remove the sleeves himself, and from the shoddy workmanship Benny guesses he must use very blunt scissors.‡

Lastly, he takes out the two camera lenses. They're dripping, the glass fogged. He examines them in the torchlight.

'They're ruined.'

'What about the case? Didn't you have a case for them? That swanky leather one?'

---

\* How could you reach this age and still be unaware of the concept of *ankle socks*?

† Cheers, Ben.

‡ Yeah, man, that was sort of the point. They were supposed to look *distressed*, you know? It was part of their charm . . .

'They weren't in the case.'

'Why not?'

'I didn't put them in.'

'Why?'

'I just didn't.'

*Pause.*

'Well, you know . . . That would have been a good idea, Ste . . .'

*Pause.*

'Maybe I could use the rice?'

'What?'

'That's a thing, isn't it? Like when you drop your phone in the bath. You leave it in rice overnight and it absorbs the moisture. And rice is one thing we actually have . . .'

'Only a couple of packets, Ste.'

'Well, noodles then. Noodles'd work too . . .'

'You're not using our noodles for that.'

'Why not?'

'Because we need to *eat* them.'

*Pause.*

'What am I going to do? Look at all my fucking stuff, man. What am I going to wear?'

*Pause.*

'You'll just have to borrow some of mine.'

Stephen paws through Benny's pile of clothing. He's still dripping wet and his fingers leave smudges on everything he touches, but Benny doesn't mention it. He wants to make more of an effort to ignore Stephen's bad habits. He has a feeling that this is important, if they're both to survive this trip.

Stephen winces at the choice of clothing before him. For a moment it's as if he's in actual, physical pain.

'Jesus. This stuff, Ben. Did you want to look like a wanker?'

'This is proper walking stuff, Ste. This is what you should be wearing.'

'Army print? Are we, like, *camouflaging* ourselves?'

*Pause.*

'Just think of them as ironic.'

'Don't think any amount of irony could make this look good, man.'

Stephen dons a clean T-shirt, a fleece, a pair of walking socks. Benny says he's sorry, he doesn't have any spare trousers. His own are waterproof, so he didn't think he'd need a spare pair. Stephen says it's fine, he'll do without. He sits there, bare-legged, shivering.

It's strange, seeing Stephen like this – in a humble T-shirt and fleece combo. It's like he's reverted back to the old Ste, the pre-uni Ste, especially with his hair flattened into that old, familiar bowl. Stephen's style of clothing was much simpler back in school. He wore jeans and band T-shirts, mostly (usually either The Beatles or Pink Floyd) and on nights out he'd spike his bowl up with gel and wear a smart shirt and a pair of leather brogues, like everybody else their age did. It wasn't until he went to London that he started styling his fringe that way, shaving the sides. It wasn't until art school that he started wearing women's shorts and baggy-fit tracksuits and Nike Airs with no socks.*

In general, Benny tries his best to ignore this stuff. He could tell, that weekend in second-year uni when he went down to London to visit, that Stephen was relishing showing off his new student lifestyle – his new clothes and hair and opinions and quirky friends, his house-share complete with empty wine bottles and half-smoked joints; the skeleton in the shower, the murals on the walls, etc., etc. – and so Benny had made a conscious effort to act unfazed, as if this was nothing, as if he hadn't noticed any change at all. The whole time he felt this pressure to react, rile against these things or give them his blessing, but Benny held his tongue. (Until later that night, that is, when he'd had a few drinks and found himself unable not to call out that Garth guy on his ridiculous tracksuit.)

Still, it's nice to be with this Stephen again now. The old, dorky Stephen. Even if he isn't wearing any trousers.

—

* ANKLE SOCKS.

118

'How do I look, man?'

*Pause.*

'Warmer.'*

Benny sets up the gas heater in the porch and they huddle there together. It's a tight squeeze – the porch has little floor space as it is, even less with Stephen's wet clothing. By now they're both shivering and they're glad of the warmth from the heater. Benny fleetingly imagines it tipping, the entire tent engulfed in flames. Camping Shop Mike said all of the new tents were fire retardant, but Benny's not sure whether they had the same safety standards back when his dad purchased this one. He tells himself it wouldn't happen. And even if it did, the flames would soon be doused by the rain.

They brew coffee first tonight. Benny's theory is that coffee-flavoured noodles will go down easier than noodle-flavoured coffee. The coffee is brown and bitter and far too watery but still, it's hot and helps with their shivering. They boil more water, add noodles and curry flavouring, watch the strands swell. After a

---

* This whole irony/fashion thing – I'm not sure you're quite getting what it actually *means*, Ben. I remember you first latching on to the word 'irony' that night you came down and stayed at the house. It was weird for me, that night – you meeting my new friends, them meeting you. The merging of two worlds. It was . . . *uncomfortable*; especially when you got drunk and started mouthing off. And so, when I said that, about you having no sense of irony, I was only trying to defend Garth. We were at Kamya's by this point and you'd started on the whiskey, and you made that unnecessarily cruel comment about Garth's look being 'chav chic'. I mean yes, he was wearing a tracksuit, but even you must see that there is a difference between Garth – a stunningly beautiful, twenty-something art student, with a glorious, bleach-blond mullet, Christian Louboutins, and a gold, Versace tracksuit – and some scally in town? Because context is important here, Ben. So is attention to detail. Fashion is nuanced, it's a lot like art in that way; it's all about juxtapositions, about playing with society's presuppositions to make a statement. Most of this happens subconsciously, a gut-instinct appreciation of a certain aesthetic. Garth understood this more than anyone. During those three years in London I honestly don't think I ever came across someone with a style quite as refined as his.

while they decide enough is enough, hunch over the mess tin with foreheads nearly touching, dipping their sporks and slurping away. There's a bit of a crunch to the noodles, the water not quite boiled yet, but they're still delicious, a warmth sliding down their throats. The curry flavour's the strongest yet and therefore the best, overwhelming the aftertaste of the coffee. They swallow every last strand, share the warm, curried noodle-water, then discard the mess tin in the porch, next to Benny's boots and Stephen's scattered clothing.

Afterwards, Benny rolls a cigarette. He can feel Stephen looking, can tell he wants one too, but supplies are running low and anyway, Stephen shouldn't really be smoking, not if he's having to use an inhaler. Benny kneels in the porch again, unzips the front of the tent and smokes, being sure to exhale out into the rain. Once he's finished he stubs the butt out in the damp grass, then slots it into his coat pocket with all the rest.

'No chance of building a fire tonight then, I'm guessing?'

'Ha.'

'I mean, Jesus. That *rain*, man.'

'We need to be up early. Best get some sleep.'

'How can we sleep with this racket?'

'You'll get used to it.'

'I'm still a bit wired, to be honest. You know, after all that . . . *stress.*'

'We need sleep, Ste. We need to pack up early. We need to be out of here before the park ranger shows up.'

'Park ranger?'

'Or, you know, whoever.'

'Like on *Yogi Bear*?'

'Like, as in we're at a park, so there's most likely a park ranger.'

'What was he called? Officer Dibble, was it?'

'Let's just sleep.'

'No, that was *Top Cat*. Did the *Yogi Bear* park ranger even have a name?'

'Let's just get some sleep.'

*Pause.*

'Can't we smoke? That'll chill us out a bit, a nice smoke . . .'

'I just smoked.'

'No, not that. *This* . . .'

Stephen rummages in his camera case, takes out the little bag of marijuana, waggles it at Benny. This is also a part of the new Stephen, this affinity with drug-taking. He was 100% anti-weed back in sixth form, wholeheartedly bought into his mum's bullshit about it being a gateway to a heroin overdose,* and would often get holier-than-thou at Cal for selling to the year sevens (even if most of the time he was just conning them with small quantities of dried herbs). But maybe he's right, maybe they've earnt a little smoke tonight. Maybe it'll bring down their adrenalin, after their run down the mountain; allow them to get some sleep.

Benny examines the bag in the torchlight. It has one of those pop-seals, which appears to have protected the contents from the rain.

He opens it, inhales the familiar scent.

'OK. Just one.'

They sit in the porch, right by the entrance. Benny rummages in his pack for his tobacco pouch. Maybe Stephen's right, maybe it will help them relax. His uncle used to smoke weed sometimes, especially at the end of a long day's walk. Sam smoked it too, usually before sex. She always insisted that it wasn't because she couldn't perform without it, it was just that it helped her drift into the most perfect sleep afterwards. Benny never quite believed her – especially considering how cold she could be if he'd come on to her when she wasn't drunk or stoned. Who knows, maybe she was telling the truth. And maybe Stephen's right, maybe a spliff before bed will be just the thing to get them off to sleep.

Benny tosses Stephen the tobacco pouch. He's never seen

---

* Yes, marijuana was one of the few new-age clichés Mum and her friends never really bought into. University was different though. (I mean, it was an art course FFS. Even the *tutors* were smoking weed during the breaks.)

Stephen roll before, but he figures after three years at uni he must at least have the basics down. At first, he does OK – licks the edges of two skins, joins them to make a large one, tears a strip of card from the packet of skins to make a roach. He takes a pinch of tobacco and a pinch of weed from their respective bags and crumbles them along the paper. But then things take a turn for the worse. There's far too much spit on the seams, making them practically see-through, and he's added twice the necessary amount of tobacco. When the time comes to actually roll the thing, the skins split. The tobacco and weed spills on his lap. He backs up instinctively, allowing it to scatter.*

Benny takes over. He's not got much tobacco left and he can't afford to have Stephen wasting it. He gathers what he can from the groundsheet, pinches it into a new skin, then rolls a tight little spliff. The whole time Stephen sits, watching.

Benny lights up, inhales. He holds the smoke in his lungs for a few seconds. It's been a while since he smoked anything other than tobacco and immediately he can feel that lightness, that recognisable blooming at the back of his skull, a hit of pure relaxation. It takes him off guard and suddenly he coughs. He reaches for the flap at the entrance, hoping to release most of it out into the storm, but he's too late – the smoke billows around them.

Benny coughs some more, apologises. Stephen coughs too, says not to worry, it happens to everyone. Stephen takes the next drag. He's gives the spliff a few short, sharp sucks, then ducks to the entrance to exhale out into the rain. The action seems effortless, much smoother than when Benny's seen him smoking in the past. He passes the joint back to Benny, then follows up with a few *hiccchhht*s of his inhaler.

'Eish, Ste. That's um . . . that's some *good shit*.'

---

* Yeah, TBH Olga usually rolled for me. She was the stoner of the house. She always got incredible weed too – plenty of connections from her rich Russian friends.

They lie there for a while, smoking and listening to the rain. Occasionally Stephen *hoik*s into his handkerchief. It's getting dark now – properly end-of-day dark, not just the shadow of the storm clouds – and the torchlight is fading. Benny's hair is drying. He brushes it with his fingers again, can feel it starting to curl. He hates curling; he needs his fringe to remain straight for adequate recession coverage (a feat he usually accomplishes with the help of his mum's hairdryer).

Stephen offers him the spliff again. Benny takes it, has another drag, then passes it back. Stephen holds it in front of his face, examining the burning ember.

He asks if they're going to talk about *him* at all.

Who? Benny asks.

Him.

Who, Benny asks, *Cal*?

Stephen shakes his head. He points at Benny's pack with the flared end of the spliff: *him*.

Benny turns. The tub of ashes must have slipped out whilst he was rooting for his tobacco. There it is, lying upside-down on the groundsheet: his father's powdered remains, now in full view.

'Oh. That.'
   *Pause.*
   'Well?'
   'Well what?'
   'Well, that's why we're here, right? That's what this is all about?'
   'What?'
   'This trip.'
   'This trip is about many things, Ste.'
   'And one of those things is *him*.'
   'I guess.'
   *Pause.*
   'It will help, you know. Talking about it.'
   'Ste, please.'
   'I know you think it won't, but it will.'
   'I don't really—'
   'I know what it's like, you know.'

'I know.'

'My dad . . . I've been there.'

'And I appreciate it, Ste. I really do. I'm just not in the mood right now.'

'OK, OK. Fine.' *Pause.* 'Well, anyway. Things could be worse.'

'What do you mean?'

'Than this. Right now. I mean, we're here. We've found a camp. We're relatively dry. We're having a smoke. Things aren't too bad.'

'True.'

'And at least we've got the tent.'

'What do you mean?'

'Well, imagine those poor homeless people we saw yesterday, man. Imagine what *they're* going through right now.'

'Right.'

'Sat out in the street, in *this*.'

'I'm sure they'll find somewhere.'

'Where?'

'All kinds of places. There are shelters. And, like, charities.'

'That the official government line, Ben? Is that what you tell people when they phone the call centre? That there are *charities*?'

'Sometimes.'

*Pause.*

'Can I ask you something?'

'I'm sure you will anyway.'

'Right.'

*Pause.*

'So?'

'Well, it's about yesterday . . . The homeless people . . . You know, when they kept asking us for money . . .'

'I remember, yeah. What about it?'

'Well, I was just surprised is all.'

'Surprised?'

'I thought you would have given them some.'

'I only had twenties, Ste. Not going to give them a twenty-pound note, am I?'

'At first, yeah. When that first guy asked us. But then you bought those Mars bars in the Tesco, so then you had change, loads of it. And yet, when you were asked again, you still wouldn't give them anything.'

'And?'

'And I was just surprised is all.'

'Why?'

'I just thought you would have.'

'OK. Well, I didn't.'

'Why?'

'I don't know. I just didn't.'

'Do you ever?'

'What *is this*?'

'I'm just wondering.'

'Wondering what, Ste? How much of an *arsehole* I am?'

'No, it's not that. I'm just interested. Not just in you. I'm not talking about you, specifically. It's more to do with people in general. It's just something I started noticing in uni. Like, there've always been homeless, right? Especially in the city centre. But this increase over the last few years . . . it's been *phenomenal*. It's crazy in London. We'd see them all the time, gatherings of them. There was this park by ours that resembled a refugee camp sometimes. And there was a shelter, a new one that had been opened by the uni, in one of the buildings they didn't really use, we'd pass it every time we went to Kamya's. It was huge, like an old sports hall kind of thing. And each time I'd pass it there was just, like, a *sea* of people. Like packed in, you know? Sleeping on the floor in rows, head to toe. It was *insane*. Anyway, that's when I began *Doomed Youth*.'

'*Doomed Youth*?'

'My project.' *Pause.* 'You know, Frank . . .'

'Oh, right.'

'Well, it was in second year that Garth and I began to notice more and more homeless people *our own age*. That's when we realised we should be doing something about it. Using our art to make a political statement, you know? Highlight injustice in our society. We began to use them as a source of inspiration for our work.'

'And?'

'And what?'

'Did it work?'

'What, did we *end the homelessness crisis*?'

'Did it help your work?'

'It helped, sure. In some ways. But still, it was also a bit of a shock. The reaction to it, I mean. You'd think the levels of homelessness would make people *more* charitable, right? You'd think there'd be others campaigning. Protesting. Or at the very least, like, handing over a bit of spare change once in a while. But in fact, *the opposite* was true. You could see, just walking around, how people became less charitable. More . . . *hostile*.'

'That's London for you, Ste.'

'Yeah. Well, maybe that's part of it. Like, I know there's that reputation, that people are less friendly down south. But there was more to it than that. It's as if the larger the problem is, the more people feel they are absolved of having to do anything to solve it. I came up with this theory: the more homeless there are, the less people give a shit about homelessness.'

'Makes sense though.'

'Why?'

'You know what it's like, Ste. When you're out and about, when you just want to get on with your day. The amount of them in the streets now . . . you can't give to them all. It's too big a problem.'

'Is that what your dad thought?'

'What's that got to do with anything?'

'Well, wasn't he always doing stuff for the homeless? I remember at Christmas he'd do that raffle, wouldn't he? And the own clothes days and stuff. He was always the one organising those sorts of things.'

'He was, yeah.'

'And there were pictures on Facebook, I think. Of him protesting outside the call centre.'

'And?'

'Why can't we just talk about him? I don't get it . . .'

'Ste.'

'I'm a good listener!'

'I know. I'm just tired.'

'But I don't see—'

'We need to be up early tomorrow.'

'Stop making excuses.'

'I'm not.'

'It sounds very much like you are.'

'Ste, I—'

'I know about cancer. My Aunt Ellen had it. Well, in her case it was breast cancer, but still . . .'

'I know, Ste.'

'She's the one with all the kids. My cousins. Five sons and apparently none of them knew how to talk to her about what she was going through. The only people she had for that were me and my mum . . .'

'Right.'

'And I know all about losing a parent too, Ben. My dad left before I was even *born*.'

'I know.'

'He just upped and left. I never even got the chance to say goodbye, you know?'

'I know.'

'He just went. Walked out on Mum and me—'

'I know, Ste, you've told me this.'

'And it was hard, man.'

'I remember. You've told me this. You told me at the funeral. You told me back in sixth form.'

'I'm just saying, it was—'

'But it's not the same.'

'What?'

'It's not the *same*, Ste.'

'What do you mean?'

'My dad didn't walk out.'

'I know, but—'

'My dad didn't up and leave. He . . . *faded away.*'

*Pause.*

'What do you mean?'

'I had plenty of chances to say goodbye. That's what those last few months were, one long chance to say goodbye.' *Pause.* 'You don't understand, Ste. You could never understand.' *Pause.* 'It was completely different, OK?' *Pause.* 'It's not something I want to talk about.'

*Pause.*

'Is it to do with your job?'

'*What?!*'

'Is that why you're so funny about all this?'

'Just *stop*, Ste.'

'Because he was totally against all that, wasn't he? Austerity . . . the cuts . . . the PIP assessments . . . all of it. He was always going on about the DWP. I remember in school, the anger in his voice when he'd discuss it in class . . .'

'Ste—'

'I mean, it must have been hard for him, you working for them . . .'

'Just stop it, Ste.'

'I mean, I don't really understand it. How you can go there each day and work for them. I mean, I wouldn't—'

'JUST *FUCK OFF*, STE, YEAH?'

Stephen looks away. He stares into the corner of the tent, into the darkness. Into nothing. His eyes stay fixed there for a good ten seconds. The spliff has long since burnt out – a cluster of ash scattered on the groundsheet.

Benny sighs, turns to his pack. He slides the plastic tub to the very bottom, next to the hatchet. He gets out the sleeping bags – gives Stephen his, then wraps himself in his own.

After a few minutes the torch flickers out. The two of them lie there in the darkness.

'I'm sorry, Ben.'

'It's OK.'

'I didn't mean to . . .'

'It's fine.'

'I mean it. I'm sorry, I—'

'Let's just get some sleep, yeah?'

# X

*Achieving sleep (then not) – Stoned – Snoring
Stephen – Balding Benny – Forums –
The day-to-day reality of the call centre –
The intricacies of the benefits system – That
same old memory of his father – An unending
torrent of rain – Silence – Sleep.*

Benny's not aware of achieving sleep in those few hours after
he's told Stephen to fuck off, but he must do, because by the
time he remembers to switch his phone on to set an alarm it's
half one in the morning. He squints against the light of the screen.
He's down to 53% battery now. No signal, no new messages. He
sets the alarm for six. That should give them enough time to
pack up and leave before anyone shows up.

He switches his phone off again, stares into the darkness.

It's not darkness though, not when he looks properly. Benny
can see shapes, spirals of colour, clouds of flashing static. He
remembers, as a child, pressing his thumbs into his eyes to
produce a similar effect. He's not sure of the cause here – an
after-effect of the light of the screen? Or could he in fact be
stoned? He doesn't *feel* stoned, doesn't feel much of anything
except a sense of heaviness. Fatigue. He's very aware of his body;
not as a whole, but each part individually. It's as if his mind
is able to slip from its usual residence in his head to other
areas. One moment he's inhabiting his neck, the next his lower
back. One moment he's in his right shin, the next the little toe
of his left foot. At the same time, he's acutely aware of the various
ailments in each of these areas – the aches, the blisters, the
sunburn and irritation from nettles and brambles. He suddenly
feels an overwhelming sense of guilt over what he's subjected his

body to. He feels like he could cry at any moment. Maybe he *is* stoned.

Stephen's snoring doesn't seem as loud tonight, what with the storm still raging outside. The wind screeches. The walls of the tent shudder. Outside is chaos, like clashing drums, like shattering glass. Benny runs his fingers over his fringe. It's not just curling now, it's *frizzed*. He was afraid of this. When he's able to blow-dry it, he can at least give his fringe the appearance of thickness, but when it dries on its own it ends up wiry, which makes the hair there look even thinner.

Benny's never really escaped his impending baldness, not since that moment of realisation in the bathroom mirror, that night of his dad's first bout of chemo. Benny's mum had made some comment that night about the possibility of Benny's dad going bald during treatment, and Benny's dad had laughed it off, said with mock-horror that (*gasp*) he'd end up looking like Uncle Ian, and they'd all laughed at that. It was only later that evening, when he was pulling back his own hair in the bathroom mirror, trying to picture what *he'd* look like bald, that it had dawned on Benny that he might not have all that long to wait. It had never occurred to him before, but his hairline seemed much higher than it should have been. There was now a definite V shape and it was thinner at the front, so thin in fact that he could see right through to the scalp. It was only when he retrieved his mum's portable mirror and held it up at the back of his head that he noticed there was a spot thinning at the crown too, the size and shape of an egg. Benny's almost certain now, thinking back, that this was the starting point for the disconnection he would feel in the months to come, the mental numbness he would later come to think of as 'The Fog'. If he had to pinpoint a moment when The Fog began, it wouldn't be the day Sam went back to Ireland, or the night with Cal and Christine, or even the morning they got the call from the hospice, telling them to rush down ASAP. It would be *that* night: him stooped over the sink, fringe pulled back tight, examining his hairline in that harsh, white, bathroom light.

Since then he's regularly lost entire evenings, stressing over his dying follicles. He'll lie there for hours, researching male pattern baldness on his phone, occasionally stopping to examine his hair-line in the front-facing camera of his phone. He trawls through forums too – there are plenty of websites where men post advice and home remedies, alongside pictures of their thinning hair. He remembers his uncle once warning him that a man reaches a certain age when he doesn't have a hairstyle any more; when his choice of hairdo becomes whatever makes him look the least bald. Benny had laughed at this at the time, as had his dad. Uncle Ian's head was shaved to the bone and Benny had no idea how anything could possibly make him look balder than that. Nowadays, of course, Benny's much more aware of the reality of his uncle's warning.

Sometimes Benny wonders if his thinning hair was a factor in Sam distancing herself near the end of the relationship. Many of the forums claim that research shows the vast majority of women don't find balding a turn off, but still, it'd be nice to know what Sam thought about it, one way or the other. She was all over him back in first year, when his hair was still thick, but then she'd grown distant as the relationship wore on. (Another way Sam was like a cat: she was contrary when it came to giving affection. Another: Benny never owned her, she owned him.)*

---

* For the record, Ben, yes, everyone knew you were going bald. You had been for years. Cal was always cracking jokes about it, saying how your hair 'wasn't long for this world', although apparently he never said anything to your face. I'm not sure why. It seems an uncharacteristic act of compassion on his part, although I guess you were always his favourite. Anyway, the fact that your impending baldness was only just dawning on you at this point is . . . *surprising* . . .

Although at the same time *not*, right? I doubt it's a coincidence, this becoming an issue for you just at the point you're having to face your father's (and therefore your *own*) mortality. I guess that's how it goes with these things. I remember having insecurities about the way I looked back in school and I think a lot of them stemmed from my dad leaving – those deep feelings of rejection, etc. It seems hilarious now, doesn't it, that I put so much effort into not being noticed in school? That even after years of name-calling and ritual beatings, there I was, still convincing myself that I was managing to somehow *fade into the background*. So much so that when I left for uni, I was still that same chronically shy, bowl-cut introvert I'd been since we first met at your mum's Sunday school classes. So much so

Still, he doesn't want to think about any of this. He needs *sleep*. He rolls onto his back again, stares at the ceiling. He tries not to fixate on his curling fringe. He tries not to think about his dad, or Sam, or Cal and Christine – all varieties of fuel for The Fog. He keeps busy, usually. He cooks, he cleans, he watches the quiz channel, he masturbates. Even in work, Benny's managed to distance himself from the day-to-day reality of his existence. He's found he can get through his shifts OK, so long as he maintains a state of continued emotional detachment. Often the people who phone up have all sorts of problems; endless questions and complaints regarding disability support or benefits sanctions or delays in payments, but so long as Benny avoids empathising too much with whatever their particular issues happen to be, he tends to get through it OK. He found this difficult at first (especially as he also has to make sure his calls remain under the call time average) but recently he's found he can speed through these conversations no problem. He knows the script off by heart; knows how to navigate the calls in a way that delivers the required outcome. And sure, some of them have a tendency to come back to haunt him (especially the more harrowing ones – the criers, the personal stories, the ones who plead again and again and again that they need more money to feed their children), but mostly he manages to get through it on autopilot.

Benny never really gave much thought to the intricacies of the benefits system, not until he finished uni and realised how few jobs were available. Sure, he remembered a lot of fuss when Universal Credit was first introduced, but that was back when he was in sixth form, when his mind was on other things. His dad was always ranting about the government (it was around then that he attended the protests outside the job centre), but Benny

---

that halfway through first year, when Garth asked to paint me, I found myself caught in this kind of horrible double-bind, wanting to please Garth and agree to anything he asked, whilst at the same time feeling mortified at the prospect of another human being examining me in such intense detail. (This was in Kamya's, the first night I ever went drinking with him. Maybe this isn't the time to be getting into all that . . .)

never quite understood how this new system was any different to the old one. Then, when Benny was at uni, they announced the new call centre was opening just down the road from his old school, and his dad had joined the protests outside there too. Benny still remembers the pictures on Facebook: his dad and a group of other middle-aged people, all in high-vis jackets, waving anti-austerity flags in the car park at the front of the building.

Benny never considered he'd end up *working* there. Not until his employment advisor had suggested it during one of his weekly appointments. He knew a lot of people from school were at the call centre, so he thought why not? He needed the money. His mum needed it too; Benny's dad wasn't reacting well to the chemo by that point and he'd had to pack in work completely. So Benny applied. He began his training at the end of January. His dad never said anything about it – never gave any indication of how he felt about it, one way or the other. Until that night in the kitchen that is, the night Benny arrived home after his first shift.

And here it is again, that same old memory, nudging its way into the forefront of his mind: his father sitting there, cigarette in hand, glaring up at him from the kitchen table.

Benny rolls onto his front again. He wishes he had a pillow he could submerge his face into. He wonders if he'll ever get back to sleep now, with this unending torrent of rain.

Then, without warning, the rain stops. The noise just ends. It's like someone flicked a switch. The only sound is an occasional tapping – scattered droplets from the trees.

Benny pictures those same words again, his dad's old breathing technique:

**IN**.

**OUT**.

**IN**.

**OUT**.

Eventually he manages to get to sleep.★

---

★ OK, so maybe this is a good time to interject. I feel like I need to rewind here, Ben, give a little context to my situation, especially when it comes to all this political stuff. I need you to know how much of a driving force my time in uni was when it came to my opinions here. Otherwise certain things (e.g. all that drama over my refusing to work at the call centre) aren't going to make much sense to you.

First, try to understand – like you, I wasn't particularly politically minded when I started at university. Sure, I had that same working-class, anti-establishment attitude as everyone else in our sixth form (*fuck the Eton elite!* etc.) but I'd never really given much thought to the ideology behind the government austerity programme, or its real-world ramifications. I should have done – Mum was receiving several state benefits, and she lost her part-time job at the library as a result of the public-sector cuts – but I'd never really considered the political decisions behind these things. I was too busy being a teenager, getting drunk with you and Cal. I was ignorant, and as a result my art was ignorant. I was still sketching, mostly, although nothing of any importance. It was a much-needed creative outlet, but it wasn't *art* per se, just entertainment.

It was during those first few months down in London that I began to lose faith in my skills. My work began to feel uninspired – wholly under-whelming compared to that of my peers. I was suffering from small pond syndrome; for most of my school art classes I'd been producing various mediocre canvases (the dead animal stuff), but still, I was the best in the year, constantly praised by Mr Watt for my sketches, and I got comfortable in that role. Being accepted for a position on such a prestigious course gave me a huge confidence boost (getting accepted on *any* course would have been – as you mentioned earlier, no one else in my family had ever been to university). Still, I can see now that I was feeling safe, which is never a good place for an artist to be. It was only once I was doing my introductory modules, when I was bearing witness to the radical canvas work the likes of Garth and Olga were producing, that I realised how unskilled I really was.

My course was based at the arts centre. This was the site I'd shown you pictures of – an enormous redbrick with spires and arched windows, nestled between oak trees and surrounded by wrought-iron fencing. It was pretty much what you'd expect from such an institution, but Mum had gasped when she'd seen it on the website, said it reminded her of *Harry Potter*. My accommodation was close by. I remember I arrived too early that first morning. I'd taken the overnight coach (six hours trying to sleep in a seat too cramped to slouch in, crammed between an icy pane of glass and a middle-aged man who smelt like cheese-and-onion crisps) followed by an 8:30 train across London. Just picture it, Ben: rush hour in Victoria station, a terrified eighteen-year-old me, shuffling through the crowds, suitcase in hand. By the time I got to my accommodation I was exhausted, and as a result I slept through the afternoon, missing the arrival of my new flatmates entirely (by the time I woke up they'd already unpacked and left for the pub, which was enough to ostracise me for the rest of my time there). Those first few weeks were the loneliest of my entire life. I went for walks down by the river. I took the tube to Piccadilly and Charing Cross and Soho – all the places you're constantly hearing referenced on TV – but I always felt a certain sadness, whilst doing so. It made it worse, that it was so *busy*. That there were so many people about. It was all so overwhelming. It made me feel even more alone.

The course was overwhelming, too. The first semester mostly consisted of a series of introductory lectures, given by either Coleman (the old, moustachioed head of department) or what he jokingly referred to as his 'young protégés' (the sessional tutors, exclusively white males in their twenties or thirties). These lectures were probably littered with fascinating insights into the history of art, as well as a forensic study of the craft, and to get the full benefit of my tuition I probably should have attended each and every one of them and made copious notes on the topics they were discussing, but the truth is a lot of it went right over my head. I wasn't ready for the academic stuff; the distinctions between Orphism and Futurism; the criteria for aesthetic and formalist theories. There were set texts to read but I'd found them hard to get hold of. Several were out of print and only available for highly inflated prices online. I'd been able to find one in the library – a book about Minimalism in the 60s and 70s – but again, I couldn't get my head around much of it. I'd only managed to get halfway through the introduction. There was one quote that stuck out to me, though (attributed to John Cage) and it was this: 'I have nothing to say and I'm saying it.' I liked that quote. I would often drop it into conversations with my fellow students, several of whom found it funny and insightful in a way that suggested they too hadn't done much of the preliminary reading. But that was as far as my studies went. I just wanted to draw. To paint. To *create*. All that academic jargon meant nothing to me.

I was a bit more hopeful when it came to the studio classes. They called them 'Art Bites': a series of practical exercises, usually provided by one of the sessional tutors, with the intention of making us think more experimentally about the artistic process. One class we had to make a portrait of a loved one out of pencil sharpenings, another we moulded abstract concepts out of clay. Unfortunately for me, only a few of these were painting tasks, all involving some sort of debilitating apparatus that thrust them well out of my skillset (e.g. creating a self-portrait whilst wearing a pair of oven mitts, or strapping our paintbrushes to the end of a broom handle to work on canvases fixed to the ceiling). Whilst the majority of the other students were using this opportunity to bond over the risk-taking thrill of true experimentation, I appeared to be in the unique position of failing at each and every task.

The only friend I made during these early days was Jess. She was a fellow painter, though of a much higher quality than myself. She did landscapes mostly, bleak scenes of northern town centres in the rain. You'd have liked Jess. She was down to earth, that same sort of cynical no-nonsense attitude as you and Cal. She was a classicist who never bought into the idea of conceptual art, and she hated the Art Bites even more than I did – outright refused to participate in most of them. Her only wish was to improve her craft and she was very outspoken when she thought the set work was impeding this. Jess claimed to appreciate all aspects of the art world, but her appreciation seemed to go no further than the post-impressionists. She liked Picasso's early stuff but drew the line at Cubism, and she wouldn't give conceptual art the time of day. The whole time I knew her I never came across a modern piece that she didn't consider a pretentious piece of shit.

And then there was Garth. He was also in our seminar group, except he (of course) excelled at everything with an infuriating air of apathetic detachment. He was hard not to notice, floating from one class to the next with his bleach-blond mullet and that black-and-gold tracksuit, always accompanied by Olga. The two of them were a constant source of derision for Jess, who would often snort within earshot of them, usually as a response to what they were wearing. As I've already mentioned, fashion was important to Garth. He showed up in an array of different outfits those first few months, although (as with you) it was the tracksuit that seemed to bother Jess the most. Sportswear was very on-trend at the time – tracksuits, baseball caps, trainers, etc. – and Jess claimed this was distasteful, an appropriation of traditionally working-class clothing, especially considering the fact that most of our fellow students came from extremely well-off families. She said it was something that really got under her skin, when private-school types played at being poor. Jess and I appeared to be the only genuinely working-class students in the group, which in turn affected their treatment of us. I'd often see Garth and Olga looking our way, whispering, giggling.

That first term continued to be difficult. I'd created this idea of London in my head and the reality was nothing like I'd imagined. I missed Mum. I restricted my calls home to once a week because I wanted her to think I was having fun – I didn't want her to worry. I hardly spoke to my flatmates. I've never found it easy talking to strangers – hiding away in my tiny room came more naturally to me. I knew they'd think me a recluse – a reputation confirmed daily by the silence I received upon entering the communal kitchen – but I found the situation unavoidable. I didn't make any friends on the course either, other than Jess, and that friendship mostly consisted of sitting next to her in lectures and seminars, followed by the occasional pint in The Albert (a pub just round the corner from our main lecture theatre). Jess had a job there, was always taking extra shifts to try and claw back some of the debt she was falling into, and a few times I went along to keep her company. But the drinks were so expensive, I couldn't keep it up. It was hard to branch out into other friendships because of Jess's unwillingness to befriend any 'arty types'. The rest of the class fell into cliques and it was interesting to see how the school hierarchy came into play even here; Jess and I at the bottom, Garth and Olga firmly at the top.

I first spoke to Garth one evening at the start of the second semester. We were at one of the university art shows. Sebastian, one of Coleman's 'young protégés', was exhibiting a piece – an enormous set of teeth made from thousands of compressed polystyrene packing chips. Projected onto the teeth was film footage of 1960s factory workers. It was over in the viewing gallery and everyone from class showed up, attracted by the promise of free wine and an opportunity to suck up to the lecturers. Jess was working, so I went alone.

I genuinely liked the piece. I told Garth as much when he appeared beside me, Olga on his arm, whispering something for him to giggle at. It was purely on impulse, I think, my speaking to him. I was fed up of his and Olga's constant mutterings. He seemed shocked at first, that I'd even dared speak to him. Then he began to nod – as if it all made sense now, as if he wasn't at all surprised by my liking of Coleman's work. Olga turned and left without a word and it was then I knew I'd made a mistake in talking to him.

Garth asked what particular aspect of the sculpture I liked. I facetiously answered, 'The teeth,' but Garth accepted this without humour, asked exactly what it was I liked about them. I sighed, shook my head.

After a few minutes of silence Garth spoke again. He declared that the only reason I liked the piece was because it reminded me of my own work. I disagreed. 'But that's your whole thing, right?' he said. 'Death? Decay? The whole *absurdist drama*? What better symbol of decay than *teeth*?' I was shocked that he knew anything about my work. I figured he must have noticed my canvas pieces in class, although he never came near Jess and me, so I wasn't sure how.

That's when he asked if I'd like to go somewhere for a drink. He said he'd like to discuss my opinions on the piece in detail. I declined. I figured he was just trying to gather material with which to later mock me with Olga. Besides, there was nothing to discuss. If I liked something, I liked it. I couldn't define why in a way that would satisfy him (and I knew from our lectures and seminars that these sorts of discussions tended to just entrench people in their original opinions). But Garth insisted. He said we could talk about anything, we could avoid the subject of art all together if I preferred. He said he detected a hint of animosity in my tone and he couldn't have that. He needed to woo me with his winning personality, prove that he was really a pussycat. Then he grinned and gave me this clawing-cat hand gesture. I shrugged. I had nothing else to do that night so figured why not. If nothing else I could at least gather material with which to later mock him with Jess.

Garth said he knew a bar nearby. Somewhere cool, artsy – the kind of place that's quickly disappearing in a city inhabited by ninety percent Russian oligarchs. We walked for forty-five minutes, didn't speak the entire journey. He navigated the streets like a practised Londoner, slipping through the crowds instinctively, whilst I trailed behind, apologising each time I cut in front of someone. I was still getting used to life in the city, the vastness of it, the herds of people, the fact Londoners considered a bar forty-five minutes away to be 'nearby'. The bar was Kamya's, that 'secret bar' that would soon become our local. (We went there that weekend you visited, if you remember, although you were pretty drunk by that point.) From the outside it looks like any other closed office building, but knock twice and a doorman grants access across the foyer and down some stairs into the humid basement where incredibly loud dance music plays whilst a single barman struggles to serve cocktails to a horde of thirsty twenty-somethings. Garth was right, it was an amazing place, unlike anywhere I'd been to back home – strobe lighting, 1920s fetish-ware photography on the walls, an atmosphere so joyous and depraved it felt like anything was possible. I'd never really explored the nightclub scene back home (my only friends being you and Cal) and so this felt like a revelation of sorts. Garth told me to get a seat whilst he forced his way through to the bar. I saw no seats (I never saw a seat the entire three years we went there) so stood over by the doorway, where the crowd thinned a little. The doorway led to a courtyard packed with smokers. I never did work out the layout of the place, how we could descend a winding set of stairs yet still have access to what appeared to be a ground floor courtyard, but right then I didn't let it bother me. I just enjoyed the breeze.

Garth returned with a couple of lime-green cocktails. It had been an incomprehensibly short amount of time, but he explained that he knew the barman. He knew a lot of the punters too; the first few minutes consisted of constant interruptions by drunken London lovie-types who each had to lean in and kiss both of Garth's cheeks (a few leant in to kiss me too, as I was introduced: 'Oh wow, it's so nice to meet you!' / 'Have we met before?' / 'Isn't Garth *the best*', etc.) before leaving with promises to catch up soon. We barely had a moment to say a word to each other, or even sip our drinks. As a result, we didn't talk properly until Garth led us out to the courtyard for a cigarette. I'd never smoked before, but Garth had this way – when he offered you something you didn't even think, you just said yes. It was the first cocktail I'd ever tried and, although I was a bit overwhelmed by the overbearing sweetness of it, I swallowed it all down.

I can't remember our conversation in its entirety (I don't have your skill in transcribing dialogue verbatim – each word uttered, the length of each

'*Pause*' etc.) but I do remember most of it consisted of Garth firebombing me with questions: Where did I grow up? How big a family? Hobbies? Favourite artists? Favourite writers, musicians, directors? Favourite drink/month/colour/type of pasta? How many friends? How many enemies? etc., etc. He had this annoying habit of interrupting, too – just when I'd get into a subject, he'd cut me off, ask me something totally unrelated. It was a complete mental workout. I would later learn that this was a common technique of his. According to Garth, life was too short for small talk. If he took a genuine interest in someone then it was important to learn as much about them in as little time as humanly possible.

Throughout all of this, I was trying (and failing) to maintain my hatred of him. I had this weird loyalty to Jess, I don't know why. Maybe it was the fact she reminded me of you and Cal. I spent the first part of the evening silently judging each of Garth's mannerisms, e.g. the way he'd bare his teeth when he smiled, or how he'd run his fingers over the top of his mullet, or the way he'd pout as he sucked through his straw – not to mention his constant use of the word 'man' at the end of every sentence. It was only when he asked about my art that I began to really open up. He asked about my feelings of inadequacy in class. I've no idea how he knew I was harbouring such feelings, but that was Garth – he seemed to know *everything*. Against my better judgement I nodded, admitted I was struggling. Lack of self-belief was a problem I couldn't seem to overcome. I don't know why I told him this. I can't remember the exact cause of that shift, when I became unguarded with him. Maybe it was the alcohol. Maybe it was the excitement of finally feeling I was *there*, in the heart of London life. Or maybe it was because I'd never had anybody I felt like I could say this stuff to, no one who genuinely wanted to hear it.

Inadequacy was something Garth claimed to have plenty of experience with. He'd spent his whole life not living up to people's expectations of him, the most pertinent example being his father. His dad was also an artist – an acclaimed sculptor who'd taught at several universities, both here and in the US (at that point he was in residency in San Francisco). He'd always been hyper-critical of Garth's canvases and the two of them often ended up in heated debates about the validity of his work. His dad was an alcoholic and it was during one of these debates that he'd hurled a whiskey bottle at Garth. I'd later come to respect Garth's father and his work, and even met him once, when he came to speak as part of a series of guest lectures the university held during its Adam Chodzko retrospective, but that night I despised the man, especially when Garth leant in to show me the bump still visible at the bridge of his nose. His father later claimed he hadn't meant for the bottle to actually *hit* him, although Garth said he still brought it up from time to time, when he needed to extort a little money from the old man.

Garth said it was around that time that he'd really found his artistic muse. He'd been experimenting a lot before then, but it was only when he was hiding away, nursing his broken face, that his canvas work manifested into something worthwhile. His breakthrough came via an expressionist piece entitled *Fucking My Father*. According to Garth, this was his greatest work. He'd somehow channelled all that bitterness and anger, all the self-loathing his dad had caused him over the years, into something truly powerful. I could only imagine. I had been in awe of what I'd seen of Garth's canvases in our workshops. Typically they'd begin as a series of rounded shapes, painted in delicate pastel colours that suggested tenderness and femininity. Then he would layer the canvas with a series of violent red and black brushstrokes, spearing the shapes from all angles; a manifestation of pure sexual aggression. Apparently (and rather ironically) *Fucking My Father* had been the first piece of work Garth's dad had actually *liked* (although he had been slightly lost for words when Garth revealed the title). I asked if I'd be able to see the piece, but Garth said he'd destroyed it not long after it was finished. He and his dad were in agreement on that; although it was an important step in his artistic progress, it was too *raw*, too powerful to live out in the real world.

It was then Garth asked why *I* had decided to become an artist. By this point we were slumped against the wall at the back of the courtyard and I still remember that moment – nursing the empty glass in my lap, trying to summon an adequate response. I tried out my John Cage quote on him, the one I'd learnt from the introduction of that textbook: 'I have nothing to say and I'm saying it.' But Garth just laughed. He told me he also liked Cage – that was one thing we finally had in common. 'And anyway, that's not true,' he said. 'In fact, I see it as quite the opposite. You've got plenty to say, you're just not managing to articulate it yet.'

I shrugged at that. The truth was I didn't have any real motivation, other than the fact that art was the one thing I was actually good at. I had drawn since I was a child and over the past couple of years I had begun to take on more macabre subject matter, copying images of decomposition I'd researched online. It had unlocked something within me – a certain mindset that gave life a sense of purpose. It seemed to me that, without some sort of creative outlet to express myself, there was little point in living *at all*. I told Garth all of this and he nodded, took one final sip of his drink and stood up. For a moment I thought that was it, my answer was so unsatisfactory that he was leaving. He must have seen the horror in my face because at that moment he laughed, told me he was just going to sort us some more drinks.

The time he was away felt like torture. There was this creeping feeling of shame over how pathetic my answer had been. Although I'd been professing to share Jess's hatred of Garth and Olga, I was secretly in awe of their work in the Art Bite sessions. I felt that, if anyone knew what direction I should take next, artistically speaking, it was Garth. It seemed like he was gone for ages (he was actually buying cocaine off somebody in the toilets, but I wouldn't know that until later on). I noticed he seemed a bit jittery when he got back, but I didn't mention it. I took my cocktail – purple this time – thanked him and took a sip.

It was then that Garth asked if he could paint me.

At first I was dumbstruck. I (of course) wanted to refuse, but for some reason I found myself unable to just come out and say so. Instead I laughed, hoping maybe he was joking. Or else that, by making out that I thought he was joking, this would somehow dissuade him from the idea. This didn't work though, he just kept staring at me, waiting for an answer. In the end I relented. I shrugged – that was my answer. The only answer I found myself able to give. I didn't know what else to do.

Garth smiled. It was then he asked if I was a virgin. I couldn't bring myself to answer that either. Although, after a few seconds he began to nod, as if my silence confirmed his suspicions. That's when he asked if I'd like to have sex. I knew from the way he said it that he wasn't speaking in general; he meant would I like to have sex *tonight*, would I like to do so *with him*. I sat up straight, began to explain to him that I didn't think it was appropriate. I told him I wasn't gay. And Garth laughed. (That was his reaction – he genuinely thought I was joking.) And I laughed too. And in that moment, it was like this huge weight was lifted, you know? What did it matter, if Garth and I had sex? I was in London. I could do anything. I could be anyone I wanted.

We did end up sleeping together that night. After a few more cocktails, and a few lines of coke, we went back to the house Garth shared with Olga. This is that same Georgian house where I'd end up living throughout second and third year, the house you stayed in when you came down to visit. That night was the only time Garth and I slept together, in all the time I knew him. Sure, there were plenty of other one-night stands during that period (Garth and Olga had plenty of hangers-on – 'fuck boys' was their term, although I never cared for it myself) but the furthest Garth and I ever went together was that one-time drunken quickie. It felt natural, that night. He'd just finished the preliminary sketches for the painting, and sex felt like the inevitable climax to our growing intimacy. It didn't last long (he warned me of that as soon as we lay down on his bed – that he couldn't maintain an erection after that much cocaine) but still, it was a liberation of sorts. Something momentous I can look back on now. A definite highlight.

It was also a crucial turning point in terms of my evolution as an artist. I remember sitting there the next morning, in the kitchen with him and Olga. I found that house so exciting. Sure, it was dilapidated, but that added to it, the once-grandness of it; an architectural marvel now cracked and crumbling. It was more of a studio than a living space – the pallets and brushes, the paint-smeared walls, the huge canvases propped up in every corner – not to mention the giant mural that spanned the living-room wall. The place radiated this buzz of creative energy (later, Olga and I would joke that we could actually *hear* the buzz, if we listened closely, although it was most likely just the refrigerator).

I remember literally dropping my spoon when Garth asked me to move in (we were eating Cheerios at the time). I asked if it wasn't all a bit sudden, but Garth just laughed. We weren't in a *relationship* or anything, he said. It wasn't like that. He just thought it'd be good for me. For *him* too – both of us. He said he liked to surround himself with artists of integrity.

'And that's what you see me as?' I asked. 'An artist of integrity?'

He never answered that (too much sentiment involved), but Olga gave me a wink and the three of us continued with our breakfast. I began to move my stuff in that very same day. I still had to pay rent in my student accommodation for the rest of term – there was no way of getting out of the contract – but Garth didn't mind that I was broke. The arrangement was that I would just pay him what I could spare, whenever I was able, and he subsidised my rent in the same way he subsidised much of my three years in London; he was often giving me cash for things. He never finished the painting of me, never got beyond those preliminary sketches, but we always worked together from then on, our canvases positioned across from each other in the centre of the living room.

Maybe I'm not explaining this very well. I'm trying not to overdo it, or to get too sentimental here (I know that'll only serve to annoy you) – but those years that followed, that house with Garth and Olga, it's almost as if I was 'born again', you know? It was the closest I've ever come to a religious experience, a true *awakening*. And yet, at the same time, it felt like this was the real me. It's not so much that I was reinventing myself, more like I was finding out who I'd really been all along. I'd been living a lie. Which was a coping mechanism, I guess – a way to survive the horror of our schooldays (not that it ever worked, of course – not that it in any way saved me from a single fucking *minute* of those daily rituals of ridicule and humiliation). But then Garth came along and showed me that all of those clichés about going to uni were right: I'd finally 'found my tribe'. I was able to 'live my truth'. I mean, do you understand how powerful that was? How liberating? Not only did I have confidence and social acceptance, but at the same time I was succeeding in my potential as an artist. It was a dream come true, Ben.

It was towards the end of our second semester that Garth's work began to get more political. He was very passionate in his hatred of the current government (austerity and Brexit and all the far-right shit that came along with it). It was Garth who showed me the multifaceted potential of art; how it was not just an aesthetic form, but could in fact be utilised as a political weapon. We had a duty, he said, to fight this cruel and repressive system in any way we could. This was around the time of the general election. I still remember that night. Garth had one of his infamous ARTies at the house, and after everyone had exhibited their work, a group of about twenty of us stayed up, awaiting the results. We were drinking champagne at first, eating vegan caviar. Some people were in fancy dress, came as parodies of their least favourite politicians (although this proved difficult, to be honest, by then most politicians had passed the point of satire to such an extent that it was difficult to portray them as more extreme and ugly than they already were). There was plenty of hope at the time, a belief that no government this incompetent could survive another election. The polls insisted they would, but we didn't believe them. We were so sure of ourselves. I still remember the feeling of horror that descended when the results came in, our belief in basic human decency shattered. And the fact we were partying – the caviar, the wigs, the silliness of what we were doing – it just made it all the more distasteful.

Garth didn't say a word for the rest of the night. He retreated into himself. This would happen more and more regularly over the next two years, these short spells of introspection that preceded a sudden burst of artistic fervour (the analogy Olga used was that of a spring, coiling). He disappeared to bed as soon as it became clear what the result was going to be, which made things a little awkward for me (these were still early days and I didn't really know a lot of the guests). The first time he spoke was the next morning, during one of Sebastian's workshops. We were supposed to be working on a group sculpture task, but Garth said he couldn't concentrate, not with all that was going on. He said it was times like these that artists were tested, we needed to take a stand. We had to leave campus, head out onto the streets. I was worried – wouldn't we get into trouble for leaving class? – but Garth insisted. He'd had a moment of inspiration born out of a need to fight a corrupt system. We needed to follow this up.

And that's exactly what we did. We left the studio – Garth, Olga, and I – headed out onto Peckham Road. It was a warm spring day, but I remember a bleakness to it; the sun seemed to bleach the colour out of everything. Garth was determined, dragged us in and out of endless department stores, homeware stores, used furniture shops. He wouldn't tell us what we were supposed to be doing at first – all we could fathom was that he was seeking out as many mattresses as possible. We managed to get our hands on six or seven altogether, dragged them out into the street. Olga and I sat with them whilst Garth nipped over to a DIY shop, came back with tins of paint. We were to paint the mattresses; one half black to match the tarmac, one grey to match the pavement. The third tin was yellow, with which we painted two stripes across each mattress, a continuation of the double yellow lines that ran down the street. 'No Parking', Garth called it. His first artwork on the homelessness crisis.

The whole thing took about two hours. I remember there were a couple of homeless shelters along Peckham Road (I think that's why he chose it) and a few people came out to watch, curious as to what we were up to. They were perplexed at first, but more encouraging once they realised the purpose of the piece. Garth delivered a short speech about it, explaining how the recent rise in homelessness was only going to increase with those fuckers still in power. This stuff needed to be highlighted. We were letting the most vulnerable people in society slip through the cracks and statements like this made a difference. Before long a parking attendant showed up, followed by a couple of community support officers. One of the officers informed us we could end up being fined for fly-tipping, but Garth just shrugged. 'Fine,' he said, and took out his wallet.

They were about to call the police when Sebastian showed up. He made a big deal about being a tutor at the uni, how this was all just part of his class. He looked terrified, kept apologising profusely, all the while trying to placate Garth. He kept telling us the work was great, distinction-worthy. Which worked, in the end – he sweetened Garth up enough to agree to shift the mattresses back to the studio. It took four black cabs, but we managed to transport them back. They stayed there for the rest of our time on the course, a reminder of the true power of rebellion.

It was around then that my own work began to find its political edge. It wasn't like I was *copying* Garth – more that we were both feeding off the same creative energy. Which is what led to the sculptures, the T-shirts, the photography – the Canon EOS, and Frank – *Doomed Youth* collections 1–7. Which eventually is what led to my decision to join you out there on the Welsh mountains, trying to get photos.

Anyway, I'm getting off topic here. I'll try not take up any more of your time, Ben. I just thought I'd try and explain some of this to you. Because we never talked openly and honestly about stuff like this, did we? Even all those nights we drank together in the Miners, I don't think I ever really spoke to you about Garth, or my art, or my time at uni. I don't think I ever clarified the purpose of Frank – the universal representation of the blood on the hands of our current political class. I've been trying my best to figure out my own purpose here, why it is I find myself hitching a ride on this little recollection of yours (I doubt it's merely to annoy you with these constant interruptions) – and I'm still not sure how much I should be saying, with regard to all of this, but I figure I might as well try to provide a little context for what happened on that trip.

After all, this is as much my story as it is yours, Ben.

# DANCE

# XI

*Thin Lizzy – 'Snooze' – First date with Sam –*
*'Cancel' – Morning glory – Wet T-shirts – Packing*
*up – 'I'll carry the tent' – Descent to the road –*
*A single sheep, watching – Climb through ferns –*
*Bogged ground – Barbed wire – Two runners –*
*A reckless use of the day's energy – Park ranger –*
*Rain – Tree.*

The song 'Dancing in the Moonlight' begins rhythmically – the clicking fingers, the funky bassline, the steady kick of a floor drum, all merging to create that atmosphere; the air of 1970s coolness that Benny's uncle loved so much (often tapping the car dashboard, insisting this was the good stuff . . . *real* music). Then, after two bars, suddenly everything stops and there's a short drum fill and a beat of silence before the vocals come in, and it's at this moment each morning that Benny's hand gropes under the pillow for his phone, the screen flashing an alarm bell symbol with the options '**Snooze**' or '**Cancel**'. Benny tends to hold out on making a selection because he has this superstition where he can only hit '**Snooze**' after the first couple of lines of the song. Sam hated this song, would often complain about it being Benny's ringtone (it being, according to her, a 'real cheesy piece of shit') but Benny still had a soft spot for it. In his opinion, it's one of the few 70s rock songs Uncle Ian listened to that actually stood the test of time. Sometimes, even in his half-asleep state, Benny finds himself drumming his fingers on his chest to the beat.

It was with the help of this song that Benny first got a laugh out of Sam. This was on their first date, at the Odeon. Benny had finally asked Sam out after weeks of messaging each other.

They met at one of the university's many freshers' events, and they were both drunk at the time, which had given Benny enough confidence to ask for her number. Sam had seemed keen at first, was happy to flirt in their messages (at one point sending him an assortment of suggestive emojis that included a pair of lips, a drooling face, and that phallic little aubergine symbol), although, when they met in person, the real-life Sam seemed to have none of this enthusiasm. From the moment he'd picked her up she'd been wholly preoccupied with her phone. Later he'd found out that she was awaiting results from the vet that afternoon regarding a suspicious looking growth on one of her cat's rear paws, but at the time Benny thought maybe Sam just didn't like him. He knew the first date was critical. He had to nip any awkwardness in the bud ASAP. He just had no idea how to do this.

And that's when 'Dancing in the Moonlight' came on. Sam had been in the queue at the time and Benny was making his way across the foyer from the refreshment stand. Whatever had been playing on the Odeon in-house radio before had been indistinguishable amongst the din of peak-time Saturday-night chatter, but it must have been the polar opposite to Thin Lizzy, because it was this change in tone that made the intro to the song so amusing. That, coupled with the fact that their eyes met just at the moment the bassline kicked in. Benny knew he had to make Sam laugh. He'd read an article about it once; how, as a man, showing a sense of humour was an evolutionary obligation, a chance to demonstrate the required level of intelligence and self-awareness. Which was why, right then, he began to sway, thrusting his pelvis and clicking his fingers to the recording like one of the dancers in *West Side Story*. He spilt some popcorn, but it was worth it – Sam *laughed*. That was all it took, this stupid moment between the two of them. A random instance of nonsense humour. By the time he reached her in the queue and offered her a coke, she was still laughing, was practically doubled over. And Benny found himself laughing too.

They still talked about that moment years later. Sam said it had really cheered her up, taken her mind off of Maggie's lump (which turned out to be benign). Plus, when they got out after the film had finished, they found there was a full moon that night, basking the Odeon car park in its silvery light. On the walk to the car Benny had kept singing the song over and over, dancing around Sam as the laughter consumed her entirely. Later, Sam remembered it as an entirely different song, a song also called 'Dancing in the Moonlight', by some band from the early 2000s.* No matter what Benny said he couldn't convince her that it was Thin Lizzy that had been playing that night, a song he remembered from his youth, when his uncle would play mixtapes of 70s hair metal in the car.

This was why he'd downloaded it. Why he'd saved it as his ringtone. It was just some stupid private joke of theirs that nobody else would even understand or care about.

He should change it.

He will do. Soon.


At 06:10 a.m. the song sounds again. Benny waits for the familiar opening lines, then selects '**Cancel**'. He blinks at the screen. It takes him a few seconds to work out why his alarm's set so early. Why he's in such a cramped, huddled, position. Why there's another person beside him, breathing loudly.

He sits up. His neck aches, as do his elbows, hips, buttocks, thighs. He's fully clothed and suddenly remembers waking in the night again, shivering – attempting to don his spare clothing only to find that there wasn't much left, that Stephen was wearing most of it.

Benny has an erection.† It's visible even through the sleeping bag, a definite nub in the dark-blue fabric. He went through a stage in his teenage years where he'd wake up every morning like this, but it had stopped during that first year with Sam, probably due to how much sex they were having. Recently it's started happening again, although he doesn't know why. He masturbates every day without fail now, often multiple times, usually as a way of keeping his mind off The Fog. There are at

---

* I think they were called Toploader.

† Of course.

least two more weeks of camping and walking ahead of them, two more weeks of shivering through the night, two more weeks of waking beside Stephen, cramped and bruised in his sleeping bag – is he really going to have *this* to contend with as well?

Suddenly he remembers last night's storm. The mountains. '**NO CAMPING**'.

They have to pack up. They have to leave as soon as possible. This is a priority.

'Ste?'

'Hmm.'

'Wake up, Ste, it's time.'

'Huh?'

'We've got to go.'

Benny tucks his erection under his belt, puts on his boots. He steps out through the porch, accidentally trampling Stephen's assortment of skeleton T-shirts in the process. At first he feels guilty (his boots are quite muddy and now so are the T-shirts) – but then he realises they're all still damp, so they won't be any good to Stephen now anyway. He'll have to pick up some more in Llangollen. Sensible shirts this time. Thicker, with proper sleeves.

Benny stretches. He checks his phone. (41%. No new messages.) He removes a cigarette from his tobacco tin, lights up. He tips his head back, exhales. It's a dull morning on the mountains. The air is icy, the sky thick with cloud. At first Benny doesn't recognise the park; everything's so still now, the grass, the trees, the fern bushes. The only sounds are baaing and birdsong. The '**NO CAMPING**' sign stands firm.

Stephen appears, crouched in the porch. He's wearing his Adidas track pants again and is now topless, his white chest especially pale next to the patches of sunburn on his arms and neck. He gathers his T-shirts. He doesn't mention the boot prints, just lifts a couple of the shirts and sniffs them.

He folds each in turn and stuffs them into his pack.

—

'You should really bin them.'

'Hmm?'

'The shirts.'

'It's OK.'

'They're still wet. They'll go mouldy in there.'

'It's fine, Ben.'

'Plus, you know, less to carry.'

'I'm not binning them.'

'They're just clothes, Ste. We'll get more tomorrow. Aren't most of them from Oxfam, anyway?'

'I mean these, the T-shirts. I'll bin the socks and shorts and the jumper, if it makes you happy, but I'm keeping these.'

'Why?'

'They mean something to me.'

'They're just a few—'

'They're not just T-shirts, Ben. Don't say they're just T-shirts.'

'So, they're what? *Artworks*? Because you've stuck on one of your pictures they're now, like, *pieces of art*?'

'I'm not getting into this. I'm just not getting rid of them. OK?'

'But they'll go mouldy. Is that what you want? A mouldy pack?'

'The pack's wet too. It's just as likely to go mouldy with or without them.'

*Pause.*

'You can pick up some new stuff when we reach Llangollen.'

'I know.'

'New T-shirts too.'

'Whatever you say.'

*Pause.*

'And you can get a fucking rain mac while you're at it.'

Benny packs up too, then sets about disassembling the tent. Last night he was ready to argue with anyone about their right to set up camp here, but now the idea of confrontation makes his stomach lurch. He just wants to get walking. Speed is a priority.

He drags the flysheet from the tent, shakes out the rainwater. He unhooks the poles, slides them from their fabric tunnels, folds them away. He lights another cigarette and places it between his lips, allowing it to bob there as he works. Stephen joins in, unties the guy ropes from the '**NO CAMPING**' sign, gathers the pegs, still scattered from last night's frenzied erection.* Stephen's still shivering. His limp is worse than yesterday. His nose is completely blocked now, each breath ending with a slight rattle. At one point he leans forward, presses one nostril closed and *hoik*s through the other. Not even into a tissue any more, just *hoik*s straight onto the ground. A slug of mucus sits there glistening in the grass.

Benny tells Stephen to bag up the rubbish. The packets from the noodles have blown across the grass and are caught in the fence, along with a few of their wet wipes. Also, there's Stephen's socks and jeans and his jumper, which he's abandoned over by the signpost. They must be sure to adhere to the Countryside Code at all times. This means they can't leave any trace of their visit.

Once the tent's disassembled Benny bundles the sheets and pegs and poles, then presses them into the tent bag. This seems harder each day, as if the tent is growing (or the bag shrinking). He has to clutch the sides in his fists, force the contents down with his knee, before he can zip the thing shut. He removes the cord, begins to bind the tent bag to the bottom of his pack when Stephen tells him to wait, stop, just hang on a sec. Benny stops, looks up. Stephen says not to bother. He'll carry it today.

Benny immediately drops the tent. It's a reflex – possibly shock, although maybe also born out of some deep subconscious relief (he has been released from the burden of the tent and so his body refuses to carry it a moment longer). Stephen just stands there, holding his weight on his right leg. His hair has curled so much it's formed two greasy horns that sprout from under the white band of his sun visor. He's donned one of his wet T-shirts (the one in which the skeleton's wearing a strap-on) and there's a muddied smear across its grinning skull, a bootprint from Benny's careless trampling. He's left the fleece unzipped, as if to display the art beneath.

---

* Enough with that word already, Ben.

His hands are outstretched and quivering. He repeats himself, says he'll carry the tent.

Benny shakes his head, says no, it's fine, honestly – he's carried it this far, he doesn't mind a little further – but Stephen insists.

'I'll. Carry. The. Tent.'

Benny shrugs. He tosses over the tent bag. Stephen pitches forwards to catch it and in the process puts too much weight on his bad ankle and stumbles. He lands on his knees, breathes through the pain for a moment, then sets about attaching the tent to his pack. There are no specific straps on Stephen's pack to hold it in place, so he has to improvise, bind it to the bottom of the handles. It takes a few attempts but eventually he manages to fix it in a way that the whole thing doesn't unfurl when he rises to his feet.

He hoists them – both pack and tent bag – onto his back. A second later his face drains of what little colour it had. He stands there breathing for a minute. Just breathing: in and out. In and out.

Benny asks if he's sure he's OK and Stephen insists that yes, he's fine. He's all set.

'Let's go.'

They exit the park and descend the hillside towards a road. Beside the road there's a layby and a single red car. Benny wonders aloud who it belongs to. Stephen huffs, points out that last night they thought they were stuck out here, miles from civilisation, when in fact they probably could have requested an Uber. There's a single sheep, perched a little up the hill on the other side. It glares down at them as they cross the road and continue to the next signpost.

The sign points up, a steep incline to the top of the next peak. One side of the fence is overgrown with long grass and fern bushes. The other side is pretty much clear. The arrow on the sign appears to be directing them up the overgrown side. Stephen asks which path they should take, and Benny says to trust the sign. It's part of the Countryside Code, to follow the signs. Plus, he'd hate to get to the top and find they've made a mistake, have to trek all the way down again.

They climb. Benny watches his legs tear through the grass. The dew is icy – sharp at first, then soothing on his sunburnt shins. It's a steep incline, especially harsh on his thighs, this being their first ascent of the day. Stephen asks if this was part of the schedule, to climb a mountain before breakfast. Benny tells him he should expect more of the same. The majority of the map today is mountainous, although they already did a lot of the hard work last night, ascending into the Clwydian Range. Now they just have to cross the peaks, enjoy the views (plenty of landscape shots up for grabs).

Stephen doesn't reply. He makes no sound at all except for when he puts too much strain on his left ankle and stifles a squeal. Benny asks if he's sure he can cope with the weight of the tent and Stephen replies yes, he's fine.

The ferns thicken the higher they get. Soon they find themselves waist-deep in leaves. Benny forgot to search for a bin back in the park, and so there are now two plastic rubbish bags tied to his pack. Every few seconds one of them catches on the ferns and he has to stop and untangle himself. Still, he's grateful not to be carrying the tent.

The further up they get, the more obvious it becomes that the sign was wrong. The other side of the fence now has a clear cobbled pathway with steps, whereas their side gets more overgrown by the second. Benny doesn't mention it. Hopefully the paths will merge further up. Besides, Stephen's too busy with the tent to notice. He's wincing now, straining at the weight on his shoulders. He keeps falling behind and Benny has to stop every few minutes to let him catch up.

'This tent, man.'

'Heavy, huh?'

'Fuck *me*.'

'You want me to take it?'

'No. I'm not saying that. It's just . . . I don't know. I just can't figure out how the hell you've been carrying this thing.'

'It's not so bad. You get used to it.'

'It's like having a person on your back, man. A *human fucking person.*'

A little further up Benny spots a gap in the fence. It's only small, and there are still a couple of strips of barbed wire, but it'll have to do. They need to stick to the path – and not just for the sake of the Countryside Code. It's steep here. If one of them slipped they could end up seriously injured.

Benny tells Stephen they have to stop, climb through the fence to the other side. Stephen doesn't argue, appears happy for this excuse to unburden himself from the tent. Benny holds the barbed wire apart whilst Stephen stoops through. Then Benny passes Stephen the packs, before wriggling through himself. His boots are wet and as he tries to find his footing he slips on one of the steps and his left leg catches on the wire. He cries out. There's a tear in his zip-off trousers.

He sits and examines his shin. The skin is cut – not deep, but enough to bleed. Stephen says maybe they should stop and get the first-aid kit out, but Benny says no, he's fine. He puts his pack on again. Blood trickles down his leg, pools at the lip of his fresh, white, walking sock. A few phrases flash through his mind – wound, infection, gangrene, tetanus shot – but he keeps telling himself it's nothing. Just another ailment.

Stephen asks if he's sure he doesn't want a plaster, he's more than happy to stop for a bit, but Benny says no. It's fine. It'll scab. Just keep walking.

Soon they're saddled up, ascending again. It's an easier climb now. They have proper steps and no foliage to contend with and there's less of a psychological burden now that Benny knows for sure they're on the right path. He's glad not to have the tent, but there's still plenty of other aches and pains to occupy him, e.g. the stiffness of the muscles in his legs, or the chafing of the shoulder straps against his sunburnt neck, or the inflamed skin on his shins from the nettles and the brambles and the rubbing of his boots. There are fully formed blisters on his toes now and the balls of his feet seethe with every step. The cut on his leg soon stops bleeding, although there's a pulsing there, as well as a stickiness (which, whilst not particularly painful, is certainly unpleasant). Plus, the headache's getting worse. That'll be withdrawal symptoms – he's had this before, when he's cut down on his intake of cigarettes or coffee (Sam was always on at him to cut down on cigarettes and coffee). Still, he's trying his best not to fixate on any of it. *Ailments*, he thinks. *Just ailments*.

Stephen is still limping, still puffing his breath. Now they're ascending side-by-side, Benny notices Stephen's arms are trembling too, his fists gripping the straps of his pack as if to steady himself. Maybe Benny should suggest a break. Maybe they should boil up some noodles or something. Maybe it's finally time to offer the ibuprofen. It's been a tough half-hour since they left the park and Stephen's hardly complained at all – surely that deserves some kind of reward.

They soon arrive at a gate that marks the top of the hill. Benny suggests they stop for water. Before he's even finished speaking, Stephen's slid off his pack. It hits the ground with a crunch and Benny has to catch it with his foot to keep it from toppling back down the hill. They sit against the gate and sip from their flasks. Stephen takes a *hiccchhht* from his inhaler. The path ahead is only more mountainous terrain, Benny knows this from the guidebook. From here they can't make out much of it, just a dark bank of land steadily rising. The valleys below seem so distant it's almost like they belong to another world. There's a patch of trees to the left of the path, surprisingly leafless for the time of year; limbs twisted and black against the sky.

'Can I . . .' *Pant.* '. . . have . . .' *Pant.* '. . . some water . . .' *Pant.* '. . . please . . .' *Pant.* '. . . man?'

Benny fills their flasks from the 2-litre bottles. He tells Stephen he's got some ibuprofen in his pack, if he wants some, but Stephen says he doesn't know if he should. He isn't meant to take certain painkillers because the side effects can be bad for his chest. Benny nods. He can feel his headache swelling. It doesn't seem right now, popping pills in front of Stephen, so he tries not to think about it. He just keeps sipping his water.

After a few minutes a pair of runners approach from the opposite direction. Benny stands, holds the gate open, steps aside to let them pass. The runners are a middle-aged man and woman – water bottles, iPods, spandex. The woman has her hair in a ponytail. The man's is brushed forwards into an attempt at a fringe, although there's not much to work with (his hairline's even worse than Benny's). The runners appear unsure at first, when they notice Benny and Stephen perched there at the gate, but as they pass the woman gives a slight nod of thanks, and so Benny nods back.

The couple descend the mountain path. The red car is still parked there in the lay-by. Could they have driven here, just to go running? It seems so contradictory and plain *wrong*. What makes people go running anyway?* Benny never understood Sam's obsession with it. She claimed she found it empowering, although never actually explained what she meant by that. She loved her early morning runs because they 'rejuvenated' her, although she was always exhausted afterwards (any chance of morning sex was out the window once she started with those runs). If anything, it seemed to Benny that running was rather a reckless use of the day's energy.†

There's a truck heading up the road. Benny points it out to Stephen and the two of them watch it park up at the bypass and a quintessential park ranger emerges – brown anorak, aviators, Stetson hat. He shuts the car door and heads up the hill, towards the park where they were camped last night.

'I can't believe it.'
   'I told you, Ste.'

---

* Probably the same thing that makes people want to walk across a country: stupidity.
† Whereas crossing Wales by foot is what . . . a *good* use of energy?

'A park ranger. A real-life fucking *park ranger*.'

'It was probably those runners.'

'What do you mean?'

'Probably saw the tent when they parked up earlier, phoned the council.'

'Arseholes.'

'Yeah.' *Pause.* 'Well, whatever. It's done now.' *Pause.* 'Plus, you know, it *is* part of the code, to obey the signs. The rangers are only there to make sure people obey the rules.'

The runners get in their car and drive off. The park ranger descends again, does the same. The single sheep still watches, although it's now the other side of the road. (Can it really be the same one? Did it really cross and climb the adjacent hillside, just so it could keep on glaring at them?)

It's starting to rain. Only spitting, but the sky has darkened above them. Benny suggests sheltering under the trees. They could cook some breakfast.

Stephen nods. He says that's the best idea he's heard all day.

# XII

*Rain on leaves – Rice – Tin of beans – Curled edges – Five pages left – Mountainous terrain – Today's mantra – The unbearable weight of the tent – Fully grown men – Bowel movement – Passing school class – Walking sticks – 'It's just too heavy . . .'*

They sit beneath the trees. Benny gets out the gas heater and what's left of their water and sets about boiling them up some breakfast. He rolls another cigarette, lights the tip on the heater's blue flame, smokes as he cooks. Stephen lies back against the tree trunk. He stares out over at the valleys. From here they can just make out the fields below, fading into the distance.

The rain's getting heavier. It rattles on the leaves above. Occasionally it drips onto Benny's head or forearms, or plops into the water bubbling in the mess tin. Breakfast is rice. They have plenty of noodles but only a couple of packs of rice and so they have to ration it for when they've reached the point they can no longer stomach noodles, and this is one of those times. Stephen asks if when they stop at Benny's uncle's they can get something else, something more flavoursome, maybe some tins of beans or something, but then Benny reminds him of how much tins weigh, compared to packets of rice and noodles. Plus, instant rice and noodles were all he remembers having those nights he'd go camping with his dad and Uncle Ian.

The rice is chicken flavoured, that same not-quite-chicken-taste as the noodles. The only real distinction is the texture, but it makes all the difference.

Once they've finished Benny stows what's left of the water, wipes out the mess tin and brews some coffee (just half a cup each to save on supplies). He stashes the rubbish in one of the plastic bags, then reties it to his pack. He's only got enough tobacco to roll two more cigarettes, and he does so now, stowing them away in his tobacco tin. He considers smoking again but decides he's best off saving his final cigarettes for later in the day. The act of rolling is enough to ease his cravings for now.

Stephen sips at his coffee, winces. He says he hates instant coffee – he'd kill for an oat milk latte right now.

Benny takes out the guidebook. He does his best to uncurl the pages, bending them back as far as he can without damaging the spine. He skips through to today's map.

'How far today, then?'

'Far.'

'Great.' *Pause.* '*How* far?'

'Hang on, I'll show you . . .' *Pause.* 'See here? We're here . . .'

'OK.'

'So today we just have to cross this page . . .'

'Right.'

'And then this page . . .'

'OK.'

'And this one, and this one . . .'

'Erm . . .'

'. . . right down to this bottom corner. Llandegla.'

'So, five pages?'

'Five pages.'

'And how many pages did we cross off that first day?'

'Erm, let's see.' *Pause.* 'About . . . two?'

'And yesterday?'

'Erm . . . hang on . . .' *Pause.* 'About the same. Well, *just over* two.'

'And what are all those . . . erm . . . those lines.'

'Lines?'

'The squiggly brown lines.'

'That's the gradient.'

'The . . .?'

'The terrain. The mountains. The lines mean *mountainous terrain.*'

'Right.' *Pause.* 'So, today we have to walk the same distance we've walked the last two days combined, across mountainous terrain?'

'Pretty much.'

'Great.'

*Pause.*

'But that's not necessarily a negative, Ste. Being in the mountains, I mean.'

'It's not?'

'Well . . . just look at it. Look at the view.'

*Pause.*

'And?'

'And so, there'll be plenty of views like this. It's an area of outstanding natural beauty. These views, they'll like *spur us on.*'

'It's the same view as yesterday, Ben.'

'But isn't it beautiful?'

'I guess . . .'

'Isn't this the whole reason you're here? For the views? Just look at that landscape.' *Pause.* 'Anyway, there's nowhere else to really camp before Llandegla. That's our best bet. Plus, if we make it there, we get an easy day's walking on Monday. Reach Llangollen just after lunch. Get to my uncle's in time for an afternoon Guinness.'

'Right.'

'And in Llandegla they have, like, proper camping places. I mean like, with facilities.'

'Facilities?'

'Showers. Toilets.'

'A shower would be nice.'

'Exactly.'

'And, you know . . . a shit.'

'Well, just keep thinking of that, Ste. A shower and a shit. That can be today's mantra. *A shower and a shit.* That can get us through.' *Pause.* 'Plus, mountainous terrain's not so bad. I mean, look at us this morning. We climb mountains *before breakfast*, Ste. We got this.'

*Pause.*

'It's just the tent, man.'

'Hmm?'

'Think how much better this'd be if we didn't have *this* fucking thing to lug round.'

'True.'

'Did they not have any lighter ones?'

'Lighter what?'

'Tents.'

'Where?'

'In the camping shop.'

'Yes.'

'Yes?'

'Yes, they had lighter tents in the camping shop.'

'They did?'

'Of course they did.'

'So . . . I mean . . . like, why the fuck have we got *this* thing then?'

'This isn't from the camping shop.'

'Oh?'

'It's my dad's tent.'

'Right.'

*Pause.*

'You think I should have bought a new one?'

'Well, maybe. I mean this thing . . . it's *heavy*, you know?'

'I know, Ste. Believe me, I know.'

'Well then . . .'

*Pause.*

'You could have come too, you know.'

'Hmm?'

'To the camping shop. You could have come along. I did invite you.'

'I know.'

'You could have weighed in on the whole tent situation.'

'It's just that day—'

'You were having a breakthrough.'

'Yeah.'

'Right.'

'And I have to be loyal to that. When breakthroughs come, I have to ride them out, you know?'

'Not really.'

'Well, I do.'

'Right.'

'But maybe I could have come . . .'

'It doesn't matter.'

'I could have got some proper shoes.'

'You could have got a lot of things.'

'It's just that stuff . . . it's *expensive*, man.'

'You could have got a rain mac. They're not expensive.'

'I had a mac. I told you, I left it in your mum's car.'

'You could have got a proper backpack. And a tent of your own, if you'd really wanted one.'

'Yeah, right. I can't *afford* all that stuff, Ben, I told you.'

'But I chose to stick with this tent. I made that call. And I know it weighs more, but I figured if my dad and Ian were strong enough to carry this, so are we.'

'Yeah, but weren't they, like . . .'

'What?'

'Well, they were, like, *fully grown men*, Ben.'

'So are we.'

'Yeah, OK . . . but they were *blokes*. I mean, your dad was a big guy. They were proper *men*, man.'

'They did plenty of camping when they were our age.'

'Right, but—'

'You know what my dad had achieved by the time he was our age, Ste? He had a wife. He had a child. He had a mortgage, a job as a teacher. A whole history. And he'd done this walk. The whole thing. And plenty of others like it.'

'OK.'

'And he'd carried this tent across them all.'

'Right.'

'And if he could, there's no reason we can't.'

Benny fetches the 'shit-kit', heads deeper into the patch of trees to perform his morning bowel movement. He chooses a spot beside the fence, where the soil is damp and easy to dig. It's only as he's squatting there that he notices a group of children over on the path by the gate. There's a middle-aged woman, most likely a teacher, standing at the front talking to them.

Benny's not sure if he's quite finished, but he decides he's best aborting partway through, rather than risk being seen. He wipes and quickly buries what he's managed to squeeze out. Luckily the teacher is still holding her class's attention, although Benny can't hear what she's saying from this distance. There are twelve children in total – Benny counts nine boys and three girls. The teacher wears a pink beanie and carries a long, dark, wooden stick with a curved handle, like a shepherd's crook. She uses it to point in their desired direction before they proceed onward, down the mountain path.

Stephen's been productive in Benny's absence; has packed away the gas stove, bagged the rubbish, tied it beside the other two bags on the back of Benny's pack. Benny says they're best moving on. Stephen asks if they're going to brush their teeth, but Benny tells him they don't have time. He gives Stephen some gum to chew instead.

The rain has died down now. A couple more walkers pass by, over on the path – a family consisting of a mum, dad, two boys and two enormous huskies. They also have hiking sticks and Stephen asks why he and Benny don't have some of those and Benny thinks back to the teacher and her wooden stick and suggests maybe they could fashion a couple of their own from the fallen branches that surround them in the grass. Benny spots a decent-sized one, sprouting near the foot of one of the trees. He briefly considers the hatchet but in the end it's easier to just pry and kick at it until the branch snaps off. He hands it to Stephen, then selects another amongst the debris in the grass. Shorter, thinner, a bit more gnarled than the first, but still a respectable stick.

Benny dons his pack. Stephen just stands there, stick in hand, staring down at the tent. Benny asks if he's OK. He nods.

Benny says they need to get moving. Stephen looks him in the eye.

—

'Man, I'm sorry . . . I don't think . . .' *Pause.* 'It's just so *heavy*, you know?'

'Don't worry.'

'I'm sorry. I really wanted to. Honestly.'

'I know.'

'It's just too heavy . . .'

'I know.' *Pause.* 'Honestly, it's fine, Ste.' *Pause.* 'I got it.'

Benny unties the tent from Stephen's pack, binds it to his own. He raises the pack-and-tent onto his shoulders, grimacing at the almighty weight of the thing. He fastens the buckle across his chest.

Stephen waits over by the tree trunk, picking at the grass. He murmurs a couple more apologies, but Benny tells him it's OK. He doesn't mind carrying it. It's fine.

The two of them set off again, Benny a little more stooped than before. He allows his stick to take the weight as he walks.

It helps, a little.

# XIII

*Jubilee Tower – Old photos – Uncle Ian's hair –*
*A happier go-to memory – Winding path –*
*'Catastrophic digestional consequences' –*
*Unintentional humming – A dot on the horizon –*
*Water break – Ibuprofen – Incline – Sun –*
*Vanishing tower – Kafka's castle – 'Too*
*mountainous terrain' – Another not-so-proper*
*rest stop – Passers-by – Thoughts of Sam.*

They continue across the mountaintops for the rest of the morning. Benny keeps an eye out on the horizon for any sign of Jubilee Tower. The tower is a 'place of significance' according to the guidebook, which means it's represented as a yellow star, slightly larger than the other icons on the map. Apparently this is one of the only landmarks of any interest on the northern leg, a ruined monument from the 1800s. All that remains is the base, but it's atop one of the highest peaks on the mountain range, and the views are supposedly some of the best of the whole trail.

Jubilee Tower was significant to Benny's dad too, enough for him to mention it back when they were first planning the trip. This was not long after the diagnosis, an evening Benny had discovered his father up in his study, sorting through a stack of old photographs. Most were from before Benny was born, his father's early walks. A lot of the pictures were of scenery – fields, valleys, mountains – there was just the odd shot of his dad or uncle, both much slimmer, with moustaches and thick black hair. Benny found himself fixated by that: the sight of his uncle with hair. He calculated Ian to be in his early twenties when those photos were taken and he couldn't help but wonder when his uncle's hair had begun to fall out.

It was then Benny's dad first cited Offa's Dyke as his all-time favourite trail. He said there was something amazing about the dyke, the sense of achievement that came from crossing an entire country. He picked out a few photos to show Benny – a castle, an aqueduct, the ruins of an abbey near Abergavenny – all of which Benny was sure to make a mental note to seek out later in the guidebook. There was only one highlight on the northern leg, his dad said, and that was Jubilee Tower. He had a few photos of it; the mossy ruins of the base, the views of the hillsides from the top.

Benny wishes he could remember more of that conversation. It's certainly a happier go-to memory than what was to follow over the next few months.

The trail descends here, winds to the east. Patches of heather spread and thicken, bruising the hillside a dark purple. Ahead there are entire peaks covered in it, with white lines – stone walls and other trails – scoured chaotically across. The path here is grit-ground, a stony strip of pure mountain where the grass and heather have worn away, the cumulative scuff of decades of ramblers' boots. The clouds have thinned now and the sun breaks through and Benny stops for a moment to find his sunglasses. He slips off his raincoat and unzips the bottoms from his trousers. Stephen takes off the fleece and ties it around his waist.

The variations in the terrain are more gradual along the mountain path. Hills rise and fall almost imperceptibly, although Benny can still feel the effects – the aching in his thighs on the inclines, the stabbing in his ankles on the de-. Even without the tent, Stephen is shaking, sweating. He says maybe it's the rice. Maybe his stomach has become so used to a strict coffee-noodle diet that even such a slight deviation can cause catastrophic digestional consequences.

Benny suffers the extra weight of the tent. It's as if the hour without it this morning has tricked his body into a false sense of security. He tries unbuckling and rebuckling the chest clip. He tries to steady the rhythm of his walking. This was something his uncle used to suggest on their trips, that they should maintain a steady march, that this would somehow distance their minds from the physical act, force their bodies into autopilot. Sometimes his uncle would even sing – usually a medley of the 70s rock songs he'd played on the drive over.

There's already a song playing in Benny's head, although he can't quite grasp what it is. It's only when he catches himself drumming his thumbs against his chest that he realises it's Thin Lizzy again. That same song has been repeating in his internal jukebox for hours. It's just the intro and the first two lines, on a loop, occasionally breaking into the chorus. He tries to think of something else – *anything* else – but it's hopeless. No matter what other song he thinks of, it soon morphs into 'Dancing in the Moonlight'.

'What's that?'
  'What?'
  'That song.'
  'What song?'
  'You were humming.'
  'What? No, I wasn't.'
  'You were, man. I swear.'
  'I wasn't humming.'
  'I could swear I heard humming.'
  'I wasn't humming, Ste. OK? There was no humming.'*

It's another hour or so before Benny spots the Jubilee Tower up on one of the peaks ahead. To them it's a dot, about the same size as the stones they picked up back at Prestatyn. According to the guidebook the trail passes right by it and so Benny suggests they make this their next proper rest stop. Stephen agrees, although he suggests maybe now would be a good time for a not-so-proper rest stop.

They de-pack, take a five-minute water break. Stephen takes

---

* Liar!

a few *hiccchhht*s from his inhaler. Benny uses this opportunity to retrieve the first-aid kit. The cut on his leg is throbbing and he wants to apply some antiseptic and a plaster. Whilst he's at it, he swallows down a couple of ibuprofen and Stephen notices, asks if he could have some too. Benny asks if that's wise – didn't he say it might make his breathing worse? Stephen shrugs. By now it's a risk he's willing to take.

Benny's been taking ibuprofen more and more over the past couple of years; an attempt to soothe his near-constant headache. He tries not to think about what Sam used to say about this; how the headache could actually be a *result* of the ibuprofen, a sort of withdrawal symptom. He briefly remembers his father's various pills during chemo. His dad had this special plastic tray for them, foil windows he'd open each morning, like an advent calendar, and Benny still remembers the weak smile he gave each time one of the care assistants would comment on the amount of pills he took, make that same old joke about swallowing so many he'd rattle.

Benny gets out the guidebook, tries to locate their current position on the map. It's hard to tell exactly where they are, he can only estimate between yesterday's campsite and the star that represents Jubilee Tower. Once they've reached the tower, they'll have done two-and-a-half miles. Nearly a quarter of the day's walk.

'Can you believe that? A quarter of the mountain range, *over*.'

'How far is it though? To the tower, I mean. It looks pretty . . . *distant* . . .'

'Not far now, I'm sure.'

'I don't know. Seems pretty far to me, man.'

'We'll be there in no time, Ste. Trust me.'

'Right.'

*Hiccchhht.*

'Don't you want to take some photos? You know, the valleys? Some landscape shots?'

'What's the point?'

'Well, you know . . . the *beauty*?'

'It's the same as yesterday.'

'Yeah, but isn't taking the same photo over and over again your *thing*. Isn't that how you make your art?'

'No.'

'Oh.'

*Pause.*

'That only works if I'm chasing something. If I'm riding a wave. If I'm feeling it. And this view . . . I'm just not feeling it.'

The path inclines for another half a mile, then continues to curve eastward, alongside a wire fence that snakes up through the mountains. Stephen keeps asking to stop: he has a stone in his shoe, he has to redo his laces, he has to refill his flask from one of the 2-litre water bottles. At first Benny thought maybe it was Stephen's sprained ankle* that was giving him trouble, although that doesn't account for the sweating and shaking. Benny tells him they can't break for long, not until they reach the tower. They can't let the schedule slip.

The clouds have dispersed now, the sun is glaring. They keep an eye on Jubilee Tower. As the path bends, the position of the tower changes. Sometimes it's on their left, sometimes their right. Stephen says maybe there are several towers. Or maybe they're *imagining* it, maybe they've finally cracked.

Stephen says maybe it's like Kafka's castle – no matter how much they walk the tower will always appear the same size, the same unreachable distance.

'You're absolutely sure the path leads past this thing?'

'It's right there on the map, Ste. I showed you.'

'I know. It's just that it still seems so far off.'

'It's because of the terrain.'

'The terrain?'

'The mountainous terrain.'

'You said the terrain was good, man. You said it would *spur us on.*'

---

* So, you finally admit it then? It *was* sprained?

'It's just *too* mountainous. If we were on flat land it'd be different. If this was all flat, we'd be making good progress. But all this up and down . . . everything takes so much longer.'

Soon Benny agrees to de-pack again (another not-so-proper rest stop). They sit with their backs against a wire fence, stare out over the valleys. Benny smokes half of one of his two remaining cigarettes, then stubs it out and stows the rest for later. There are flocks of sheep in the distance. Benny's mind flits back to this morning, to the sheep that was staring at them, and once this thought's taken root it's hard not to imagine these sheep are doing the same. It's impossible to tell – the flocks are mere dots, too far away to gauge where they're looking – but Benny can't shake the feeling he's being watched.

Two girls approach from the path behind. Both look like they're in their mid-twenties. One is an attractive brunette in good shape, the other an incredibly muscular blonde with tattoos. Benny says hello as they pass. The blonde scowls but the brunette gives Benny a half-smile. He combs at his fringe with his fingers. He finds himself wishing they'd passed by when he was still smoking; there's something about holding a cigarette that gives him more confidence around girls.

It's only as they're walking away that he realises that, from behind, the brunette is the double of Sam. She's even got the grey leggings, just like Sam used to wear to go running. Benny gets a sudden image of Sam from behind. In his imagination, Sam is on her hands and knees, slowly raising herself towards him.* This is one of Benny's go-to fantasies when he masturbates and, once this image has established itself, he knows it'll be impossible to stop thinking about it.†

---

* Urgh.

† I get that you're horny, Ben, but is there any need for these repeated, hyper-sexualised imaginings of Sam? Was she not also a three-dimensional human being? Did you not have any connection with her other than via your dick?

If you ask me, this way of thinking is *extremely* problematic. I mean, you've got to admit, the female representation as a whole thus far is pretty

The two girls continue along the trail, disappearing over the next mound.

'You OK, Ben?'
   'Hmm?'
'You know her or something?'
   'Um . . . er . . . no.'
'You sure?'
   'Yeah.'
*Pause.*
'You seem lost in thought, man.'
   'No. I'm fine.'
'Right.'
*Pause.*
'How about you?'
   'Hmm?'
'Are you OK? That ibuprofen kicked in yet?'
   'I don't know, really. I'm OK though.'
'You sure?'
   'I'm coping, man. I'm coping. Let's just leave it at that.'

---

piss poor. The only women you've mentioned up to now have fit perfectly into the male-psyche, archetypal gender roles – i.e. The Mother (your mum), The Maiden (Christine), The Whore (Sam). Are you not in the least bit worried about this? The fact that you're being so overtly misogynist here?
   Do these things ever even cross your mind?

# XIV

*The tower vanishes – Steep incline – Walking vs wanking – Sick joke – A little further – Two boys – Day-trippers – 'Jubilee Mound' – Noodles – Make-shift cigarettes – Atop the tower – Caught leering – Altercation – History class – Pursued by dogs.*

It's nearly midday when Jubilee Tower disappears completely. Benny keeps telling himself it's just over the next hill, that it will appear any minute. By now they've been crossing the mountains for three hours. Stephen asks what will happen if they don't make it off the mountainous terrain today. Benny says it will be like last night, trying to find somewhere to set up camp. That there probably isn't anywhere sheltered and safe from the wind. That this is, after all, a fucking *mountain range*.

The path gets steeper. There are rocks for footholds and, further up, stone steps carpeted in grass. It's becoming harder and harder for Benny to ignore Stephen's panting, harder and harder for it not to conjure up images of Sam in *that* position, raising herself for him. There's something in the sound and rhythm of it – the sharp gasps of pain-that-could-be-pleasure.* It's been three days now since Benny last masturbated. His regular output is three or four times a day and he longs for it, here on the mountains. He misses how easy it is, how mindless, how focused on the simple task of pleasure. Walking is the opposite of masturbation. Walking is a hard, drawn-out slog. Walking is all about the long-term goal, with nothing in the way of short-term satisfaction.†

---

* Erm . . . ?

† If you'd have just told me how horny you were, I'd gladly have given you some alone time in the tent, Ben.

Soon they have to stop and rest again, catch their breath. The ibuprofen has eased the aches in their muscles, but they're still exhausted. Stephen asks if this is really the path, if the national trails actually expect people to walk this, or could this in fact be some sort of elaborate joke on the part of the guidebook publisher? Benny doesn't say anything. He just sips from his flask, checks his phone for signal and smokes the rest of his penultimate cigarette. Behind them lies the mountain range they've crossed this morning, a series of heather-patched bumps, like the spine of some gigantic creature. Beyond that, the towns and fields, the rivers and forests. Beyond that, the sea.

After another short break, they* decide to keep climbing. The steps zigzag from side to side here, perhaps to lessen the steepness of the hill. Benny concentrates on his footing, only occasionally gazing up at the ridge ahead. The stick doesn't help much. He's keeping up the pretence, spearing it into the grass to try to support his weight, but his hands are so sweaty it keeps slipping.

Stephen appears to have given up on his own stick. He drags it along behind him. A couple of times he makes as if to lift it, flails it about as he tries to get some purchase, then allows it to fall and drag again. It seems much too big for him now. It reminds Benny of a children's cartoon his sister used to watch, about a young King Arthur lifting the sword from the stone. That's the image Benny keeps getting: a child trying to lift a grown man's sword.

'I can't take this, man. I can't.'

'You said you were doing OK.'

'I was lying. It's my ankle, it's killing me.'

'We'll be there soon.'

'Plus, my stomach's not great. I still don't think the rice is sitting right . . .'

'Not much further now.'

'You keep saying that.'

---

* (You.)

'We'll be there any minute.'

'That too.'

'But it's true. Just a little further . . .'

'It's always just a little further, just a little further. And then there's always further to go.'

The sun is high now, there's not a cloud in the sky. Benny squints against the brightness. It's giving him a headache, but he doesn't want to have to stop and search for his sunglasses again. He can feel the steady glare on his forehead, the heat on his already-sunburnt skin.

Something appears on the crest above. Benny shades his eyes with his hand, tries to make it out, thinking maybe it's Jubilee Tower. Once his eyes adjust, he can see it's actually a bench. There are two young boys sitting there. Or two of the same boy (he could be seeing double). A little further up he realises one of the boys is older than the other, they're just dressed the same – both in full Manchester United kits and white trainers. They glare down at Benny. One of them points, turns, whispers something to the other.

Then suddenly there it is, just beyond the bench. The landmark they've been aiming for the past few hours: the ruined base of Jubilee Tower. All that remains is a crumbling stone building, about the size of a bungalow, overgrown with grass and patches of moss. Still, Benny can't keep from grinning. He laughs, a laugh that quickly develops into a cough. Then, once he's finished coughing, he finds himself laughing again. The boys are laughing too, scowling down at him – matching giggles and snarls of derision – but Benny just laughs even more, he can't help it. His ankles ache and his legs are stiff and his feet sting and his shoulders are raw from the straps of the pack, but overall he feels magnificent, alive. This country. The air. The path behind that led them up to this highest of mountaintops. The world, laid out below them, so tiny and insignificant. This feeling is what it's all about. This feeling is why they're here. *This feeling*.

—

'Ste, look! Ste, we're here!'

'Hmm?'

'Look Ste, there it is!'

'Hang on, man. I—'

'We're here, we're actually here!'

*Pause.*

'That's *it*?'

The path leads straight across a patch of grass to the northern face of the tower. There's an entrance at either side, a staircase at each corner where the walls meet, leading up to a small viewing platform. There are people scattered about. Some are up top, taking advantage of the extra few feet of elevation. Others are on the tiered rock walls or on the surrounding grass, basking in the sun. Benny recognises a few: the class of schoolchildren; the muscular blonde and Sam-like brunette, making their way up the steps; the family with the huskies, sitting on a wall on the western side.

These people are day-trippers. It's their cleanliness that gives them away; a lack of stubble on the men, an amount of competently applied make-up on the women. Plus, the dogs, the children, the picnic hampers, the small backpacks. There's no way any of them are walking the dyke, not in its entirety. The biggest giveaway is that they're all smiling. It's unnerving, this new buzz of chatter and laughter. It seems louder than it should do, up here. Still, at least there's a slight breeze, a little respite from the baking heat.

Benny leads Stephen across to the eastern wall, away from any dogs or children. A few of the day-trippers are staring at them. One of the huskies barks. Benny ignores it, sits with his back against the cool stone.

Stephen slips off his pack and collapses on the grass beside him.

'I thought you said it was a tower.'

'It *was* a tower. The tower part blew down. Now there's just the base.'

'Wow.' *Pause.* 'Great.' *Pause.* 'It's still called "Jubilee *Tower*" though . . .?'

'Well, they're not exactly going to change its name, Ste.'

'I just think it's misleading, calling it a tower. That's all.'

'Well, what would *you* call it?'

'I don't know, man. A mound. "Jubilee Fucking *Mound*".'

'Well, write to the council if you want. We're here, that's the important thing. We've made it.'

'Right.'

*Pause.*

'Shall we eat now?'

They cook up a couple of noodle packets. They're nearly out of water again – they only have what remains in their flasks – so this is once more a priority. Stephen says it'd be nice to be able to wash, too, at some point – they stink. Benny sniffs his armpit. It's hard to assess just how bad the smell is, but he knows Stephen's probably right. Neither of them has had a proper wash for two days, just wet wipes and deodorant. Plus, they smoked weed last night, which they probably still reek of. Their shirts are grass-stained, yellowed with sweat, their shoes and trousers caked in flaking soil. Stephen's skin is red and blotchy in patches, his nose beginning to peel. Benny assesses his own face with his fingertips. There's a spot swelling on his forehead and his chin is roughly coated with stubble. His sunburn hasn't started peeling yet, but it's only a matter of time.

Another school class approaches. It's a different class from before, this one led by a short, stocky teacher – bald with a 1930s RAF-style moustache. The class are all girls, each wearing matching navy-blue skirts and raincoats, clutching clipboards and pens. They look like they're in their early teens. Their faces convey a mixture of a) resentment at being there, b) shock there are *other* walkers there, and c) disdain towards these other walkers, including Benny and Stephen, for *choosing* to be there. Stephen *hoik*s again, right in front of the class. A slug of mucus wobbles in the grass. One of the girls laughs. Others stare at it with looks of abject horror.

The teacher leads them up the steps to the viewing platform.

—

'You OK, Ste?'

'Yeah. It's just not sitting right today.'

*Hiccchhht.*

'Is there a right way for mucus to sit?'

'Well, there's certainly a wrong way.' *Hoik.* 'What's with all the *kids*, man?'

'I don't know. Some sort of school trip?'

'For what – punishment? Extreme detention?'

'Probably Geography.'

'Oh right, yeah.' *Pause.* 'Yeah that makes sense, actually.' *Pause.* 'No wonder they look so fucking miserable.'

By this point the noodles are swollen enough to be deemed edible, so they take it in turns to spork themselves a mouthful. Stephen only manages a couple of sporkfuls, then has to admit defeat. He says his stomach's still not right. Benny tries his best to carry on, but he keeps glancing at the mucus slug on the grass beside them, can't help associating the salty slime of the noodles with Stephen's phlegm, glistening in the sun. In the end he too gives up, leaves the noodles to steam in the mess tin.

Benny considers smoking but he's on his last cigarette now and there's something sacred about this. He feels he should save it, that there will be a time and place for him to smoke it and it's not here and now. Then he remembers the cigarette butts. He's been collecting them this whole time with a mind to binning them somewhere along the trail, adhere to the Countryside Code. He scours the pockets of his trousers and raincoat, gathers about fifteen in total, then splits them one by one, retrieves the remaining tobacco. This is a trick he learnt from the homeless in town; there was often a gathering of them outside the Tesco on Hankin Street and there would always be at least one of them scouring the car park for discarded ciggie butts. Some still have a good amount of tobacco inside (most probably Stephen's, considering his habit of stubbing them out well before they're finished).* Benny gathers enough to half fill his final two skins, sets about rolling two pitifully

---

* So, you were glad in the end, that I was such a piss-poor smoker?

thin cigarettes. At one point he notices an old lady watching him from the bench over at the eastern side of the tower. He ignores her, concentrates on the task at hand.

Once he's finished, he has three cigarettes in total – two to smoke, one as an emergency. He lights one up, inhales.

By now the class of school children are making their way back down the steps.

'I might go up, Ste. Check out the view.'

'OK.'

'You coming?'

'Nah, it's OK.'

'Really?'

'It's fine, man. I'll stay here.'

'There's a good panoramic up there, you know. Great for landscape shots.'

'I'm good, man.' *Pause.* 'Thanks though.'

*Pause.*

'Ste, this is like, the *perfect* place for photos.'

'I know.'

'So?'

'I'm just not feeling it today.'

'Feeling what?'

'The landscape. You know, artistically speaking. I mean, I know it's pretty. It's just . . . I don't know.' *Pause.* 'It's like, the more I think about it the more I just see a load of towns and fields, just *really far away*. I mean, that's it really, isn't it? It seemed cool at first but . . . I mean, is that really why people trek all the way up here? To see things from far away?'

'It gives perspective, Ste. All this, it makes you think *big picture*.'

'I know. It's just, we've had this for days now. These views. And it's like, how much perspective do we need?'

*Pause.*

'So, you're really not coming?'

'I'm just going to rest up here, man. The view's good enough from here.'

—

Benny heads around the side to the steps. There's an old man coming down, so he waits at the bottom, so as not to have to squeeze past him. The man is short, bow-legged. He has a comb-over of yellowing hair, blown into disarray by the wind. He takes his time descending the steps and Benny spends the wait wondering how the hell this old man got up here in the first place – there's no way he trekked the path he and Stephen just took.

Benny takes the man's wrinkled hand, helps him down the last few steps. The old man looks him up and down, gives a slightly reserved nod of thanks. Benny nods back. He wonders what's making everyone so edgy today. Could Stephen be right? Could it be how rough they're looking? Could it be the *smell*?

Benny climbs the steps to the viewing platform. There's an even stronger breeze up here but it's still hot, the sun glaring down. The two girls are there – the blonde scanning the horizon with a pair of binoculars, the Sam-like brunette beside her, waiting her turn. Benny forces himself not to stare at the brunette, tells himself to take in the landscape instead. This is the perfect place to take stock of how far they have come, how far they've left to go. The path splits off at each side, shrinking into the heather-topped mountains, which makes for a sort of plateau here – the hills and fields laid out below. There are a few clouds creeping in over to the west, each leaving a corresponding blotch of dark-ness on the landscape. The sea is barely visible now, a thin grey line in the distance.

Benny considers getting the guidebook out. He could probably decipher which of the towns are Bodfari and Rhuallt, which of the mountaintops is Moel Arthur, which of the clusters of forest was the one they'd so foolishly planned to camp in. He doesn't bother in the end, just stands there, taking it all in. After all, that's the whole point, isn't it? That's why he's here. To take it in. To get some perspective.

Benny's dad had talked a fair bit about Jubilee Tower when they were first planning the trip. It's situated at the highest point of the Clwydian Range, so even without the actual tower, Benny's still able to see all the way across to Snowdonia, if he squints, or

Liverpool, if he looks back the way they came. Benny's father had said that on a clear day they'd be able to make out Blackpool Tower, though when Benny asked why anybody would want to do that his father had just laughed, told him he'd no idea. He said that, back when he'd walked the dyke with Uncle Ian, he'd managed to convince him it was Paris they could make out in the distance.

Benny had half thought this might be a good place to scatter some of the ashes. His plan was to distribute them at various landmarks along the trail and he figured this might be an appropriate first stop. He pictured himself, climbing to the highest point, tossing handfuls into the wind. He'd never considered the possibility that the tower would be such a hotspot for day-trippers. Also, he can't get Stephen's words out of his head. That this view is nothing special. That it's just a load of *stuff* far away. He wonders what his dad's response to this would have been. His dad loved the views, it was the main reason he'd go on these walks, to appreciate his place in the immensity of the natural world. He said there weren't enough words to describe such sights. It was a pet hate of his, people using grandiose words too frequently, words like 'awesome' and 'amazing'. He complained about how they were dropped into everyday conversation to describe films and restaurants and flavours of ice cream. It meant there were no words left to describe stuff like this: *this view*.

And yet Benny still can't concentrate on it. He finds his eyes drifting to the brunette girl, to the awesomeness and amazingness of her arse.* All he can think is how much she looks like Sam.

It's only after a few seconds that he realises the muscular blonde is staring at him.

'Can we help you with something, mate?'

'Um . . . *sorry*?'

'I said can we help you with something?'

'No . . . erm . . . I'm sorry, no . . .'

'Carrie, leave it, it's fine.'

---

* *Sigh.*

181

'Pretty sure I could kick the shit out of you, mate, if it came to it.'

'Carrie, leave it I said.'

'Why should I? I'm fed up of people like him, thinking they can look at you like that.'

'I wasn't, honestly . . . I just—'

'Let's just go, yeah?'

'Why should we? We were here first!'

'We've seen it now though.'

'And so's he, by the looks of it! Really *taking in the view*, aren't you?'

'Carrie, please . . .'

'I'm really sorry. I didn't mean—'

'Didn't mean what? To check out my girlfriend's arse?'

'Carrie!'

'I'm sorry, I wasn't. I mean, I didn't *mean to*.'

'Look at his fucking pants, Jen. What is that, a hard-on?'*

'No. It's just the trousers, I—'

'Fuck it, we're leaving. But just to warn you – yeah, *you* – I'm a nice person, so I won't, but if I wanted to, I could kick the shit out of you, yeah?'

'Carrie!'

'I mean, the state of you. You're a fucking *tramp*.'

'Carrie, come on!'


The brunette takes the blonde by the hand, drags her over to the eastern stairway. The blonde glares at Benny the whole time, until her head sinks out of sight behind the stone wall. It's not until after they've left that Benny takes stock, realises he's shaking. He doubts this is wholly due to fear – he didn't really believe the blonde girl would hit him – most likely it's a mixture of adrenaline and exhaustion. He takes a cigarette from his tobacco tin, rests it between his lips. He stoops, manages to create a shelter between himself and the wall, enough protection from the wind to allow him to strike a match and burn the tip of the roll-up.

---

* FFS, Ben.

He's down to one cigarette again now, but he doesn't care. He needs to smoke.

He's about to turn and leave when a schoolboy appears at the top of the stairs. He's followed by another. Then another. Soon the viewing platform is full. It's the class from earlier – the female teacher with the pink beanie and walking stick being the last to ascend. Benny considers making a break for one of the other staircases, but then the children are told to spread out by their teacher, and as they do they block all available exits. Benny half smiles at the teacher then looks away into the distance, as if this will compensate for the awkwardness of his presence.

The teacher begins to explain the history of the Jubilee Tower, shouting so the whole class can hear. She tells them how it was built in the early 1800s to commemorate King George III, how originally it was to be an Egyptian-style structure with three obelisks. She asks them to picture the tower's collapse, the strength of the storm that brought it down, a mass of stone crashing into the mountainside. Benny wishes Stephen was around to hear this, perhaps it would inspire a little enthusiasm in him. He realises he's still smoking, and it feels wrong to be doing so in front of schoolchildren, so he dabs the tip of the cigarette against the stone wall, places what's left behind his ear for later. Eventually the teacher finishes talking. She says the children can stay up here, admire the view, make their own way down whenever they're ready. The children break into groups, begin to wander about. Benny sees his chance and makes his way back over to the staircase.

He's surprised when he arrives at the base of the tower to find Stephen is gone. At first, he thinks maybe he's in the wrong place – with all the confusion at the top of the tower he could have come down a different set of steps – but then he notices his pack, resting there against the wall. He scans the horizon, shading his eyes against the sun.

A few seconds later Stephen appears from the south side. He's doing a circuit of the tower, limping slowly under the weight of his pack. He keeps glancing over his shoulder, as if he's being pursued.

And then suddenly he is. The two huskies from earlier are trotting behind him, followed by the two boys in Man United kits. The huskies are sniffing at Stephen's pack, one of the dogs going as far as to take a bite at it. The boys find this hilarious. One of them is filming it on his phone. The Countryside Code specifies that all dogs should be kept under 'effective control' and Benny feels a need to go down and apprehend the dogs, inform the boys that they're breaking the rules. And yet, he just stands there. He finds himself laughing along with them. There's something so pathetic* about it: Stephen's lopsided limp, the look of genuine fear in his eyes. Plus, he's *so slow*. He may as well just stop and let the dogs sniff him. He's done a whole other lap before he spots Benny, standing there at the bottom of the steps. He waves over to him.

Benny's about to step down and intervene when the boys' mum appears. She catches the two huskies by their collars and drags them away. Stephen thanks her between struggled breaths, but she doesn't reply. She shouts at the two boys to stop their laughing.

Stephen hobbles back over to Benny. He retrieves his inhaler, takes a good few *hiccchhht*s.

'What was *that* about?'

'I don't know, man.' *Pant. Pant.* 'They came over whilst you were up on the tower.' *Pant. Pant.* 'They wouldn't stop following me.'

'So I saw.'

'I don't know what it was . . .' *Pant. Pant.*

'They seemed to like you.'

'I know.'

'They seemed to like your pack. What you got in there, dog treats?'

'Nothing, man!' *Pant. Pant. Pant.* 'Let's just get out of here.'

---

* Thanks, Ben.

# XV

*Southern path – Day-trippers – Car park – Ice cream van – Calippos – Loose change – Schoolgirls – Extra Flake – Tenderised tongues – Promise of a restaurant – Acting strangely – Photos – Teacher's scorn – The finger – A kiss (blown).*

They follow the trail south, a well-worn path that leads down through balding grass and patches of dark heather. More and more day-trippers pass them by, hiking uphill to the ruins of the tower. Benny has no idea where they're all coming from. There must be something nearby, some sort of facilities, although he doesn't remember seeing anything on the maps in the guidebook.

Amongst the day-trippers are families, children, old couples with walking sticks. None of them are panting. None of them are stooped under the weight of their packs. Instead they talk and laugh. An old man whistles. Two boys run ahead, brandishing sticks like guns, spitting sounds like bullet fire. It's getting hotter. Benny can feel the midday sun, the sweat gathering on his forehead. He can feel eyes upon him; each passing person offering a smile and a hello. Benny finds himself avoiding eye contact. He can detect a little derision in their smiles, probably because of how dishevelled he and Stephen look. Benny's hair always looks thinner in bright sunlight, especially if it's wet from his sweating – maybe they're looking at that.

At the foot of the hill is a road, a passageway between the two mountaintops. There's a car park, the biggest they've seen so far – a substantial patch of concrete sectioned off by grass and knee-high drystone walls. Benny feels a small jolt of panic; why does he not remember this from the guidebook? The car park is nearly full, family cars mostly, hatchbacks, four-by-fours, a couple of caravans. Most of the cars are clean, barely a trace of mud on the tyres. Some families are still unpacking; a mum zips up her children's raincoats; a dad checks the contents of a picnic hamper, ready for the short trek up to the tower. There's an ice cream van over by the entrance, decorated with hand-painted cartoons of Minnie Mouse, Buzz Lightyear, Snoopy – all distorted, faces elongated, clothing the wrong colours. A group of schoolchildren queue at the van. The sun is out now and most have removed their blue coats, opting to tie them round their waists instead. They fan themselves with their clipboards.

Stephen asks if they can please stop and rest again. Benny says no. He wants to keep moving. He doesn't tell Stephen this, but the truth is he wants to get away from all these people, wants it to just be the two of them again. He doesn't like being stared at by everyone. He doesn't want to be seen. Stephen motions to the ice cream van. Maybe they could get something? An ice lolly? Cool off a bit? Benny glances up at the mountain ahead. The trail is more grassy here, less definable. But still, it looks steep. The temptation for something cold is hard to fight.

'Do they have Calippos?'
  'I don't know, Ben.'
  'A Calippo might be nice.'
  'I'm sure they do. *Everywhere* has Calippos.'
  'You sure you're up for this? Isn't your stomach dodgy?'
  'Feeling a bit better now, man. Think the sugar might do me good, y'know?'
  *Pause.*
  'OK. Maybe. So long as they have Calippos.'
  'Really?'
  'If they have Calippos we can stop.'
  'OK, hang on. I'll go check.'
  *Pause.*
  *Pause.*
  *Pause.*
  'Well?'
  'Success, man! Calippos! Two-fifty each!'

186

Benny rifles through his pockets, empties out his remaining change. He has £5.45 in total. Stephen checks too but says he has nothing in the way of change; he gave it all to the homeless that first day.

Benny tells Stephen to wait with the packs, then goes over and joins the queue. He's behind a group of schoolgirls, all on their phones. He tries not to dwell on the fact they appear to have signal.

One of the girls turns to face him, her eyes widen and she leans in to whisper with her friends. The others peer over their shoulders then huddle again, giggling. Benny tries not to look at them. Instead he focuses on the ice cream van, on the middle-aged woman who is serving. She has dyed red hair, tied into a bun. She's wearing a grey T-shirt, sweat patches darkening her chest and armpits. The schoolgirls laugh again and Benny looks up at the sky. Not a cloud now. The sun stings his face. Beads of sweat edge down his back. The coins grow hot and heavy in his hand.

'Next!'

The girls order four 99s and the woman takes out four cones and sets about crafting them – piping ice cream, sprinkling hundreds and thousands, drizzling raspberry sauce. She pinches each cone daintily between her finger and thumb and Benny can't help but wonder how much of her sweat is absorbed in the process. She finishes them off by inserting the trademark Flake, then hands them over to each of the girls, who hurry across the car park, still giggling, to join the rest of their class.

Benny steps up, orders two Calippos, hands over the money. The woman fetches them out of the freezer. He's turning to leave when he notices Stephen waving, calling over to him. Stephen doesn't want a Calippo any more, he wants what the girls had. He wants a 99. And he wants two Flakes (make sure to get an extra Flake). Benny nods, turns back to the woman, asks if he's OK to change the order. She sighs, takes back one of the Calippos, sets about making another 99. She sighs again when she finds she has to open a fresh multipack of Flakes.

She hands the cone over, asks for an extra seventy-five pence. Benny only has forty-five pence left. He asks how much a 99 costs and she tells him it's £2.75, plus fifty pence for the extra Flake. He asks if he can opt out of the second Flake and she doesn't bother sighing this time, just takes the ice cream back, removes the flake and drops it with a thud somewhere below the counter. Benny places the rest of the coins on the counter, tells her to keep the change.

He turns and heads back over to Stephen.

'Awww, lovely stuff, man. Nice one.'
  'I don't think any of this is vegan, Ste.'
  'I'm making an exception. I think we've earned it.'
  'Right.'
  *Pause.*
  'Only one Flake?'
  'There wasn't enough for two.'
  'That's a shame, man. A real shame.'

They sit on the stone wall. Benny holds off starting his Calippo. He likes to wait, let it melt in his hand a little, let the juice gather at the bottom of the carton. Stephen has none of this patience. He's devoured his ice cream within seconds, Flake and all. He stops momentarily to complain about brain freeze, then crunches away at the cone.

Finally, Benny decides the time has come to peel back the lid. He squeezes the sides until the frosted tip edges out, then presses his tongue against the ice – that familiar tang and burn. Sam told him once that the reason the Calippo ice burns like that is to do with enzymes. They attack your tongue, effectively start to cook it. Apparently there was some health food chef she liked who once used a similar technique to tenderise steak (another way she was like a cat, Sam liked her meat *bloody*). Benny can still picture Sam, those summer nights he'd walk her home after uni, when they'd stop at the Tesco for an ice lolly. This was the Tesco where all the homeless gathered and Benny always felt guilty making such a luxury purchase whilst they were all out there, asking for change. Still, seeing Sam eat her Calippo made it all worthwhile. He can picture it now: her peeling back the lid, her cat-like laps at the orange ice inside. He remembers one time the two of them made out straight after, the sweet iciness as they explored each other's mouths with their newly tenderised tongues.*

Benny knows he shouldn't dwell on it. He's not sure it's healthy, that every memory of Sam is so overtly sexualised.† Instead he gets out the guidebook, flicks through to their current page, seeks out their position on the map. He can't believe he wasn't aware of this car park, but there it is – a huge blue '**P**', just beyond Jubilee Tower. He scans the pages ahead for any other landmarks, anything else he could have forgotten.

Stephen sips from his flask, then carries on chomping at his cone.

'You OK, man?'

'Yes. Fine.' *Pause.* 'Why?'

'Just checking.'

*Crunch.*

'How about you?'

'I'm all right. I think. That ice cream helped. Bit of a cooldown. Bit of an energy boost, you know?'

*Crunch.*

'Says here there's a restaurant up ahead.'

'A restaurant?'

'Well, by *up ahead* I mean another mile or so. We have to get over this next mountain first.'

'Right. Of course.' *Crunch.* 'You mean, like, a fancy restaurant?'

'It doesn't say.'

'What sort of food?'

'Doesn't say, Ste. There's just the restaurant symbol. A little blue knife and fork.'

'It'd be nice to have a proper meal.'

'That's what I thought.'

---

* Urgh.

† Agreed!

189

'You think they'll let us in? I mean . . . you know, with *the smell.*'

'I don't know.'

'Ah, fuck 'em, man. We'll eat there whether they like it or not.' *Crunch.** 'I hope they have vegan stuff. Some falafel. I'd kill for falafel.'

'I'm sure they will.'

'Or a spicy bean burger.'

'Yeah.'

*Pause.*

'Aren't those cartoons amazing?'

'Huh?'

'On the van, man. The ice-cream van.'

'Oh, yeah. Creepy, aren't they?'

'You reckon they're *meant* to be that bad?'

'Probably. How could they not be? Look at them. Even *I* know that's not art.'

'They're terrifying.'

'I think it's for, like, copyright reasons. You know, so Disney can't sue . . .'

'I'll have to get some photos of them, man. I *need* some photos of that shit.'

*Pause.*

'Ste?'

'Hmm?'

'Can I ask you something?'

'What?'

'Well, do you think people have been acting . . . *strangely* towards us?'

'Like, how?'

'Like weird. Looking at us weird.'

'Weird?'

---

* How many bites of this fucking cone did I take, Ben? Strange, isn't it – all these *crunch*es and not a single *slurp* mentioned? I'm certain you were slurping that Calippo all the way through this conversation, yet mysteriously you choose to omit this . . .

'Yeah.'

'Don't know, man. Maybe some of those schoolkids. I think that's just schoolkids though. It's an awkward age, isn't it?'

'I meant more . . . erm . . . other people . . .'

'Like who?'

'Like . . . I don't know. Did you see those girls?'

'What girls?'

'The ones that passed us this morning. They were up on the tower when I went up.'

'The lesbians?'

'One of them, like, *had a go* at me.'

'A go?'

'Yeah.'

'What about?'

'I don't know.'

'Was it about the tower? Did she say, "This isn't a tower"? Did she say, "We've been lied to by the National Trails Association"?'

'No, she just went nuts for no reason. Said I was looking at her girlfriend.'

'Really?'

'Yeah.'

*Pause.*

'And were you?'

'No!'★

'That's weird then.'

*Pause.*

'She called me a "tramp" too.'

'Really?'

'Yeah.'

'Wow.'

'What do you think *that* means?'

'You're asking me what "tramp" means?'

'Well, yeah. I mean, like, was she saying she actually thinks I'm homeless?'

---

★ Liar!

'What do you mean?'

'Do we *look* homeless?'

'Well, yeah. I mean, I guess we *are* homeless. For the next couple of weeks anyway . . .'

'But is that why people keep looking at us?'

'I don't know, man.'

'You've not noticed people looking at us?'

*Pause.*

'I think you're just being paranoid, Ben.'*

\*

* Of course, thinking back, we *did* look homeless, didn't we? As you've pointed out (repeatedly . . . mercilessly . . .) I was still dressing in the manner I had been at uni, aspects of which . . . (how can I put this?) . . . aspects of which *shared certain similarities* with the growing homeless population. My fashion sense was something Olga brought up early on, when I first moved into the house (I think her exact words were, 'We need some sort of intervention here.'). When I started at uni, I was still holding on to that same aesthetic as you and Cal – plain T-shirts and plaid shirts, jeans and Converse. It's almost like I was doing everything I could to fade into the background.

It was Garth and Olga who first opened my eyes to how exciting and expressive fashion could be. It was Olga who explained to me that our generation didn't really *have* an identifiable style of its own, that we were living in a post-fashion world, where all that remained was an appreciation of what had gone before. She said this was beautiful; it was emancipating; it meant that we could wear *anything*. She likened this to art: how post-modernism had freed the form from the shackles of tradition. Then she took me shopping. We went to a few of her favourite renewal stores in Soho, where they freshen up vintage clothing. The prices were outrageous, although luckily the first trip was on her. (Garth once told me that her father is a literal Russian oligarch, so I didn't feel too guilty letting her pay.) It was only later, when I was broke, that I began to frequent the charity shops instead.

As I mentioned earlier, it did strike me as odd at first, how much sports-wear was currently on-trend. I'm talking tracksuits here, peaked caps and trainers, all the brands we wore when we were younger, Reebok and Ellesse, Fila and Le Coq Sportif, all the stuff we'd long since labelled the uniform of the chav. By the time I got to uni this had been reclaimed by people in the know, people like Garth and Olga, people with enough money and influence to make it ironically pleasing on the eye. Like art, a lot of their fashion relied on juxtaposition – combining disparate elements to create a

Benny swallows the remains of his Calippo and bins the carton. He remembers the half-a-cigarette tucked behind his ear, lights up. The tobacco tastes sour against his tenderised tongue.

Stephen gets out his camera, takes a few photos of the cartoons on the back of the ice cream van. He remains distant at first, then edges closer with each picture, until he's kneeling only a foot or two from the paintwork. Eventually the woman steps out of the van, tells him to pack it in, and Stephen apologises and returns to Benny.

Just then the teacher with the moustache appears, instructs his class to follow him. He glares at Benny, shakes his head. It takes

---

brand-new emotional response. It was nuanced and deliberate. They had many . . . (what's a good phrase here?) . . . many *irony signifiers*, I guess you'd call them. Mostly what this involved was enough attention to detail to curtail any assumptions that they could actually *be* working class, e.g. Olga would wear an Ellesse T-shirt and jogging pants with a choker, heels, a full face of flawless make-up; or Garth would wear a tracksuit-and-trainer combo that, on closer inspection, consisted entirely of expensive designer brands. Plus, ankle socks (never was there a better signifier of irony than *bearing one's ankles*). Some of the others (not me or Garth, granted, but a few of his followers) had facial hair, only it wouldn't be the shabby, unkempt facial hair of actual homeless people; instead they'd sport Vandykes or pencil moustaches, or lumberjack beards styled at expensive barbers', glossy with moisturising oil they'd sourced from specialist websites.

I know all this is probably boring to you, Ben, but what I'm getting at is this: although we may have looked unkempt to the untrained eye, this stuff was curated. Our outfits were thought out. It was *fashion*. Hence the Adidas tracksuit. Hence the Nike Airs. Hence the T-shirt of Frank in his strap-on dildo. Of course the problem was, on the walk, this all got muddled. This style only really worked on a well-groomed art student. After a few days in the wilderness I was losing that aesthetic. Especially with the mud and the sheep shit and that stink of sweat and weed coming off us. Especially with my greasy hair and lack of glasses and that fucking *fleece* tied round my waist.

And then there was you, with your zippable trousers and camo T-shirt and those bin bags dangling from the back of your pack. I mean, think about it, Ben. Just picture it for a minute – these two dishevelled walkers, clad in such a disparate combination of styles. Is it any wonder people might have thought we were tramps?

Benny a few seconds to realise that it's the cigarette he's glaring at; that he's watching Benny raise it to his lips, watching him exhale. Stephen notices too, asks Benny if he can have a puff and Benny hands over the cigarette and Stephen inhales, all the time maintaining eye contact with the teacher. He exhales into the air, then gives the teacher the finger. Some of the kids laugh. The teacher shakes his head again, leads them over to a minivan at the far side of the car park.

They wait another few minutes, watch as the school class files one-by-one into the van. Benny recognises the girls from the queue, still giggling. One of them blows him a kiss. The teacher barks at them and they disappear inside. The teacher gives Benny and Stephen one last scowl, then slides the door shut and makes his way round to the driver's side.

They watch as the minivan rolls out, shrinks along the mountain road. The sun is fading now. A bank of white cloud is moving in. Stephen says maybe ice cream wasn't such a great idea. He hasn't eaten dairy for a while and it's sitting funny in his stomach. Benny says he'll be OK. He just needs a proper meal in him, something more substantial. He'll be fine once they reach the restaurant.

It occurs to Benny just at that moment that they no longer have their walking sticks. They must have left them up at the tower. He doesn't mention it. He's sure Stephen will agree that it's best to leave them there.

After a few minutes they set off again across the car park, re-join the trail.

# XVI

*The homeless of Hankin Street – Purchasing
donations – A grassy incline – Steps – Miniature
ice cream van – A path around the mountain –
A mile laid out – Downhill running – Mammoth –
A fall – 'Daft bastard' – Corridor of trees –
Goodbye sun visor – Sheep – Sheep – Sheep – Sheep
– Sheep – Sheep – Sheep – Sheep – Sheep – Sheep.*

It was back in uni, when Benny was spending most of his time at Sam's student accommodation, that he began to notice the growing homeless population. Back in first year, he and Sam were occasionally accosted by *Big Issue* salesmen on their way into campus, but Benny knew their usual spots and would plan his route to avoid them. By second year this was becoming more difficult. There seemed to be beggars on every street corner. They were impossible to avoid.

It was around that time that the little community began to grow outside the Tesco on Hankin Street. They were the usual type; typically in caps and hoodies, cocooned in sleeping bags. Most were in their forties or fifties, although Benny found it a little unsettling, as time went on, that there seemed to be more and more that were his own age. Their huddle was usually decorated with cardboard signs, scrawled declarations of how hungry they were, how the system had failed them, how many wars they'd served in. It was as winter approached that the little campsite appeared. It was a good site for them there: a patch of grass big enough to peg their tents, a supermarket to provide plenty of passers-by (and with them, the promise of spare change), although Benny always wished they'd chosen somewhere else. That Tesco was the only decent-sized food shop within walking distance of Sam's flat.

There were occasions (usually when she'd just received a bank transfer from her dad) that Sam would get this sudden sense of generosity regarding the city's homeless, would insist on picking up a bag of essentials from Tesco to bestow upon them. Benny found this distasteful, at the time. It seemed patronising somehow, to actually *buy* the shopping on their behalf. But he could never articulate this to Sam without sounding like an uncharitable monster. So he'd end up going along with it, traipsing around the aisles with her as she filled their basket with sausage rolls and sandwiches, toothpaste and bottled water, shampoo and wet wipes (she'd read online that homeless people always appreciated wet wipes). Benny was pretty sure the essentials they'd really appreciate were over at the booze and fag kiosk. Whiskey, cider, vodka, maybe a bottle of rum, as well as twenty Lambert & Butler to keep the tips of their noses warm.

It's not that Benny didn't sympathise. He was always sure to hand over spare change, at first. But once the numbers rose it became awkward. How could he give to one person, without giving to next? Plus, what good was it doing, the odd fifty pence here and there? It wasn't going to fix the problem, was it? It became easier just to pat his pockets, shake his head, pretend he didn't have anything to give – although as time went on, he began to detect a little animosity towards this response. There was an undercurrent of resentment there, he was sure of it. It was like they knew, even before asking, what his answer was going to be. And yet, they still asked, just to make him feel guilty. Plus, they were getting sneaky in their asking; they'd make sure to do it in front of Sam, as if trying to shame him, or else they'd linger at the collection point when he was returning his trolley, ask for the pound coin he'd used to unlock it.

The number of tents began to dwindle after a while. Benny could only assume that something was being done about it by the relevant authorities (although 'being done' was a euphemism he tried not to give too much thought to). Still, he was pleased to see them go. Sometimes he still thinks about them, especially at work. He can't help but associate the homeless on Hankin Street with the people who phone the helpline.

They continue across the car park and up a grassy incline onto the mountain path. It is steep but manageable, especially compared to some of the terrain they encountered this morning. At least the sun's not so bright now. At least there's no barbed wire. At least there aren't any day-trippers. A little further up there are more stone steps. Benny wonders who installed them; they've come across a few different sets of steps along the trail and it's hard to imagine someone dragging all those lumps of stone up, digging holes and setting them in the ground, all with the noble aim of aiding future walkers.

Halfway up, the path veers to the right and curves round the side of the mountain and they stop for a few minutes to catch their breath. There are a few sheep dotted across the hillside here and one is standing amongst the heather a few metres up, staring down at them. Stephen burps, then spits into the grass. He says all this climbing's not good for his stomach. He says it feels like the ice cream is *curdling* in there. Benny tells him not to worry – he's pretty sure that isn't scientifically possible. Also, they're doing well today, miles-wise. They'll be over the mountains in no time. This is a lie, but he doesn't think admitting the truth will help either of them.

Already the car park has shrunk into a tiny patch of grey. It is speckled with a variety of different coloured cars, a miniature ice cream van. Jubilee Tower is returned to its former state: a mere speck in the distance, beyond which lie the peaks of the mountains they've crossed this morning. It's a shame Benny hasn't managed to scatter any of the ashes; he wishes he'd been able to dispose of some on the tower. He reconsiders the word *dispose*, that's probably not the best way of thinking about it. Maybe he could sprinkle some here? It's certainly a peaceful spot, and the views are nearly as good as they were atop the tower. But Stephen will probably have questions, will want to talk about it. Plus, Benny doesn't like the way those sheep are staring. He figures there'll be plenty of chances later on. There are, after all, two more weeks of walking ahead of them.

He's surprised he forgot about the car park. He's read the guidebook cover to cover, again and again, and he thought by now he'd managed to memorise most of the maps. He thought of this as an integral part of his preparation; excessive, yes, but he figured if they lost the guidebook then at least he would be able to summon a mental image of the basic shape of the trail they were taking; what lay ahead in terms of landmarks and facilities. Still, his head's been all over the place these last few weeks. No need to be too harsh on himself. They're doing OK, so far. They're about halfway through today's allotted maps. They'll get off the mountains today, he's sure of it. They'll make it to Llandegla. They just need to keep walking.

They follow the path around the side of the mountain. There are more steps, wooden this time, even steeper than the stone ones below. With each step comes that ache, the burning and tearing in their thighs. They stop a few times to catch their breath. They take a five-minute water break at the top. Benny says not to de-pack. They can't de-pack until they've reached the restaurant, he says. Stephen doesn't reply. He stares straight up at the sky and breathes.

The next signpost directs them south, down into a valley. From here they can see the next mile of their journey laid out before them, the hills below, the patches of forest, the path curving to the left through a bank of trees, then a sharp right through fields of sheep.

Stephen says he needs to stop again, catch his breath. Benny takes this opportunity to retrieve the guidebook, seek out their position on the map. From here the scale is spot on, the patches of light and dark green to represent the fields and forests, the wavy lines indicating the gradient of the terrain. He can't help smiling at how good a representation it is – a testament to the art of cartography.

He decides to show this to Stephen. He thinks he might appreciate it, being an artist himself.

Stephen examines the map. He looks out at the valley, scratches at his cheek. He looks at the map again.

—

'That's *it*?'

'What?'

'All this ahead of us and that's it? That *tiny bit of map*?'

'Well . . .'

'I mean, this whole valley. Look at it! It goes on for miles. And it's just, like, *an inch* of map.'

'It's like *one mile*, Ste.'

'You know what I mean, Ben. Look how far it is!'

'It won't take that long.'

'Are you *kidding*?'

'Honestly.'

'And how many pages are left?'

'Erm . . . three?'

'*Jesus*, Ben!'

'Honestly, Ste, we'll be there in no time. Look how far we've come today already. Behind us, all those mountains . . .'

'Those mountains nearly killed me!'

'It won't take that long. Honestly.'

'Right.'

'Honestly, Ste.'

'Great.'

'We'll be there in no time.'

'If you say so.'

By this point it's nearly four o'clock. Benny suggests they continue down the hill, get this valley out of the way. Just beyond the valley they'll arrive at a main road, which'll lead them down to the restaurant. It's not that far, not really. Stephen says nothing, just *hoik*s onto the grass, then struggles to his feet again.

Stephen totters a little way down the hill. Benny tells him to be careful not to slip. It's a steep decline and the grass is still a little slick from the rain and it's easy to imagine Stephen buckling on his bad ankle, tumbling down headfirst. Benny turns side-on, to edge his way down. Stephen copies. They've only managed a few steps before Stephen shrieks. Benny turns just in time to see his leg sliding forwards, as if he's doing the splits. Benny grabs his arm, steadies him.

Benny says maybe they should jog down. At first Stephen laughs at this suggestion, but Benny says he's serious, they did it all the time when he used to walk with his dad. They'd jog the really steep parts because often it was easier than walking them. Stephen says he doesn't have the energy. Benny says it's not really about energy, it's about letting go. Giving way to gravity. He says he'll demonstrate.

Benny takes a moment to psych himself up. He closes his eyes, straightens his back. He reaches out for balance, arms spread, as if he's offering himself to the world (as if he's being crucified). He takes a deep breath, inhales the collective tang of sweat, marijuana and sheep shit. He raises his left leg. He can feel Stephen's eyes upon him. He can feel the eyes of the sheep, up on the mountain.

He opens his own eyes. Rocks back on his heels for a moment, then allows himself to tip forwards.

There's a moment when it's as if he's falling. He gets that tinge of panic at the bridge of his nose, as if his face is bracing for impact. But then his right boot hits the ground and his left boot kicks out in front and suddenly he's charging down the hill. This isn't even something he has to think about any more. His body does it auto-matically. It has to; with the momentum he's building, if he wasn't running he'd have already pitched too far forwards, would be rolling head-over-heels. The first few strides are painful. There are aches in his ankles and shoulders and a steady thumping at the point where the pack butts his spine. But soon these pains numb, the fears subside. The ground glides beneath him. A few seconds and he's found his rhythm, a galloping pace. The landscape bounces ahead: the stile, the patches of heather, the trees and fields beyond.

There are fleeting images of his father. Benny remembers how strange it was, those times his dad and Uncle Ian jogged down the hills. It was a rare event, to see his dad running (he rarely engaged in any sort of physical activity beyond walking). If Benny were to compare his father to an animal it would have been a mammoth – large, hairy, reverential.* Mum used to call him lazy. She used to complain Benny's dad didn't get enough exercise,

---

* Extinct?

that he should stop smoking and drinking so much and join a gym. She was always saying his bad habits would catch up with him one day. (She stopped saying these things after the diagnosis.)

Still, they're happy memories, those occasions Benny's dad would charge down the hillside. He looked ridiculous, arms flapping, belly bouncing, hair slipping loose from its bobble. He'd usually laugh as he ran and it's this that Benny pictures now, his father laughing. He hears it, that deep chuckle. And, although it's only for a second, it's a welcome change from the recurring image he has of him, sitting there that evening at the kitchen table, after Christine had phoned the call centre.

Stephen is calling out now. He's shouting for Benny to slow down, but Benny can't, there's too much momentum. He's not been paying attention and suddenly he's almost at the stile. And the speed he's reached, the weight of the pack, there's no way for him to stop. He tries nonetheless and, in attempting to stop, he slips, pitches forwards. The world spins. There's a sharp pain as the ground slams into his left shoulder. Another in his tongue, as he bites down hard.

Then everything stops. All is still.*

*Pant. Pant.*
*Pant. Pant.*
*Pant. Pant.*

———

* Sorry, I take that previous comment back. About your father, I mean. It was a cheap shot. I'm not trying to be unnecessarily cruel here, Ben, in spite of what you might think. I'm aware how devastating his illness was for you and your family and I didn't mean to make light of your suffering.

In fact, for the record, I always liked your dad. He wasn't bad, as far as teachers go. I had him for Year 9 English, which was a nightmare class, but he was always good at picking out those who were the most severe bullies, punishing them accordingly. He was an imposing presence, slumped there at the front of the room, with that glare he'd aim over the brim of his glasses. (Yes, you weren't the only victim of 'The Glare', Ben – anyone who'd ever had your father as a teacher had experienced it at some point.)

Still, in my defence, I'd say I'm entitled to a little gallows humour here, right? You know, given my current situation . . .

Benny opens his eyes. His head is tipped back. He can see the hill he's just charged down, beyond it the clear blue sky.

He tries to roll onto his front. But he can't, the pack won't allow it. He's like a turtle, stuck on its back. He breathes, **IN** and **OUT**. **IN** and **OUT**. **IN** and **OUT**.

After a minute or so Stephen appears, upside down, still a fair distance off. He's edging his way down the hillside. He's laughing; he shouts something and Benny shouts back between breaths, informs Stephen that he can't hear a word he's saying.

Stephen shouts again.

'I SAID, YOU'RE A DAFT BASTARD!'

Benny laughs. With his head tipped back the laughter gathers in his throat, manifests as a deep chuckle. This only makes him laugh more. By the time he's composed himself Stephen is standing over him.

Stephen sighs, shakes his head. He reaches out and helps Benny to his feet.

'You OK?'
'Fine. Never better.'
'*Christ*, Ben. For a second there I thought you were dead.'

Benny brushes himself off. There are plenty of ailments: aches in his shoulders and back and his calves and ankles are still raw and tender, although none of this is a result of the fall. The only new pain is the throbbing in his tongue, but even that is fading fast. Plus, they're at the bottom of the hill now, so in a way his plan worked, they made it down quickly.

He tries explaining this to Stephen, but Stephen doesn't agree. Stephen says it was dangerous. Plus, he couldn't join in with the running even if he'd wanted to, because of his bad ankle. He asks Benny not to do that again, please.

Stephen suggests they have another dose of ibuprofen. Benny knows this is really about Stephen's pain, about *his* need for ibuprofen, but he dishes a couple of tablets out anyway. They still have a little noodle water left, just enough to wash them down. Benny should have brought more painkillers – they only have the one packet and so there's only a couple more doses before they run out – but the fact they're now out of water is probably a more immediate problem.

They keep walking. This is the same part of the trail they'd been examining earlier in the guidebook – the curving path, the patch of trees, the fields beyond. They climb the next stile then veer south, towards the forest. The path takes them through a corridor of sorts, trees on one side and a wire-mesh fence on the other – a mass of nettles and thorn bushes beyond. They follow this for the next fifteen minutes. Further along, the branches lower and they're forced to stoop – and stooping isn't easy, what with the weight of the packs. Benny can feel the extra pressure on his thighs and lower back.

They come to a clearing and Benny decides to stop for a minute, straighten up, allow his body a little respite from the prolonged hunching. Stephen goes on ahead. After a few feet, his sun visor catches on one of the low-hanging branches. Instead of stopping and untangling it, Stephen tries to keep walking, and suddenly the branch flings back, and in one fluid motion the visor is torn from his head, catapulted over the fence. There's a couple of seconds before it descends, landing with a rattle amongst the nettles.

Stephen sighs. He turns back to Benny. His hair is in complete disarray by this point, his fringe bursting forth from the side of his head like the exit wound from a gunshot. Benny can't help but laugh. He's still buzzing with adrenalin from his freefall down the hillside and the sight of Stephen sets something off inside him.

Stephen asks if his visor counts as littering. Benny laughs again. No, he says. He's more than happy to leave *that thing* behind.

They soon arrive at another stile. Beyond it the landscape opens out, a valley of grassland. The path runs through a slight dip here, which Benny realises could well be the dyke itself, rising into hills at either side.

The sun is blinding. It's lowered a little by now and Benny has to hold his hand up, squint against it. He can just about make out sheep on the surrounding hills. It's only as his eyes adjust that he realises there are in fact hundreds of them, entire flocks of the things, spanning across the valley, shrinking to specks of white in the distance. They remind him of a crowd at a sporting event, gathered in expectation. There's an apparent mix of breeds – black, white, long-haired, short- – although they're all gathered there together.

There's something about this image that brings Benny to a halt. Stephen stops too, gives a small gasp. Benny can't quite figure it out at first. Then it hits him: the sheep aren't baaing. Not a single one of them. They aren't shuffling or chewing the grass. They're perfectly still.

Also, every single one of them is staring in their direction.

What's most surprising of all, though, is the seriousness of this image. A few minutes ago Benny was laughing at Stephen's sun visor. Now he's standing here, with *this* – an army of glaring sheep – and for some reason it doesn't seem funny at all.

'Erm . . .?'

'I know.'

'Are we still stoned, man?'

'I don't think so.'

'I mean, do you see what I'm seeing?'

'I see it, Ste.'

'But . . . *why*?'

*Pause.*

'Come on. Let's keep walking.'

'Maybe we should turn back, Ben.'

'Back?'

'Yeah, I don't like the look of this.'

'We can't turn back, Ste. Not because of some sheep.'

'But *look at them*!'

'Keep your voice down.'

'Right OK. Sorry. I just . . . I mean . . .'

'I know, Ste. It's weird, I know. But let's just keep walking, OK?'

—

They follow the path down between the two hills. There is no breeze now, no birdsong. The only sound is their breathing, their feet shuffling through the grass. The whole time Benny can feel the eyes of the sheep upon him, their gaze fixed – heads turning as they pass.

The path leads over another stile and alongside a fence, beyond which is a patch of woodland. There are sheep lounging across the path here, basking in the shade of the trees. They too are staring. There's something empty in their stares. They don't have the curiosity of the cows, the hunger of the dogs, the distaste of the day-trippers. Their expressions are hollow – impossible to read. They make no effort to stand and hobble out of the way and so Benny and Stephen have to veer from the path to step around them.

At the edge of the field an acorn sign leads them right, alongside another fence. Benny wishes he could stop for a minute, de-pack, cool off a little. But there's no way. Not here. Not with all these eyes upon them.

The field beyond the fence is inhabited too. An entire flock has gathered at the wire mesh, just to glare at them.*

———

* And there was an *intensity* too, right? I'm not sure you're quite getting that across, Ben. Yes, there was a blankness, an expressionlessness to the flock's glare, but there was a certain power to it as well. It's hard not to sound like I'm exaggerating when I say this, but it was like they were staring *deep inside us*; like they could see right into our *souls*. The closest equivalent would be back in school, the crowds of onlookers that would gather when I was being bullied. There were always plenty of bystanders there to witness those ritual humiliations (e.g. the shower-room piss-dousings, or Cal's obsession with trying to pluck out my nipple hairs, or that hot summer's day when that gang of year elevens held me down in front of the whole playground and wrote 'SHIT STABBER' on my shirt in what I always hoped and prayed was chocolate spread). It's actually the crowds that I remember most of all now – their expressionless faces – even more so than the actual bullies.

And when it came to the sheep, well, there was a similar sense of judgement to it. I think that's what I'm trying to get at here. It was as if those sheep knew something about us, something they considered fundamentally humiliating and dehumanising, and the fact that they knew this and could

*[Whispered.]* 'What. The. Fuck.'

*[Whispered.]* 'I know.'

*[Whispered.]* 'What the actual *fuck*, man.'

*[Whispered.]* 'I know, Ste. Just keep walking.'*

They spot a gate ahead, find themselves quickening towards it. Stephen reaches it first, struggles with the bolt. Benny tells him to relax. The sheep aren't approaching like the cows were; they're not being *chased*. Still, Benny feels it too, how unwelcoming their glare is. He too wants to be out of there as soon as possible.

Stephen drags the gate open and they hurry through, slamming

---

still look upon us with such a peculiar mixture of intensity and disdain was all the more damning than if they'd summoned the energy to show us what they really thought. (Which, thinking about it now, is similar to that look your dad gave you, right? The one you keep going on about, in the kitchen that night . . .)

* You know, before we embarked on that trip, I actually *liked* animals? My veganism is another one of those things we never really discussed in much detail, isn't it? To be honest there isn't much of a story there – it just sort of happened. When I first moved into Garth's, he and Olga made the assumption I was vegan, the same as everyone else in their circle of friends, and so I went along with it. I took trips with him to the wholefoods store. I had oat milk on my cereal, avocado spread on my toast. I ate lentils and soysages and this crumbly vegan cheese that smelt like sick (but actually tasted OK, once melted). And, you know what? I didn't mind at all. I was surprised by how little I missed my old diet of cheeseburgers and Nutella sandwiches. I mean, maybe it was because there was so much else going on at the time; the drinking, the drugs, the sex – not to mention the excitement of making genuine progress in my artistic journey. Sure, maybe I wasn't as committed as Garth and Olga were (hence my willingness to devour that ice cream earlier) but it felt like an important part of the lifestyle we were cultivating during our uni days – the feeling that we were fighting for something. There was this underlying self-assurance that we would be on the right side of history.

Still, *Wales*, man. I mean, *Jesus*, did we ever come across another sentient being that whole trip that wasn't an utter arsehole? First the cows, then the dogs, now *this*. I still remember that moment just as clearly as you do, stood there in the sheep fields with all those black eyes upon us. I mean it, Ben, I can honestly count that face-off with the flock as one of the most disturbing moments of my adult life.

it shut behind them. Stephen gasps – it's a shock to both of them, the clatter of the thing. An explosion in the thick silence.

They follow the path down for a quarter-of-an-hour or so. Neither speaks a word. They pass through another patch of trees, come out onto a dirt road. They pass over a cattle grid and Benny feels immediate relief – another obstacle between them and the sheep.

After a while, Benny realises he can hear the sound of traffic. Soon a main road appears, running parallel on their left, the noise of the road getting louder and louder as they follow the path down. It's a welcome change from the silence up on the fields. The speeding cars, the screeching and honking, the smell of the exhaust fumes – it's wonderful.

'What *was that*, man?'

'I don't know.'

'Did you see the way they were looking at us? Did you see *those eyes*?'

'I saw.'

'Fuck me. That was *horrible*.'

'I know.'

'I mean it, man. If I never see a single sheep again, I'll die happy.'*

---

* Incidentally, have you ever looked into the symbolism of the sheep, Ben? It makes for interesting reading. Of course, there are the obvious modern associations – a crowd-following majority, conforming to societal norms, etc. – although it's important to remember that this interpretation only came about in the progressive, anti-religious era. There's also a flipside to this, sheep originally being considered a spiritual animal, especially in Christian tradition (remember those Sunday school classes with your mum, 'The Good Shepherd' and all that?), especially regarding a sort of *collective spirituality*, which is something I'm certain we both felt lacking, by this point in our lives.

Garth was more familiar with the modernist interpretation, from what I remember – 'sheep' being his go-to insult for what he also referred to as the 'unthinking masses'. More specifically anyone that didn't understand the need for art, or the importance of the creative spirit. It was also how he'd describe anyone who dared to criticise his work in class (which became quite a common occurrence near the end, when he became increasingly obsessed with his *Unstill Life* pieces – began building tiny galleries in the parks and underpasses, labelling *actual homeless people* as works of art). It's also what he'd say about Jess, if I ever brought her up. That she was unimportant; a 'sheep'. That she didn't know art, she just knew painting. That she was destined to end up in a high school, back in some shitty northern town, teaching a bunch of scallies how to paint bowls of fruit.

To be honest, I never really knew where Garth stood on the issue of the class divide. He was one huge contradiction when it came to such things. On one hand he considered himself an ally to the working classes, forever angry at the current government and the cruelty of the austerity programme, but at the same time he was a massive snob who hated the general public with a passion; there's no way he would have given the time of day to a member of the ordinary, working-class majority. He scoffed at them regularly – always the first to point out their poor fashion choices, their limited vocabulary, their hairstyles or beer bellies or badly designed tattoos, with what can only be described as a sneering sense of derision. He saw them too as 'sheep' – a mass of easily led, braindead followers.

Which is where I came in. I think I was the missing link, his way of connecting a deprived underclass with the modern art scene. I was far from a typical member of the underclass (sure, Mum and I were hard up after Dad left, but we were never *starving*). To Garth though, I was the closest thing to an actual poor person he'd ever met. Certainly, I was the only working-class person he considered a friend. Which is why he was so keen on helping me out financially during my time at uni. Why he bailed me out each time my student loan payments ran dry. He kept insisting that this was a golden opportunity for me, a once-in-a-lifetime chance to fully immerse myself into my work. The last thing he wanted was for me to have to quit and get some crappy job. Sell out.

And back then, of course, I believed him. Above all else it seemed like I was heading towards something. That I was gaining some kind of momentum with my sculptures. That I was dissociating myself from the unthinking masses.

We made it a point of principle. Garth said it was essential we did our best to always stray from the flock.

You know what happens to sheep when they stray from the flock, Ben?

# XVII

*Road to the restaurant – Closed for business –*
*A search for water – Vantage point – Fences –*
*Axe-wielding – Breaking and entering –*
*Anti-vandal paint – Water – Front terrace dining*
*experience – Poetry – Kafka – 'The futility of life'*
*– The night before the funeral – The loft –*
*A priority above all other priorities.*

It's approaching late afternoon when they eventually arrive at the road and continue along the embankment to the restaurant. There's not much in the way of a path here, just a slither of pavement, the traffic speeding by. Benny shouts for Stephen to be careful, watch his footing. Stephen doesn't reply. He's fallen behind. His limp's getting worse. Hopefully any minute now the ibuprofen will kick in.

A grass verge appears on their right, which steadily rises into an embankment. There's a driveway leading up to a long, grey building, a car park out front and a patio along the side, adorned with rows of wooden picnic tables: the restaurant. There are no cars. There are no diners. The windows along the front are suspiciously dark. Stephen laughs, shakes his head. Benny says it means nothing. It's half past four, not exactly a popular time for restaurant-goers. It doesn't necessary mean the place is closed.

They ascend the path to the front entrance. The doors are shut, windows boarded, handles bound with thick chain. The windows along the patio area are boarded too. It's a beautiful location, overlooking the Welsh valleys. It probably had a great view out of those bay windows, when the place was open.

There are clouds now, rolling in from over the mountains to the west. The sun is swallowed, suddenly. The landscape dulls.

'What now?'
    'We eat. We said we'd have a meal here and we will.'
    'Eat what?'
    'The same thing we always eat.'
    'We have no water, man. We going to eat them *dry*?'
    *Pause.*
    'Let's take a look around.'

They dump their packs in the porch and head around the back. There's another grassy incline, a scattering of trees at the top, a couple of houses beyond. At the bottom is a red fence, blocking off a yard at the side of the restaurant. There is a door, but it's chained and padlocked, a bright-yellow sign nailed to it with an exclamation mark and the words: 'WARNING: ANTI-CLIMB PAINT'.

Benny seeks out a vantage point, further up the hill. He stops at the trees, where he can make out the restaurant's backyard. There are bin bags piled up. There is yellowed patio furniture. There is an old oven, its hob puddled with rainwater. There is a back door, most likely to the kitchen, and a length of hose, coiled and knotted in places, running the length of the pavement up the side of the wall, attached to the building via an outdoor tap. Benny points this out to Stephen, who squints, nods.

'How do we get in, though?'
    'We climb.'
    'What about the paint?'
    'We're filthy, Ste. What's a little anti-vandal paint going to do?'
    'Dirt washes out, man. Paint doesn't.'
    'Really? You're worried about paint? Aren't you supposed to be an artist?'
    'It just . . . it feels *dodgy*. Can't we just knock at some houses or something?'
    'That worked a real treat back in Rhuallt, didn't it?'

'Yeah, but . . .'

'We'll not make it to Llandegla without water, Ste. I don't know what else to suggest.'

'It just seems . . . extreme . . .'

'No one will know. No one will care.'

'I'm sure this must be against the Countryside Code, breaking and entering.'

'The code says nothing about breaking and entering. The code is ambivalent where breaking and entering's concerned.'

'I just . . . I don't know, man. I just don't know.'

Benny walks down to the wooden door at the side of the fence. It's bound with the same type of plastic-coated chain as the front. Parts of the plastic have split and the metal beneath is bleeding rust. Benny tugs at it but there's no give. He backs up, wipes the rust residue on his trousers. At first, he thought maybe he could climb it, although on a second glance this is unlikely. The fence is easily seven-foot high, with nothing to use as a foothold. He taps one of the fence panels with the toe of his boot. It seems solid. He checks his boot to see if the paint has stained, but there's nothing. Then he taps the next panel. The next. He works his way along, tapping each panel, only to find it as sturdy as the last.

He turns to Stephen, up on the hill. He gives an exaggerated shrug. Stephen shrugs back. Benny gives a thumbs up and Stephen scans the area then replies with a nod: coast's clear.

Benny turns back, raises his boot, stamps heel-first at one of the boards. There's a bang and a shudder from the fence – a yelp from Stephen, up on the hill. Benny stamps again. Again. Each time the violence of it comes as a shock to him, yet no cracks appear, no splits, no visible weakening of the wood.

Benny stamps at the next panel. Nothing. He tries the next, then the next. There's a tackiness to the surface of the wood now, and he can tell the paint is wet; is more-than-likely staining the sole of his boot. He doesn't care. He makes his way around, stamping at each fence panel, but none of them show any sign of weakness.

Somewhere behind, Stephen is calling to him.

Benny heads back round to the front of the restaurant. He kneels at the packs, unbuckles the top and slips his hands inside, down past the cooking equipment and clothing, past the empty water bottles and packets of noodles, past the plastic tub of ashes, to the hatchet nestled at the bottom. As he pulls, it catches, needs to be eased through the bag's assorted contents. By this point Stephen is there too, standing over him, lip raised in that wince-face, asking what on earth he's doing. Benny ignores him. He struggles with the hatchet for a second, wriggling it free of its plastic packaging, then rushes back round to the fence.

He takes a run-up and swings at the fence as hard as he can. The first couple of strikes produce nothing but that now familiar bang-and-shudder – and a sharp pain in his shoulder at the force of it. It's his third attempt that yields a satisfying *crack*; a few more hacks before a slit appears, spreading vertically down the seam of the wood. Benny steps back, kicks at the panel – once, twice, three times – and it splits right down the middle, the left half tumbling inward, the right pitching forward onto the grass.\*

With a panel missing there's now just enough space (a little snagging-of-clothes and a smearing-of-paint aside) for Benny to squeeze through into the yard. He kneels at the tap, disconnects the hose. The tap itself is cold and stiff but using both hands he manages to turn it. At first there's nothing. He turns it again and again and eventually a rumbling comes from somewhere deep within. There's a slight chugging before water gushes forth, rusty brown at first, then clear and foaming. He shouts for Stephen to fetch the bottles – they've got water.

A minute later Stephen appears, passes the bottles through the gap. Benny fills them one by one, passes them back. Once they've collected all the water they can carry, he rinses his hands, scrubs at the paint and rust residue. Stephen's complaining again, some-

---

\* You were in full berserker mode here, Ben. It was *scary*. I mean, imagine it from my perspective: I was exhausted from the mountains. I was totally freaked out by the incident with the sheep. And now here you were, going full Jack Nicholson on me with a fucking *axe*.

thing about getting paint on his T-shirt, but by this point Benny's not even listening.

He turns off the tap, squeezes back through the gap in the fence, and the two of them ferry the water back around to the picnic benches at the front of the restaurant.

Benny takes a seat and sets about boiling up some noodles.

'Um . . . is this wise, Ben? You know, staying here?'

'What do you mean?'

'Well, what if somebody shows up? What if somebody sees the fence?'

'I fixed the fence. You can't tell anything by looking at the fence. Not from a distance.'

'But what if the owner shows up?'

'Does it look like the owner ever shows up here? We won't be long, Ste. Just long enough to eat.' *Pause.* 'Plus, we're lucky you know. That there's an outside tap. That it's still running.'

'No man, lucky would be burgers. Lucky would be Guinness. We have coffee and noodles.'

'Well, we have to make do with what we've got.'

'Right.'

'What else can we do?'

*Pause.*

'Saying that, I don't even know if I could eat any of that shit. I feel rough, man. That ice cream fucked me over.'

'You just need something more substantial, Ste.'

'Like noodles?'

'Yes. Exactly. Like noodles.'

*Pause.*

'I can't stop thinking about those sheep, man. All those fucking *glaring* faces.'

'I know.'

*Pause.*

'How we doing now? Miles-wise, I mean. How much further?'

'We're making progress.'

'Really?'

'Yeah, look . . . here . . . I'll show you.' *Pause.* 'Just let me get

213

the . . .' *Pause.* 'Here. Right. We've crossed to this side of the map now. Just these few inches to go . . . See? I told you we'd make it.'

'What's that?'

'What?'

'That writing in the corner.'

'Nothing.'

'No, on the inside cover . . .'

'It's nothing.'

'Let me see.'

'It's nothing, Ste.'

'Is that . . . is it . . . a *poem*?'

'No.'

'It *is* . . . it's a poem!'

'So?'

'You wrote a poem?'

'It's my dad's.'

'Your dad?'

'Yeah.'

'He wrote poetry?'

'Sometimes.'

'Wait, is that the one you read at the funeral? The one about walking?'

'Yeah.'

'That's where you found it? Written in the guidebook?'

'It's the only one left.'

'What do you mean?'

'The only poem. He got rid of the rest.'

'Really?'

'He must have, I couldn't find any. I think he burnt them.'

'Burnt them?'

'Yeah. Well, I'm only guessing here. But not long after the diagnosis he made this big bonfire out in the garden. He was burning bags of papers. I thought it was old schoolwork or something. It was only later, when I was looking for something to read out at the funeral, that I realised I couldn't find any of his poetry.'

'Wow.'

'He didn't want anyone reading them after he'd gone, I suppose.'

'I mean, I guess you have to respect that.'

'What?'

'There's something noble in it, isn't there? In not wanting to lose control. Like I said yesterday, I do the same thing with my photos. It's like with Kafka, isn't it? He wanted all his stuff destroyed too.'

'What?'

'Kafka.★ The writer. He wanted all of his work destroyed when he died. He asked his editor to destroy it.'

'And?'

'Hmm?'

'Did he?'

'Nah. The bastard went and released it anyway. Can you believe that?'

'Right.' *Pause.* 'So . . . I mean, what's that got to do with anything?'

'Well, it's the same.'

'It's not, Ste.'

'It is. Your dad didn't want his work to be read after he died. Like Kafka.'

'Right.' *Pause.* 'But isn't Kafka meant to be, like, *really good*?'

'Well, yeah.'

'So, isn't it a good thing that his work wasn't burnt?'

'Yeah, but that's not the point. It was *his* work, so it was his call whether to release it or not. It's got to be the artist's call, always.'

'Right.' *Pause.* 'And *is* he good?'

'Who, Kafka?'

'Yeah.'

'Never read any. But, like I said, that's not the point. You have to respect the wishes of the artist. Especially when they die. I mean, it's their legacy. And burning it: that's pretty cool. I mean, kudos to him on that. Very dramatic.'

---

★ By the way, yes, if you're wondering, it was Garth who introduced me to Kafka.

*Pause.*

'Well, if all it takes to make you an artist is burning all of your own work, I guess you can get there pretty quickly, Ste.'

*Pause.*

'Can I read it?'

'What?'

'The poem.'

'I'd rather you didn't.'

'Go on.'

'No.'

'Please?'

'What about *respecting the wishes of the artist*?'

'Well, you did read it at the funeral, Ben. I'd just be rereading it, really.'

*Pause.*

'You know what, *fine*. Here.'

'Really?'

'Knock yourself out.'

'Thanks!' *Pause.* '"When you feel alone—"'

'In your head.'

*Pause.*

*Pause.*

*Pause.*

*Hiccchhht.*

*Pause.*

*Pause.*

*Pause.*

'Hey, that's pretty good!'

'Yeah?'

'I don't remember it being that good. You know, at the funeral.'

'What's *that* supposed to mean?'

'Well, it's just . . . I don't know . . . Sometimes it works better on the page, doesn't it?'

'If you say so.'

*Pause.*

'Did he write this . . . erm . . . *near the end*?'

'Why?'

'Just wondering.'

'What makes you think that?'

'Well, that's what it's about, right? The cancer?'

'What?'

'It's about his . . . you know . . . "The road that's ending . . ."
the *futility* of life . . .'

'No.'

'You sure? I mean . . . that last line . . .'

'What about it?'

'"We die . . ."'

'And?'

'And so . . .'

'It's the exact opposite of that, Ste. It's about the *beauty* of life.
It's about the joy of his time on earth.'

'*On earth*?'

'You know what I mean.'

'If you say so.'

'What do you mean, *futility*?'

'It doesn't matter.'

'No, go on. I'm all ears, Ste. What do you mean by futility?'

'Look, I'm not meaning to upset you here. It's just that I think
I can see some parallels between what your father's written here
and my own work . . .'

'Oh, God.'

'No, seriously.'

'Let's move on, shall we.'

'I'm not meaning to upset you, Ben, honestly.'

'Let's just talk about something else.'

*Pause.*

*Pause.*

*Pause.**

———

* I know this is probably the wrong moment, but you're aware that a pause
is an indefinite amount of time, right? So, repeating the word 'pause' over
and over like this is actually, like, *grammatically incorrect*.

Benny sighs. The sky is darkening now. There's a chill breeze. He roots out the zippable bottoms to his trousers, but can only find one of them (the left one, with the rip from the barbed wire) – the other one has vanished. There's an ache swelling in his forehead. He rubs at his face, massages his eyeballs with his thumbs. He can feel a slight pain in the tip of the index finger on his left hand and on closer examination there's a splinter there, burrowed beneath the skin. He tries to squeeze it out, but it won't budge.

It wasn't until the night before the funeral that Benny found the guidebook. It was up in the loft. Until Amy moved away, Benny's dad hadn't had the luxury of a study, and so he'd kept all kinds of things boxed away up there. On occasion he'd still go up to fetch things and Benny would have to assist him. Benny's role was holding the ladder, plugging in the lamp, perching on the edge of the bathtub until his dad's face appeared at the black hole in the bathroom ceiling, usually with cobwebs coating his hair and beard. His dad had his own system of organisation. He claimed he was the only one who knew the weak spots in the ceiling, the places where, if you trod too heavily, you'd crash through into the bedroom below.

Climbing up alone that night had been a little disconcerting; partly because Mum was asleep at the time, and so Benny had no one to steady the ladder, but also the underlying sense that he was intruding. The study was different, Benny felt at least partly permitted there (perhaps due to the fact it had once been his own bedroom), whereas the loft was home to huge parts of his dad's past: photo albums, journals, flyers from his Free Cymru days. Also paintings, odd bits of furniture – stuff Mum wouldn't let him keep down in the house. Benny found old board games, boxes of VHS tapes. He found a bag of those *Sun* page three calendars Uncle Ian bought him every Christmas with the sole intention of pissing Mum off. The box labelled 'WALK' was over in the corner, behind the artificial Christmas tree. At this point Benny had decided he wasn't going to attempt Offa's Dyke, not now his dad and Cal were both off the scene. He wouldn't have had a clue how to go about something like that alone. But there was the box, sitting waiting for him, a discovery that seemed too fateful to ignore. Especially when the guidebook was there, right at the top. Especially when he found the poem his dad had penned on the inside cover.

Stephen closes the guidebook. He hands it back.

Benny tells him to pack up, they need to keep moving. They need to reach the campsite before dark. This is a priority* above all other priorities.[†]

---

* Another thing: I know how hopeless I was with regard to this stuff, and that it was a godsend, really, your levels of organisation and overall preparedness, and the way you'd think ahead with regards to rationing our resources etc., and so believe me when I say that I don't mean any disrespect here, and am only pointing this out now with a genuine desire for logical consistency, but, I mean, surely *by definition* one can only have a limited number of priorities?

† Also, just another quick note, re: Garth and the Kafka connection. I was a touch flippant, perhaps, when I made that remark about never having read Kafka. Be aware; this doesn't mean I didn't understand him, or that I wasn't at all influenced by his work. I've never been the most well-read person, it's true, but I did learn a lot from Garth during those years we lived together. That's one thing you have to understand about Garth, he was an expert on *everything*. I don't know how he'd found the time to have crammed in so much culture in his two decades on this earth, but he somehow managed to be a connoisseur of every major art form, including literature, film, theatre, music. Then there were the psychology books, the philosophy, the politics . . .

At first I found it all a little intimidating. Here was this incredible artist with this wealth of knowledge and experience, all of which had helped shape a unique viewpoint he was now bringing to his work. When it came to my own artistic process, I'd always just painted what I felt like, regardless of any artistic or cultural context. I just painted what I thought looked *cool*. At first I tried to hide my ignorance – I would disappear into the bathroom each time Garth name-dropped an artist, so that I could look at Google images and memorise a few facts from their Wikipedia page – although Garth soon caught on to this. He told me not to worry. 'Reading all of those books, watching subtitled films, studying all those dead painters, it doesn't make a difference,' he said once, during one of our late-night painting sessions. 'It won't make you a better artist. The reason you're so good is because you're *real*, untouched by all that stuff. You're *pure*. So many of these students are fakes, just taking note of what their lecturers like and imitating it to improve their grades. Just keep doing what you're doing, man. Trust me, I'll clue you in on anything you need to know when it comes to the theoretical stuff.'

And he did. We'd often end up discussing these sorts of things whilst we were painting. Olga wasn't interested, would usually work in the kitchen with her headphones on, but Garth and I would set up together in the living room, and throughout the night he'd regularly take the time to talk to me about his favourite books, films, plays, etc. We'd discuss plots, characters, the various interpretations and philosophical ideas. We'd talk about music too – his favourite composers, his favourite recordings of certain pieces (often he'd end up playing me something from his vinyl collection). He had an eclectic taste, where music was concerned. His upbringing had educated him in the classics (Mozart, Beethoven, Tchaikovsky, Brahms), yet he also adored pop music; his favourites inhabiting that juncture where art, fashion, and music collide (Bowie, Jones, Nico, Gaga).

And then there was *art itself* – his greatest love of all. He could talk art history for hours (and often would, during these sessions) – the various movements, the turning points, the shift from classical painting and sculpture to the modernist abstractions we were seeing play out in our workshops. In the early days, the tutors would sometimes try to correct him in class – assert dominance, so to speak – but Garth never stood for it. Garth could have embarrassed the university's most verbose and stately lecturers with his expertise. We were always trying to get him to take on Coleman in a debate, although he claimed to admire the man too much to ever do such a thing. The sessional tutors were fair game though, and whenever they would clash it would soon become obvious that whichever one of them Garth had decided to argue with didn't stand a chance.

It was different when we were alone. Sure, watching Garth outsmart a tutor in front of a class of students was entertaining, but it was only in our private painting sessions that I'd see the genuine enthusiasm flood forth. It was heart-warming to bear witness to that. Most of the time Garth had this apathetic, detached air about him – wholly cynical of everyone and everything – but during those painting sessions he'd be discussing his theories on the chaos of Pollock, or the balance of humour and horror in Dalí, or the beauty in the simplicity of Creed, and suddenly his whole energy would shift. In those moments he'd transform completely, become an excited schoolboy, bouncing around the room with genuine *glee*. Plus, I got to witness first hand how this passion fed into the work. The more he'd talk about the art he loved, the more heated he'd become in the creation of his own. His method of painting was wholly reliant on 'the chance of the brushstroke', and by the end of these discussions he'd be taking more and more chances, attacking the canvas with increasing levels of violence. Until it all became too much. Then he'd have to stop, stick the kettle on. Ask Olga to roll a spliff, calm us all down.

Of course, it seems a little naive, now I think of it, that I so willingly accepted Garth's opinions on these things as my own, but that's how it played out. To me the most important movements became those that put forth the idea of concept over form – i.e. Pluralism, Dadaism, Abstract Expressionism. To me, the three most important events of the twentieth century became Duchamp's urinal, Warhol's soup tin, and Emin's unmade bed. To me, Hirst was a sell-out. Bacon was a god. Kafka's *The Castle* was the greatest novel of the last hundred years, Tchaikovsky's *Symphony No.6* the best piece of music. *Hamlet* became my favourite play, *Un Chien Andalou* my favourite film. Garth's influence also became more and more apparent in my own creative work. Hence Frank. Hence *Doomed Youth Pt 1–7*, etc., etc.

And it turned out Garth was right. It didn't matter that I was wholly undereducated in this stuff. I'd still join in with the discussions in class, still spout opinions in a way that suggested a certain level of cultural competence, even if these opinions weren't wholly my own. And no one seemed to notice. Not the teachers or the other students – not even Olga (or if she did, she never mentioned it). If I'm honest, pretty much all of my cultural knowledge came second-hand through Garth. 'Fake it till you make it,' that's what he told me once, as we were painting together. And so, I did. And, at the time, that was good enough.

It's easier now, of course, to look back with a bit of perspective – see how much I must have missed out on. See how maybe it would have made for a more fulfilling existence if I'd actually gone ahead and *engaged* with this stuff, formed a few opinions of my own. It's something I have plenty of now: perspective. I guess that's one of the horrible ironies of the whole transcendental experience – you never really get to appreciate things with the clarity of true hindsight until it's all over and done with. At which point, of course, it's too late to actually *do* anything about it.

# XVIII

*Quad bikes – Uphill – More mountains – Various
rituals – Chewing gum – Pale Stephen – Phlegm
– Autopilot – Sex on the brain – Farmer's field –
Dog – Passing truck – A break for freedom –
An empty inhaler.*

They cross the main road and follow a country lane. The rest of
the day's route doesn't seem too problematic* according to the
map, minimal wavy lines suggesting nothing too steep in terms
of the gradient of the terrain. Further down the lane they pass
a couple of bungalows and Benny feels a wave of regret about
what happened up at the restaurant. Maybe Stephen was right,
maybe they should have just tried knocking and asking for water.
Maybe it was avoidable, smashing that fence panel. Still, it was
a good way of releasing some tension. It felt like a test of some
kind, obtaining the water. After the lack of fire that first night,
then his failure to scatter the ashes up on Jubilee Tower, it felt
good to finally succeed at something.

The lane ends at a padlocked gate, an enormous sheet-metal
barn in the field beyond, with a couple of muddied quad bikes
chained out front. Alongside is a pathway, leading to a large
farmhouse. Stephen jokes that maybe they should continue with
their crime wave and steal the bikes. It would certainly speed
things up.

Benny spots a stile and they climb over, ascend through a field
of knee-high grass. With this new steepness come the old familiar
aches, the slow tearing of muscles in their thighs and shoulders.
Just when they think they're reaching the top of the hill there's

---

* You're using my word!

another stile, another incline. Beyond that, another. The path winds through patches of heather and fern bushes. It soon becomes apparent that these aren't a mere succession of hills – they're climbing another mountain. Despite the lack of wavy lines in the guidebook, today's mountain range hasn't quite finished with them, probably won't for the next few hours. Benny focuses on his thighs, his legs tearing through the grass, only occasionally glancing up at the expanse of hill ahead.

There are regular stiles along this part of the trail and each time they reach one Stephen asks to stop for a break. This becomes routine; Stephen continually de-packing, then having to re-pack after each break. It requires more energy overall, although no matter how many times Benny explains this to him, Stephen still goes ahead and unbuckles his shoulder straps, enjoys the short-lived burst of relief. Maybe this brief sensation of lightness is important to him, psychologically. He must attain enough satisfaction to make it worth his while. There are rituals to everything. Benny, for example, keeps catching himself reaching for his back pocket, seeking out his tobacco tin, checking the final cigarette is still stowed away inside. He also chews gum. For the last few months of their relationship Sam had him on nicotine gum and, although he hated it at the time (still longed for the process of rolling and smoking), he did find that it eased his headaches a little. Here he just has Wrigley's Extra, but he chews it anyway. He's hoping there'll be enough associations there to trick his body into believing he's offering it some sort of nicotine-based relief.

Benny's current list of ailments goes as follows: there are the usual aches in his thighs, his hamstrings, his lower back, his upper back, his neck. There are the blisters on his heels and his toes, the balls of his feet. The cut on his shin from the barbed wire has now faded to a dull, sticky throb that merges with the other pains, i.e. the bramble scratches, the nettle stings, the chafing of his boots. There's the splinter from the fence in the index finger of his left hand. There's the hot pulse of the sunburn on his arms and legs and neck and face and especially on his forehead, in the peaks of his receded hairline (as well as a piercing burn on the little bald spot at the crown). Plus there's his stomach, the noodles squirming away in there, the occasional wave of nausea that comes as a result of three days without a proper meal.

After a while Stephen asks for more ibuprofen.* Benny obliges. They're within the six hours they should wait between doses, but what does it matter? Stephen seems OK. He doesn't appear to be having any adverse side effects.† Sure, there's his paleness, his lack of appetite, his limping, his breathing troubles, but he was suffering all of these ailments already. Maybe more ibuprofen will help. Maybe it will make all the difference in getting them to Llandegla before nightfall.

The ibuprofen makes no difference. Stephen's losing colour at the same rate as the sky, which by this point has darkened under a blanket of grey cloud. It looks like it could rain again at any moment. Stephen keeps coughing, sniffing, *hoik*ing wads of phlegm onto the grass. Stephen's never made it through that initial wall of pain and exhaustion. It's been two and a half days now – Benny's sure he's got to break through soon. They just need to keep going.

They stop at the next stile and Stephen collapses against it, mouth open. A string of white saliva bungees down and hangs there for a moment, connecting his lips to the stile's wooden step.

He spits, *hoik*s, spits again. He mumbles something.

'What?'

'It's the noodles.'

'What's the noodles?'

'My stomach, man. Shouldn't have walked straight after eating.'

'I don't think it's the noodles, Ste. You hardly even touched them.'

---

* I'm pretty sure that by this point ibuprofen was the only thing keeping me going. That stuff was amazing, man. We should have been dosing up on it that entire trip.

† Although, thinking about it now – are there any digestion issues listed in those side effects? Is there any chance the ibuprofen could have played a part in the eventual voiding-of-my-bowels on World's End the next day? Because trust me, Ben, if so there's no way I should have touched the stuff. That was one humiliation I could have done without.

'It's the . . .' *burp*, '. . . noodles, man, I'm telling you.'

'Maybe they're just digesting. The ibuprofen will kick in soon.'

'You sure there's no meat in them?'

'I'm sure.'

'I react badly to meat. Can't digest it any more.'

'There's no meat, Ste. You'll be fine.'

'It's feeling *wrong*, man. It's just feeling wrong in there.'

'Let's keep on, we'll be there soon. I promise.

'I can't do it, man. I just can't.'

'We'll be over the worst of it soon. Just another half a mile or so, then it's all downhill from there.'*

Stephen spends most of the next hour hunched, stumbling along. He nurses his stomach with both hands, occasionally spitting or *hoik*ing wads of phlegm onto the path. Soon his *hoik*ing isn't powerful enough. All he can manage is a slight dribble that runs down the front of his shirt.

They descend into a valley. There's a lake to their left, skirted by a patch of woodland. To their right is some sort of radio tower, a huge metal spike aimed at the thick grey sky. There they sit, sip from their flasks. Benny uses the landmarks to locate their position on the map. He tries to show Stephen, but Ste remains balled, head-in-hands, rocking on his heels.

Benny allows a few more minutes' break before they continue. They pass along a dirt road, which soon joins a narrow country lane, hedges on each side. Occasionally a car approaches and

---

* TBH, that afternoon is all a bit of a blur. Which is odd, really, isn't it, given that recollection is pretty much all I've got right now, in terms of a continued existence? I know my stomach was churning more and more as the day wore on, although the actual physical sensation is now impossible to recall. I guess pain can be like that, it's the most awful thing imaginable when you're going through it, yet any memory of it will fade given time. All I can really remember are my *thoughts* on the pain, the predominant one being that I was going to die. And don't get me wrong, Ben, these aren't the melodramatic imaginings of the weak, ill-prepared caricature you're painting me as here. I mean it. Whatever was happening in my stomach that afternoon, it felt *terminal*.

they have to back against the hedge, allow space for it to pass. By now Benny is on autopilot, numb to the pain, oblivious to the rhythm of walking. It's something his body just does, without any thought required. The same cannot be said for Stephen, whose skin has faded to near-ghostly levels of paleness. He's sweating. His breathing is heavy. He's still taking his weight on his left leg, which causes his right trainer to occasionally scuff the tarmac. Each time this happens he yelps at the pain in his ankle.

Benny asks if he's OK. Stephen nods. Benny says they can't stop for a break, not on a road like this – where would they even sit? Stephen nods again.

The road bends to the right. Benny spots a stile in the hedge on the other side, the acorn plaque marking their way. They cross the road and Stephen slumps against the stile, head bowed. He doesn't bother removing his pack this time, just lies there, hunched under its weight. Benny waits there beside him, the only sound being the occasional roar of a passing car. The surrounding fields seem so quiet. There hasn't been any baaing for ages now.

'Can we . . .' *Pant.* 'Can we talk about something, man?'

'What?'

'I don't know.' *Pant. Pant.* 'Anything.' *Pant. Pant.* 'I think it's making it worse, this silence.' *Pant. Pant. Pant.* 'If I could just take my mind off my stomach, you know?'

They continue across the next field. Benny doesn't talk. What's the point? Going over the same old shit, time and time again. Maybe they could play a game, I Spy or something, would that make Stephen happy? Would that keep him from complaining?* What a shit game. Benny never liked it, even as a child. And anyway, what would they be able to spy, with their 'little eyes'? The sun? Grass? Clouds?†

---

* Or you could have just, like, *talked* to me.

† I mean, was that really too much to ask, Ben? That you *talk to me*?

Instead Benny thinks about sex.* This is a technique he uses when he's on the phones at work, to help pass the time. He responds to his calls on autopilot whilst his mind goes off somewhere else, into some imagined sexual encounter. Most of the calls are routine anyway – by now he's used to the various quirks of the claims system, and if it's something more difficult he can always pass it over to a supervisor. Often he finds he doesn't even have to think about what he's doing. So instead he imagines Sam. It sounds seedy but it isn't, not really.† He just likes to remember their good times together, and where's the harm in that? It's skin he thinks of mostly, the feel of Sam's skin against his. Her body was always so much warmer than his (another way she was like a cat – she seemed to *radiate* heat) and it's nice, sometimes, to summon that warmth. Usually these thoughts lead to others, of course. Sometimes he plays out whole sexual encounters (whether real or imagined). Sometimes he maps out her entire body in his mind, each mound and crevice.‡ He has plenty of material from that first year, when sex was pretty much all they did together.

He thinks about this stuff when he's masturbating too, although then he finds it helps if he pretends he and Sam are still together, as that way he can avoid that horrible swelling in his chest like his heart's about to rupture. Sam is all Benny has to go on, in terms of sexual experience. Sure, there's porn, but he finds that it's lost its edge now since experiencing the real thing. He can't seem to make the necessary leap, transport himself into the scene. He can't think of porn as anything but manufactured, can't imagine that he's anywhere but in his own bedroom, lying back on his own, single bed, dick in hand. He still resorts to it, night after night, but usually it's not the porn itself that's turning him on, but rather the *thought* of porn. He imagines he's watching it with Sam (which is something they used to do in the early days) and that *she's* getting off on it. And it's this – the thought of

---

* Of course.
† If you say so, Ben.
‡ *Crevice?*

Sam's enjoyment of the porn (her cries of pleasure, her eyes ravenous) – that brings Benny to a climax.

Benny tries not to think about later, when the passion began to dwindle. Because the truth is Benny and Sam's sex life wasn't the constant fuck-fest he likes to pretend it was. This hypersexualised, cat-like, nympho of his fantasies doesn't amount to much in the long run because he knows it's not the real Sam. Sure, there *was* a time Sam enjoyed sex, but this was when they were first going out. It was much more intense then and, looking back, it's easy to see how this momentum was unsustainable. Even though Benny likes to pretend otherwise, the passionate stage of their relationship burnt out before they'd even reached their one-year anniversary. At the time Benny attributed this to bad timing. The workload was picking up at uni and they both had to knuckle down (less sex, more study). They were virgins when they'd met; they'd admitted this to each other on that first date, walking back from the Odeon. They'd become overexcited at the possibilities of a sex life. They'd binged – now they had to ease off a little. As far as Benny was concerned, there was no reason things couldn't heat up again once the exam period was over.

But he was wrong. At the end of the semester Sam went back to Ireland for a few weeks and when she returned things weren't the same. This was when all the healthy lifestyle stuff started – the runs, the Instagram photos, the charcoal stick in her water bottle. She gave up drinking and smoking weed. Sure, they'd still have sex once in a while, but Benny could tell she wasn't into it. He was forced to take on the role of instigator and, over time, increasingly felt like he was pestering her. Sam acted like nothing was wrong, repeatedly claimed she was just tired or had a headache, but Benny found himself being invited to stay less and less. It's hard for Benny to think back over this stuff now because of how strongly his own libido is tied to his memory of Sam. For the sake of his own masturbation-as-coping-mechanism he can't allow himself to give too much thought to the tired, headache-prone Sam that refused his advances, has to instead imagine Sam as that same hungry-for-sex deviant she was when they first met. Because without this Benny can't masturbate, and often this is his only way of achieving sleep. And if he can't sleep then he just lies there, The Fog descending, and all the stuff he's trying his best to avoid thinking about comes tumbling down with it.*

It's nearly six o'clock by the time they arrive at the farm at the bottom of the valley. A rusty gate with a sign, handwritten and laminated: 'PLEASE **CLOSE** BEHIND YOU'. The laminate has bubbled and the ink has run at the bottom, but the message is still clear enough and Benny's sure to carry out the instruction, making a big deal of rattling the lock in place. They need to present themselves as good, Countryside Code-abiding ramblers, especially when they're entering private land.

Benny tries to maintain a steady pace as they pass through the farm. It's hard with Stephen there, Benny finds himself

---

\* It's time for that word again, Ben. ('Give me a P . . .' / '**P!**' / 'Give me an R . . .' / '**R!**' / 'Give me an O . . .' / '**O!**') This is **P R O B L E M A T I C**. Without even delving into the obviously unhealthy psychological aspects of your need for masturbatory endorphin kicks, let's just get straight to the glaring misogyny on display here: it's really *not OK* for you to think about Sam in this way. I get that you're hurting, Ben, I really do, but Sam was (is!) a human being, deserving of respect. She is *not* a fucking *SEX DOLL*. I mean it, man, this is a dark, dark path you're treading here, the sort of Cal-like behaviour I know you're too good for. I mean, can you not hear how you sound when you spout this stuff? Can you not appreciate how fucking *offensive* it is?

You always had a slight tendency towards that hetero-male perviness, though. I remember when you came to visit me in London – how you stared at Olga all night (you were still dating Sam back then, too). You thought no one could tell, but you'd had a few drinks by that point and it was obvious that you couldn't take your eyes off her. Garth noticed too, I'm sure of it. It was embarrassing. But even back then I would make excuses for you. I blamed the alcohol. I blamed Cal's influence (I thought his constant objectification of women must have rubbed off on you over the years). I can see now how generous this was, on my part – justifying your failings this way. I should have called you out on this stuff more.

Still, on the walk you weren't drunk, Ben. Cal had been off the scene for months. Not only that, but we'd both borne witness to where this sort of misogynistic objectification could lead.

By then you should have known better, man.

constantly having to stop, wait for him to catch up. There's a house up ahead, beside it a barn with a tractor and a couple of trucks outside. In Benny's imagination the farmer who lives here varies from a pleasant Old McDonald type, who invites them in for tea and sponge cake, to a shotgun-wielding maniac, who only speaks Welsh and can't understand the words 'public' and 'footpath', only the words 'trespassers' and 'die'. It's only when they're a bit nearer that it becomes clear the farmhouse is abandoned. One of the windows is smashed and the vehicles outside are old and rusted and lacking enough wheels to be deemed roadworthy.

Benny waits for a comment from Stephen, something about how even the farms out here have fallen victim to government cuts, how the evils of capitalism will one day be the death of them all, etc., etc., but Stephen doesn't say anything. He's too busy concentrating on walking and breathing. Right now, this appears to require all of his concentration.

'You OK, Ste?'
*Pant. Pant. Pant. Pant. Pant.*

Suddenly a dog scampers out from behind the farmhouse, makes a beeline for them. It's hard to tell what breed of dog it is. One of those stocky, fierce-looking types, probably a staffie or a pit or a mongrel mix of the two. It's only small (about half the size of what Samson used to be) but it's wild-looking, its skin black, tight against bone and muscle. Its jaw is fixed into a constant, shark-like smile. Something flaps from its teeth as it runs, long and black, like an eel. As it gets closer Benny realises it's a strip of tyre, torn from one of the trucks.

The dog gets to within a few metres of them, then stops on the path ahead. It sits there, panting, watching them approach. The strip of tyre dangles there, like a black tongue. Stephen isn't paying attention and Benny has to pat him on the shoulder, point out to him what's there, waiting for them on the path ahead. Stephen halts the moment he sees it. He just stands there, glaring. Benny stops too. After a minute or two he tells Stephen it's probably not the best idea, you know, for the two of them to stand there, staring it out. Best to just keep walking. Ignore it.

They continue along the path. Benny crosses to Stephen's right, puts himself between Stephen and the dog. Stephen breathes, concentrates on his feet. The dog watches as they approach. It yawns, allows the tyre to fall to the grass. It pants.

It's only once they've passed that the dog stands up again.

It begins to follow.

'Don't panic.'

'I'm not.' *Pant. Pant.*

'It's OK.'

'I know.' *Pant. Pant.* 'I'm fine.'

'Just keep walking. We just need to keep walking.'

The dog crosses over to Stephen, trots alongside him. It sniffs at his pack. Its teeth are yellow in parts, black in others, gums a violent red. Its forehead is speckled with scars, black holes that could be old cigarette burns. As soon as it notices Benny looking, the dog lets out a bark. Stephen yelps in response. Benny turns away, keeps focused on the stile ahead.

The dog barks again, louder this time, obscene in the silence of the farmer's field. Benny thinks back to the Countryside Code: 'Keep all dogs under effective control.' By now Benny wants a farmer to appear. Or anyone in fact – a day-tripper, a park ranger – anyone who's able to distract this creature long enough to allow them to get away.

There's another gate at the edge of the field and Stephen must find some extra burst of energy because as soon as he spots it he speeds up, powers on towards it. Benny holds back. He thinks maybe the dog will stay with him. Maybe he can keep it occupied whilst Stephen makes his escape (if anyone's going to have to fight this thing, he'd rather it was him than Ste).

But it's useless; the dog's clearly much more interested in Stephen than Benny. It sniffs at his pack, lets out another bark. It's drooling now, strands of saliva dangling as it trots.

—

'Nearly there, Ste. *Nearly there.*'

Stephen arrives at the gate. His hands shake as he fiddles with the lock. The bolt must be stiff because he tugs and tugs but he can't seem to open it. Benny waits a good distance away. He doesn't want to overcrowd the dog. He remembers this from when Samson was younger, how reactive dogs can be to body language, how susceptible they are to changes in people's moods. He calls over for Stephen to take it easy. Slow and careful, no sudden movements. The whole time the dog just sits there, at Stephen's feet, growling.

Stephen hammers the bolt with the heel of his hand and finally it jolts free. He opens the gate a crack, just enough to edge through, making sure not to allow the dog enough of an opening to follow. Only then does Benny approach. He skirts the dog and follows Stephen through the gate. The whole time the dog just sits there – watching, drooling. Benny shuts the gate. The dog remains still. It's only when the bolt clanks back into place that it finally reacts – a wild eruption of barking and snapping and leaping up at them. Benny and Stephen both jerk back instinctively. It comes as a shock, this outburst of violence. It's like a switch has been flicked and suddenly this torrent of pure hatred has come tearing forth. Benny can see it in the dog's eyes.

Stephen asks if they can please leave now.

The two of them hurry up the path, the dog still barking behind them.

'That was close, man. Too close.'

'I know.'

'That was insane! Fucking *insane!*'

'I know.'

'It shouldn't be so dangerous, should it? Just taking a walk in the countryside?'

'I know.'

'That thing would have had us, man. Would have torn us to shreds!'

'I know.'

—

Stephen is shaking. He rubs his eyes. He's not necessarily crying – it's possible his eyes are just watering due to his various ailments.

After a few minutes the barking stops. They slow to a walking pace again.

Another few minutes and Stephen's tugging at Benny's sleeve, motioning with his eyes to the ground.

There's the dog, trotting alongside them.

'This is a joke, man. This is someone's idea of a joke.'

'Must be a hole in the fence or something. Just keep walking. We'll come to another gate soon.'

'I can't see one.'

'Just keep walking.'

*Pause.*

'But what if . . .'

'Don't panic. Just ignore it.'

'OK.'

'Don't look at it either, look ahead. Just keep walking. Slowly. Like with the cows.'

'We ran from the cows.'

'True, yes. OK. Fair enough. But don't run this time. Just keep walking. If we run it'll only get it excited.'

'It's already pretty excited, man. Did you *hear* it back there?'

'Just listen to me, Ste, all right? Just don't run, OK? Whatever you do, *don't run.*'

Benny doesn't remember such hostility from the local wildlife back when he used to walk with his dad and Uncle Ian. The sheep, the cows, the dogs – as far as he remembers, there weren't ever any issues with any of them. Maybe this was his father's influence. Benny's dad was good with animals, especially dogs, with whom he seemed to have some deeper level of communication. It was him who had – without any prompting from the rest of them, without even *telling them* – gone down to the shelter and picked up Samson. And, although it was Mum who'd claimed ownership and named him, it was Benny's dad who would always take him out for his walks, twice a day. It was his dad who would eventually bury Samson as well, at the bottom of the garden, when his arthritis got too much and they had to put him down. He dug the hole alone, a mammoth task that Benny later felt guilty for not helping with.

At the far side of the field the grass has worn away into a makeshift dirt road. Benny remembers this road from the guide-book – there are no acorn signs as far as he can see, but they take a right here, the path veering west for the next half a mile. Surrounding them are open fields, nothing in the way of discernible landmarks. Further up, the grass is balding away entirely and soon enough they're walking along another dirt road.

The dog is still beside them. The clacking of its claws accompanying their every step.

'I can't, man.'
  'I know.'
  'I just . . . can't.'
  'I know.'
  'It keeps staring at me.'
  'Just keep walking, Ste. Keep walking.'

A vehicle appears on the horizon. At first Benny has to squint to see it, but it's travelling at a decent speed and is soon identifiable as a truck, light grey in colour, with mud splattered up the sides. The inhabitants are impossible to make out, due to the reflection of the sun on the windscreen. Stephen says they should flag it down for help. Benny laughs. What could they say? *Can you take this dog off us?*

Keep walking, Benny says. It'll be OK. The dog'll get bored and leave. Eventually.

They step aside as the truck speeds past. The dog turns, bounds after it. It charges alongside, barking and snapping at the wheels. Then suddenly it begins to gyrate, its head twisting, around and around and around and around and with a certain amount of horror Benny realises the dog has bitten into one of the truck's tyres. The truck's not stopping. The dog isn't letting go. It just keeps spinning.

Benny turns to Stephen. The two of them share a look.

'Run.'

Neither speaks. The only sounds are those of their thudding boots and bouncing packs, their heavy breathing. Running exaggerates every ailment in Benny's body. The aches in his legs and the rub of the shoulder straps and the butting of the pack against his spine. But still, he keeps going. He doesn't stop, not even when they've crossed over a cattle grid, not even when they've turned off through a gate and reached the cover of some trees.

He only stops when he hears Stephen fall. It's a horrible succession of sounds: Ste's cry, the *crunch* as he hits the ground, the gurgling moan as he tries to communicate this new level of pain and exhaustion. Benny hurries back to him, kneels at his side. Stephen is panting. His fringe is stuck flat to his head. Sweat streaks down his face. He's searching his pockets, a panicked expression on him now.

Benny asks what he's looking for, but he doesn't answer. He finds it eventually: his inhaler.

He rattles it, presses it to his lips, breathes in. But there's nothing; no *hiccchhht*, no sound at all. His eyes widen in horror.

He tries again. Nothing.

'I'm . . .' *Pant. Pant.* 'I'm out, man.'

'Out?'

'My . . .' *Pant. Pant. Pant.* 'My inhaler . . .'

'You've run out of inhaler?'

'It's gone.' *Pant. Pant.*

'I didn't know you *could* run out of inhaler.'

'It's all gone, man.' *Pant. Pant. Pant.* 'What am I going to do?' *Pant. Pant. Pant. Pant. Pant.*

# XIX

*Pat on the back – Return of the dog – The last few fields – Bending river – Corn – Crickets – B&B – Graveyard – Sunday opening hours – Girl in tutu – Papier-mâché – Unconscious Stephen – A concerned citizen.*

They wait another half an hour in that small patch of woodland outside of Llandegla. Stephen spends most of the time on all fours, wheezing. There's a rattle in his throat. Every thirty seconds or so he tries to *hoik* the phlegm free, but it isn't working. Benny kneels beside him, slaps him on the back. He's aggressive at first, thinking it might help dislodge the mucus, but after a while it begins to feel as if he's literally hitting Stephen whilst he's down, so he softens his touch. He pats the spot between Stephen's shoulder blades in a manner that he hopes is at least somewhat reassuring.

After a while this also feels inappropriate, so Benny relocates to the tree opposite. He sits with his back against it, sipping from his flask. He removes the final cigarette from his tobacco tin and places it between his lips. Not to smoke – not yet – just to hold there. Pretend.

Soon the dog shows up again. It stands there panting for a few seconds, staring at the hunched figure of Stephen with what seems like genuine concern. Then it goes over and sits beside him, its head resting upon its paws. There's a new scratch on its forehead – a result of its altercation with the truck – but aside from that the dog seems relatively unharmed.

Stephen's wheezing slows. Eventually it stops. He sits up, cross-legged, his hands covering his face.

—

'You OK?' *Pause.* 'Ste?' *Pause.* 'You OK?' *Pause.* 'You good to go?'

Eventually Stephen nods. He climbs to his feet. Benny asks a few more times if he's OK and Stephen nods again. Benny asks if he's able to keep walking and Stephen gives a half-hearted thumbs up, and so Benny helps him get the pack back onto his shoulders and the two of them follow the trail south, out of the trees and across another field.

The sun is setting now and Benny keeps telling Stephen this is it, the final few fields that'll lead them into Llandegla. According to the map, there's a river that cuts across their path and once they reach the footbridge that crosses this river, they're pretty much there. Stephen's face remains locked in frowned concentration. His breaths are drawn out, still with that rattle of phlegm. The dog still trots along beside them. Stephen hasn't mentioned the dog and Benny half considers that maybe he hasn't noticed it yet.

They reach the bridge, pass over the river. They cross a field. Just through the trees at the far side there's another bridge. Beyond that, another. Benny says he must have miscalculated. The river must snake a bit before they reach the town. But still, the fact that they're at the river is a good thing – it means they'll reach Llandegla any minute. They'll soon be at the campsite, luxuriating in the facilities (shower and a shit . . . shower and a shit . . . shower and a shit . . .).

Benny asks if Stephen wants to talk. Maybe they could discuss people from school again. He brings up the gym-obsessed guy from Stephen's maths class. He namedrops the girl who went to Ibiza, the other girl who's always changing her Facebook relationship status. He even brings up Cal. But Stephen doesn't give anything in the way of a response. He just keeps shuffling along, his heavy breaths accompanying the panting of the dog.

*Pant.*      *Pant.*        *Pant.*        *Pant.*
*Pant.*      *Pant.*        *Pant.*        *Pant.*

—

The next bridge leads into a field of knee-high corn. By this point the sun is sinking into the trees behind. Furred corn-tops blaze in the orange light. A rattling surrounds them, as if the field is infested with sets of tiny maracas. The path is overgrown with long grass and nettles and scatterings of buttercups and it's not until a little further on that Benny realises he can actually *see* the crickets, nestled there amongst the vegetation. They're bigger than he'd thought, darker too, like elongated cockroaches. Some hop from stalk to stalk, others just cling there bobbing in the breeze. Benny wonders if these are in fact crickets, or maybe grasshoppers . . . and what's the difference, anyway? He asks this out loud, on the off-chance Stephen knows the answer, but when he turns back, he finds Stephen and the dog are gone.

Benny scans the meadow. He spots them back at the bridge. Stephen is huddled, head in hands again. The dog beside him, waiting.

'You OK?' *Pause.* *[Rustling of grass.]* 'Ste?' *Pause.* *[Rustling of grass.]* 'We need to keep on, the sun's setting.' *Pause.* 'We need to keep moving.' *Pause.* 'Come on, Ste, not much further now.' *Pause.* 'There's proper facilities at this place. Showers. Toilets. Shit and a shower, that's what you need. Another intake of noodles.' *Pause.* 'We can rest as soon as we get there, I promise.' *Pause.* 'Maybe I can even get a fire going. You're allowed, in these places, sometimes.' *Pause.* 'Ste?'
*Pause.*

Benny retrieves the guidebook. He double-checks the map. He seems to remember there being other accommodation in Llandegla, apart from the campsite. And he's right, there's a blue bed there, right in the centre of the gathering of grey rectangles that represent the rest of the town. He checks the key, confirms this means what he thinks it means: a B&B.

He sits beside Stephen, points this out to him on the map. Maybe they can treat themselves tonight, book a room? Forget the campsite and its shower cubicles – maybe they sleep in a bed for a change? Have a bath?

The dog's ears prick up at this. (*Not you*, Benny thinks.) Stephen raises his head a moment later. His eyes are bloodshot, glassy from tears.

He nods, spits, then nods again.

'A bath would be n-nice, man.'

And so, this becomes their new mantra: *A bath and a bed*. And for now, it's enough to get Stephen up and walking again. Which is enough, in turn, to make the dog get up and follow. The three of them skirt the cornfield for another ten minutes before arriving at a passageway, a pebbled path with hedges either side. This is it, Benny says, they're here, they're finally here. And this time he's right – the passage leads right out into the centre of town.

They arrive at a T-junction, the road splitting off at either side. Ahead is a large stone building with a bright-yellow door, a clock built into the wall above like the steeple of a church. Benny remembers a church from the guidebook (represented by a little blue cross). He thinks this must be it. He soon realises he's wrong – across the road is the actual church, a small medieval building, surrounded by gnarly old trees. There's a graveyard out front and the gravestones look medieval too – lopsided crosses and stone slabs, the epitaphs faded or obscured by moss. There are a few over in the corner that look more modern; black and white marble, gold lettering, bunches of fresh flowers potted at the base. Surrounding the churchyard is a stone wall, against which Stephen is already leaning. He *hoik*s a wad of phlegm onto the ground. The dog sniffs at it.

Benny crosses to the building opposite. He wonders if this corresponds to the other symbol he remembers from the guide-book; a little blue envelope that represents a post office. He was hoping it might also be a shop, somewhere he could stock up on cigarettes and ibuprofen. He thought maybe they could pick up some beers too, that'd cheer Stephen up. As he approaches, he sees that he's right, it *is* also a shop – he can see shelves of fruit and veg inside, as well as a cash machine in the far corner. There's a sign beside the yellow door that says something in Welsh, beneath it: 'Community Shop'. Beneath that there's another sign: 'Closed'.

Benny steps back, squints up at the clock. It's ten past eight. It's Sunday. Of course it's closed. *Everything* will be closed.

When he turns back there's a young girl there, leaning against the stone wall of the church. She's wearing a parka coat, the underskirt of a pink tutu pluming beneath. She's holding a tray with what looks like some sort of large cake on it, smeared with red icing. She stands perfectly still, glaring open-mouthed at Stephen. From the look of horror on her face you'd expect Stephen to be some kind of zombie, recently unearthed from the graveyard. Which, to be fair, is a pretty apt comparison, now Benny thinks of it. Stephen is wheezing, sweating. His hair is greased down the side of his face, glistening like blood. The girl's eyes flit to the dog, then back to Stephen.

Stephen turns, presses his back against the wall, then lowers himself into a sitting position. He tilts his head back, face to the sky, offers a series of coughs to the clouds above, then slumps forwards, chin to chest. The girl keeps on staring.

Stephen pats his pockets, roots out his inhaler. Three times he tries to summon a *hiccchhht* from it, before giving up, tossing it to the ground.

The girl turns to Benny. She closes her mouth, frowns. Benny smiles (he doesn't know what else to do). He gives her a thumbs up.

She turns the other way and stares across the street, into the distance.

'Right, Ste, I'm going to try and find the B&B. You stay here, OK? Guard the packs.' *Pause.* 'OK?' *Pause.* 'Ste?'

*Pause.*

Benny unclips his pack, lets it slip to the ground. He stretches. His shoulders have numbed over the past few hours and it's only now he's free of the pack that the cramp begins to surge in his spine. The dog sits beside Stephen, as if guarding him. Benny's unsure whether it's a good idea, leaving Stephen here with this unpredictable dog and a young girl, but right now he's not sure what else to do. He roots out the guidebook, double-checks the location of the B&B, then limps off up the road to find it.

There's not much to the town, just a few rows of terraced houses, all built from the same grey stone as the shop and the church. The streets are lined with hedges, all neatly trimmed. There's no litter, no gum on the pavement. Everything's pristine and quaint in a way that reminds Benny of the towns from his uncle's train sets. He keeps an eye out, but all the houses are much the same and he can't see any signs or plaques or anything else that might indicate a B&B.

Beyond the terraces are a couple of detached buildings that look as if they might be part of a farm. Beyond that: nothing, just a hedge-lined country lane. Benny turns back, retraces his steps, this time stopping to examine each house as he passes. It's only on a second lap that he notices one has a small, handwritten sign in a front window – some unintelligible Welsh words and 'Bed and Breakfast' written beneath. Below that, there's a propped-up piece of card – more Welsh and then the words: 'No Rooms Available'.

Benny jogs back around to the church. The little girl has shifted along the wall, away from Stephen and the dog. It's only now that he realises it's not a cake that she's holding, but rather a papier-mâché volcano; that the splattered red on top isn't icing, but paint, representing the lava. Stephen is slumped on the ground now, a little further along from where Benny left him. His head is tipped forwards, chin to chest. There are white streams of saliva down the front of his shirt and trousers and a frothy puddle on the pavement, a mixture of ice cream and undigested noodle strands. The dog licks at it.

Benny sits down next to Stephen. His shoulders are still aching. There's a swelling in his thighs, an itchy stinging on his shins, the culmination of three days' worth of sunburn and nettle stings. The headache is getting worse now and he wonders if there's anywhere he can get cigarettes, maybe a pub with one of those old-fashioned cigarette vending machines or something. Then he remembers he has no change and that those machines aren't likely to take card payments and he sighs and tries to imagine the word '**A I L M E N T S**' spread out before him in huge black letters, as if this will in some way diminish his suffering.

Suddenly the girl hurries up the street, volcano raised overhead. A man is approaching. He's tall, well built, wearing one of those thick woollen jumpers with the arm patches. His hair is blonde and shoulder length, parted at the side in a way that shows off a perfect hairline. The man kneels, embraces the girl (careful to avoid crushing the volcano) then stands there, one hand on her shoulder, staring over. The girl points to Benny and the man squints, frowns. He kneels and says something to her, only partly audible (and Welsh, by the sounds of it), and she nods, remains where she's standing as the man approaches.

Benny shakes Stephen. He hisses for him to wake up, but there's no response.

The dog begins to growl.

'You OK there, fellas?'

'Hmm?'

'Y'alright?'

'Yeah . . . um, fine thanks.'

*Pause.*

'Your friend looks in a bad way, there . . .'

'He's fine.'

'You sure?'

'He's just tired, that's all. We've been walking all day.'

*Pause.*

'You . . . erm . . . doing a trail or something?'

'The dyke.'

'The . . .?'

'Offa's Dyke.'

'Oh yeah, I know the dyke.' *Pause.* 'How's it going?'

'It's OK.'

'Yeah?'

'It's good.'

'Nice route?'

'Yeah.'

'Where you start from?'

'Prestatyn.'

'Right.' *Pause.* 'Mountain range today then, was it? Moel Famau?'

'That's right, yeah.'

'Still a long way to go, then.'

'Yep.'

*Grrrrrr.*

'Your . . . um . . . your *dog* doing it with you?'

'No.'

'Not too friendly, is he?'

'No.'

'He's looking in a bit of a bad way, too . . .'

'It isn't ours.'

'Eh?'

'The dog. It's not ours.'

'Oh, right. Whose is he?'

'Don't know. Just started following us.'

'Really?'

'Yeah, a few fields back.'

'Wow. Strange.'

*Pause.*

'We're not homeless, if that's what you're thinking.'

'Eh?'

'We're just a bit dirty. You know, from all the camping and that.'

'Yeah, I figured.'

'And the dog isn't ours.'

'Right.' *Pause.* 'I wasn't . . . erm, I mean . . . it didn't even occur to me that you might be *homeless* . . .'

'Well, good. Because we're not.'

'Right.'

'In fact, we're going over to the campsite in a minute.'

'The old Higgins place you mean?'

'I don't know what it's called. It's just up the road . . .'

'Sorry to be the bearer of bad news here, but if it's the Higgins place you're after, I think you'll find it closed. Has been for a couple of years now.'

'Oh.'

'They used to run a farm shop out of there too, but the recession hit them pretty hard, I think.'

'Right . . . of course. Brilliant.' *Pause.* 'Well, I guess we'll find somewhere else then.'

'You got somewhere in mind?'

'I don't know. Somewhere.'

'I'd say come back to ours, but my daughter, she's a bit scared of dogs, y'know?'

'It's not our dog.'

'Right. But still . . .'

'And thanks, but we don't need your help. We'll be fine. Don't worry.'

'You sure?'

'I'm certain.'

*Pause.*

'Look, I'm just checking you're OK here. You seem a little agitated. And your friend, he's . . .'

'He's fine.'

'He doesn't *look* fine.'

'He's just tired. He needs some rest.'

'Yeah?' *Pause.* 'Tell you what, why don't you come back to the house. You can rest up there. It'll be getting dark soon.'

'No, we're fine. Thanks.'

'You could camp on our lawn, if you wanted?'*

'We're fine, honestly. We'll find somewhere.'

'It's getting dark.'

'I'm aware of that.'

'Well, I can't just leave you out here in the street. My conscience won't allow it . . .'

'Look we don't need charity, all right? We're fine.'

'Really?'

'Yes, very much so.'

'I'm sorry, but I just. I don't believe that.'

'Well that's not really any of your concern.'

---

* Wait, *what?*

*Pause.*

'Look, I don't live far. How about this. I'll walk my daughter home, then come back with the car. Won't take more than fifteen minutes. Then we can drive over to the campsite, see if its open?'

'We don't need charity.'

'And then, if it's not open, you can always set up the tent at the back of ours.'

'We're fine.'

'I know, I know. You're fine. But just wait here anyway, OK? I'll bring the car around.'

The whole time the man is speaking, the dog is baring its teeth. It's only when he's finished that he reaches to try to stroke it. The dog snaps at him, erupts into a similar outburst of barking and snarling that it displayed back in the farmer's field. The man backs up so quickly he stumbles. He laughs nervously. He nods at Benny, then turns and walks away.

The little girl is still standing across from them, staring straight down at the erupting peak of her volcano. The man takes her by the hand, leads her up the street. Occasionally she turns back to glance at Benny.

A few minutes later and Benny is alone again. Just him and the dog and Stephen, snoring softly beside them.*

---

* So wait, let me get this right, Ben. We were offered a lawn to sleep on . . . and you *turned it down*?

*Why*, man?! A lawn would have been luxury compared to what we had to put up with! A lawn would have meant a house, which would have meant warmth and safety and running water and maybe a hot meal that wasn't just boiled carbs with no flavour! Surely you could see the state I was in? Surely you knew by now the toll that day's walking had taken on me? I needed help, Ben. We both did. At that moment we were struggling.

And that's OK! Despite what your toxic-masculinity-riddled brain might think, you're *allowed* to struggle sometimes. Imagine how differently things could have turned out if you'd taken him up on his offer. Imagine how much a night properly rested would have meant to us right then.

Maybe, if you'd just swallowed your pride here and accepted his help, things wouldn't have turned out how they did the next morning – ever think of *that*?

# XX

*Sunset – Starlets – Headache – Shaking Stephen – Drunken teens – Stumbling Stephen – Twitching curtains – Torchlight – 'C mp n ' – Snoring Stephen – Drunken walks – 'A little further'.*

The sun has nearly set behind the church now, the orange light just about breaking through between the branches of the trees. From this angle the gravestones are mere silhouettes, their shadows elongated across the grass. The whole thing reminds Benny of a set from one of his uncle's old horror films. He only has vague memories of those films (sometimes his uncle would play them in the background, whilst he was packing for one of their walks), but Benny remembers a lot of graveyards, blood-red sunsets, big-titted starlets in wholly inadequate nightgowns. Benny was always frightened of those films as a child, but also a little thrilled, as he knew there was no way his mum would have ever allowed him to watch them at home (a point his dad was always sure to make if he ever came into the room and saw what was playing).

Benny looks down. He realises his hands are trembling. His headache has swelled to occupy the entire frontal cavity of his skull. He pats down his pockets for gum or ibuprofen – anything that could potentially ease the throbbing – but he's all out. All he has left is his final cigarette and it's not the time for that. No matter how tempting the relief of that last smoke, the thought of afterwards, of having no cigarettes at all, is too much to bear.

Instead he closes his eyes and lets his head fall back against the wall.

He breathes. **IN** and **OUT**.

**IN** and **OUT**.

They need to keep moving. Benny doesn't want to wait for

the man and his car. It's not much further to the campsite. They've come this far, they can manage the final stretch on their own. That was the plan and they should stick to it. Maybe the man was wrong, maybe the site isn't closed (the guidebook is a fairly new edition, after all, and surely they check these things when they bring out a new one). And anyway, even if it *is* closed, maybe they can get inside somehow, use the facilities – or at least find a patch of grass to pitch up on.

Plus, there might be firewood. A fire would do Stephen the world of good. Sure, he's in a bad way now, but most likely he's just exhausted. Benny used to get like that too sometimes, on those walks with Ian and his father, and he'd always feel rejuvenated by the warmth of a good campfire. If that man comes back and takes them to his house, Benny knows Stephen will insist on sleeping inside, and the two of them will probably end up getting a lift to Llangollen in the morning, and he doesn't want that. They need to do this properly.

Stephen just needs to break through that wall of pain. If they can just keep going, Benny's sure he'll turn it around. If they can just make it to Llangollen, then Benny knows everything will be OK.

Benny climbs to his feet. Stephen's still slumped there, snoring softly. The dog is laid out beside him. A bubble of phlegm balloons from Stephen's left nostril. He must have been edging down the wall these past few minutes because he's nearly flat across the tarmac now, just his head propped upright. His left arm is draped on the pavement, his fingers resting in the puddle of sick. His throat gurgles with each breath.

Benny kneels, shakes Stephen by the arm. He pats the side of his face.

'Ste?' *Pause.* 'Come on, Ste. Snap out of it.'
　'Hmm?'
　'It's not time to sleep yet.'
　'Urgh.'
　'Come on, we need to keep on to the campsite.'

—

Back when they were in sixth form, Stephen would often drink too much, end up in a state. These were their teenage years, when they'd binge-drink every weekend – usually at Cal's, if his dad was working nights, or else in the Miners, seems the bar staff would turn a blind eye to the fact they were still underage. Cal never wanted to invite Stephen along on these occasions because of how awkward and dorky Stephen was, and how drunk he'd get, and how he'd sometimes challenge Cal on his homophobic remarks, but Benny would always feel guilty and end up bringing him, and on these nights there'd always come a time when Stephen had drunk too much and had fallen asleep somewhere – be it on Cal's couch, or in one of the booths in the pub, or, on one occasion, on the floor of the gents' toilets – and Benny would have to revive him, walk him home.

This is the Stephen Benny's now having to contend with. A stumbling mess; panting, burping, veering into the road as he walks. Occasionally he mumbles something. Occasionally he snorts. Occasionally he stops, stoops forwards, hands on thighs, to spit. This isn't a Stephen Benny's missed these past few years. He tends to be better at holding his drink these days, paces himself on their nights at the Miners, often ordering himself halves whilst Benny's still on full pints.

Benny concentrates on the road ahead. He's double-checked in the guidebook and it's not far to the campsite, they just follow this one road. Benny has got both packs now; it was obvious that Stephen was in no shape to carry his own, so Benny's taken one on each shoulder. The streetlights have come on and the road ahead is now lit like a runway, guiding them in to land. There are a few more houses along this stretch and as they pass Benny's sure he spots curtains twitching. He tries to imagine how he and Stephen must look to the families of Llandegla, observing from their living rooms this Sunday evening: two young men, soiled from three days' walking, one loaded like a pack mule, the other swaying in the road like a drunk. And the dog, that scabby little dog, trotting at their heels. Benny keeps expecting headlights. He's waiting for that guy from earlier to appear in his car, but he doesn't.

Before long the weight of both packs is too much. Benny has to stop, de-pack, regain his strength. He shifts stuff around, attempts to carry Stephen's pack on his front instead. Benny's seen walkers do this before, one on the front and one on the back, so they're encased, like a turtle in its shell, but he can't manage it somehow. The front pack keeps slipping, the straps garrotting his forearms. The base bashes his knees as he walks. In the end he has no option but to drag both packs along the ground by their straps, one in each hand. He ignores the strain in his arms, the hideous scraping of the fabric along the tarmac. He just concentrates on the sense of relief he feels in his shoulders.

Soon the houses disappear and the road reverts to a hedge-lined country lane. Benny is pleased (he could do without an audience), although this means they're out of the residential area, which in turn means there aren't any streetlights. By now it's too dark to safely navigate the road, so he has to stop again, rummage through his pack for the torch. He still has his hands full dragging the packs and so he has to hold the torch between his teeth.

They come to a junction at a main road and Benny crosses with the packs, waits for Stephen and the dog to shuffle into sight. This is now a regular occurrence; Benny having to stop and wait for them. It just makes things harder – each time they catch up Benny has to re-summon the strength to continue. He decides to push on ahead. It's *one road*, he thinks. It's not like Stephen can get lost. He'll catch up.

Benny speeds up along the country lane. The packs scrape and bounce along the ground. The torch is making his jaw ache. He concentrates on the fading beam of light. He tells himself that he has to reach the campsite before the torch runs out of power. Partly this is because he doesn't want to have to stop and wind the thing again, but there's also a superstitious quality to it. It's as if the torchlight is a metaphor for his own energy. It *has* to last. He *has* to make it.

Ten minutes later the torchlight flickers to nothing. Benny stops, dislodges the torch from his jaw. He winds it again and slots it back in place, keeps on walking.

A little further ahead there's an opening – a waist-high wall with a sign for the campsite. It's supposed to say 'Camping' but some of the letters have peeled away, so what it actually says now is 'C mp n '. There are also symbols: a tent, a caravan, and an arrow that points to a field on the left.

The field is overgrown with long grass. Debris is scattered: rubble, plastic bags, vinyl sheeting. There are a few old tractor tyres the size of paddling pools. Beyond the field is a chain-link fence. Beyond that, a few buildings barely visible in the moonlight: a house, a long white shower block, a metal silo the size of a small cottage. There are no cars or people. There are no lights on in the house. Everything is still.

Benny dumps the packs next to the 'C mp n ' sign and crosses the field to the fence at the far side. There's a gate but it's chained and padlocked. The chains are flaking with rust. There's another sign: '**NO ENTRY**'. Benny rattles the gate. He continues along until he's opposite the house. There's a small wooden hut to the side that could be a log store, although the torch beam isn't anywhere near powerful enough to properly light it, so he's no idea if there's any firewood inside.

'Hello?' *Pause.* 'Hello!' *Pause.* 'Is there anybody here?!' *Pause.* 'HELLO!'

Benny returns to the 'C mp n ' sign. He sits on the wall, feet up on the packs. He knows Stephen was walking at about half the speed he was, which means he's due to appear any minute now. He listens out for the sound of shuffling trainers, the clicking of the dog's claws, but all he can hear is crickets.

He takes out his tobacco tin, examines the final cigarette inside. He holds it to his face, breathes in that sweet tobacco tang. With his other hand he massages his forehead, hoping the combination of tobacco-scent and massage might help ease the aching. After a few minutes he gives up, stows the tobacco tin away in his pocket. He checks his phone instead. Still nothing from Sam. Still no signal. He's down to 29% battery. He switches it off.

The torch is dying again. He winds it for a minute, then stands, crosses the road to see if he can spot Stephen. He can't. A car passes and for a moment Benny thinks maybe it's the man from earlier. He has this horrible feeling he'll have Stephen with him in the passenger seat; that Benny will have no choice but to go along with them. He soon realises this isn't the case – the car is going far too fast for that. It speeds by. Benny hopes that Stephen is sensible enough to keep close to the hedge. That he's not still veering into the road like a drunk.

It's only then that it occurs to him that Stephen doesn't have a torch of his own. That, by pushing on ahead, Benny's inadvertently abandoned Stephen somewhere back along the road. That right now Stephen is out there, stumbling blindly through the darkness with only that savage little dog for company.

'Fuck.'

Benny hurries back up the road. His legs are quivering now. On reflection, sitting had been a bad idea – his muscles have grown used to the comfort of inaction and now he can hardly walk. Another car approaches, its headlights blinding, and Benny has to back against the hedge until it passes. The car roars by, its light shrinking into the distance, the growl of the engine fading amongst the buzz of the crickets.

Benny keeps up the pace. He's not so much running (there's no way his legs are able to do so at this moment); it's more of a fast limp than anything. The torchlight bobs ahead of him. He tries to ignore the trembling in his knees. He tries not to imagine Stephen lying there, a lanky strip of roadkill spread across the tarmac.

*[Whispered.]* 'Don't be dead. Don't be dead. Don't be dead. Don't be dead.'

A little further along he spots something in the torchlight; Stephen's body, hunched beneath the branches of an overgrown hedge. A little closer and Benny can see him more clearly: the fleece, the scruffy hair, the Nike Airs. The dog sitting there patiently by his side.

Stephen is huddled foetal, his face nuzzled into the crook of his elbow. He's alive at least – his back rising and falling in a steady succession of breaths. Closer still, Benny can hear his snoring. There's a small pool of vomit on the road. No noodles this time, just froth and bile.

Benny kneels, shakes him again. His eyes open.

'I'm sorry, Ben . . . I . . .'

'Don't worry.'

'I thought I was stronger than this. I thought I'd be all right. I . . .'

'Honestly, Ste, don't worry. Let's just get you out of the road, yeah?'

He drapes Stephen's arm over his shoulder, counts to three, then rises to his feet. He stoops slightly under this new, awkward weight.

Stephen belches, apologises, then belches again. Benny says it's fine, tells him to take a minute. Something screeches in the distance, possibly an owl. Stephen says he needs water. Benny tells him the flasks and bottles are at the campsite.

Stephen says it's OK. He's OK. He can walk.

They shuffle up the road. Again, this is very much like those days in sixth form, when Benny would help Stephen home drunk. If Stephen was especially bad, he'd need carrying, and they'd have to walk like this: his left arm wrapped over Benny's shoulder, his right side slumped, his head bobbing against Benny's chest. Sometimes Stephen would ramble on about his art. Sometimes he would sing or tell Benny how great a friend he was. Sometimes he would start laying into Cal, about how he was such a narcissist and a psychopath and would probably end up sexually assaulting one of those girls he was lusting after in school.

Sometimes he would stop to hug Benny, saying he really cared about him, and the hug would go on for a more-than-appropriate amount of time, and Benny would have to gently ease him away, patting his back, telling him to come along, he was drunk.

This time there's none of that. This time Stephen just breathes.

He's bigger than he used to be – back in their schooldays his head would barely reach Benny's elbow, but after his growth spurt in uni they're now about the same size. His breath is hot and sour against Benny's face. Benny can smell other stuff too, not just the cloying mix of sweat and bile, but also that unique *Stephen smell* he remembers from their childhood, the smell Stephen's bedroom had on those bygone days when they'd sit playing Xbox together – that combination of Lynx and cheese Wotsits and those cinnamon incense sticks his mum was always burning. Stephen's shivering now. His skin's cold and tacky with sweat. He's hobbling as best he can, although he no longer seems to be able to permit even the slightest weight on his ankle.

Occasionally he shudders. Occasionally he spits. At one point Benny has to stop to wind up the torch and to do this he has to unburden himself of Stephen, guide him into a sitting position on the road, where he waits, head slumped, staring at the tarmac.

The whole time the dog follows. It stops when they stop. It sits when Stephen sits.

'We're nearly there, Ste.'
   'Really?'
   'Just a little further.'
   'You promise, man?'
   'I promise, Ste. Honestly. Just a little further.'

# XXI

*Campsite – Fly-tipping – Erecting the tent
(again) – A broken pole – Extreme pins and
needles – A journey through the darkness –
Breaking and entering – Slit thumb –
Boosters – Constructing a step –
A difficult climb – A drop.*

Eventually the 'C mp n ' sign comes back into view and Benny sits Stephen on the wall, then fetches one of the 2-litre bottles from his pack. Stephen chugs at the water. The whole time the dog sits there panting, its pink tongue hanging from the side of its mouth. It occurs to Benny that maybe the dog is thirsty too, and so he retrieves the mess tin and decants some of the water, and the dog laps away at it. Meanwhile Benny scans the field with the torch, searches for a good place to set up camp.

The amount of rubbish here makes it difficult. There are plastic bags, beer bottles, even a couple of torn sleeping bags. There's the industrial waste too – the abandoned tyres, bags of rubble and old kitchen units. Benny decides they're best choosing some-where over by the fence. There's less junk there and besides, he doesn't like the idea of the tent being visible from the road.

He helps Stephen to his feet again, transports him past the gate to the far corner of the field. The dog follows. It sits beside Stephen on the grass, its head resting on one of his trainers. Stephen's shivering more and more now and so Benny takes off his raincoat, drapes it over Ste's shoulders. He asks Stephen if everything's OK – makes that OK sign with his fingers, like divers do to communicate underwater – but Stephen gives no reply.

Benny says he's going to set up the tent now. He just needs

Stephen to do one thing, and that's hold the torch. He places the torch in Stephen's hand, aiming the beam of light at a relatively junk-free spot at the edge of the field.

'That OK?' *Pause.* 'Ste?'

'Hmm?'

'Just keep the torch steady, OK?'

Benny then ferries the packs over and sets about erecting the tent. He kicks away a few plastic bags and empty beer bottles, clears enough of a patch of grass so that he can peg the groundsheet. Everything is still muddy from the night before – he'd hoped he'd have been able to clean it before they set up camp again but there's no chance of that now, they'll just have to make do.

He lays out the inner tent, drags out the poles, links them together. Suddenly the torchlight dips and Benny calls over to Stephen. It rises again.

Benny manages to construct the tent quickly. He only struggles when it comes to the tentpoles. The first couple slide through no problem, but the third catches on that familiar snag in the lining. Benny tries to force it. He thinks, fuck it – what does it matter if he tears a hole in the thing? He can always repair it tomorrow at his uncle's. But this time the snag won't give. He presses harder and suddenly there's a crack and the tentpole splits, the elastic rupturing the plastic casing. Benny has to slide the pole back out, feed it through the other way around, extra careful this time to make sure none of the splintered shards of plastic catch on the lining.

The torchlight dips again and Benny calls out. It rises.

Finally, the poles are in place and Benny's able to raise the roof. He attaches the various hooks, joins the inner and outer sections. He pegs the tent to the ground. By now the crickets have stopped chirping. There are occasional screeches in the distance from what Benny keeps telling himself are owls.

Once he's finished, Benny stands back to admire his work. It's only then he realises how crooked the tent is – the snapped pole jutting off at an unnatural-looking angle. But it'll have to do. It'll keep them dry if it rains. That's all that matters.

The torchlight dips a third time. Benny calls to Stephen but there's no response. A second later the torch thuds to the ground, the light shrinking to an ember. Benny makes his way over. He trips on one of the guy ropes but manages to steady himself without falling. He kneels at the ember of light, picks up the torch.

He can make out Stephen now. He's still sitting there, eyes open, the dog still beside him. His legs are straight out in front and he's clutching his thighs with both hands. A strand of white drool hangs from his chin.

He looks up at Benny in horror.

'I . . . I don't know what's happening to me, man . . .'
'It's OK. You're OK, Ste.'
'I feel bad . . . I feel really b-bad . . .'
'We just need to get you warmed up.'
'My l-legs . . .'
'Let's just get you inside the tent, yeah?'

Benny takes Stephen by the hand, attempts to drag him to his feet. But Stephen squeals for him to stop. His legs are seized, he says, he can't put any weight on them. The dog whines and stands back as Stephen aggressively rubs at his thighs. Stephen says he's never known his legs to be like this, like extreme pins and needles.

In the end Benny has to get behind him, hook his hands under his armpits, drag Stephen across the grass like he would a corpse. It's no easier when they reach the tent. Benny tries to back in through the porch, but Stephen objects, says he can climb in himself.

He's wrong; he can't kneel to stoop inside like he usually would, so instead he has to lie flat on his belly and attempt a crawl. He can't manage to crawl either though, and for a minute Benny just sits there, watching Stephen writhing at the porch. The dog watches too.

Soon Benny intervenes. He grabs Stephen by the collar and drags him through. Stephen looks up and nods in appreciation. As if to say: *OK, I admit it, that was necessary.* As if to say: *thank you.*

Benny ties the torch to the fabric loop on the ceiling. He drags the packs inside, dumps them in the corner, then opens Stephen's pack and begins to rummage inside. Stephen asks what he's doing, and Benny tells him he's getting his sleeping bag, and Stephen says no, pass him the pack, he'll search for it himself.

Benny shrugs and slides the pack over.

Stephen carefully removes his camera bag, places it to the side. He searches for a minute or so before finally removing his sleeping bag, draping it over himself. Benny gets out the mess tin, places it beside Stephen, in case he needs to vomit again.

He roots out the hatchet, slips it through one of the belt loops in his trousers. He pulls on his raincoat, zips it to his chin.

'Right, now I'm going to have to leave, Ste, OK?'

'W-what?'

'Just for a few minutes.'

'Why?'

'I need to take a look around. Will you be OK?'

'I don't know, man. I feel pretty b-bad here.'

'I saw some firewood, just the other side of the fence. I'm going to see if I can get it. Make a fire, warm us up.'

'Right.'

'Also, I'm sorry, but I'll need to take the torch.'

'W-what?! *Why*?!'

'I need it, Ste. It's pitch-black out there.'

'But it'll be pitch-b-black in here!'

'I'm sorry. I won't be long.'

'I'm scared, Ben. What if there's something wrong with me? Like, *seriously* wrong?'

'You'll be OK, Ste. You're just cold and tired. You need some rest. A fire will get you warmed up.' *Pause.* 'I won't be long, OK? I promise.'

Benny steps outside again. The dog is still there, perched sphynx-like at the entrance to the tent. It looks up at Benny, its jaws hanging open, its white breath blooming in the torchlight. Benny reaches down, strokes its head. The dog allows it. After a few seconds it begins to wag its tail.

The sky is clear tonight, stars like pinpricks in a great black canvas. Below, the buildings – the farmhouse, the shower block, the silo – are only silhouettes, grey shapes basking in the moonlight. The torch is dying. It seemed brighter in the tent, where the enclosed space magnified the light. Benny winds it for a few minutes, listens to it *whirr*, watches the yellow beam thicken before his eyes.

For the first time Benny thinks maybe he was wrong to turn down that man's offer of a lift. Maybe Stephen's worse than he thought. Either way, it's too late now. He can't go back. He has to get a fire going. That's the only way to help Stephen: get him warm and fed. If he can get over the fence, then he can search the house and raid the log store.

'Right.'

Benny makes his way back across the field, over towards the house. He examines the fence in the torchlight along the way, but can't see any breakages or openings. The only entrance appears to be a padlocked gate, and the padlock is one of those heavy-duty types, like his dad used for locking the shed, encased in black rubber to protect it from rust. Benny shakes it. He scans the path beyond in the torchlight. He considers calling out again, to see if anyone's there, but for some reason he decides against it.

Instead he slides the hatchet from his belt. The blade glitters in the torchlight. He runs his thumb along it, thinking somehow this is a good way to assess how sharp it is. He's wrong: there's a slitting pain and suddenly he's wincing, gritting his teeth against this new, all-consuming ailment. He makes a fist, clutching the thumb in the palm of his hand. He counts his way through the next few seconds, breathing steadily, trying to distract his mind from the searing pain. There's a stickiness as he eases the pressure. The cut must be deep because when he checks it's still bleeding.

He raises the hatchet, brings it down on the padlock with all his strength. The subsequent *thud* is surprisingly quiet; an anti-climax to the violence of his attack (probably the rubber, deadening the blow). He hacks again. Twice more. Nothing. The lock doesn't give. On closer examination there are a few slits along the rubber casing, but that's it. He tries hacking at the chains instead. Unlike the padlock, this produces a clatter worthy of his efforts, but still they don't break.

Benny sits on the grass and catches his breath. He knows now there's no other option, he's going to have to try and scale the fence. It isn't too high – in theory it's climbable. In practice, after a day's mountaineering, he knows it's going to be near impossible. The chain-links will probably make good handgrips, but there's nowhere for his boots to gain any sort of purchase.

What he needs is a booster. They were always giving each other boosters, back in school. It was a part of everyday life back then – binding your hands together whilst one of your mates placed their foot (and with it their full weight) into the palm of your hand. He used to give Cal boosters to get up on top of the sports hall, so he could spy on the girls in the changing room.

Here, now, who does Benny have to help him? *Stephen*? Regardless of his current state of exhaustion, there's no way Stephen would have had the strength to give Benny a booster.

*Sigh.*

Benny inspects the debris that's scattered there. He figures maybe he can collect some of the larger rubbish to stack by the fence, build some sort of platform, something he can climb to give himself a step up. He knows if he could just get a few feet higher he'd be able reach the top of the fence, drag himself over.

Firstly he considers the bags of rubble. They would be easy enough to stack – like those walls of sandbags they have in old war films – although it's only once he kneels and tries to lift one that he realises they're far too heavy. He can't budge them a foot, never mind dragging them across the field or piling them up against the fence. Next he spots the old kitchen units, wonders if they'd take his weight, but once he reaches them he finds the wood wet and rotten, crumbling in his hands.

Then there are the tyres. There are three of them in total, dumped at the far side – enormous tractor tyres with weeds and long grass sprouting up through them. Up close they're even bigger – lying flat they nearly reach up to his knees. He clasps the torch between his teeth, squats by one of them, prises his fingers underneath and lifts. He's expecting there to be some weight in it, but the tyre isn't heavy, in spite of its size. He has a bit of trouble tearing it from the weeds, but he soon manages to stand it on its end, roll it across the grass to the fence.

He's grateful he doesn't have to do any heavy lifting. His arms are aching now, especially his right shoulder, which had to take the weight of Stephen during that final stretch. His legs are aching too, as is his jaw from holding the torch. His thumb is throbbing, his right hand now sticky with blood. (*Ailments*, he thinks.) He wishes he'd picked up one of those strap-on torches he'd seen in the camping shop, the ones that fix to your head like on a miner's helmet. Camping Shop Mike hadn't particularly pushed for a sale, with regards to the head torches, because he said they were mostly for rock climbing or mountain biking, but now Benny realises how useful one would be.

Once he's fetched the other two tyres, he stacks them, one on top of the other, then steps back to assess his handiwork. It's pathetic – a crooked mound of rubber that even the smallest nudge of his toe would set wobbling. But still, it's worth a try. He needs firewood. This is a priority. To get firewood he needs to climb the fence, so this too is a priority.

Plus, what else does he have? There is no plan B. This is it. This is all he can think of.

He slots the torch between his teeth again, places his foot against the top tyre. This is a difficult task in itself – it's quite a height and the stretching involved causes a succession of tearing pains in his thighs and hamstrings. Even before he's stood straight, he can feel the tyres slipping.

And so, he lunges – one hand gripping the chain-links of the fence, the other grasping at the bar above. The pile gives way, the tyres topple, and Benny slams into the fence, gagging as the torch jabs back into his throat. The chain-links bite at his fingers. The cut in his thumb flares with pain. Various aches swell in his biceps and shoulders.

But with this comes a final burst of adrenalin. It's enough for Benny to find the strength to raise his leg, hook it over the top of the fence. He gasps, balances there for a few seconds. He breathes deep through his nostrils – **IN** and **OUT**, **IN** and **OUT**. After a few seconds the torch slips from his mouth. It hits the ground with a crunch and the light goes out. Suddenly everything is black.

Benny closes his eyes. He can feel himself slipping. He can feel the weight of his own body, dragging him down.

He lets go.*

---

* And meanwhile I was left there lying in the darkness. Do you realise how long you left me for, Ben? It felt like *hours*. I had assumed that my eyes would adjust to my surroundings eventually, but I was wrong, it remained pitch-black the entire time you were gone, so dark it made no difference whether my eyes were open or closed. I was lying on my back staring up at what should have been the ceiling but was now just a void. There was no definable sound either; no cars passing, no crickets chirping, not even any breeze. Just a thick, black silence.

I remember once, years ago, Mum received a gift card for one of those isolation tanks, complete with full colour catalogue of the 'Isolation Centre' – a birthday present from one of her new-age yoga friends. She never used it (said the thought of it freaked her out) but her friend had insisted it made for a truly worthwhile meditative experience. I remember seeing the pictures of the tanks in the catalogue; plain white capsules, probably about the same size as those one-man tents you saw in the camping shop. As far as I could tell, the idea was that Mum would just get in and lie there, bobbing on a shallow pool of saltwater, completely sealed off from all other sensory influences. She'd be left alone with her mind – for hours. Apparently it'd help clear her thoughts. Some people said they began to hallucinate ('receive visions' is how the catalogue phrased it). Mum's friend had said it made her feel as if she was *back in the womb*.

My time in the tent made for a similar experience. Before long I became very emotional. I remember crying. I still felt relatively calm, but it was this *horrifying* calmness, like I'd suddenly found myself at the bottom of the ocean and there was no way I could reach the surface. After a while I began to lose my sense of spatial reality. This varied: sometimes it was as if I was on an open field, exposed to the elements, staring up at a starless sky – other times I felt as if I was trapped inside a coffin. At first this panicked me. I kept reaching out just to test the distance between myself and the walls of the tent. Which wasn't easy, by the way. The reaching, I mean. At this point my whole body was seizing, the stiffness spreading rigor mortis-like. It was as if nobody'd told my body it wasn't actually dead yet.

Still, after a while I began to relax. It occurred to me that lying there in isolation was the closest to death I had ever experienced; an unending void, with time and space rendered entirely irrelevant. This may sound overdramatic, but honestly, Ben, it didn't feel so at the time. I knew at that moment what I'd later confirm to be only partially true, that the worst aspect of the transcendental experience, the real torture of it, wasn't atoning for one's sins, or meeting one's maker, or contending with Dante-esque imps jabbing blazing pitchforks up people's rectums, but rather a state of constant, inescapable darkness. An unending nothing, with no sort of mental or sensory stimulation whatsoever. An eternity of staring into a yawning blackness, without anything there to stare back at you.

Although lying there in the tent there was one crucial difference: I was still *in pain*. Not only my ankle, or the aches and blisters from walking, but also that swirling and grinding in my belly. This was the only thing that assured me that I was still alive, my one connection to the physical realm. I couldn't be dead because to be dead would be to be put out of my misery, and at that moment I was wholly miserable. (The philosophical certainty of a cross-country walker: *I ache therefore I am.*) Honestly, that sickness, Ben, it was like nothing I'd ever felt in my life. Like a washing machine filled with rusted cutlery, churning away inside me. Waves of nausea so strong I had to concentrate on breathing just to keep myself from throwing up. That time you were off exploring just dragged on and on.

The only thing that broke it was the screaming – your screaming (although I didn't know this at the time, I didn't know who the hell it could be, out there in the wilderness, screaming) – which occurred a little later on, and which echoed across the field, instilling within me its own unique brand of blood-curdling terror.

# XXII

*House in darkness – Broken window – A scurrying something – Chopping wood (failing at) – A shuffling something – Pursuit to the shower block – A new darkness – Self-reflection – First shift – Rick – Following the script – Christine – The Miners Arms – A celebration – Home late – Dad in the kitchen.*

Benny doesn't remember hitting the ground, but the next thing he knows he's face down on the gravel, bits of which are embedded in his cheeks and forehead. His eyes are open, but everything is black. He's trembling; the cold seems to have breached every cell of his body. He's not sure how long he's been there – maybe seconds, maybe hours – but all he can think is that at least he's made it to the other side of the fence.

He gropes for the torch. He turns the handle, sighs in relief as the light flares to life. He keeps winding until there's enough of a beam to see his breath billowing out. The view ahead is much the same: a gravel path leading to the house, the outlines of the silo and the shower block lurking behind. There's no wind now. The crickets have ceased their chirping.

His boots crunch against the gravel as he makes his way over to the house. At first he's a little self-conscious about it, but he decides not to worry. If there's anyone still living here, he's going to have to disturb them at some point. He needs food and firewood and he's probably going to have to ask for permission, offer to pay something towards it (although hopefully not, given that he has no money left).

The house is in darkness. It's built from a similar stone to those back at the village, although it's twice the size, and as he gets closer Benny can see it's more dilapidated than those previous. There are splatters of mud on the brickwork at the front, as well as weeds and tufts of moss in the grouting. The front door has a large brass ring knocker. The paint is peeling, dark green with a silvery undercoat. There are a couple of windows at each side, one of which is smashed, and its shattered fragments glitter on the ground in the torchlight. Benny is aware that the glass is on the outside, which suggests the windows were broken from within, although he has no idea whether this is of any real significance.

He raises his hand to knock. For the first time he notices how much blood there is from the cut on his thumb – his entire fist is red. He swallows. He tries not to give it too much thought. He raps against the wood, lightly at first. He gives it a few minutes then tries again, a little harder this time. Flakes of paint flutter in the torchlight. They stick to the blood on his fingers. His hands are numb and with each knock there's a dull ache against his knuckles.

He decides to try the door knocker instead, although the screech of the handle is louder than the actual impact, which is less of a knock and more a dull *thud*. He makes his second knock extra hard, a single satisfying *bang* that stabs through the silence.

A couple more minutes creep by in silence and in the end he decides to take a look through one of the windows. He approaches the one that's still intact. It feels more appropriate somehow, less invasive.

He raises the torch to the glass.

In the centre of the room is a large table, strewn with rubbish. Plastic bags, crisp packets, cans and beer bottles. There are plates and cutlery and a couple of mess tins balanced on old gas heaters, their shadows stretched across the back wall. At the far side is a sink, the floral wallpaper behind it patched with grey rectangles where units and appliances once lodged. There is rubbish scattered on the floor too. More cans and food wrappings, some empty boxes, even a few odd items of clothing. There are some papers over in the far corner, amongst them a couple of books.

One of these resembles Benny's own guidebook (that same blue cover) and it's just as he leans closer to the glass, squinting to try and make out the title, that something black darts out from under the table.

Benny jerks back.

When he seeks it out again, whatever it was has already disappeared into the shadows.

'*Shit.*'

He heads round the side of the house. He shouldn't be wasting time like this. He has no idea how long he's been out here but he's sure he's left Stephen for too long already and he knows his priority is to collect the firewood and get back.

Luckily there are still a few large logs housed within the log store. Benny kneels to lift one. The bark is dry on top, but the underside is slimy, infested with centipedes and woodlice, which squirm and peel themselves from the surface, as he drags it out onto the grass. He knows he has no chance of getting logs this size over the fence – he'll have to chop them here, transport the firewood in pieces.

There's a chopping block to the side of the log store – a section from an old tree trunk, sunk into the ground. Benny balances the torch on top of the log store, angles it in a way that he can make out the block. He saw his father chopping wood many times on their old camping trips. There's no axe here but that's fine, he has the hatchet. That's all his father ever needed.

He balances the first log upright on the block. He holds it in position with one hand, raises the hatchet over his head with the other. He knows he has to time it so that he moves his left hand away a fraction of a second before the hatchet strikes. Timing is everything, when it comes to chopping wood.

First attempt and he's too quick releasing, and as a result he misses, the log pitching forward onto the grass. He stands it up again. Second attempt and the hatchet bounces off to the left, the log tipping to the right. Benny sighs, stands it up again. Third attempt and the hatchet hits the target dead on. Still, it barely makes a dent. Fourth attempt is the same. Fifth he misses again, nearly catches his own leg.

That's when he loses his patience, tosses the hatchet onto the ground, collapses there on the grass with his head in his hands.

Benny lies there for a while in the darkness. He stares up at the moon. He wonders what would happen if he stayed there indefinitely. Would Stephen come and find him, eventually? (Would anyone?)

Suddenly he hears a shuffling sound from behind. He sits up, reaches for the torch and winds it. He scans the field at the back. He calls out, asks if anyone's there, but there's no answer. He tries to remain calm, control his breathing. He's not sure if maybe he'd been sleeping when he thought he heard the sound. For the first time it occurs to him he could have a concussion as a result of his fall from the fence earlier.

Then suddenly Benny thinks he can see something, out there in the darkness. Some black shape that looks like it could be an animal. He tries to catch it in the torchlight, but it eludes him, scuttles towards the shower block at the back of the site.

Benny stands. He feels this compulsion to follow – he doesn't know why. His boots rustle against the grass as he crosses the field. He keeps an eye out for the thing – whatever it may be – but he can never quite catch it in the torchlight. He wonders if it's the dog. How it got into this part of the site, he has no idea. (Maybe there's a hole in the fence somewhere, although he's sure he'd have noticed.) He doesn't give much thought to what he's going to do if he actually catches up with the thing. There's just this vague awareness that he needs to follow.

Over at the edge of the field is the silo, imposing and space-ship-like in the torchlight. It must be eight foot in height, constructed from some sort of corrugated metal, which is rusted in places. There's a door around the side but it's padlocked and there's no indication of what's housed within (chances are it's grain or something – doubtless it'd be of little use to them).

Behind the silo stands the shower block; a long, white, window-less building with an entrance at the far end. Somebody has spray-painted swear words at various points along the wall, as well as several gigantic penises.

There's no sign of the dog anywhere – and Benny knows it's unlikely it would have gone inside the shower block – and yet, still, he feels this overwhelming obligation to enter. The door is open – beyond, a blackness the torchlight seems unable to pene-trate. There's a familiarity to the odour of the place, a mixture of mould, urine and bleach. The night is eerily quiet. Benny knows he should head back. He needs to chop the wood, climb the fence, get back to Stephen. He needs to light a fire and get them both fed. And yet, still, he finds himself approaching the doorway. He finds himself covering his mouth with the back of his hand and following the torchlight inside.

The interior is pitch-black. Outside there's still the moonlight, but within the shower block the darkness is contained, and it feels *closer* somehow. The only thing cutting through it is the yellow beam of the torch, and with that Benny can make out a long, redbrick corridor – a row of sinks along the left-hand wall, half-a-dozen grey shower cubicles on the right. One of the cubicles has an out of order sign. Another has a missing door. Several have severe cases of mildew on the doorframes, black spores that have spread like liver spots. The floor is a mosaic of tiny grey and black chipped tiles. The urine smell is even stronger now.

There's a light dancing at the far end of the corridor. Benny holds still. He squints. He can just about make out a black figure, standing facing him. The figure is also holding a torch. Benny sputters a *hello*. His voice echoes across the cubicles. The figure remains still.

Somewhere a pipe is leaking and this is the only sound, a steady drip.

Benny searches for the figure's face with his torch, but finds the outline is doing the same, and suddenly he is blinded by the light.

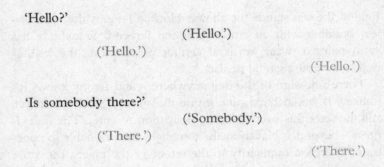

'Hello?'

(‘Hello.’)

(‘Hello.’)

(‘Hello.’)

'Is somebody there?'

(‘Somebody.’)

(‘There.’)

(‘There.’)

Benny takes a few more tentative steps, the figure does the same. Then he realises the corridor is actually only half the length it appears. The wall is taken up by a full-length mirror.

'Fuck.'

(‘Fuck.’)

(‘Fuck.’)

(‘Fuck.’)

Benny approaches the mirror. He hardly recognises himself. This is partly due to the distortion in the glass, which is cracked and smudged in places, as well as the light, which shines from below, highlighting his jaw and eye sockets. Mostly, however, this change in his appearance is the result of three days' walking. His skin is pale, his cheeks dark with stubble. His shirt and trousers are crusted with dirt and anti-climbing paint. His hair is parted too far at the left in a manner that emphasises his receding hairline and, in the white light of the torch, what's left of his fringe looks incredibly thin. (*Ghost hair*, he thinks.)

He raises the torch, holds it directly under his chin. Uncle Ian used to do this on those nights around the campfire. He always opted for these clichéd horror tropes during his ghost stories – the upturned torch, the firelight, the lowering of the voice to a throaty whisper; an homage to those old films he loved so much.

Benny stares at his reflection. He rotates the torch, watches his face distort, his skin now white as bone. A shadow stretches from his mouth like a grin. His eye sockets swell to two black pools. The face reminds him of someone but he can't think who.

Then he realises – it's his father. He looks like his dad did, that night in the kitchen. That image that keeps coming back to him, over and over, his dad's frail figure at the table with that cigarette in his hand – that look of utter disdain as he peered over the top of his glasses.

Benny lets out a laugh at this – a single *ha* – then allows himself to slump forwards, his forehead pressed against the glass.

He closes his eyes. He switches off the torch.

He stands there for a while, swaying in the darkness.

It was Benny's first proper shift at the call centre, the morning Christine phoned the helpline. After weeks of training Benny was finally up on the third floor; an enormous open-plan office with its rows and rows of workstations. He was feeling stranded at first, unsure who he was supposed to report to, where he was supposed to sit. Until he spotted Rick.

Rick was Benny's supervisor; a short, middle-aged, gym-type with that same fixed smile a lot of the supervisors had. It was Rick who explained to Benny how it worked, with regards to the workstations. It turned out it didn't matter where Benny sat, each desk was identical – same keyboard, same call unit, same shining flat-screen monitor – all with their cables bound, fed through specially drilled holes, to give a clean and clutter-free aesthetic. This was the whole point of the workstations, their uniformity. No personal items were allowed, no trinkets or family photos. The idea was that any call handler could take a seat at any of the workstations and feel they were at exactly the same desk they sat in every day.

So Benny took a seat at an empty desk and donned his headset. He took a few deep breaths. His application, his interview, his training schedule with Rick, it had all led to this moment. It was only now that he began to really contemplate what was happening here; the fact he was about to have a real-life claimant on the other end of the line.

Benny was nervous. He knew all calls were recorded and there was a rumour that management listened to them at random. Supposedly this was for 'training purposes', although everyone knew it was the higher-ups keeping tabs on people. It was a sensitive time, politically. There was a lot of stuff in the newspapers: whistle-blowers, personal accounts of how Universal Credit was failing the most vulnerable in society during their time of need. Benny and his fellow call handlers were the frontline of this, the human face (or voice) of the system, and there was a lot of emphasis on what Rick referred to as their 'brand image'. Everyone had to be as polite as possible when talking with claimants. Everyone had to stick to the script. But most importantly, everyone had to be as quick as they could; keep down their call time averages.

So that's what Benny did. He stuck to the basics, kept his eye on his call times. And at first, he found he got through it OK; his initial calls went surprisingly well. They were mostly new claimants with questions about filling out their applications (they have to do this themselves online, and there are plenty who aren't tech-savvy enough to manage it without assistance). Benny dealt with their queries as quickly as possible, then ended with a polite goodbye. There were a few other issues – delayed payments or inconsistencies in the amounts they'd received, usually a result of errors in the system – but Benny found he was able to navigate these calls satisfactorily, keep the claimant onside. He gave the relevant information and they accepted it gracefully. And, at first, it seemed like this was all his job consisted of: answering questions to perfectly reasonable people who were genuinely grateful of his efforts.

It was a few hours in when he started getting the more difficult calls. These interactions usually began in the same way; the person would start by insisting there had been some sort of mistake – they had been paid late, or given the wrong amount, or they'd been sanctioned without cause, etc., etc. – and Benny would have to try and offer up a worthwhile explanation. The longer he took to do this, the angrier they'd get (as if he was supposed to just take their word for it, process a full repayment right there and then). Then came the pleading, the sobbing, the all-too-personal tales of woe. Some wanted to discuss illnesses or disabilities, problems with childcare or other domestic issues. Benny did his best to sidestep these issues, stay on topic, but it all amounted to the same thing, really. They needed more money. Whether it was to feed their children or pay their rent or help them crawl out of the debt they'd found themselves in, it didn't matter. The answer was always the same: they couldn't have any. This was also something they'd gone over in the training. It was Rick who had pointed out that the stages people go through with this – denial, anger, bargaining, depression, acceptance – were the same as the five stages of grief.

Still, each time, these conversations were a struggle for Benny. He tried his best to calm the callers, remembering the tips Rick had given him (maintaining composure, a logical viewpoint, repeating their name back to them as much as possible) but it was harder than it seemed. For one thing, the more desperate the callers were, the less logic there was to their arguments. Usually they resorted to repeating the same mantras – that they were doing their best, that they would try harder to find work, that the government couldn't do this to them, it couldn't do this to them, *it just couldn't do this to them*, no matter how many times Benny pointed out that the government *was* in fact doing this to them, and there was nothing he personally could do to change that. But the people at the other end of the line, they didn't want to hear this. Instead they just kept repeating themselves, over and over, whilst Benny nodded along (always nodding along), until he had no choice but to summon Rick over to assist.

And this was the most frustrating thing about the day-to-day reality of the call centre. Some days Benny just wanted to be honest. He wanted to say to the people on the other end of the line, 'Look, no one gives a fuck. You're on your own.' But that wouldn't fly with Rick. He was all about 'brand image'. Benny had to somehow be compassionate, without being able to offer any real assistance. He had to appear understanding without becoming emotionally involved; to remain logical without seeming cold, sympathetic without straying into empathy. He was not allowed to make false promises or give any sort of adverse reaction to the abuse he received. Instead his role mainly consisted of waiting it out. This, too, was a contradiction (he was constantly trying to bring down his call time average). And yet, he could never hang up. That was Rick's one golden rule: never hang up. If anyone became too difficult to handle, Benny had to pass them over to his supervisor.

It was just after his morning break that the call came through from Christine. Benny had only just managed his introductory *hello* when the sobbing started from the other end of the line. Somehow, he knew straight away that it was her. She'd already reached stage three on the grief index: pleading for a reversal of her sanctions. She hadn't recognised Benny's voice, not at first, and he was surprised, really, that he'd been so quick to recognise hers, after all they'd only actually met a couple of times (the most notable being that Halloween party she and Cal had thrown, not long after moving in together). Benny tried to convince himself that he'd made a mistake. It was impossible; of all the times she could have called, all the people she could have been put through to, somehow it ended up being *now*, it ended up being *him*. It was too much to accept.

And yet, here she was. And Benny had a job to do. So, he waited it out. He tried his best to answer her questions, to combat Christine's emotions with logic. She told him she'd been sanctioned for three months without payment and had got herself into debt and now she was struggling. Benny cut in, tried to talk her through her options, but Christine wasn't really listening. Instead she was telling him about her boyfriend, about how they'd argued and he'd attacked her, and Benny felt that familiar cold dread gathering around him. Benny had been doing his best to avoid thinking about that night, about what Cal did. This was near the start of the mass-avoidance of any form of negative thinking – the early days of 'The Fog' (although at this point, he still hadn't named it as such). He was trying his best not to dwell on the fact that they'd gone back with Cal to the flat that night, seen the state of the place – the wine stains on the wall, the coffee table on its side, the TV broadcasting a chaos of white static. The blood was mostly confined to the bathroom, on the tiles and the bathtub and in the sink, where Cal's shaving stuff was still scattered. There were a few splashes in the hallway too, Benny had noticed, once his eyes had adjusted to the darkness, although at the time he was still in denial about how serious it all was. It was only later, when he'd gone on Facebook, when he'd seen *that photo*, that he realised the significance of what Cal had done to her.

Christine was now referring to Cal by name. Cal was the one who'd ruined her, she said, but he was also the one who'd saved her. She'd been staying with a friend since the fight, but her friend had since moved away, and Christine had nowhere else to go. She was technically homeless (and with her face fucked up like that it's not like she could find someone else to take her in). And so, that's how she'd ended up back at the flat. And, to give him his due, Cal had been great with her. He'd been treating her like a princess; takeaways and film nights and all sorts of extravagant gifts – his way of apologising for what had happened. Of course, it was all on credit, but he didn't seem to care. He even offered to pay private for plastic surgery – see if they could do a better job on her nose than the NHS had managed. He was always staring at her face, obsessing over it – the scar on her eyelid, the bump in her nose. He was feeling guilty. He was fine, she said, when he was sober, but now he was drinking more and more. The guilt about what happened, coupled with the debt he was falling into, meant he was falling off the wagon. He was getting snappy again. It was only a matter of time before all that resentment boiled up. Then what?

At this point Benny placed his forehead on the desk. He closed his eyes. He tried to concentrate on his breathing. There was a pause. Benny thought maybe he'd accidentally muted the call or disconnected his headset or something but no, Christine had stopped talking. She'd stopped because she'd asked Benny a question, he could tell as much from the silence. There was an expectation there. He was supposed to respond, to give her advice or a few words of comfort or something. He thought back to what Rick had said during his training. *Don't get involved in personal stories. Keep the call time to a minimum. Stick to the script.*

And so, this is what Benny did. He tried to explain Christine's options to her. She'd already been sanctioned several times over the past year, which is why her latest had been so severe. She wasn't going to receive any money now for the best part of three months, and her only option was another advance on future payments, although by the looks of it she'd already had a few of those, so that might be difficult. There were always foodbanks and . . .

That's when she gave a sharp intake of breath.

'Benny?' she said. 'Is that you?'

Benny didn't reply, not at first. He didn't have to, the pause that followed was more than enough to confirm his identity. This whole time he couldn't shake the thought that maybe management were listening in. He glanced over his shoulder at Rick.

Suddenly Christine was sobbing. It was like this realisation that it was Benny at the other end of the line had broken something within her, let forth a flood of hysteria. The worst thing was her constant use of his name. Benny hadn't used Christine's name this whole time – despite Rick's tip to repeat callers' names back to them. And yet now it was Christine who was repeating *his* name, over and over – 'Please, Ben, Benny, please, I need this, Ben, please, Benny, I need your help, Ben, please . . .' – and the whole time he was imagining management listening in, the sense of curiosity as to how Benny would continue with the call. Christine was asking if Benny could pull a few strings, get her payments started again. At least then she would be independent, have some money of her own. At least she could stand up for herself, if the worst came to the worst. At least she could find a way out.

'Please,' she said. 'You know him,' she said. 'You know what he's capable of. *Please.*'

That's when he hung up. It was easy on the headset, not much drama to it. No slamming down of the phone. Just the quick push of a button, followed by the cold vacuum of silence. It came as a shock, after all Christine's wailing. Like he'd been plunged underwater.

He scanned the room. All around him were other operators,

nodding and talking. But, thanks to the noise-cancelling head-phones, Benny could hear none of it. All he could hear was his own breathing:

**IN** and **OUT**.
**IN** and **OUT**.
**IN** and **OUT**.

Benny got home late that night. He'd ended up going to the Miners with his new colleagues after work. Rick had insisted it was a tradition for each new batch of call operatives to go for a pint together to toast their first shift, and Benny didn't want to be the only one to say no.

He hadn't meant to stay long. Rick only stayed for one round (which he insisted on paying for) but there were still about fifteen of them, gathered around that cluster of tables at the back, by the fruit machines. These weren't people Benny would end up keeping in touch with beyond this initial get-together. There were a few Benny recognised from high school, but no one he knew well enough to make their schooldays a viable topic of conversation. Still, it was nice to be with them that night. To feel part of something. They were in the same position he was, all slightly in shock from the nature of some of the calls they'd received, and there was a desire amongst them to share what they'd experienced. They ended up having a laugh that night, discussing the more colourful characters – especially the ones they judged to be rude or workshy or in some other way deserving of the problems they were facing. Benny didn't say much himself (he certainly didn't mention Christine), although he was happy enough listening to their stories. A couple more Guinnesses and he decided to leave his car there, take the bus home.

Christine was never far from his mind that night. He couldn't help imagining what would have happened next. She would have called back, most likely, and somebody else would have answered, probably a more experienced call operative. They would have listened to Christine, discussed her issues, offered the numbers for the services on hand to support her, whilst simultaneously ensuring she was under no illusions that the government itself would be willing to give her any more money. She'd have hung up having received all the guidance available to her, even if Benny hadn't been the one to give it.

He left the pub around ten thirty. He figured that was a good time to say his goodbyes – late enough not to seem rude, without overstaying his welcome. He got home just after eleven and by that point the house was in darkness. This wasn't unusual – Mum always went up to bed early, and recently Benny's dad had been joining her, what with the chemo eating up so much of his energy. This was something his dad regularly complained about when he got home from the clinic: how he could sit there for hours on end with nothing to do but watch the IV slowly empty into his arm, and yet somehow still come home exhausted. It was only when Benny stepped into the kitchen, smelt the cigarette smoke, saw the little red ember floating in the darkness, that he realised his dad was sitting up, waiting for him.

Benny flicked the lights on. It was not a pleasant sight. His father had lost a lot of weight by this point and the spotlights in the kitchen only served to highlight this. He'd begun to shave recently, seems his beard was getting patchy, and Benny wasn't used to how small and round his head looked. What was left of his hair was greasy, tied back tight, and the whole thing reminded Benny of one of those shrunken heads he'd seen in pictures of old Amazonian tribes.

From the moment Benny entered the room his father had been giving that stare of his, peering over the top of his glasses like a disgruntled librarian. Benny could never figure out if this was deliberate; if he purposely placed the glasses at the end of his nose to achieve this, or whether they just didn't fit that well (a problem further exacerbated by his weight loss). Still, there was something in this look that seemed defiant. At this point his father had promised never to smoke again and yet he seemed in no way ashamed of the cigarette smouldering there between his fingers. There was something in that look of his that was challenging Benny to even mention it.

He held this stare for what felt like minutes. Benny looked away a couple of times, glanced around the room. There were a few things scattered on the kitchen table: cigarettes, a lighter, an empty wine bottle, a newspaper (which there was no way his father could have been reading in the darkness), as well as that pill box he had to pop the lid of each morning, the one he called his 'advent calendar'. But Benny's dad wasn't looking at any of that. The whole time his eyes didn't leave Benny's face.

And that's when Benny realised: his father *knew*. It was impossible, of course. The only people who could have known about what happened that day were Benny and Christine (and possibly management, if they *had* been listening in). But right then Benny was sure of it; somehow his father knew what Benny had done. Somehow he'd heard Christine begging for help. He'd seen his own son, sitting there, listening to her pleas. And then he'd seen him reach for his headset, disconnect the call.

It defied all logic, of course. There was no way his father could have seen this. There was no way he could ever have known. And yet, Benny was certain of it. More certain than he'd been of anything in his entire life.*

---

* Interesting you actually believe this to be true, Ben. I mean, it's understandable really, that your feelings of guilt would manifest this way; your relationship was being pushed to its limits and the lack of resolution must have made things difficult. As ever though, what remains a mystery to me is how you can have such little insight into your own psychology here. Because you continued to go there, didn't you? Week-in week-out, answering calls for those fucking *vampires*. I mean, surely by the time you were in that shower block, engaging in this little moment of self-reflection (no pun intended), it was obvious that the toll of your work was causing immeasurable damage to your own mental health?

And yet, you still had this sort of weird *pride* in your work there, didn't you? Only a couple of hours later – just before the explosion, when the two of us were arguing outside the tent – there you were, demanding that I *also* apply for a position at the call centre, as if this would in some way be good for *my* spiritual wellbeing. I mean, can't you see how fucked up that is, Ben? Can't you see this point where this sort of behaviour becomes nothing short of masochistic bootlicking?

Is anything I'm saying here registering *at all*, Ben?

# XXIII

*Chopping wood (take two) – Screams (memories)*
*– Gathering wood – Climbing the fence –*
*A too-still tent – Awaking Stephen –*
*Several attempts at fire – A new companion –*
*Keeping warm – Open-fire cooking –*
*Feeding time – Fogged (or smoked) –*
*Stephen's bedtime.*

Benny is running. The pain flares in his thighs and ankles with each step, but it doesn't matter. He's bounding across the field – hatchet in one hand, torch in the other – and as soon as he reaches the log store he's down on his knees again, mounting the torch in place, replacing the log on the chopping block. He raises his hatchet, brings it down upon the log.

Nothing.

Again.

Nothing.

Again.

Again.

Each strike sends a shockwave through his arm and a series of images play through his mind: Stephen, laid out like roadkill at the side of the road; that crazy dog, bounding along the dirt road, snapping at the wheels of the truck; Sam on all fours on the bed, her bethonged rear slowing rising; Camping Shop Mike's concerned face as Benny emerged from the suffocating confinement of the one-man tent; Benny's own distorted face in the shower-block mirror.

And his father. Always his father, again and again. That fucking cigarette between his fingers. That fucking pill box. That fucking glare of his, over the top of his glasses.

Benny finds it helps if he screams whilst he chops.

'AGGGHHHH!'
*Thud.*
'GAHHHH!'
*Thud.*
'NAGGAAHAHHHHHHHHHH!!!!'*
*Thud.*

And then suddenly he strikes lucky. He catches the log at an angle, blade tilted forwards, and the whole thing splits clean down the middle, the two halves toppling each side of the chopping block. Benny stares in disbelief for a good few seconds. Then he picks up one of the halves, stands it upright on the tree stump and hacks at it again. He's sure to angle the blade in the same way, to give it that same short, sharp impact, like a karate chop. And the same thing happens, the wood splits.

And it dawns upon Benny that there's an *art* to this. That it's not at all about brute strength, but rather technique. It's not about having enough power to hack through the entire log, but catching it at just the right place, with just enough force to split the seam already running through the wood.

And so he keeps on, splitting and screaming. From each piece he derives two smaller pieces. Until the log is reduced to a pile of firewood.

Then he fetches the next log.

'NGAHHHHHHH!'
*Split.*
'GAHHHHH!'
*Split.*
'RAAAAAAAAA!'

—

---

* Even at this late stage, it's nice to finally have an explanation for all the screaming.

Once all the wood is chopped, Benny gathers as much as he can, ferries it round the front of the house, over to the fence. He finds that some pieces slot through the gaps in the chain-links, the rest he tosses over. It's only then that he realises he has no way of getting *himself* over.

He weighs up his options. His best bet is to attempt to climb again, although he needs something substantial to stand on. He heads back over to the house. He has to be quick, he's wasted too much time out here already. He briefly considers that there may be a ladder somewhere inside, although the thought of entering through the kitchen window isn't particularly appealing. Then he spots the log store. It's perfect: a solid, waist-high structure that appears to be moveable. It's only when he actually starts dragging it, that Benny realises how heavy it is; how much noise the act of dragging it makes. He remembers earlier, how self-conscious the crunch of his boots on the gravel had made him, and laughs to himself, because that was nothing compared to this – a churning, scraping *roar* of wood and rock. And yet, what does it matter? He's been screaming his lungs out for the past few minutes – who gives a fuck how much noise he makes now?

He pushes the log store in place, steps up onto it. He hooks his leg over the fence and drags himself over, gritting his teeth against his various aches and pains. His ankles take the force of his landing and there are sharp, stabbing pains as he hits the ground, but it makes little difference, overall. By now his whole body is in pain; one all-consuming *ailment*.

He gathers the firewood and hurries back across the field to Stephen.

The tent has continued to sink in Benny's absence, much of the porch now sagging. The dog is gone and everything seems unusually still. For a moment Benny gets this strong feeling that Stephen is no longer inside the tent, that he's going to unzip the front porch only to find an empty sleeping bag abandoned in the darkness. A sense of dread swells within him. What would he do, if this turned out to be the case? Would he go out into the darkness and look for Stephen? Or would he just wrap himself in the sleeping bag . . . give in to his own exhaustion . . . sleep . . .?

He reaches for the zip. He swallows.

Stephen is still there. He's laid out on the groundsheet over at the far side of the tent. He's on his front now, his arms stretched out at each side. The sleeping bag has bunched at the top, his feet poking out the bottom. He's managed to kick off one of his trainers completely, but the other is half on, jutting out at an unnatural angle, as if his leg's on back to front.

Benny asks if Stephen is awake, but gets no response. He tells Stephen that he's managed to chop some wood, they can light a fire now, warm up a bit, but Stephen remains still. He's not shivering any more and there's no sound coming from him either. No struggled breaths, no snoring.

Benny asks if he's OK. Nothing.

He gives it a few seconds, then asks again, louder this time. Nothing.

Benny edges closer. He places the tip of his boot against Stephen's hip, rocks him gently. He kneels beside him, shakes him by the shoulder.

Benny's breathing fast now. He can feel that sense of dread again, ballooning in his chest. He shakes Stephen again, harder this time.

Then he panics, grabs Stephen by the shoulder and rolls him onto his back.

Stephen coughs, cries out.

'What the hell, man!'

'I thought . . .'

'I was s-sleeping, Ben.'

'You weren't snoring.'

'What?'

'You weren't snoring. Usually you snore.'

'Well, I'm s-sorry, man . . . *Jesus.*'

—

281

Benny steps out. He takes a deep breath of the cold night air. He's shaking all over. He's not sure if it's the cold or the adrenalin, but he can't seem to steady his hands.

The dog is back. It's on guard outside the tent again, that same position as before. It squints up at Benny in the torchlight. Benny asks where it's been, but the dog doesn't answer. He asks if the dog was over at the house, leading him on that wild-goose chase into the shower block.

The dog just sits there, panting.

Benny sits down beside it.

He takes out his penknife, selects one of the smaller pieces of wood, and shaves off strips of tinder, which coil and flutter onto the patch of grass between his thighs. The dog watches. Benny's hands are still shaking, but he soon gets into the rhythm of it. There's something about the simplicity of the task that he enjoys. It reminds him of peeling veg. He tends to cook dinner, now it's just him and his mum, and he finds the routine of it relaxing – the peeling and chopping, boiling pasta, frying meat. They usually eat in front of the TV with the quiz channel playing and never say a word to each other, but that's OK. Benny's grateful, in a way, that his mum doesn't feel the need to offload her grief onto him. It would only be more fuel for The Fog.

After a few minutes there's a hiss of polyester against canvas, followed by a series of short, sharp breaths as Stephen drags himself out into the porch.

'Ben?' *Pause.* 'You OK?' *Pause.* 'I'm s-sorry. You just s-scared me is all.' *Pause.* 'B-Ben?' *Pause.* 'What . . . what was that sound before? The screaming?' *Pause.* 'I heard s-screaming . . .' *Pause.* 'About t-ten minutes ago. There was screaming . . .'

*Pause.*

Benny keeps whittling away at the strips of wood. He wonders if Stephen's really expecting him to answer, with the torch there between his teeth. The edges are slicked with saliva and he has to bite down to keep it from slipping. A strand of drool runs down his chin – he rubs it off against his shoulder. His right thumb is pressed into the base of the wood and with each knife-stroke the cut there throbs. There's a thumbprint of blood on the wood, but he ignores it. His legs are cramping, he ignores them too. He can feel Stephen watching, waiting for an answer – he ignores him too.

Soon Benny's gathered what he deems a sufficient amount of tinder, a tennis-ball-sized mound. He crawls on knees and elbows with the kindling cupped before him, lays it sacrificially a good distance from the tent. He selects a few of the smaller pieces of wood and props them over the mound in a makeshift pyramid structure. He reaches for his pack, scours through the clothing and cooking equipment, the noodle packets and water bottles. Eventually his fingers arrive at something small and icy, the length of a pencil – the flint. He sighs, pitches it into the darkness. He doesn't even hear it land. The split in his thumb throbs. There's blood smeared on the side of the pack. It's all over his fingers, probably staining all his possessions, but Benny keeps searching until he's sought out the tiny, stubble-edged box at the bottom. It feels light; nearly empty. It sounds it too, when he lifts it to his ear and shakes. He slides it open: five matches left.

He nearly prays, kneeling there beside his fire-in-waiting – *let there be light*. His mum would often make him and Amy pray before bed, back when they were children, although he never knew what to ask for. Right now he can think of plenty.

He strikes the matches one by one. The first is a dud. The second flares out instantly. The third he's able to preserve, cupped between his palms – the flame stroking the tinder, the edges of the shavings glowing red. But there's no climax to it, no blaze of light. The match burns all the way down to his bloodied fingers, then dies. The embers fade. The shavings are probably too big. It could be that they're damp. If the tinder is too damp it isn't going to light, he remembers that much from his uncle.

Then he has a thought. He removes the guidebook from his pocket. He flips to the back pages – the maps of Prestatyn and Bodfari, the path already trodden (the furthest possible pages from the poem) – and tears them from the spine. Stephen gasps, but Benny ignores him. The dog watches, intently. Benny carefully shreds each page into strips, nestles them amongst the tinder. He strikes the penultimate match, holds it to the paper, watches the slight flare as one of the strips catches. At first it seems his plan is working – the flame makes its way along the strips, each one lighting the next. The paper curls, blackens, withers in the heat. But soon the flame flitters out. All that remains is a few thin strands of black smoke.

Benny has another idea. He scours his pack again, this time for his washbag. He unzips it, slips out the can of deodorant. Benny holds the can a few centimetres from the tinder, presses the button for a good five seconds, holding his breath to keep from inhaling the fumes. He's certain this'll work. He remembers in school, how people would spray their names on the tarmac in the playground then set the letters alight. He's sure Cal did it a few times; can picture a blazing **C A L**.

He strikes the final match, drops it onto the bark, then watches as a crown of blue flame spreads. The bark begins to crackle. Embers vein the surface like a series of tiny fuses. There's a pop, a blaze of light as the wood catches.

And there it is: fire.

'Woah, it w-worked, man. It really worked.'

'Uh-huh.'

'You did it.'

'Uh-huh.'

'It's warm, man. I can f-feel it already, nice and w-warm.'

Benny selects the thinnest pieces from the woodpile, places them one at a time on the fire. Start thin and gradually thicken with the fuel, that's the idea – it's important not to choke the flames. He realises he still has the torch in his mouth, removes it. His jaw aches. His thumb throbs. He can feel the pain in his thighs from squatting.

Stephen's at the edge of the porch now. He's lying on his front, head protruding turtle-like from the crumpled tent. He looks a little healthier in the firelight, not as pale as he did under the glare of the torch. He's eyeing the dog, who is at that moment standing and approaching the fire. It stops there for a few seconds, awestruck, the reflection of the flames dancing in its widening eyes.

It sighs and slumps to the ground, then rolls over, its belly basking in the heat.

'That dog, man. Jesus.'

'I know.'

'You think it'll ever stop f-following us?'

'Probably not. Especially now it's discovered we can make fire.'

'What'll we feed it?'

'I don't know. All we have is rice and noodles. I don't think dogs can survive on rice and noodles.'

'I don't think p-people can either.' *Pause*. 'Jesus, just look at it. Remember earlier, when it went c-crazy? Never thought we'd see it like this.'

'I know.'

'It's as if it thinks it's like . . . joined our p-*pack* or something.'

'I know.'

'You reckon it's a boy or a girl?'

'Hard to tell.'

'Yeah, don't really want to get close enough to it to f-find out.' *Pause*.

'You should get a little closer to the fire, Ste. You need to keep warm.'

'I'm OK.'

*Pause*.

'I mean it, you need to get closer. You're not well. You need to warm up.'

'I'm OK, Ben. I'm fine. Honestly, I'm w-warm enough here.'

The flames flap wildly. It's as if a wind is blowing, although the night is still. Benny selects a few thicker pieces from the woodpile, tosses them into the centre. They blacken as the flames curl over them. There are a couple of pops and sparks – pockets of sap exploding. The dog lifts its head, glances over.

After a few seconds it lies back down, its belly rising and falling with each breath.

Another few minutes and it begins to snore.

Benny unzips the front pouch of his pack, retrieves the wet wipes, scrubs the blood from his hand. There are only a couple of wipes left and he uses both, although he finds it hard to get the little moons of dried blood out from under his nails. He tosses the bloodied wipes onto the flames where they crackle and curl. Then he seeks out his mini first-aid kit, unpeels a plaster, binds his thumb as best he can. He tosses the plastic backs off the plaster at the fire too, watches as they rise in the heat, dance in the air for a second, like butterflies, before descending into the flames.

He sits for a few minutes, watching.

Then he stands and walks over to Stephen. He clutches the top and bottom of the sleeping bag and drags him out onto the grass.

'Aggh! W-whaddayadoing?! Ben?! W-w-whaddayathinkyadoing?!'
    '*Urgh.*'
'Ben! Man! Jesus!'
'*There*, that's better.'
'I said I was f-fine, man!'
'You're better here.'
'It's too hot here, man. I'm b-burning . . .'
'You need to warm up.'
'I *am* warm.'
*Pause.*
'You need to eat, too.'
'I *can't* eat, Ben. My s-stomach . . .'
'You need to.'
'I threw up, Ben. Remember? I'm not w-well, I . . .'
'I remember, Ste. You threw up your entire lunch and more. That's why you need to eat.'

Benny gets out the mess tin, fills it to the brim with a mixture of noodles and rice – two packets of each – topping it up with the remaining water from one of the bottles. They're having a feast tonight, he says. They need the energy. Plus, he'll cook a little extra for their guest.

Benny pokes at the fire with a stick from the woodpile. He spreads some of the embers, places the mess tin onto them. He doesn't want to set up the gas heater; doesn't want that thing anywhere near the open fire. He still remembers one of his uncle's stories about a friend of his throwing a gas canister onto the fire for a laugh when they were drunk, how it had exploded in his face and a shard of metal had torn one of his eyes right out of the socket. Benny never knew if this was a genuine story, or maybe a scene from a horror film retold as one of his uncle's campfire tales, but it was a warning that always stuck with him.

The sides of the mess tin blacken within seconds. It starts to smoke as the flames whip up around it. Benny's not worried though, he's seen this done before – the placing of the tin directly onto the flames. He's sure he remembers his dad doing so at some point on one of their walks.

It doesn't take long until the water begins to boil. Benny has overfilled the tin and there's an angry hiss each time the broth bubbles over into the fire. The dog looks up, eyes the food, licks its lips.

Benny gives it a few more minutes, then wraps the hem of his shirt over his hand, grasps the tin by its handle and deposits it onto the grass. He gets out the sporks, offers one to Stephen, although Stephen's arms are still tucked away in the sleeping bag, so Benny drops that on the grass too.

Stephen stares down at the contents of the tin. He swallows.

'I can't.'
  'You can.'
  'I can't, man, I . . .'
  'Eat.'
  'Ben. I . . .'
  'Eat.'
  *Pause.*
  'I m-mean it, man, I . . .'
  'Just fucking *eat*, Ste.'

—

Benny takes the lead, scoops up a sporkful of the steaming mixture. Despite the intensity of the boiling, the rice is still luke-warm and gritty. He should have just used the gas heater, set it up a safe distance from the fire and boiled the noodles at a lower but more consistent temperature. Plus, he realises now that he's eating that he hasn't added any of the flavour sachets.

But whatever. Benny swallows. He takes another sporkful, keeps chewing. Even when blood drips from the plaster on his thumb, blooms there in the water, he just keeps slurping the mixture down. He doesn't feel any hunger. He feels nothing but the desire to get this over with.

He doesn't stop until he's eaten roughly a third of the contents of the tin.

Then he turns to Stephen.

'I'm sorry, Ben. I just can't m-manage it.'

Benny picks up the spork, scoops at the mixture, raises it to Stephen's mouth. Stephen stares down at it. The shadow of the spork flickers across his face in the firelight. His eyes flit to Benny's.

He shakes his head.

'No.'

Benny places the tip against Stephen's lips. He tries to back away.

'N—'

Only this time, the moment Stephen's mouth opens, Benny forces the spork inside. Stephen turns his head. Rice and noodles spill onto the grass. He presses his face into his shoulder, mumbles about not wanting anything, about feeling sick, whilst Benny scoops up another sporkful.

Benny places his other hand on the back of Stephen's head, pries it from his shoulder. Stephen wriggles. His arms are still encased in the sleeping bag. His hair hangs down over his face. A noodle-strand is clinging there on his fringe. The dog stands, suddenly alert to what's happening. It begins to growl.

Benny tightens his grip, presses the spork to Stephen's lips.

'Ben, please. I . . .' *Pause.* 'Mnnmn.' *Pause.* 'Nnn-nn.'
    'Eat it.'
    *Pause.*
    'Mnnnmn. Nnnn-nnn.'
    'Eat it.'
    *Pause.*
    'Mnnnnnn! Mmmnnnnn!'
    'Eat it.'

Benny straddles the sleeping bag. He presses the spork against Stephen's lips, finds his teeth still clenched beneath. Stephen is squirming now. Benny has to tighten his grip and he can feel this new pressure in every muscle of his aching body. He clasps his palm over Stephen's mouth, pinches his nose closed. Stephen writhes in the sleeping bag, but his arms are pinned, and he can't manage to free himself, and so Benny just has to wait for him to open his mouth, to breathe. Eventually he does – a deep, gasping breath – and Benny forces the spork inside.

Stephen continues to struggle but Benny holds his mouth closed, tells him to swallow. The dog is barking now. The wound in Benny's thumb throbs. The warm blood trickles over his tightened fist, runs down the side of Stephen's cheek, like a tear.

Benny says the same word, over and over.

'Swallow.' *Pause.* 'Swallow.' *Pause.* 'Swallow.'

Eventually Stephen swallows.

Benny loosens his grip. He picks up the spork again, dips it back into the mess tin.

'You've got to eat, Ste. It's important.
    'P-please . . .'

'It's for your own good.'

'Seriously, Ben. I c-can't. P-please.'*

This carries on in much the same way. Soon Benny abandons the spork, it's easier to just scoop the rice and noodle mixture into Stephen's mouth with his fingers. Stephen coughs, splutters. Occasionally he tries to turn away, but Benny manages to maintain a steady grip of him.

Soon the dog begins to bark. It scuttles back and forth as if it wants to join in the fight but doesn't quite know whose side to be on.

A few more handfuls and Stephen vomits† – a thick, white mixture, like rice pudding. Some of it lands back in the mess tin, the rest on the grass in front of him. He manages two more mouthfuls before he spews it up again. At this point, Benny stops. Enough is enough.

Benny sits back, wipes his hands on the grass. He throws a few more pieces of wood onto the fire. He sips water from his flask. Stephen stares straight ahead, over the puddle of sick into the flames. He says nothing. Benny sips some more water from the flask, offers it to him: nothing.

Benny pushes the mess tin over to the dog. This seems to sedate it a little.

He and Stephen watch as it laps at the remains of the food.

'I n-need to.' *Cough.* 'N-need to go inside.' *Cough.* 'I need sleep.' *Cough.*

---

* And I meant it, Ben. About being sick, I mean. I was feeling awful by this point, I really was. The sight of that mixture in the mess tin – that slop of rice and noodles, bobbing there in the water – *urgh*. (All I kept thinking was *worms and maggots, worms and maggots* . . .) I mean, what *was* that? You know how awful it is to be force-fed when you're nauseous? You realise how fucking torturous an experience that was for me? You were full-on psychotic at that point, Ben. It was like earlier, when we were down at the restaurant, when you were going at the fence panels with that axe – it was like you were *possessed* or something.

† Hate to say I told you so.

'You need to keep warm.'

'I need sleep.' *Cough. Cough. Cough. Pause.* 'I can't stay out here, Ben. I just can't.'

Benny turns back to the fire. Suddenly the smoke changes direction and in that moment they're fogged. Stephen erupts into a coughing fit. Benny closes his eyes, holds his breath.

'Fogged' is the wrong word – it's *smoke*, not fog, and this distinction is important. Benny doesn't want to be thinking about fog. Smoke is different – a positive – a consequence of the fire he made. Smoke is proof that they're safe and warm. Smoke also has certain comforting nicotine associations, a taste that simultaneously soothes and irritates the back of Benny's throat.

He opens his eyes again. Too soon: he sees nothing but a blanket of swirling grey. It stings his eyes. He squints against the tears. He waits until Stephen's coughing has died down, then takes another look, and by this time the smoke has dispersed. Stephen is huddled, face pressed into the grass. His fringe has wilted into the pool of vomit. The dog is there beside him, licking its paws.

Benny sighs. He nods, stands. He says yes, Stephen's right, he needs sleep. They both need sleep.

He squats over Stephen's sleeping bag, clutches the top corners, then drags him back across the grass into the tent.

# XXIV

*Feeding the fire – Old messages – Headache –*
*Final cigarette – Smoking in the house – The*
*hospice – The quiz channel – Possible dreams –*
*Searching for weed – A grim discovery – Fight –*
*A revelation – Fight / flight – An explosion.*

Benny stays up a while longer feeding the fire. He sees this as an important role. He figures that, even from inside the tent, Stephen's going to gain at least some benefit from being in the general proximity of the heat. Plus there's a chance Benny is concussed from that fall earlier. He decides he's best giving it a few hours before he tries to sleep.

The dog has no trouble sleeping. It seems to have abandoned its guard duty in favour of a lazy night in front of the fire. It's snoring loudly now, its belly inflating and deflating like a bellows. Benny wonders if the dog will try to get inside the tent with them once the fire dies out. Will it curl up at their feet? Or maybe nuzzle beside him, like Samson used to?

Benny retrieves his phone from his pocket, switches it on. He scans through his messages. Most of his recent conversations with Sam have been arguments, but scrolling back he finds a text from last September that ends **'i love u anyway u idiot'**, and he reads those words aloud to himself a few times. There aren't any new messages and he's on 12% battery now. He's no idea how he can be losing power so quickly. Maybe it's all this turning the phone off and on again.

Still, he switches it off. He sits back, watches the stars.

He retrieves the final cigarette from the tin, places it to his lips. He lets it bob there for a few seconds before changing his mind and stowing it back in the tobacco tin. His headache has eased a little now, possibly as a result of the fire (the inhalation of smoke, the associations with cigarettes). The pain has retreated to a dull throb – like a stone, lodged somewhere behind his right eyeball. He can't help but imagine it as the very same stone he picked up in Prestatyn two days earlier. He had images of himself skimming that stone out into the sea at Chepstow, although this is seeming less and less likely. He's not even sure he still *has* the stone – it's no longer in either of his trouser pockets. Possibly it's in his coat or his pack, but right now he doesn't have the energy to search for it.

He knows he should cut his losses, smoke the final cigarette. What's he saving it for? He's smoked for six years straight and in all that time this is the longest he's ever gone without nicotine. He used to refrain from smoking in front of his parents, although recently he's started lighting up whilst watching the quiz shows. His mum drinks hot wine and Benny smokes his roll-ups and neither of them mentions the various health implications. Not that he needs her to remind him; the photos of blackened lungs are right there on the front of the packet. Benny's father smoked for as long as Benny can remember, although he did his best to hide it from Benny's mum too, often sneaking to the shed to light up in secret. After the diagnosis he made a big deal of quitting – the gum, the patches, the ceremonial toilet-flushing of his cigarettes, etc., etc. – but even that didn't last long. He was holding a cigarette that night in the kitchen, wasn't he? Plus, Benny caught him at it again, a few weeks later, kneeling at the tiny window of his room in the hospice. (Although what did it matter, really, by that point?)

It's pathetic now, thinking back, but even during those weeks at the hospice, even when his father was sleeping eighteen hours a day and walking with the help of a stroller, even when he'd given up eating and given up talking and was needing to piss so frequently he had to keep a collection of plastic bottles at the side of the bed, Benny was still hoping that one day they could do this walk together. It was a notion he held on to throughout – no matter the opinions of the medical staff, Benny could never quite manage to extinguish this one spark of senseless optimism. The hospice was torture for his father. It wasn't too bad in the hospital because there was a lot going on, but in the hospice he was all alone in that tiny room on the third floor. It was a lot of sitting and waiting; blocks of time broken only by an offer of a cup of tea from one of the palliative care team.

That's when they started watching the quiz channel. Initially, Benny's dad had refused to pay for the TV in the hospital – he said it was a disgrace that some private company would leech off NHS patients – but once he got to the hospice, the boredom forced him to relent. He didn't read anymore, didn't write, didn't engage with the news (he said politics only made him feel more hopeless). The quiz channel was something easy – a distraction. He kept it on constantly. Even near the end, when he was drifting in and out of consciousness by the minute. And that was fine, none of them really knew what to say to each other by then anyway. At least with the quiz channel blaring they didn't feel the need to make small talk.

Benny sits up. It feels much darker suddenly. The fire has faded to embers. The dog is back on guard duty beside the tent. Benny switches his phone on. An hour has passed since he last checked, which seems impossible. He must have slept. His hoodie and shorts are covered in grass and shavings of firewood and he realises he's had his sleeve in Stephen's puddle of vomit. He wipes it on the grass.

He has a feeling he was dreaming, although he doesn't know what about. Ever since the arrival of The Fog he's not been able to remember his dreams. It's been this way for months now.

He throws the last of the firewood onto the embers, then crawls into the tent.

Zzzzzzzzzzzzzzzzzzzzzz.
   Zzzzzzzzzzzzzzzzzzzzzz.
   Zzzzzzzzzzzzzzzzzzzzzz.

—

Stephen is sleeping on his back again. Benny was right to keep the fire going – it does feel warmer in here. He zips the porch closed and wriggles into his sleeping bag. He feels better knowing that Stephen is sleeping, that his body is finally resting. Benny should sleep now, too. He needs to keep his strength up if they're going to make it to Llangollen tomorrow.

He climbs in his sleeping bag and closes his eyes. He pictures Sam's words on the screen again: '**i love u anyway**'. He tries to imagine Sam speaking these words aloud, but can't quite manage it. He wonders how many times they must have said they loved each other back in uni, the various amounts of significance they'd attributed to those words.

He tries his dad's old breathing technique – **IN** and **OUT** and **IN** and **OUT** – but soon his mind returns to Sam, to a different set of connotations for that mantra, and he laughs, sighs, feels that throb of regret ballooning in his chest. He tries to recall the message he sent to her three days earlier. Did he make any suggestive comments in that message? Did he tell her he still loved her? At one point he knew that message off by heart, but right now he can't even remember the opening line.

He wonders if he could get away with masturbating.* He probably could,† Stephen's well out of it. Still, there's something about it that feels . . . *icky*.‡ Plus, he's got a feeling that those depraved images of Sam are the only thing keeping him going. If he succumbs to his urges then he might lose that desire and tomorrow he'll have nothing to distract him whilst he's walking.

He tries not to think about it. Instead he concentrates on breathing. **IN** and **OUT**. **IN** and **OUT**.

**IN** and **OUT**.

It's then he remembers the weed. Maybe that would help, a spliff before bed. That could be exactly what he needs. Sure, there's no tobacco left, but he could always smoke it uncut. After all, that's how Sam used to smoke it, each time they were going

---

* Erm . . .

† NO.

‡ Yes. Very icky. No wanking, please.

to have sex, and she always said it sent her off to sleep nicely afterwards. Once she even fell asleep *during* sex, although that's not a memory Benny's particularly fond of recalling.

Benny sits up. He reaches for Stephen's pack. He knows he should ask, really, but he doesn't want to disturb him. He unbuckles the top as quietly as possible, slides his hands inside. There are plenty of Ste's sodden T-shirts still in there and Benny has no choice but to ignore how cold and slimy everything has become. He remembers Stephen stowing the bag of weed in his camera case, and so he pushes on through to the bottom. He drags out the case, unzips it, takes out the separate lens case and unzips that too.

He stops as his fingers arrive at something smooth and hard. It's about the size of a rugby ball, but it's delicate. Brittle.

It's only when he feels the horns and eyeholes that he realises what it is.

He lifts it from the lens case, raises it before him in the torchlight.

'Ste?'*

Zzzzzz.

'Ste?'†

---

* OK, so yes, I took the skull. You told me to leave it, up on the mountain, but I ignored you and I went back and took it. To be honest, I'm still not entirely sure why. It just felt . . . *necessary*. It's important to trust your intuition, when it comes to these things. It's not like I had a concept planned in my head or anything. But there was something about it – that death stare – I just knew that I had to have it.

And yes, I'm aware that it's a little macabre as far as souvenirs go – but is it really such a *crime*, Ben? Does it really warrant waking me in the night like this? You knew how rundown I was. You knew I needed rest – you've said as much yourself. Could this not have waited until morning?

† Because just imagine this from my perspective. I'm annihilated from that day on the mountains. My body is shutting down. I've been in and out of consciousness all evening. I've suffered illness, abandonment, not to mention my supposed best friend subjecting me to a prolonged session of *waterboarding by noodles*. My dreams are filled with images of glaring sheep and snarling dogs, and I'm still rattled from that series of disembodied

Zzzzz.

'STE!'*

Stephen's eyes open. He squints in the torchlight. His expression crumples into that wince-face, top lip rising to reveal a good half-centimetre of gum. His eyes dart from Benny to the skull, then back to Benny again.

Suddenly Stephen's mouth hangs open. It's only after a second or two that Benny realises he's trying to scream. It's a horrible image: Stephen lying there, silent-screaming in the torchlight. It's a few more seconds before Benny's able to get it together enough to respond; waving his arms in an attempt at reassurance. But Stephen's eyes are fixed on the skull, and in the process of waving, Benny is inadvertently flailing the thing in his face, and Stephen is shifting back now, right up against the wall of the tent. He's still bound in his sleeping bag, but he's squirming, trying to free himself from the fabric. Benny is telling him to stop, wait, it's only him, it's only Benny, *don't panic.*

And then suddenly one of Stephen's arms is free and he must have found some reserve of energy because, before Benny even gets the chance to drop the skull, Stephen's at his neck, choking him. His mouth is still open and his eyes are streaming and outside the dog is barking, and Benny topples backwards, trying to hold Stephen off with one hand, whilst raising the skull with the other. He crashes, shoulder-first into the side of the tent, feels the canvas give under his weight.

---

screams earlier. Suddenly something is coming through to my unconscious mind . . . it's a voice . . . familiar, but laced with anger . . . it's speaking my name, softly at first . . . but then louder . . . and louder . . .

* And then my eyes open. And there *you* are, Ben. Looming over me. Not only that, but there's that fucking *skull,* hovering there in the darkness. I mean, what would *you* do? Because I'm telling you, what came next was all instinct. A will to survive. It wasn't anything personal. It wasn't an act of aggression. It was self-defence on a purely *adrenal* level. It was a fight or flight moment at a time when, due to my exhaustion / my encasement in the sleeping bag / my position in relation to the entrance of the tent, the option of flight had been rendered an impossibility.

A pole snaps. The ceiling drops, blanketing them both.
The torchlight flickers out.


'GAAAAAGGGHHHHHH!'
'WHAT THE FUCK, STE!?'
'AGGGHHH-HA-HAAAAAA . . .'
'STE? CALM DOWN. STE!'
'I . . .' *Pant.* '. . . can't . . .' *Pant.* '. . . I can't breathe . . .' *Pant. Pant.*
'What the actual *fuck*!'
'I mean it . . .' *Pant.* '. . . Ben . . .' *Pant.* '. . . I . . .' *Pant.* '. . . can't . . .' *Pant.* '. . . b-breathe . . .' *Pant. Pant. Pant.*
'We need to get outside. Can you get out? Come on, follow me . . .'
'What . . .' *Pant. Pant.* '. . . were you . . .' *Pant. Pant.* '. . . doing?!'
*Pant. Pant. Pant.*


Benny climbs out through the porch. The heat from the fire hits him immediately. He didn't realise how much life there was in those last few pieces of wood, but now the flames are roaring.

The dog is over at the side of the tent, barking. It stops when it sees Benny, gives out a low, rumbling growl. It's baring its teeth and its ears are back and there's wildness in its eyes again, like back in the farmer's field. It turns to watch Stephen, wriggling out from amongst the wreckage of the tent.

Stephen collapses onto the grass. He's gasping for air now. He ignores the dog, glares up at Benny instead. No, not at Benny – at the skull. Benny is still holding it aloft, as if to protect it. In the firelight he can make out a crack along the cheek (his thumb must have snagged one of the eye sockets). One of the horns has snapped too, it's now hanging loose at the side.

Stephen points at it.


'That's mine.'
'What the *fuck*, Ste?'
'It's mine!'

'Why in fuck's name are you carrying around a fucking *dead animal*?'

'Give it back.'

'No.'

'It's mine!'

'No, Ste. This is not OK.'

'Why does it matter so much?'

'It's just *wrong*, Ste. OK?'

'Why? Because it's against the *code*?!'

'Not just that.'

'I don't give a *fuck* about the cunting country code!'

'I *told you* to leave it, Ste! I *told you* to have some respect . . .'

'It's for my work! I need it for my work.'

'So, what? You're going to *take photos of it*? Put it on a fucking *T-shirt*?'

'Maybe.'

'Why?'

'Because!'

'*Why*?'

'Because I want to, OK?'

'No, I want to know why. I want to know what the fucking point is.'

'It's got nothing to do with you!'

Stephen attempts to stand, make a grab for the skull. His legs still aren't ready to support his weight, and so all Benny has to do is back up a little and watch as he stumbles onto all fours. He lands with his hand in the puddle of sick and his arm slicks off to the left. His face hits the grass.

Benny's right up against the fire now. He can feel the heat against his back. He's sweating.

'Just leave it, Ste.'

'Why can't I just have it, man? Why does it matter?'

'Because enough is enough! Are you really going to keep on with this shite? You've got to grow up. You've got to stop all this.'

'It's my *life*, Ben!'

'Enough already! This fucking . . . I mean, what even *is this*?'

'It's art, Ben. You wouldn't understand.'

'Then explain it to me.'

'I can't, man. That's the whole . . .' *Cough. Cough.*

'What?'

*Cough.* 'That's the whole *point*.'

'You're collecting dead things, Ste. This is, like, serial killer behaviour.'

'And what about *you* Ben?'

'What?'

'What about that plastic tub?'

'What about it?'

'You're carrying round bits of a dead *human*, for Christ's sake!'

'That's not the same thing!'

'Look, I'm sorry, Ben. I really am. I get that you're all fucked up about your dad and everything, and that maybe mortality is a bit of a sore subject for you right now, but this is my *work*, OK?'

'Ste . . .'

'This is my *art*.'

'Ste, just stop. You're not an artist, OK? You're a grown man, living in your mum's attic, taking photos of a fucking Halloween decoration.'

'That's low, Ben. That's really—'

'But guess what, you've still got time. You can still find a job, turn it around. You just need a fucking *job*. You just need to stop fucking around with these fucking skulls and *get a job*. You've got a degree now. Use it. You can't just waste your life like this.'

'I haven't.'

'What?'

'I never got my degree. I dropped out.'

'What?'

'That's how much this *means* to me, Ben.'

'Hang on a minute, you—'

'I never finished the course.'

'You *dropped out*?'

'In second year.'

'Why?'

'For my *art*, Ben. The course was just getting in the way of what I was trying to achieve. That's how seriously I'm taking this. That's what I mean when I say *it's my life*.'

'*What*?!'

'I don't want to get into all this, Ben. Can't we just—'

'You dropped out of uni?'

'I needed to, Ben. I—'

'That's it, Ste. I'm getting you a job at the call centre. I'll get you another application form.'

'I can't, Ben. I can't do that.'

'But you don't need a degree to work there. Not *yet*, anyway.'

'I know, I know. I just don't *want* to, OK?'

'Why?'

'Because.'

'Because you're too good for it?'

'*No*! It's just . . .'

'You think it's below you. You think I'm the lowest of the low for taking that job.'

'No, Ben. I—'

'But you're wrong, Ste. You're wrong. Because you know who the lowest of the low *really* is?'

'Ben, I—'

'*They* are.'

*Pause.*

'What do you—'

'*They* are, Ste. I swear to God. Those fucking people who ring up.'

'I don't—'

'I *speak to them*, Ste. I answer the phone to them every fucking day. Moaning, crying, *begging*. And for what? For nothing. For fuck all.'

'I really don't think—'

'And I know you've bought into it, this whole *Guardian*-lefty, big-bad-dystopian-government bullshit. And fine, I'm not surprised, considering that gang of twats you were hanging out with at uni. But guess what, Ste . . . it's not that simple. Because these people . . . these *fucking people* . . .' *Pause.* 'You don't want to end up as one of these people.' *Pause.* 'They're *parasites*, Ste. They're fucking waste of *life*.'

Benny stares into the darkness across the field. His headache is growing again – he can feel it, swelling. He closes his eyes, takes a few deep breaths. The air is thick with smoke.

When he opens his eyes again Stephen is lying still, face pressed into the nook of his arm. His breathing has settled now. The dog has settled too. It's staring up at Benny with a pleading look, its eyes flitting between Benny and the skull in his hand. Benny raises it, watches the dog's head rise. He moves it from side to side – the dog's head follows.

Benny slips the hatchet from his belt, weighs it in his hand. He stoops, holds the skull out towards Stephen, who looks up instinctively. There are tears in his eyes, but maybe it's just from the smoke. He glances at the skull, then up at Benny. His eyes widen. He thinks Benny's giving it to him. He and the dog are both watching with matching looks of expectation.

Benny drops the skull onto the grass. Then, before Stephen or the dog can make a grab for it, he brings down the hatchet. He's almost surprised at how easily it pops through the bone. It's not like the logs – there's no technique required. It's as if the thing were made of papier-mâché. Benny raises the hatchet again and this time the skull comes with it, hooked on the end like some giant, gnarled marshmallow on a stick. Stephen looks up, mouth open in horror. He shuffles back into the porch of the tent. For a moment it looks like he's worried he might be next.

Benny takes a final glance, then turns – tosses both skull and hatchet into the fire.

'There. It's done with.'

Stephen climbs to his feet. He stands beside Benny. The two of them stare down at the fire. It's the handle of the hatchet that catches first, flames dancing around the wood. The dog approaches too.

Benny places a hand on Stephen's shoulder. The skull just lies there, grinning from the crackling flames.

Then a few things seem to happen at once. One is that Stephen lunges forwards to retrieve the skull. Another is that Benny, purely on instinct, engages him in a hard tackle, the type he hasn't attempted since his rugby days. Their two bodies collide and a shockwave tears through Benny's shoulder as they twist and fall. They hit the ground side-on, and Benny is calling out now, telling Stephen to give in, to stop being so stupid, and Stephen is writhing on top of him, arms stretched out towards the flames. The dog starts barking again. Benny can feel every ache and ailment in his body, screaming out to him. He's in no state to be wrestling – his body needs rest. And yet here's Stephen, still reaching out, still desperate to get his hands on that fucking skull.

Benny tries to stand, but his attempt is clumsy and he slips on the smear of Stephen's sick and his foot lunges into the tent, his toes striking against something hard and cold. He looks up just in time to see something bounce from the porch. At that moment Stephen stops struggling and he too turns to watch. The dog stops barking. It's as if they're all aware something of significance is occurring.

It's the gas canister. It's on its side, rolling from the porch of the tent and out across the grass. At first it looks as if it's going to miss the fire completely. Benny almost sighs in relief.

But then it veers, rolls straight into the centre, where it stops, the flames crackling around it.

Benny and Stephen share a look.

'Run.'

Suddenly they're up. They're moving. Benny is clutching Stephen by the collar of his shirt and Stephen is hobbling beside him, and they are making their way across the field as fast as they can, away from the campsite and into the darkness.

Benny has no idea which direction they've taken – whether they're heading to the road or back towards the house – everything but the fire behind them is pitch-black. He has no idea where the dog is, whether it has any way of grasping the danger of the situation. He keeps expecting an explosion from behind. He's imagining something all encompassing, a tidal wave of heat and energy that knocks them to the ground, like in a film.

They only stop when they arrive at the fence. Stephen collapses against it in fits of lunging breaths. He coughs, *hoiks*, then coughs again. Benny watches the fire in the distance. Neither says a word.

They're waiting for a good few minutes for the inevitable explosion. Benny can feel his heart beating in his chest. He can feel the cold grass against his knees. He can feel Stephen, huddled beside him, his entire body trembling.

When the explosion comes, it's tiny. A pop like a fart, and a flutter of sparks from the flames.

Benny laughs. He can't help it. He can't make out Stephen's face, but he can hear him – he's laughing too. It's like with the cows again, the two of them crouched there, laughing together.

Eventually the laugher dies down.

'I'm sorry, Ste.'
'I know. M-me too.'
'I don't. I mean, I don't know what to say . . .'
'I know, me n-neither.'
*Pause.*
'Come on, fuck it. Let's just go to bed.'

# D I E*

<hr />

\* OK, this will be my last major interruption, Ben. I promise. I get it: this is your story. This is you exorcising your various demons, regarding what happened on that trip. And I appreciate that, I really do. But, for some reason, *I'm here too*. I can't ignore that, can I? I can't just sit this out as a casual observer. I don't know why I'm here (I don't even really know *how*) but we're approaching the end now, and I'm starting to think maybe I'm supposed to interrupt. That maybe that's my purpose. I'm beginning to feel a certain sense of *duty*, when it comes to these interruptions, a certain obligation to the principle of truth.

I won't spend too much longer on the subject of Garth. I know I've probably gone overboard as it is, trying to talk you through the development of our relationship. I'm also aware that you're not a fan of his (you've thus far made your feelings towards him perfectly clear) and so I imagine the importance I'm placing on his role in all this will more than likely only serve to annoy you. So I'll just come out and say it, OK: I *loved* Garth. I wasn't consciously aware of doing so at the time, but in hindsight I can see the objective truth of the matter. I'm also aware that this was in no way a positive, healthy type of love. That, although Garth more than anyone helped shape me into the person I would later become, he can't (and should not) withstand scrutiny, especially regarding certain life choices I made back in university. At the same time, I'd like to make clear that this is in no way an attempt to shift responsibility. I hold my hands up – failing the course was my own doing. Garth was incredibly important, in terms of my artistic and political awakening, and sure, one way that manifested was my decision over whether to continue as a student, but still, no one forced me to drop out. Ultimately, I was the one who made that choice and I was prepared to see through the consequences.

To be honest, my dropping out wasn't a particularly dramatic series of events. I mentioned earlier about my newfound political engagement, my rekindled creative spark. Garth and I were devoting a lot of time to this art-as-activism ethos during second year and we would often spend our days out on the streets with our sketch books and cameras, seeking out shelters or alleyways, parks or underpasses – anywhere the homeless were likely to congregate. We'd use these research trips to gather inspiration, then retreat to the house for all-night sessions of intense artistic outpouring. Our initial concepts mostly manifested in canvas work, but after a few weeks we began to experiment with expression and form. Garth became increasingly obsessed with 'authenticity' and by the beginning of the second semester he had begun to collect unwanted items from the places we visited; abandoned pillows and blankets, old cardboard signs or polystyrene cups. 'Homeless detritus' he called it; 'readymades' he could incorporate as parts of his sculptures and installation pieces. It was around then that I began to use Frank as a model and *Doomed Youth* began to take shape.

We took the usual route for displaying these pieces, arranged viewings at the house at one of Garth's ARTies. The ARTies were legendary by that point – became the go-to extra-curricular activity for the majority of the course – and every one of our classmates was begging to have their work displayed (everyone except for Jess, that is). We had to clear the entire downstairs of the house in order to create enough gallery space for the new work. *Sheltered Life*, we called it. We didn't allow any other artists to contribute at this point, not even Olga; it was all mine and Garth's work, our first collaboration. And it seemed to get a good response, people were congratulating us. Still, Garth wasn't happy. He didn't want people to like it. According to Garth the work demanded *outrage*, not acceptance. He wanted to challenge the status quo.

It was towards the end of second year that all this began to have an effect on our uni work. Coleman didn't like the project. He couldn't see the potential in what we were doing. He thought the whole 'working-class politics' angle had been done to death already via the Street Art movement. Which was great news, according to Garth. 'All good work is rejected by the establishment,' he said, 'that's the whole *point*. A good art movement is a *revolution*.' When it came to coursework, however, Garth had a distinct advantage over me, in that he'd been churning out canvases for years. Garth had a surplus of old material he could submit and as a result he still ended up receiving good marks. For me, *Doomed Youth* was my first proper project.

It seems strange now – ironic even – that it was due to me spending so much time working on my art that my marks began to slip, but that's how it played out. In the end it got embarrassing, showing up to class, week in week out, with nothing to show for myself. So I stopped attending. Months went by. I missed deadlines. I requested extensions, but each time I was rejected out of hand. Garth even got his dad to write to the department on my behalf, but it made no difference. Maybe I could have just bitten the bullet, submitted something from *Doomed Youth Pt 1* or *2*, but I knew these were still early days. It wasn't ready.

And then, one afternoon near the end of term, Jess showed up. It was a surprise, given her feelings on Garth and Olga – both of whom couldn't help but arrive at my bedroom, smirking, to inform me that I had a visitor. Jess and I hadn't really spoken since I'd started living at the house. It'd been during one of our workshops when I'd first told her I was moving in with Garth and Olga, and Jess hadn't given much of a reaction at the time, just shrugged and said she had to get on with her canvas work. After that she'd pretty much ignored me in class. I'd still feel guilty each time I noticed her, working away on her own at the back of the room, but she was consistent with her grades and it seemed like she was getting on fine without me (like I said earlier, she really was a good painter).

That night Jess was waiting for me at the end of the path. Which seemed odd, given how long that path was (I don't know if you remember, but the front of the house was a jungle of overgrown trees and bushes – obviously she wanted to keep as much distance from the house as she possibly could). I put on my coat and shoes and made my way out to her. She was staring up at one of the first-floor windows, and I turned just in time to see the curtains twitching, Garth and Olga desperate to eavesdrop. Jess suggested we go up the road to a pub she knew, give us a chance to talk in private. I agreed, and that was all we said to each other the whole way there. The silence lingered even after we'd arrived and ordered a couple of pints of Guinness.

Jess was the first to speak. She asked how I was doing. I told her I was fine, but it was obvious she didn't believe me. Was I sleeping, she asked? Was I eating enough? I didn't answer. I didn't want to discuss my late nights or my diet (especially the whole veganism thing, which I knew she'd have been cynical of). Instead I shrugged and stared down at my pint. Jess sighed, shook her head. She told me I looked like shit. That much I agreed with; I'd lost a lot of weight by then and I'd recently agreed to let Garth shave my head (this was in the midst of delirium brought on by one of our late-night painting sessions, so it didn't seem that big a deal at the time). I was actually looking more and more like *Frank*, which only occurred to me right at that moment, sitting across the table from Jess, staring at my own reflection in the window behind her, and it was a notion I found quite pleasing. (The use of Frank had been inspired by Van Gogh's *Head of a Skeleton with a Burning Cigarette*, and Garth had this theory that the skeleton was actually a self-portrait of sorts, and so there was a nice symmetry there, artistically speaking.) Jess was staring at me the whole time I was thinking this. It was then that it occurred to me that she too looked different. She'd cut her hair short, which suited her face more than the old pulled-back ponytail, and she was dressed a bit more stylishly too, wearing dungarees and a headscarf. She looked good.

After a minute or so Jess tried again. This time she got straight to the point, asked what the fuck I thought I was doing skipping class. Did I know I'd missed the portfolio deadline? Did I know Garth had been telling everyone to stay away, that I wasn't to be disturbed? That Coleman was considering withdrawing me from the course? I shrugged again. I knew at that moment it had been a mistake, agreeing to talk to her. I had nothing to say. I already knew what her reaction would be if I told her anything about the project, and right then I could do without that sort of negativity. It was then she asked if my mum knew about any of this and I felt a jolt of shame. I hadn't gone home for Christmas and at this point it had been weeks since I'd phoned Mum. It was too much mental energy, I needed to concentrate on the work. I didn't tell Jess that though. Instead I sat there for a good minute or two, staring at the head of my Guinness. I couldn't bring myself to drink it. I'd been up for seventy-two hours working on *Doomed Youth*. A wave of exhaustion was sweeping over me.

Jess sighed. 'Look,' she said, 'I know you believe what you're doing is, like, *worthy* or whatever, but don't let this mess up your chances, OK? Don't let yourself get swept up in all of this. This isn't a game for the likes of us.'

I looked up. I asked what she meant by *the likes of us*.

Jess smiled. 'Can't you see what this *is*?' she said.

I wanted to leave, but I didn't even have the energy to get up from my seat. I knew from Jess's earlier outbursts that she had little love for Garth and Olga, but it was that night she really let them have it. The art world had always been a game for the upper classes, according to Jess. It was reliant on the rich because without them it wasn't economically viable, and Garth and Olga were a testament to that tradition. They were using me. They weren't my friends – it was all a sham. I was a 'token working class' to them, a sacrificial lamb for their cause. 'Grooming' was one word she used (which I found laughable, at the time – we were all *adults* for Christ's sake). Still, it was hard to hear this stuff, most likely because I was aware there was a certain amount of truth to it. I just remember staring at my Guinness the whole time. I'm not sure if I ever got around to drinking it.

It was then Jess shared her theories about the course itself. According to her, the whole thing was a scam. 'A glorified pyramid scheme.' We were all tricked into applying, seduced by the promise of working in the arts. We'd enrolled, paid our fees, *bought* our degrees, but what did it amount to, really? It didn't mean anything once the course was over, not when it came to any sort of artistic career. The only purpose we served here was financial; the money that came flooding in would be funnelled up through the system to those at the top, the teaching staff (not directly, of course, but it paid their salaries). Only a handful of students would actually *make it* as artists, and they wouldn't be the likes of us. They'd be the Garths of this world – the students rich and well-connected enough to survive in London for long enough to establish themselves without ever drawing a salary. Garth's dad would more than likely call in a few favours, get him a few gallery displays, and then the next thing he knew, Garth would be invited to teach at the university, get his share of the pot. The rest of us were disposable.

'Think about it,' she said. 'Think about Garth's whole *deal.* That guy is *bred for power*, when it comes to the art world. His parents are both respected artists and collectors, both teach at major universities. Garth was probably hosting Art History seminars *in the womb*. He's destined for the top, Ste. He's the fucking Boy Pharaoh of this scheme. And we're the humble slaves, breaking our backs trying to shift a few bricks in order to enable his ascension.'

I had a slight problem with Jess's logic here. Not the pyramid analogy (sure, she got a little carried away, but she had a point where it came to Garth and his predetermined career path). What I was struggling with was that, if she was right – if the course was really as corrupt as she made out – then surely it was a *good thing* that I was on the verge of dropping out? Surely she too should walk away?

Jess didn't agree. She said we were different from the others. The only reason the rest of the class were willing to go along with this sham was because for them it didn't matter too much. They could afford to dabble in the art world. They could play at self-expression and experimentation and then return to their rich families, safe in the knowledge that they'll go on to have some lucrative career based on their current positions in society. And, if not, they had enough time and money to have a go at something else.

The two of us, we weren't like them. We had no safety net. We had to take it seriously.

'It's too late now,' she said. 'We only get one shot at this. You only get one student loan, Ste. We've made our beds here. Now we need to go ahead and get our degrees.'

'But I don't get it,' I replied, 'you just said they were worthless.'

'Well, yeah. I mean, they're worthless in the context of the London art scene, sure. But not out in the *real world*. That bit of paper, Ste, it's still a degree. It still counts for something. It's still our best route to getting a job in the future – *any* job.'

I knew she had a point. I'd seen plenty of news stories about places tightening their application processes, an increasing hysteria in the jobs market. In most jobs a degree was now a base-level requirement. That's why (according to Jess) it was important we put the work in. We'd come all this way – the only option now was to see it through to the end. And then, after we graduated, sure, we could keep on with our art in our spare time. But things had become much more competitive. We couldn't fight it, no matter what claims Garth made as part of his 'activism'. We had to play the game.

Jess put forward a good argument – I knew as much at the time. I was also very aware of Garth's lack of logical consistency. It was a running theme with him, the fact he didn't always practise what he preached. (Jess's go-to example was his veganism vs drug use; how he was so outraged by the meat industry, yet happy to fuel the much more ethically dubious drug industry through his unrelenting coke habit.) Still, I never minded too much. To me, this humanised Garth. I mean, weren't we all flawed somehow, deep down? Also, by then it all felt too late. I was so deep into *Doomed Youth*, it seemed impossible to turn back. This was important work I was doing, I was sure of it. I didn't have enough time now to produce course-work for all of my core modules. The only way to turn things around, in terms of the course, would have been to resit the entire year, which real-istically would have meant abandoning *Doomed Youth* altogether.

It felt like Garth was the only one who understood my dilemma here. He, too, was finally succeeding in fostering a political conscience in his work. And sure, he was still able to earn good marks whilst doing this, but that was unimportant in the grand scheme of things. *Doomed Youth* was my concept and I wanted to see it through to its conclusion, and Garth was encouraging of that. He'd already offered to let me stay at the house rent-free. If it reached the point where I lost my student loan, he could always help me out for a few months. I was pretty much relying on him and Olga for most of my money anyway, by that point (the loan went virtually nowhere in London), so it didn't seem like too much of a stretch.

Jess didn't agree. She thought of Garth as a wholly malevolent force in my life. I think she saw herself as a little angel, sitting on one shoulder, a horned little devil-Garth on the other. And I sympathise with her point of view; it certainly could seem like Garth was pushing some agenda here, like he was deliberately encouraging me down the path of dropping out. However, when I got home that night, shared Jess's comments with him, I could see that to Garth it was the other way around. He was trying to support my artistic truth, whereas Jess was trying to make me conform to the system. In his eyes, Jess was the devil – him the angel.

I can see now that the truth is probably somewhere in the middle. It's possible both of them thought they were acting in my best interests in this regard. But it was that moment in the pub with Jess that made me realise this was a definite choice I had to make. And once made, I had to stick to it.

So I did. I stayed at the house for another year, even after being kicked off the course. It was only when Garth and Olga graduated and moved out that I came back to Mum's. I continued with *Doomed Youth* even when I was back home, all alone in the attic. I carried on even after I'd drifted out of touch from Garth and Olga, when all I had left were those nights in the Miners with you. I had this belief that one day the project would be finished. That there would be some sort of payoff; a moment when I could finally reap the rewards for all the time I'd spent working on it.

Of course, there is a chance that all this is irrelevant. Maybe my being a jobless drop-out actually had zero effect on the events of that final day. Maybe things would have gone down the same no matter what. It's hard to say. I mean, how much unconscious bias were *you* harbouring at that point, Ben? Would you have been more likely to come back for me if it wasn't for our argument the night before? Were you, by this point, seeing me as just another one of your callers on the helpline? A 'parasite' on our country's finances? A 'waste of life'?

Are you even equipped with enough hindsight to answer these questions? Still, I guess it's a bit late for all this now, isn't it, Benny . . .?

_____

. . . Benny?

# XXV

*'A bad feeling' – Structurally compromised tent
– Fog on the field – Emptying the tent –
Dismantling – Suggestions from Stephen – 'Go
on without me' – Blackened bone – Abandoning
Stephen – A change of mind – Transferring
weight – Fog walking – Confirmation of the
existence of human life – Llandegla Forest –
Ghost trees – 'Keep g-going' – An opening – A
stile – An attempt at rest – Cold noodles –
Stephen goes on – Excessive panting.*

'. . . Benny?' *Pause.* '. . . Ben?'
  'What?'
  'You awake?'
  'Well, I am now.'
  'Right. Sorry.'
*Pause.*
  'Why? What is it?'
  'I don't know.'
  'You don't know?'
  'I just . . . I have a feeling. A bad feeling.'
  'About what?'
  'About today. Just, you know, *today in general.*'
  'What sort of feeling?'
  'Like, I'm worried.'
  'About what?'
  'I don't think I'm going to make it.'
  'You will.'

'How do you know?'

'You made it yesterday. You made it the day before.'

'Today's different.'

'It's the same.'

'It *feels* different.'

'You've just . . . hit a wall, Ste. You just need to push through it.'

'That's the thing. I don't know if I can push through it. I don't think I have it in me, to push through it.'

'You will.'

'How do you know?'

'You'll have to, Ste.' *Pause.* 'You'll just have to.' *Pause.* 'What choice do we have?'


Benny sits up. The tent has continued to collapse through the night and the porch is now dipped so low it's covering both of their legs. For a second this image takes him by surprise – as if he and Stephen no longer have the lower halves of their bodies. The snapped tent pole juts out like a hernia through the fabric of the wall, an inch or two from Benny's right cheek. He pushes it, forces it the other way, but the pole crooks back and the ceiling sinks behind them.

Benny sighs. He reaches for his pack. His hand arrives at something warm and he jerks away from it, only to realise it's the dog. It's laid out at the bottom of the tent, snoring.

Benny reaches past the sleeping dog to his pack. He takes out his phone, checks for messages. Nothing. He's on 6% battery now. He takes a sip from his flask. His hands are trembling. The headache feels like a rugby ball, lodged lengthways at the front of his skull. His thumb is swollen and angry-looking. He's lost the plaster during the night and the trench of the cut is now scabbed black. His shins are raw and tender and now almost totally hairless. His dick is pitched, hard as a crowbar. He wants, more than anything, to light and smoke that final cigarette.

Benny wriggles free from his sleeping bag, crawls out through the collapsed porch. He breathes deep as he emerges. A bright, white light blazes and he waits for his eyes to adjust, searches out a blue sky or green field, any sort of signifier of a large open space. He's expecting the same view as last night: the grass, the road, the fence and house and silo and shower block beyond. But there's none of that. There's just the remnants of the fire, a few feet of grass, and then nothing. *White*. The entire field has vanished, replaced by an unending bank of fog.

There's a rustling of canvas as Stephen emerges from the porch behind him. Benny doesn't turn to look. His stare remains fixed on the view ahead – the fog – as if his eyes will somehow adjust to it.

As if – if he stares for long enough – everything will suddenly reappear.

'Shit, man. Where'd Wales go?' *Pause*. 'Ben?'
'I . . . I don't know.'
*Pause*.
'You OK, Ben?'
'Fine.'
'You sure?'
'Yes.' *Pause*. 'It's just . . . I've never seen it so *thick* before.'
'Me neither. There's no way we can walk in this, is there?'
'We'll have to.'
'You're joking?'
'What else are we going to do?'
'We could wait.'
'For what?'
'For it to clear.'
'That might take hours, Ste. Might take all morning.'
'But still . . .'
'We need to keep going. We'll just have to walk through it.'

Benny stands, rubs his eyes. He glances around at their campsite – the island of field he can still see amongst the fog. He takes a deep breath.

Then he gets to work emptying the tent. He drags out their packs and sleeping bags, as well Stephen's scattered belongings (his camera, his flask, his soiled clothing). The dog soon gets wind of what's happening, steps out of the tent and shakes itself, before settling at Stephen's feet.

Stephen clears his throat. He asks if maybe they should leave the tent here. They could go to a camping shop in Llangollen, pick up a new one there – a lightweight one. It's fucked anyway, and it'd be one less thing to carry.

Benny doesn't reply. He drags out the broken poles, folds them as best he can, slots them into the bag. He drags out the inner awning, folds it over, flattens it with his foot.

It's not like littering, Stephen says. It's not breaking the code. There's junk everywhere here and anyway it's private land, so surely it doesn't even count.

Benny uproots the pegs, bags them too. He folds up the outer tent. He rushes it, and as a result none of it's bound tightly enough to fit inside the tent bag, and so he ends up rolling the whole thing into an unruly bundle, binding it with one of the guy ropes to the back of his pack.

Once he's done, he turns to Stephen, who still appears to be waiting for a response.

'Come on.'

'Ben . . . I, um . . .'

*Pause.*

'What is it?'

'I think I'm going to . . . you know . . . *stay.*'

*Pause.*

'Come on, Ste.'

'I mean it, Ben. I feel like I'm *dying.*'

'You're not dying.'

'I can't stop shaking. My legs. This pain in my stomach. It feels like a . . .'

'I know, Ste. I know about the pain. You've told me about the pain.'

'But I mean it, Ben. You should just go on without me.'

'How can—?'

'Just leave me here. I'll be OK. Someone will come along at some point. I can ask for help.'

'Are you *insane*?'

'Just go, man. I'll be fine.'

'Who exactly is going to come along, Ste?'

'I don't know, someone. *Anyone.*'

*Pause.*

'Look, you can't stay here. OK? I can't just *leave* you here.'

'Why not?'

'Because!'

'Look, I don't want to ruin this for you, Ben. I get it, this walk is important to you. It's fine. But I can't do it. I just can't. I'm incapable.'

'I don't believe that.'

'I don't care what you believe. *I. Can't. Do. It.*'

Benny sits on the grass, his back to Stephen. He stares into the remains of last night's fire. He can make out the gas canister; its paint peeled into ribbons, an exit wound near the spout at the top. A few pieces of surrounding wood have survived, although they're charred now, thinned in the middle, like bones. And then there's the actual bone – the crumbled husk of the skull – blackened now, but still grinning beneath a layer of white ash.

Maybe Benny should take Stephen up on his suggestion – go it alone. Don his boots, cross the field to the road, and just keep walking. If he's honest, he'd love a day by himself. A day without small talk and complaining, a day when he could stop for breaks only when absolutely necessary. He could probably make it to Llangollen by lunchtime if he was alone. But then what? His uncle would ask where his friend was. He'd have to explain that he'd abandoned him in a field, alone, and then Ian would probably drive them back to pick him up. Ian would pity Stephen and judge Benny accordingly. And he'd be right to. What sort of person would abandon a friend like that? What sort of person would even consider it?

He looks up, stares into what should be the distance, but is now very much just a blanket of fog. He can't believe the weather has conspired against him this way. British weather is insane – predictable only in its unpredictability. Suddenly he's unsure of his own ability to make it today. He isn't sure if there are enough pornographic images of Sam imaginable to avoid succumbing to the weight of it all.

The grass behind him rustles. He turns to see Stephen approaching.

Stephen stops there beside him. He sighs, kicks at the ground. He stands there a few more seconds before speaking.

'OK, man.' *Pause.* 'OK, you win.' *Pause.* 'I'll . . . I'll *try.*'

Stephen dishes out some water for the dog, whilst Benny finishes packing up the rest of their belongings. Benny decides he's best carrying the majority of the weight today. This means he's carrying the sleeping bags, the first-aid kit, the heavier items of clothing. This means he's carrying what's left of their water, as well as the flasks, the mess tin, the tub of ashes and the guidebook (which is heavy for its size) – not to mention the unholy burden of the tent.

Stephen gets the lightweight stuff. The T-shirts and socks, the empty bottles, the toilet rolls and last few packs of noodles. Stephen sits on the grass with the dog, whilst Benny empties the packs and redistributes the weight. Benny asks if he's planning on taking any photos today and Stephen takes a look at his surroundings and shrugs as if to say *of what?* and so Benny stows the camera case in his own pack as well.

Finally, Benny stands. He asks Stephen if he's ready. Stephen doesn't answer. Benny takes his hand, helps him to his feet. Stephen's still shivering. He's wearing that same T-shirt from yesterday – the photo of the skeleton with a strap-on, crusted with splotches of vomit and anti-vandal paint.

Benny takes off his raincoat, offers it to Stephen. Stephen stares at it for a few seconds, bewildered, until Benny explains that he should put it on. Stephen's sick, so he's the one who needs to keep dry. Otherwise he'll be soaked through by the fog, and that'll just make him even more sick, and *then* where will they be?

Stephen asks if Benny's sure. Benny says yes, of course he's sure, and Stephen nods and takes it from him. He removes the fleece, puts on the raincoat instead.

Benny dons the fleece. It smells like Stephen. He picks up his pack and heaves it onto his shoulders.

The dog stands there, watching.

'You OK, Ste?'
  'I think so.'
'Ready?'
  'I think so.'
'Right. Let's go.'

The three of them head out across the field. Benny glances back at the remains of the fire, although soon it fades into the mist. He tries to ignore the feeling of unmooring this instils in him. Leaving the campsite. Being *out here*, amongst the fog. Instead he focuses on his boots.

There's no point looking ahead now, not without visible landmarks – his only guide is what he remembers of the layout from last night. Stephen shuffles along beside him. His walk has an uncertainty to it now, like a toddler – each step measured, as if he's only just figuring out what his legs are for. Occasionally he wobbles to the extent that Benny feels the need to reach out and steady him.

Even accounting for their pace, crossing the field takes longer than expected. When the hedge does finally appear, Benny realises they've veered off course, and they have to skirt the field for another ten minutes until they reach the entrance to the site. There's still the same debris from last night, the bags of rubble and kitchen units. It's easier once they're back on the road, at least that's a guide of sorts, a path they can follow. They stick to the right. That way they're walking into traffic and can hopefully make out any fog lights approaching with enough time to move out of the way. Still, Benny's starkly aware of how dangerous this is. Road-walking in such conditions is far from ideal. He'll be much happier when they reach the forest.

No cars pass. No people either. At this point Benny almost

hopes to see someone. It's not like he'd communicate with them beyond a simple nod and hello, but still, it'd be nice to receive a little confirmation of the existence of human life.

Soon they arrive at a fork in the road and Benny consults the guidebook, directs them down a narrowing path between a scattering of stone buildings. They're most likely houses, although to them the buildings are indistinct shapes, mostly lost to the fog. It's here Benny spots the first signpost of the day: an acorn and an arrow directing them west across a patch of grass and up a steep cobbled path into the forest.

'You OK, Ste?'

   *Pant.* 'Yeah. I'm . . .' *Pant. Pant.* 'I'm OK.'

'You want to stop for a bit?'

'No, I'm . . .' *Pant. Pant.* '. . . f-fine.'

   *Pant. Pant. Pant.*

This is a section of the map Benny remembers from the guidebook, the stretch from Llandegla to Llangollen. He remembers thinking it would be a nice end to the first leg of their trip – the fields, the forest, the moors and the cliffside at World's End. Ian had mentioned this part of the trail too, when Benny had asked about staying over. Ian said it was a nice hike down from Llandegla, he'd done it a few times since he'd moved there. He'd even suggested he could come meet Benny along the path somewhere, join him along the trail for a few hours, although they'd never got around to arranging it.

Of course, the reality of the morning's walk is quite different. There is no view, just the few feet directly in front of them, then *nothing*. Fade to white. Still, Benny remembers the map of the forest from the guidebook – 6.5 square kilometres of densely packed conifers, its corresponding maps a nerve centre of paths and trails, winding and crossing, looping and splitting. The Offa's Dyke path channels straight through the middle but Benny knows they'll still have to keep an eye out for signposts. It'd be easy to lose their way in the fog, end up on the wrong track.

They continue through the forest for the next half an hour.

The fog makes for an unsatisfying walk. They're constantly heading towards it, without ever seeming to reach it. Benny keeps his eyes on the ground. The path here is manmade, a pebbled trench that stays level whilst the overgrown forest rises and falls at each side. The path is littered with conifer needles. Occasionally there are dark patches of moss, glistening like seaweed, engulfing rocks and fallen branches. An entire tree trunk lies flat against the side of the path, like the toppled mast of a ship.

Further on, the path grows steeper. There are scattered wooden steps to aid their footing, although Stephen struggles here, the process of climbing being too much for him. Benny goes back to help. Stephen keeps his eyes closed, wincing as Benny lifts his arm over his shoulder, moaning in pain as he guides him up the steps. Stephen's stomach lets out a series of gurgles and whines. The whole time the dog sits there in anticipation, as if it wants to help but doesn't quite know how.

Benny suggests they stop and sit on the steps for a minute, drink some water, but Stephen says no. He can't stop. He has to keep going. The only way he's going to make it today is if he keeps going.

They continue along the path. Stephen's panting has transformed into a definite wheeze now. Benny can almost hear the mucus, gurgling in his chest. The fog has condensed into droplets, glittering from his hair and jacket. Benny's sweater is soaked too, an icy dew that causes him to shiver. Benny's aware that his hair always looks thinnest when wet and part of him regrets giving Stephen his raincoat (at least the hood would have helped a little). But whatever. It's too late now to ask for it back.

*Pant. Pant. Pant.*

'You OK, Ste?'

'Yeah.'

*Pant. Pant. Pant.*

'You sure?'

'Yeah. It's just this fog, man.' *Pant.* 'I feel like I'm inhaling it.' *Pant.*' I can f-feel it on my chest.' *Pant. Pant. Pant.*

'I don't think that's how it works, Ste.'

'Eh?'

'Maybe we should . . . stop?'

*Pant. Pant. Pant.*

'No.' *Pant. Pant.* 'Keep g-going.' *Pant. Pant.* 'Need some-where . . . clear.'

*Pant. Pant. Pant.*

Before long they reach the edge of the forest, step out into fields again. The stone path is still there to guide them, and they follow it through the fog for a few more minutes, until they arrive at a fence. There's a stile here that leads onto the marshes beyond.

Benny suggests this'd be a good place to stop and cook some noodles. Stephen doesn't reply. He continues over to the stile, places a foot on the step and attempts to climb over. His legs are still hopelessly inflexible, and his bad ankle catches on the step, and he gasps and topples backwards. Luckily Benny's there to catch him.

Benny lowers Stephen to the stile, where he slumps back, face to the sky. He's sweating now. He's trembling more than ever. His fringe is thick and greasy and flecked with dandruff. A wad of mucus sits on his top lip, an almost luminous shade of green.

'Just hang on, Ste.'

*Pant. Pant. Pant.*

'Let's just sit and eat, yeah?'

*Pant. Pant. Pant.*

'Stephen?'

*Pant. Pant. Pant.*

'Ste?'

*Pant. Pant. Pant.*

Benny slides off his pack. He rummages for noodles, the mess tin, the water bottles. There's not much water left but it's enough for one packet of noodles, and they can always save the broth to drink along the way.

He dispenses the water into the tin. He peels open a pack of noodles, empties the contents. It's only then that he remembers they have no gas heater. The noodles bob there on the surface. The dog pants beside him, watching them bob. For a moment Benny considers whether Stephen would agree to chew them down cold.

Then suddenly a grunting sound comes from behind. Benny turns to find Stephen up on the stile again.

'Ste!' *Pause.* 'What the fuck are you *doing*?' *Pause.* 'Why won't you just stop and rest?'
*Pause.*

Somehow Stephen finds enough energy to haul himself over. He stumbles down the steps on the other side. The path beyond consists of a series of wooden boards bridging the marshes.

Stephen sets off along them, dragging his bad leg behind him.

A few more seconds and he's faded into the mist.

'STEPHEN!'
*Pause.*

For a moment Benny doesn't know what to do. He just stands there, staring at the path ahead, thinking maybe Stephen will reappear. The dog gives it a few seconds, then begins to lap at the noodles in the mess tin.

Benny sighs. He rubs at his eyes. He knows they need to rest. They need to stop and eat something if they're going to have enough energy to make it down the mountain to Llangollen. Surely Stephen knows this?

In the end Benny decides he has no choice but to follow. He too climbs the stile. He too proceeds along the wooden boards. After a few seconds he can hear the dog, trotting along behind him.

It doesn't take long for them to catch up with Stephen.

—

*Pant. Pant. Pant. Pant. Pant. Pant. Pant. Pant. Pant. Pant. Pant.*
*Pant. Pant. Pant. Pant. Pant. Pant. Pant. Pant. Pant. Pant. Pant.*
*Pant. Pant. Pant. Pant. Pant. Pant. Pant. Pant. Pant. Pant. Pant.*
*Pant. Pant. Pant. Pant. Pant. Pant. Pant. Pant. Pant. Pant. Pant.*
*Pant. Pant. Pant. Pant. Pant. Pant.* 'I c-can't . . .' *Pant. Pant. Pant.*
*Pant. Pant. Pant. Pant. Pant. Pant. Pant. Pant. Pant. Pant. Pant.*
*Pant. Pant. Pant. Pant. Pant. Pant. Pant. Pant. Pant. Pant. Pant.*
*Pant. Pant. Pant. Pant. Pant. Pant. Pant. Pant. Pant.* '. . . d-do it
. . .' *Pant. Pant. Pant. Pant. Pant. Pant. Pant. Pant. Pant. Pant.*
*Pant. Pant. Pant. Pant. Pant. Pant. Pant. Pant. Pant. Pant. Pant.*
*Pant. Pant. Pant. Pant. Pant. Pant. Pant. Pant. Pant. Pant. Pant.*
*Pant. Pant. Pant. Pant.* '. . . man . . .' *Pant. Pant. Pant. Pant. Pant.*
*Pant. Pant. Pant. Pant. Pant. Pant. Pant. Pant. Pant. Pant. Pant.*
*Pant. Pant. Pant. Pant. Pant. Pant. Pant. Pant. Pant. Pant. Pant.*
*Pant. Pant. Pant. Pant. Pant. Pant. Pant. Pant. Pant. Pant. Pant.*
'. . . I can't stop . . .' *Pant. Pant. Pant. Pant. Pant. Pant. Pant.*
*Pant. Pant. Pant. Pant. Pant. Pant. Pant. Pant. Pant. Pant. Pant.*
*Pant. Pant. Pant. Pant. Pant. Pant.* '. . . I n-need to k-keep . . .' *Pant.*
*Pant. Pant. Pant.* '. . . going . . .' *Pant. Pant. Pant. Pant. Pant.*
*Pant. Pant. Pant. Pant. Pant. Pant. Pant. Pant. Pant. Pant. Pant.*
*Pant. Pant. Pant. Pant. Pant. Pant. Pant. Pant. Pant. Pant. Pant.*
*Pant. Pant. Pant. Pant. Pant. Pant. Pant.* '. . . I . . .' *Pant. Pant.*
*Pant. Pant. Pant. Pant. Pant. Pant. Pant. Pant. Pant. Pant. Pant.*
*Pant. Pant. Pant. Pant. Pant. Pant. Pant.* '. . . need to k-keep
g-going . . .' *Pant. Pant. Pant. Pant. Pant. Pant. Pant. Pant. Pant.*
*Pant. Pant. Pant. Pant. Pant. Pant. Pant. Pant. Pant. Pant. Pant.*
*Pant. Pant. Pant. Pant. Pant. Pant. Pant. Pant. Pant. Pant. Pant.*
*Pant. Pant. Pant.* '. . . or I w-w-. . .' *Pant. Pant. Pant. Pant. Pant.*
*Pant. Pant. Pant. Pant. Pant. Pant. Pant. Pant. Pant. Pant. Pant.*
*Pant. Pant. Pant. Pant. Pant. Pant.* '. . . won't make it . . .' *Pant.*
*Pant. Pant. Pant. Pant. Pant. Pant. Pant. Pant. Pant. Pant. Pant.*
*Pant. Pant. Pant. Pant. Pant. Pant. Pant. Pant. Pant. Pant. Pant.*
*Pant. Pant. Pant. Pant. Pant. Pant. Pant. Pant. Pant. Pant. Pant.*
*Pant. Pant.* '. . . man . . .' *Pant. Pant. Pant. Pant. Pant. Pant. Pant.*
*Pant. Pant. Pant. Pant. Pant. Pant. Pant. Pant. Pant. Pant. Pant.*
*Pant. Pant. Pant. Pant. Pant. Pant. Pant. Pant. Pant. Pant. Pant.*
*Pant. Pant. Pant. Pant. Pant. Pant. Pant. Pant. Pant. Pant. Pant.*

# XXVI

*Marshland – Walking the plank – No view –*
*Camping shop memories – 'PISSING PLACE'*
*– River crossing – Bowel movement – The Fog –*
*The Fog – The Fog – The Fog – The Fog –*
*The Fog – The Fog – The Fog – The Fog –*
*The Fog – Behold, a pale sheep! – The Fog –*
*The Fog – The Fog – The Fog – The Fog –*
*The Fog – The Fog.*

They walk on in silence. The boards are only wide enough for single file here, which means Benny has no choice but to stay behind Stephen, maintaining the same creeping pace. It's more hazardous, Benny thinks, to be walking this slowly. The less momentum they have, the more their minds overcomplicate the act of balancing on the boards. As if to prove this theory Stephen wobbles occasionally, arms flailing to steady himself. Benny keeps expecting him to plummet into the marshes. He has this image of Stephen, sinking below the surface. A thrashing of arms, a froth of bubbles. Then nothing.

Benny's breathing is more laboured now. It's nowhere near as sharp or pained as Stephen's, but still, he's struggling. He doesn't know why. They're walking slowly and they're not going uphill, so there's no reason, really, for him to be this out of breath. Maybe Stephen's right, maybe the fog is entering their lungs. Maybe this is why everything's so much harder today: a slow smothering due to a sudden change in the weather. Benny tries not to give too much thought to the word *smothering*, which once again summons that moment back in the camping shop (the tight fabric of the one-man tent, the inner awning drawn into his mouth with each gasping breath). Once it was over, once Benny was finally freed from the twisted canvas, Camping Shop Mike had offered Benny a seat in one of the folding chairs set out amongst the faux-woodland scene beside the counter, said he could rest there for a minute, but instead Benny had lied about a prior engagement, paid up and left, still with that buzz of panic, still feeling The Fog pressing down on him. He stepped out in front of a Land Rover in the car park, had to endure the driver leaning out of his window, calling him a fucking idiot. Then he just sat there, in his car, staring at his reflection in the rear-view mirror, hair swept back in its receded V, face pale, jaw trembling. It took him nearly half an hour to get his breathing back under control. Another fifteen minutes or so before he felt ready for the short drive home.

It's hard for Benny not to dwell on this stuff. It's been bad enough the past few days, without the distractions provided by the routine of everyday life, but here, now, this morning, with *literal fog* surrounding him on all sides, it's almost unbearable. He concentrates on his breathing. (**IN/OUT. IN/OUT.**) He can hear Stephen breathing ahead of him, as well as the dog panting behind him. He knows it's not much further to Llangollen, not in the context of the distance they've travelled the last three days (a few hours, at most), and yet at the same time it feels utterly unreachable. The weight of the pack is truly horrific. The addition of Stephen's belongings has pushed it over the acceptable limit of a tolerable human burden and Benny is now hunched in a way that he can only assume is doing some lasting damage to his spine. Plus, there's Stephen himself – this new insistence on not having any breaks. In previous days Benny would have been thankful for this sudden change in attitude, but today he's aware this is going to end badly. By this point it's obvious that walking for hours on end is well beyond Stephen's physical capability.

According to the guidebook, the marshes only stretch for one mile in total, which should equate to about twenty minutes at average walking speed. To Benny it feels much longer. With the weight of the pack, the extra effort required to maintain balance, he feels every step of it. Occasionally there are patches of solid ground, a few metres of stony path, but for the most part it's boards and the boards make Benny uneasy. He doesn't like how wobbly some of them are. He doesn't like how slick they are, or that hollow clunking his boots make against the wood. He doesn't like the recurring notion that they're walking the plank – that at some point they'll come to the end, have no choice but to jump.

Eventually the marshes do come to an end and they're off the wooden boards and back on dry land. Benny is able to take the lead again now. The dog takes its place beside Stephen. Benny remembers from the guidebook that the road snakes down through the valley here, although the fog is still just as thick, and it's impossible to see what lies ahead. He's reassured a little when he spots an acorn sign, an arrow directing them to take a sharp right (which, if he's calculated correctly, means south). He can't believe this fog. It seems impossible, especially covering such a distance. It's almost as if it's localised to him and Stephen; as if it's accompanying them along the trail. From what Benny remembers, the path leads down into a valley, then up again, around the edge of the mountains. 'World's End'. He'd half thought the cliffs here might be a spot worthy of spreading another portion of ashes, but now they're approaching he doesn't like the idea of tossing handfuls of his father into this white nothingness. As they descend into the valley, he can feel the weight of that plastic tub, along with every other item that's crammed into his pack. He strains against it, tries his best to maintain a good posture – head back, spine straight. The tent has come loose and Benny can feel the canvas, flapping at the back of his legs. He can hear the rubbish bags, tapping against the sides of the pack with each step, and for a second he almost laughs (all that junk back at the campsite and *still* he's carrying these rubbish bags). He fiddles with the little chest clasp but finds the shoulder straps are now pulled too far back to enable him to fasten it.

They follow the road for the next twenty minutes. There's little in the way of landmarks. They keep to the right as usual, in case of oncoming traffic – although they haven't seen a car all morning. Occasionally there are points where the road opens out for a stretch and at each of these points there's a sign: 'PASSING PLACE'. A few of these have been vandalised with graffiti; a single black strip across the first 'A' to make it read 'PISSING PLACE'. Further on they pass another with several letters blacked out, plus an extra 'A' added, to read 'ASS PALACE'.

Soon they arrive at a river with stepping-stones leading over the water. The fog is thicker here – the river's only a few feet wide but Benny can barely make out the bank at the other side. He finds the act of stepping across, the precision required, is too much with the pack; he has no choice but to remove it, pitch it across the water, then hoist it back onto his shoulders once he's made his way across. Predictably this short spell of packlessness only serves to exaggerate the weight of the thing.

Stephen's fallen behind. Benny decides to wait, make sure he gets across the river OK, although it's a good few minutes before Stephen's bedraggled figure appears through the mist. He's looking more and more like something from one of Benny's uncle's horror films – head bowed, arms slack, body tilted to keep his weight on his good ankle. The dog follows at his heels, obedient as ever. Benny shouts over that Stephen would be best de-packing, that it'll make it easier to cross, but Stephen doesn't acknowledge this, doesn't say a word. He ignores the stones completely, ploughs straight through the water, his staggered lunges so violent Benny has to step back to avoid being splashed.

Now he's closer, Benny can see that Stephen has deteriorated rapidly. The trail of mucus has crossed his lips now, the more solidified end dangling from his chin. His T-shirt is twisted, giving the skeleton's strap-on dildo the look of a crooked pink finger, beckoning. Both of his arms are shaking and between pants he's emitting this sort of *hum* of discomfort. He appears to be a little less pale than before, although this may be due to the fact that his skin is now tinged a slight shade of green.

Stephen passes by without comment and fades into the fog. There's a stench coming off him now and it's only when he's gone on ahead that Benny recognises, with a sudden sense of horror, the unmistakable smell of human shit.

The trail takes them up through another stretch of woodland. The path is overgrown here, a combination of ferns, brambles and nettle bushes. Benny wishes he hadn't misplaced one of the zippable bottoms to his trousers. He knows it'd probably still be worth stopping to attach the other one, but it seems wrong, shielding one leg whilst allowing the other to take the pain.

Further up, the path gets even steeper. Benny takes it slow, maintains a similar pace to Stephen. This part of the trail skirts the side of a mountain – to their left a steep and stony incline, to their right a sheer drop down the cliffside. Exactly how far down a drop it is, Benny can't tell. He knows it must be a fair distance because of what his uncle said about the views here, but it's impossible to gauge with the fog. Occasionally his boot scrapes the ground and sends a few stones skipping off the edge, and he watches as they vanish into the white, listens out for the distant clatter some way down the mountainside. He tries to remember the name of the loose stones that cover the sides of mountains. It was mentioned in the guidebook. *Scree?* Is that it? It sounds wrong now but he's pretty sure the word is *scree*.

Benny thinks of the ashes again. He imagines pitching the entire tub out into the mist. He briefly considers whether the scattering of ashes would be seen as littering, in terms of the Countryside Code. Benny had thought, when he phoned his uncle, that they might have discussed what happened to his father – i.e. the cancer / the funeral / what was to be done with the remains. This was a couple of months down the line, when Benny had tracked Ian down on Facebook. Benny was a little worried about speaking to his uncle again. He thought it might have been awkward after all this time, but the truth is it was kind of nice, talking to him on the phone, especially as it was now on the level of one grown man to another. Still, Benny didn't feel like he could bring up Ian's lack of attendance at the funeral. Benny already knew about the falling out, all the stuff over Nan's house, although a part of him had hoped his father's death would transcend that. Even after the service, when they were sitting in the Miners, his dad reduced to ashes, Benny still expected Ian to show up and buy them all a drink.

At first, when Benny searched for Ian on Facebook, he had scrolled right past his profile. The thumbnail of his uncle's grinning face was the first image he'd seen of him in over ten years and Benny didn't recognise him. He remembered how Ian had once talked about growing older, about a man's haircut becoming whatever makes him look the least bald, and how Benny and his dad had laughed at this, the idea that any haircut could make his uncle look balder than completely clean-shaving his scalp every morning – and yet, somehow, now, with that bushy horseshoe of grey hair, the few strands combed over the top, Benny was shocked to find that Ian was right; growing his hair out only served to highlight what was missing. This was Benny's future, he knew it immediately. There were two paths Benny's genetic code could have taken him down, and from the moment he'd examined his hairline in the bathroom mirror, he'd known he wasn't going to grow old with a mane of thick, black hair like his father.

Stephen hasn't spoken for over an hour now. Benny thinks fuck it, if Stephen's going to ignore him then fine, he'll ignore Stephen back. Which is actually pretty hard, what with his panting and his gasping and the scrape of his bad leg as it drags through the scree. Plus, there's the smell. Stephen smelt bad enough already but ever since Benny noticed that faecal tang in the air, he can't help but envision the horror now oozing in those tighty whities. Part of him thinks he must be imagining it. Or else, Stephen must have just trodden in dog shit or something. He wouldn't let it come to *that*, surely?

Benny decides to fall back, allow Stephen to take the lead. He wants to check if there's any discolouration at the back of his trousers. Stephen passes without even looking up – without even acknowledging that Benny has slowed down – although the dog eyes him suspiciously. The raincoat covers most of what Benny deems would be the affected area, but then a sudden steepness to the path means Stephen has to stoop forwards, the hem rising just enough to display the backs of his thighs. And suddenly there it is: a seeping darkness in the fabric. Benny almost laughs. Of course it's true. Of course Stephen's shat himself. It was inevitable, really.

Benny overtakes Stephen again, powers on ahead. The path is obvious enough here to allow a little distance between them. The mountainside is much steeper now, although luckily the trail winds around the peaks, rather than crossing over them. To Benny's left is a steep bank of rock, to his right a sheer drop into the valley. The path has narrowed so much that he has to constantly watch his feet to ensure he doesn't slip. He takes a few deep breaths. The headache is like a bowling ball, there's that sort of shape and weight to it. His thumb is bleeding again, a result of clutching the shoulder straps to ease some of the weight on his back. His forehead is tight with sunburn. There's burning on his shins too, an undercurrent of stinging from the constant hostile vegetation. The blister under his big toe has popped and he can feel the rawness there, the flap of skin beneath. There are stabbing pains at his heels and the balls of his feet. He's thirsty. He suspects there might be a little water left in one of the flasks, although he doesn't have the energy to stop and retrieve it. There are other ailments too – too many to list. Because what good will it do, dwelling on this stuff? What good has that ever done?

Stephen's pant-and-scrape is fading now, as is the smell. Benny should stop, give him the chance to catch up. He knows it would be the right thing to do. Plus, if he stopped, maybe he could root out the ibuprofen and the water and maybe his sunglasses, soften the glare of the fog. And yet his legs keep striding on. It's almost as if he's no longer in control of his body – as if he's just a passenger, observing the ground roll by beneath him. His dick is hard again, pointing out straight. He has no idea why. He doesn't bother tucking it under his belt. (What's the point? Who's here to see it?) It's almost as if he's following it, like the teacher yesterday, directing the class with her walking stick. He thinks of Sam – the text message he sent the other day. Sometimes he thinks maybe he really does love Sam, and then other times he thinks maybe he just misses her, and then other times he thinks maybe he just misses having sex with her, and then other times he thinks maybe he just misses sex with anyone, and then other times he thinks he's missing something deeper and truly substantial, but he has no idea how to pinpoint this thing he misses, label it in any way that doesn't reduce it somehow, and so he tells himself it's the sex he misses, that's all, and he'll have sex again, won't he? Maybe not a whole lot, maybe not as much as someone with a full head of hair, but still enough to gather some new material with which to knock one out occasionally.

Camping Shop Mike had a perfect hairline. A straight band across his forehead, no frontal recession at all. He'd even slicked it back with gel, which Benny saw purely as showing off, a peacocking of his follicular prowess, seems (as anyone from the baldness forums would testify) any kind of wet-look products are a big no-no for those with thinning hair. Benny's almost certain that Camping Shop Mike's perfect hairline had been what triggered the incident in the one-man tent that afternoon. After Benny had got home from the camping shop, he had tried to immerse himself into the usual routine of cooking dinner and washing dishes and watching the quiz channel with Mum, but it didn't work, he found he couldn't focus, instead having to resort to an early night of masturbating himself to sleep (which had actually taken a long time and had caused him significant chafing), and during the course of this he'd found himself imagining Sam in all sorts of strange scenarios, by the end resorting to imagining her having sex with *someone else*, which is a risky strategy he sometimes resorts to because it has enough of that so-wrong-it's-right thrill to it that he finds himself climaxing after only a matter of seconds, and of course the first person he'd thought to imagine with Sam had been Camping Shop Mike, who was actually quite muscular under that uniform, and why the hell is Benny even *thinking* this stuff?

He tries to focus on the here and now. He tries to pinpoint

this exact moment as he experiences it. He is walking – he's sure of that, that much he can hold on to. He is trekking the side of a mountain in Wales. He is with Stephen, one of his oldest friends, who he can still just about hear, panting and scraping some way behind. They are somewhere between Llandegla and Llangollen. Soon Benny will be at his uncle's, smoking cigarettes, drinking beer, without this pain and the fog and this unholy weight pressing down upon him . . . but no, that's the future, for this approach to work he has to be *in the moment*, this is the only way he's going to get through it. He knows this from his routines at home. Often he can find solace in little things, household chores – cooking, cleaning dishes, hanging out washing – small tasks he can concentrate on without the risk of failure. These are his go-to ways of coping before the last-resort guaranteed anaesthesia of masturbation.

Suddenly there's a wailing some way behind.* It's almost comical – like the *woooo* a guy in a sheet would let out in *Scooby Doo* – and is followed by a succession of barks. Benny stops. He turns back. He can't make out anything. There's just the fog now. Still, he knows it's Stephen. His own personal liability, his number-one ailment. Why won't Stephen just grow up? Why won't he get a fucking *job*? The amount of times Benny's sent Stephen links for vacancies at the call centre. And Ste's intelligent, he'd have aced the interview. And working there, it's not that bad, not really. Sure, there are difficult callers, people getting angry or upset, or trying to emotionally blackmail their call handlers – Benny gets this quite often, callers asking if he enjoys what he does for a living, if his parents are proud, etc. – but since Christine he's always sure to follow procedure, reply that this is irrelevant to the caller's situation and answer their queries as best he can. He never hangs up. And sure, sometimes they don't take kindly to his answers, become abusive, and he'll have to pass the call on to his supervisor, but Rick says it's fine to do this. It's just a job, after all. It's not like Benny *likes* it. It's not as if it's a lifelong

---

* Help me.

333

career choice. But still, it's something.

He thinks of Christine on the phone, her voice cracking with emotion, how he'd recognised it straight away. Which was odd really, given that they'd only actually met a couple of times, the most memorable being at Cal's Halloween party, when she'd worn a red latex devil dress that was a couple of sizes too small, and kept having to shimmy it down to avoid showing her underwear. Sam had caught Benny staring at this and had taken offence. Another way Sam was like a cat: she could be volatile. Another: her fierce protection of her own territory. Another: she actually *dressed* as a cat for that party, ended up getting drunk, and, after they'd kissed and made up, let Benny fuck her in full costume, even purring into his ear as he came.

Somewhere Stephen lets out another cry.* This time it sounds like he could be calling Benny by name, although it's possible Benny's imagining this level of articulation. He thinks of Rick's tactic of repeating a person's name back to them in order to foster empathy, although Benny's had mixed success with it. On average Benny would estimate he passes one in twenty of his calls over to his supervisor, and each time he feels a nagging guilt, a failure on his part. He's never sure if these feelings derive from the act of passing the call over, or the content of the calls themselves. Like for instance once there was this woman who claimed she had a breadknife to her own throat, said that if she didn't have her benefits restored immediately she would sever a major artery and die right there in front of her two children. Benny passed the call to his supervisor. Another time there was a guy with a strong Geordie accent who told Benny he'd had his hours cut and he hadn't had the guts to tell his wife yet and had instead been relying on payday loan companies to survive, only now he'd found himself spiralling into more and more debt, and there was no way to pay any of it back with what he was getting from Universal Credit, and he kept apologising to Benny over and over for getting emotional about this, and occasionally there were these repeated slapping sounds

---

* Help me.

that Benny began to attribute to the caller striking his own face in an attempt to dislodge the grip his emotions had on him, and by the end he was punching a wall or a door or some other hard surface, based on the noises down the line, so Benny had no choice but to pass it on to his supervisor. Benny doesn't often give much thought to the people at the other end of the line because, as he sees it, he has so little control over their situation that it's impossible for any degree of accountability to fall on his shoulders.*

Benny keeps walking. The headache has reached a level where it feels as if his skull is literally splitting open. The fog is brighter now and he's squinting so much the path in front of him is a blur. His hair often looks worse under bright lights, e.g. those fluorescent strip-lights at the call centre, or the spotlights they had in the camping shop, or the overhead light in his car where the rear-view mirror is perfectly placed to give him a close-up of his hairline. There's a knot of pain at the top of his spine. His clothes are damp from the fog. They only have one coat between them, and Stephen is wearing it, and this is a failure in preparation. (Benny's as much to blame – he should have noticed Ste left his mac in the car.) There was a PDF of the countryside code on the GOV.UK website that could be downloaded and printed, complete with bullet-pointed rules and a colour graphic of a man with a dog on a lead, staring out over a valley. *Plan ahead*, it said. *Be prepared for natural hazards, changes in weather and other events.* Benny is simultaneously hot and cold at this moment; parts of him are burning – his armpits, his shoulders, his thighs, his crotch – but his exposed skin is goosepimpled from the chill of the fog. There's still that splinter from the fence yesterday, burrowed in the tip of the index finger on his left hand. *Leave gates and property as you find them.* He thinks back to the men in the pub on Saturday. He thinks back to the two girls yesterday, up on the tower. He remembers the man and his daughter, that papier-mâché volcano clutched to her chest.

---

* Help me.

*Consider the local community and other people enjoying the outdoors.* There is no wind now. No baaing or birdsong. The Fog is like a vacuum, nothing external can enter – although each sound Benny makes is exaggerated, like it's occurring millimetres from his ears: the crinkling of the rubbish bags, the scuffing of his feet, his breathing **IN** and **OUT**, **IN** and **OUT**. The pain in Benny's shins has an almost static-electric quality to it, a prickling from the lining of his boots. His neck is raw: a combination of sunburn and chafing from the pack. The blisters are like tiny daggers, jabbing at his toes and heels each time his foot makes contact with the ground. The blood from his thumb has trickled down inside his sleeve and is working its way towards his elbow. Another way Sam was like a cat was that sometimes, in the early days, she'd wake Benny in the night by running the tip of her tongue across his left earlobe. Benny still has the small acorn plaque in his pocket (can feel it pressing against his thigh as he walks) but the little skimming stone from Prestatyn could well be missing. His hatchet is still amongst the pile of ashes at the campsite, along with the gas canister and the charred remains of the sheep skull. *Leave no trace of your visit and take your litter home.*

The dog is barking. Stephen is wailing some way behind.\*
Suddenly Benny realises he can't smell Stephen any more, and for this he is grateful. (At least that awful, bowel-voided odour has faded, he thinks, although even from that – even from the *memory* of Stephen's smell – there comes a lurch in his stomach.) Aside from 'Dancing in the Moonlight', the only Thin Lizzy song Benny can remember now is arguably the most famous, 'The Boys Are Back in Town', which he and his uncle would also sing in the car (much to his father's dismay) and which, a few years down the line, Sam would also decry as 'a real cheesy piece of shit'; an opinion Benny found difficult to argue against. That day he noticed his receding hairline in the bathroom mirror was the same day as Benny's dad's first chemo treatment, and Mum had ordered a Chinese

---

\* Help me.

banquet to celebrate, and as Benny stood there at the bathroom mirror processing the realisation of his impending baldness, he could still taste the rich saltiness of the black bean sauce. That night at the pub, after Cal had told them about Christine and they returned to the flat with him, bore witness to the carnage there, noticed the blood on the floor, Benny tried to convince himself things weren't as bad as they looked; they'd just had one of their fights and trashed the place (maybe the blood just meant Christine was on her period or something), but then she posted that photo on social media . . . that photo . . . *Keep all dogs under effective control.* That night he masturbated over Sam and Camping Shop Mike, Benny's mind had been filled with images of the two of them, their naked bodies rutting right there on the floor of the shop, the equipment scattered, the chairs and little stove turned over, the plastic fire flickering romantically.

Sometimes Benny's memory of arriving home late to find his father smoking in the kitchen is warped to the extent that the moment of silence between them stretches out obscenely, entire minutes passing with his father's face locked in that glare of disappointment, cigarette balanced between his fingers, ash occasionally crumbling from the smouldering tip and landing there on the table in front of him.

Somewhere behind there's a scream.* Benny stops, turns back. The scream is not unlike the sort those actresses would let out in Uncle Ian's films – *bloodcurdling.* It cuts through the fog, echoes off the mountainside and down into the valley. It's followed by a crunch, like someone digging into a mound of gravel, then a clattering of scree. Benny's legs are trembling. He can feel the fog upon him, cold against the skin on his face and neck. His thumb is still bleeding within his clenched fist, little berries of blood that drip and speckle the stony ground. He knows, somehow, that this moment is of great significance. He should go back, he's sure of it. And yet, he can't. He's anchored to the

---

* Help me.

spot. He wants to shout out, ask if Stephen's OK,* but he can't seem to manage that either. There's a disconnect between mind and body. He can't do anything. He can't *see* anything either – just a few metres of the path, then *white*.

He has that feeling again, like he's being watched. He doesn't know who could be watching. He thinks back to the funeral, all that bullshit about *the Lord's eternal gaze*, and he turns from the whiteness in front of him to stare instead at the infinite whiteness above. It was probably a surprise to a lot of people, the fact they opted for a church service. Benny's dad was always clear with regards to his opinions on organised religion and Benny could feel the tension in the church that day, everyone thinking the same thing – how he'd have been the first person to point out how tasteless it all was, allowing large portions of his funeral to be hijacked by a load of indoctrinating nonsense. But it was Mum who arranged the funeral, and that stuff was important to her, and people had to respect that. The service was more for her benefit than for Benny's father's.

And then there was the poem. It was only once Benny had stepped up to the pulpit and glanced around the room at Mum and Amy and the extended family and his father's friends (a handful of whom were teachers he recognised from school) that he had experienced that sudden jolt of dread at the prospect of reading it aloud. He realised just at that moment that there was a possibility he'd completely misinterpreted it; that the various references to the arduous nature of walking might not have been metaphorical musings on the search for a meaningful life; that maybe it was only supposed to be taken at face value, and was therefore wholly inappropriate for a funeral service – a concern that only intensified at the pub afterwards, when no one even mentioned the poem, instead focusing all of their attention on Amy and how well she'd done with the eulogy (at which point Benny had been glad he didn't believe in all that stuff about Christ their lord and saviour and the kingdom of heaven, because at least it meant his dad wasn't up there looking down on them, having to bear witness to *that*).

---

* Help me.

Benny turns back to the path.* It's only then he notices that there *is* something watching.† A few feet ahead there's a sheep, standing ghostly amongst the fog. Its wool is yellowed and overgrown in a way that makes it look as if it's wrapped in a duvet. Its face is thin and clean as bone. Its eyes are staring right at Benny and, under its gaze he doesn't know what to do.‡ He could keep walking but somehow he knows the sheep won't move, and the path isn't big enough to veer around it.§ At the same time he doesn't want to turn back.¶ So instead he just stands there.** He stares out over the cliff edge.†† He wonders if, in normal weather conditions, he'd be able to make out the sea in the distance.‡‡

One thought Benny's been outright refusing to process these past few months is the possibility that the reason Uncle Ian didn't make an appearance at the funeral is because he didn't know about it. Sure, Mum put out an announcement in the paper, but what if Ian hadn't seen it? I mean, why *would* he have? No one reads newspapers any more, do they? And, even if for some unknown reason Uncle Ian *had* gone ahead and read one, what were the chances he was keeping tabs on the eulogies?

Of course, there's also a chance (and this always hits with a cold spear of dread, if Benny even dares to give it more than a moment's thought) that Benny's uncle still doesn't know about the cancer. There's a chance he doesn't even know Benny's dad was *ill*, never mind the fact that he's now dead. Benny had assumed Ian would hear about it through a mutual friend or something, but what if he didn't? What if it was Benny's responsibility to tell him? His dad was always insistent that he didn't want to see his brother because of their fallout

---

* Help me.
† H e l p   m e .
‡ H   e l p     m e .
§ H     e l p       m e   .
¶ H       e l p         m e     .
** H         e l p           m e       .
†† H           e     l       p         m       e         .
‡‡ H             e       l         p           m         e         .

over the inheritance, but shouldn't his own impending death have transcended that?

Maybe Benny's dad was just trying to save face. Maybe he was secretly hoping someone would phone Ian and explain the situation. Maybe, if Benny had gone ahead and done this – shown up at the hospice one day with his uncle in tow – he could have experienced a glimmer of joy from his father, something to remember him by that isn't that look of all-consuming disappointment he'd had to endure in the kitchen that night.*

---

\* Help me.

Benny's on the ground now.* He has no idea how or when this change occurred but here he is, slouched with his head against his pack and his hands cradled on his chest and his legs stretched out in front across the path and his dick still pitching in his shorts and he's glad, in a way, to be finally at the point where all he can manage to do is lie here. It's a relief. He's exhausted, has been for days, has been for months, and he knows it's easier, sometimes, rather than battling the relentless oppression of The Fog, to just surrender to it, let it engulf him, let it bleach his mind of all thought and purpose, and he knows now that all he has to do right in this moment is concentrate on breathing: **IN** and **OUT** and **IN** and **OUT** and **IN** and **OUT** and **IN** and **OUT** and suddenly there's this sound, this high-pitched screech, like

'Bennnnnnnnyyyyyyyyyyyyyyyyyyyyyyyyyyyyyyyyyyyy . . .'†

---

* Seriously, Ben, why not just go back and help me? At this point it isn't too late, I'm literally just lying there. My memory isn't great when it comes to that final morning (obviously by then all of my attention was required to maintain the act of putting one foot in front of the other), but I can still remember the events surrounding the fall in all their grotesque mundanity. I was trying to catch up with you, that's why I first started shouting. I had this sudden (and, as it turns out, totally justified) suspicion that you were trying to abandon me. You'd been out of sight for a while, and I was scared we'd arrive at a fork in the path or something, and I wouldn't know which way you'd gone. And so, I called out for you. Again and again, I called. And you *knew* I was calling. (What else could those sounds have been?) And I'm sorry if I didn't articulate this clearly enough at the time, but by that point those wailing sounds were all I could manage. They were a cry for *help*, man.

† Consider the state I was in. It wasn't just the aches and pains, the overwhelming fatigue. It wasn't just my stomach or my ankle or my phlegm-flooded lungs (or even the squelching indignity of my newly soiled briefs). By the time we'd arrived at the cliffside at World's End I'd reached a point of *complete physical burnout*. As I've mentioned (several times), I wasn't built for this stuff. Days on end out in the wilderness . . . it was too much. I was tired, Ben. I was so fucking tired. And I panicked, and in that state of panic I tried to catch up with you, and that's all it was: a momentary lapse on my part, a misplaced step. I still remember that jolt

from somewhere back along the path and on some level he recognises that this too is significant, something he should be acknowledging and acting upon, and yet at the same time he feels nothing. It's like when he's manning the phones at work – he can sit there and talk to the people at the end of the line for hours, dealing with callers who are often in a state of complete emotional anguish, and yet somehow none of it ever feels real. Sure, he sympathises (that's his job) but it's a surface-level sort of sympathy. A nod-along sympathy. It's like hearing a news report from a war-torn country. He knows the situation is sad, worthy of compassion. He's aware of a nagging moral obligation to be at least partly outraged. And yet, at some point, all he can do is think *oh dear* – shrug it off.

His body is numb now. He stares down at it, slumped there on the path – his torso wrapped in sodden fleece, his legs bare and scabbed and muddied, his boots finally sullied with the stain of three days' hiking – and he can't help but think of Frank, that model skeleton Stephen was so obsessed with, can't help but consider *himself* as a mere collection of bones, slotted together, layered with muscle and sinew and tender pink flesh, and suddenly the whole thing seems ridiculous, the very concept of him having

---

of dread as my trainer skid on the wet stones, my leg veering off to the right as the ground lurched up towards me. And I landed with some force, didn't even manage to raise my hands to break the fall. I seem to remember my left side taking most of the impact, shooting pains from my hip and elbow, the cold scrape of gravel across my left cheek. The first fall wasn't the *big* fall (that was still to come) but it was still a decent enough drop to put me out of action. It turned out there was a little ledge in the rock, a few metres down the cliffside, and this is where I landed. And for a while all I could do was lie there, braced, the air knocked out of me. I could hear the dog barking but there was nothing I could do. I couldn't move.

That's when I screamed your name. I knew there was no way I'd be able to carry on, not now. I'd spent that entire morning completely focused on the simple act of walking, but the abruptness of the fall was an end to all that. The tiredness, the struggle to breathe, the aches and pains and churning in my stomach – I'd managed to keep it all at a distance until then. But as soon as I hit the ground it came over me; an all-encompassing tidal wave of exhaustion.

control over any of it totally obscene, and he knows now that if he tries to raise his hand or shift his weight or make any attempt at standing and walking then nothing will happen, and it's only once he accepts this, aims his stare into the bank of fog, that the tension seems to ease a little, and the fog ceases to be this great imposing wall of fear and uncertainty and instead becomes transformative, like he's ascending into the clouds of heaven or something. He looks over at the sheep on the path ahead. A baby lamb has appeared beside it. Maybe the lamb was always there and Benny didn't notice, but he sees it now, standing to attention, its stare just as cold and indifferent as its mother's. Benny thinks of his own mum, that mug of hers with a picture of a sheep, as well as Christ her lord and saviour and the words 'Jesus Loves Ewe', faint from many dishwasher cycles. He remembers the receipts his dad kept in his books, how they faded, tucked away between the pages. He remembers his dad, how he too seemed to fade away, transformed over such a short space of time from that commanding, mammoth-like presence to a state of utter aged decay, so fragile he began to remind Benny of his nan (which is something he'd never noticed before, the similarities between them – but once his dad had thinned out and the hair and beard were gone, Benny could see how alike they really were; the nose, the jawline, the same cords in the neck, the same bony fingers and watery eyes and quivering uncertainty when attempting to stand and go anywhere by foot), and Benny's breathing heavier now, **IN** and **OUT** and **IN** and **OUT** and **IN** and **OUT**, and he's aware that somewhere out there is a fresh green valley and a blue sky and a small Welsh town called Llangollen, although, if he tries to imagine it, all he can picture is one of his uncle's model railway sets, the felt grass and papier-mâché mountains, and the little trees and cars and buildings, and how, when they'd sleep at Nan's the night before their walks, Benny was always too scared to sleep in his uncle's room due to the vast array of scary posters on the walls, and so Nan would have to arrange a bed for him in his dad's old room instead, where the train sets were set up; laying out the airbed on any free patch of carpet she could find between the strips of track, and Benny's there too, sometimes, in the camping shop fantasy with Sam and Mike, i.e. not only is he visualising this scenario playing out, but is also inserting *himself* as a part of it, standing in the darkness by the counter, observing proceedings with a sort of grim detachment, much in the same way he would watch the quiz shows with Mum, allowing his eyes to go in and out of focus, the questions and multiple-choice answers drifting in and out of legibility (**IN** and **OUT** and **IN** and **OUT**), and one problem with watching the quiz channel is the ad-breaks; because it's a channel targeted at a specifically elderly audience, each break contains several adverts for life insurance in which actors discuss the terrifying eventuality of death as if it isn't something to lie awake at night agonising over, but rather an inconvenience you simply need to get on top of and *organise*, like a trip to the dentist or a visit to the in-laws or a fucking MOT, and each time Benny and his mum have to just sit and endure this, staring straight ahead, Benny with his cigarettes, Mum her hot wine, all the while pretending that the increasing levels of poor taste aren't even occurring to them, and Benny remembers back when he and Stephen* were in that first

---

* Eventually, of course, it began to dawn on me that maybe you weren't coming back. I'd been on the ground for a while, by that point, calling out to you again and again, with nothing in the way of a response. It was strange lying there, staring up into the fog. There was an otherworldliness to it; everything was this sort of *glowing white*. I couldn't really make out anything except for the embankment to my left, the path about six foot above. The dog's head looking down at me, barking.

It was then I knew I had no choice. I was going to have to get up. I was going to have to try to climb the embankment all by myself. Which was easier said than done, right? Because in that moment I was just as out of it as you were, Ben. In that moment even the act of *standing up* seemed impossible. I knew that the only way I was likely to manage it was if I could roll onto my front, raise myself press-up-like from the ground. Bear in mind, I'd banged my head during the initial fall, was still feeling a little woozy. Also, I was still ill from whatever sickness had ravaged me the night before, and I hadn't managed to digest any noodles for about twenty-four hours (was probably a little delirious as a result). And then there was the exhaustion / the various aches and pains / the fact that I'd recently soiled myself. My head was bleeding and I remember, as I rolled

year of their friendship, how the two of them would sit in the attic room playing Xbox, and Ste's mum would occasionally appear in the little hatch entrance to tempt them with the offer of Nutella sandwiches, and how once back in school when they were out on the field at break Stephen was tackled to the ground by a gang from the year above who smeared the words *shit stabber* onto the back of his shirt using the Nutella from one of those very sandwiches, made for Stephen by his own mother as a part of his packed lunch, and how Benny had just stood there, laughing along with everyone else, although he's pretty sure Stephen has no way of knowing he'd been there, no way of being able to distinguish his laughter from the rest of the crowd, and then there was that weekend he'd gone down to visit Stephen in uni, when he'd drunk too much and made some negative comment about that Garth guy's tracksuit in the hope of impressing that incredibly beautiful Russian blonde girl that'd been with them, and it was Stephen who'd stepped in and retaliated, claiming that Benny wouldn't know irony if it'd reached out and grabbed him by the dick (which, thinking back, was pretty ironic in itself, seems this had been just what Benny had been imagining the Russian blonde to be doing) and Benny had stormed off, got a taxi back to the house, then had to sit there for over two hours on the doorstep before Stephen and his mates arrived back and let him inside, and Benny's blinking a lot now, roughly four or five blinks to each intake of breath, and the sheep are still staring,

---

over, a drop of blood making its way down the bridge of my nose, wobbling there at the tip.

I looked up. The dog was still there, although it had momentarily stopped its barking. It was looking down at me with what I can only describe as a look of hopeful expectation. I raised my arm, waved to it. Signalled that I was OK. I reached up to grab at the rockface.

And then suddenly there was a change. Something had gone wrong. Everything was shifting.

And it dawned on me just at that moment – in this sort of laughable, you've-got-to-be-fucking-kidding sort of way – that, in rolling onto my front, I had inadvertently edged closer to the cliffside. That I was now sliding, feet first, down into the valley below.

and he remembers Nan once telling him to pretend to count sheep as a way of getting off to sleep, those nights he'd lain awake, too excited at the prospect of the next day's walk to be able to drift off naturally, although he'd found it wholly ineffective, counting sheep, even though there were often little model sheep there for the counting courtesy of the fake hills of Ian's railway sets, much more reliable was his dad's method of imagining the words **IN** and **OUT** as a series of huge black letters with each in- and outtake of breath, and suddenly he remembers his uncle's bedroom again, the scary posters on the walls of those horror films, and he remembers one actually being for a film called (of all things) *The Fog*, an image of horrifying shadowy figures lurking somewhere amongst a misty landscape and the title spread out in huge black letters, and a dog is still barking, and for a moment it sounds like somewhere out there someone might be screaming Benny's name,* and he feels a slight tug of

---

* And you know, Ben, at first it didn't even occur to me how dangerous all of this was. I hadn't even considered that it could be such a long drop through the fog (as I've mentioned, I'd been paying very little attention to my surroundings up until then). This was the beginning of the fall to my death, and yet I remember being more irritated than anything, the fact that it all happened in such a slow and undramatic fashion only added to the frustration. I tried clinging to whatever I could, but there wasn't much on which to gain any sort of purchase – just gritty, wet stone – my fingers still raw from the cold. I continued to slide for a good few seconds before I noticed there were roots sprouting from the rock in front of me. The first couple I grabbed at were dried out and came away in my hands, but I gouged deeper and managed to find something fleshier, well burrowed; something with which I could maintain a more substantial grip. It was only then, as I hung there – my legs dangling freely, my entire bodyweight now at the mercy of my clinging fingers – that it occurred to me that I had no idea about the distance of the drop below.

I tried to keep focused on the path above, but it was hard by this point – the blood from my forehead was getting into my eyes, which were already blurred with tears. It was then that I began to fathom the true horror of my situation. I had this sudden image of **THE END** – not as the vague concept I'd been exploring with Frank and my photographs; not the abstract notion of the death figures of the homeless I'd been researching, murdered by the cruelty of ideological governmental policy. This time it was *real*. It

desire at this, imagining Sam screaming during sex, although the truth is he's not sure this ever actually happened, or whether it's an occurrence confined to his masturbatory fantasies (like how sometimes in the camping shop fantasy Sam has been known to scream out *Mike's* name, or else make these belittling comparisons to Benny, e.g. how Mike is much more skilled at a particular sex act, or how he's more muscular / his penis much bigger / his hair more voluminous, etc., etc.) and then suddenly Benny remembers Christine, and how she cried out his name from the other end of the line in the call centre that day, and with that he can't help but think of the photo, how it had been taken down soon afterwards, flagged 'offensive' by the social media platform to which she'd uploaded it (which meant Benny had never got the chance to go back and check if it was truly as gory as he remembers), and once when Benny was manning the calls at work a man with a Scottish accent had phoned up and just said the words *you're fucking scum* over and over, no matter what Benny had said in response, and so Benny passed him over to his supervisor, and once a woman with a very posh telephone voice had called and straight away asked to speak to Benny's supervisor, and Benny had suggested she direct her enquiry to him first to see if it was something he could assist her with, and again she had asked to speak to Benny's supervisor, and Benny had tried again to convince her, assuring her that he was able to answer any queries she was likely to have, and she asked one more time to speak to Benny's supervisor before bursting into an uncontrollable fit of sobbing, and so Benny passed her over to his supervisor, and his

---

was *me*. Right then and there, clinging to that cliff edge at World's End, I was finally having to face my *own* mortality. And suddenly it was all too horrifying to process.

Anyway, that's when I started to scream. It was all I could think to do. I was just *hanging* there, Ben. Those roots I was holding were already beginning to tear, and I could feel the strain in my arms too, and I wasn't sure which would give out first – my arms or the roots. Either way, I knew it wouldn't be long until I was taking a fall into the unknown depths of the fog.

breathing is getting heavier now, **IN** and **OUT** and **IN** and **OUT**,*
and his eyelids are heavy too, and the sheep are still just standing

---

* And it's strange, Ben, but suddenly it feels like I'm back there. As if I'm
experiencing it all over again. As if I'm *reliving* it. I keep picturing myself,
clinging to the cliffside – my hands grasping at the roots, my legs flailing,
trying to find any sort of foothold in the rock. And I'm sobbing, Ben. I'm
crying out to you. I'm a fucking *mess*, man. There are tears in my eyes and
snot down my chin and shit all down the inside of my legs, and I'm bloodied
and broken. And still, I'm trying to keep my head back, trying to keep
sight of the path. It's all I can think to do. Any second I'm still expecting
you to appear. I'm expecting your head to pop up alongside that dog's.
I'm expecting you to reach out and take me by the hand, to drag me to
safety.

And I know this is hard to understand (and illogical, given that I no
longer even have any sort of physical existence) but it's almost as if I'm
clinging to another cliff edge *right now*. I've always suspected that there's a
time limit on how long I can ride along on this little recollection of yours,
and it feels like we're fast approaching the end here, and suddenly I have
this horrible feeling that as soon as we reach that moment in the narrative
when I actually *fall*, the me that exists here and now will *also fall*, into some
even greater and more substantial abyss. I've been bound to you thus far
due to some inexplicable celestial connection, although I have a feeling that
upon my death this thread will suddenly be severed, and whatever existence
I'm still clinging to will be lost forever. That I'll be gone, Ben. Truly *gone*.
And everything I've ever been – all the memories, everything I've experienced during my short time on this earth – will be gone with me.

Because who knows what comes next? I certainly don't. I wish I could
offer you some solace with regard to that, I really do. I wish I could give
you the same reassurance your dad gave, round the campfire – his theory
that ghost stories are somehow proof of an afterlife. But the truth is, I'm
not really expecting *anything* to be waiting for me on the other side. There
have been no angels so far, no white pearly gates. I'm yet to find myself
at a cocktail party atop a cloud, sipping champagne with Warhol and Van
Gogh. Thus far, my experience of the afterlife has not given any indication
that there's a destination at the end of all this. In fact, up to now, my
experience has done nothing but confirm what had occurred to me in the
tent that previous night (my own personal sensory deprivation pod); that
death is just a long, black nothingness; a place where nostalgia and regret
are all that remain. And I'm sorry if that's disheartening for you, Benny, I
really am. I'm sorry if that happens to be a grim takeaway message from
your encounter with the other side. But sometimes the truth hurts, man.

there on the path ahead glaring at him, and he can smell them, that animal stench of wool and earth and manure, and they appear to have edged a little closer, although Benny's certain he doesn't remember noticing any actual movement on their part, and he's shaking now,* and he's cold,† and there's no screaming now, no barking, nothing but the thick silence of The Fog, and he thinks he might need to piss (although it's hard to tell, what with the combination of bodily numbness and his rock-hard erection), and his dad needed to piss a lot near the end too, he remembers, a side effect of the chemo, one that stuck around even after they'd stopped the treatment, and even when the hospice provided clear plastic containers for such occurrences Benny's dad would still refuse to use them, or else fail to inform the staff when he had, instead stashing them under his bed (possibly hoping to avoid the embarrassment of having the nurses take them away), which meant Benny would often spend entire visits trying to ignore the distinct urinal fug that gathered in that tiny room, and Benny's long since forgotten the film he and Sam went to see on their first date or what they talked about or whether they had their first kiss that night, but he can remember that Thin Lizzy song playing and him dancing in the foyer and then again out in the car park, and sometimes Sam would argue with Benny about really petty things, e.g. the varying quality of Guinness in different pubs, or how charcoal was a natural puri-fier, or how the orange Calippos weren't as nice as the seldom-seen green ones, and they'd get into real arguments about this stuff, to the extent that they'd end up screaming at each other, saying the most hurtful things, but then they'd make up with this amazing sex that would fix everything and bring them back together and would make all that arguing almost *worth it*,

---

* Because consider *my truth* here, Ben. I *needed* you. At that moment, I really needed you. This is what it was all building towards – that moment at World's End. The fall.

This was life and death, a literal cliffhanger ending. A chance for you to come back and help me.

† Why couldn't you just come back and help me?

in a way, and sometimes Benny thinks maybe that's why he wants to fuck Sam so much every waking hour of the day, as a way of throwing himself into that place of utmost intimacy again, and sometimes in the camping shop fantasy Sam and Mike will suddenly become aware of Benny standing there in the corner of the shop, although this doesn't seem to deter them from their undertakings in any way, if anything it seems to *spur them on*, (**IN** and **OUT** and **IN** and **OUT**), and sometimes when Benny's feeling particularly paranoid about his hairline he finds himself checking his fringe in the front-facing camera on his phone, which he knows is the least flattering way to assess his own appearance, but still resorts to it again and again, taking selfie after selfie, examining his hairline from various angles, until his phone's picture gallery becomes a mosaic of his own frowning face, and when he thinks back to that night he realised he was balding, Benny remembers how Mum insisted on ordering a Chinese banquet as a means of celebrating his father's first chemo session (which wasn't really the best idea, given one of the side effects being a heightened sensitivity to the saltiness in certain foods), and in fact, when Benny thinks about it now, that night was probably the last time any of them even *ate* Chinese food (them having so little to celebrate from that point on), and, in fact, when he *really* thinks about it, there's actually a strong possibility (due to his mum's habit of rinsing out and saving the tubs from their takeaways) that one of them could in fact be the very container now housing a portion of his father's remains, and Benny's not sure now if his father actually ever spoke to him directly about his position at the DWP, although his mum would sometimes intentionally discuss it with him when his dad was in earshot, some of the remarks she'd make being e.g. how it was a different world now, or how Benny couldn't afford to have such high principles, or how he needed to find his own way and make his own decisions and certain people were just going to have to get used to it (etc., etc.) and when Benny thinks back now he's certain that the look his father gave him in the kitchen that night after Christine phoned the call centre was not only a look of utter disappointment, but a look that seemed to balance that disappointment with a level of *acceptance*, as if Benny's dad knew all along that Benny was likely to fail at the little testing of morality Christine's phone call provided, as if this was actually some sort of victory on his father's part, his assumptions about his son having been proved right after all

and Benny's eyes are closed now, he's sure of it, and yet somehow, instead of the usual blackness, everything is *white*, as if the fog has somehow breached the inside of his skull, as if his brain has been bleached into pure untarnished nothingness

he can't actually feel anything at all – not the headache, nor the muscle pains, nor the cut on his thumb, nor the blisters, the chafing, the bitter chill of the fog – not a single ailment

it's almost as if his mind is a totally separate entity, unmoored from any physical existence, set adrift within a gaping blankness

and suddenly he realises that all there is left for him to do is accept this

to reassess The Fog as something positive

not a fading of his mind and soul, but rather a new beginning; an enormous unspoiled blank canvas; a great white sheet onto which he can paint these two simple words

over

and over

and over

again:

# IN

and

# OUT

and

# TIN

and

# OUT

and

# Epilogue

They enter the Miners together, Cal and Christine leading whilst Benny and Sam linger in the doorway. They'd been standing at the back during the service, which meant they were the first to leave the crematorium, and are therefore first to arrive here. The pub is relatively empty for now, just a couple of black-suited mourners over at the side of the bar where the buffet is laid out. Benny's trying not to look at them. He's looking for an appropriate place to sit, preferably a dark corner away from the entrance. Based on how many people attended the service, the place is set to fill up any second. They've managed to avoid Stephen's family so far and Benny would like to keep it that way.

They'd found each other outside the crematorium. Benny hadn't been sure if Cal was going to show up or not, but he'd spotted him and Christine as soon as they pulled into the car park. And Cal spotted them too, or Benny's car at least, had rushed over and embraced Benny as soon as he stepped out. It was strange, seeing Cal again. He looked positively dapper; his face shaven, hair gelled, his three-piece suit crisp and clean looking. Christine was even more of a shock. Her hair was red now and she was wearing a black dress that seemed a little too short for such an occasion. Her face had changed since the surgery, some crucial alteration that Benny found impossible to put his finger on, a modification to her nose or jaw (maybe both). Benny told Cal that he intended on leaving straight after the service, but Cal had insisted they drop into the Miners. After all, surely that's what Stephen would have wanted, Cal said, the two of them toasting his life over a cool pint of Guinness . . .

Benny leads Sam to a free table over at the back, whilst Cal and Christine go to the bar. Benny sits against the wall. Sam takes the seat beside him. It's possible this is the same spot he and Stephen would occupy, back on those nights they'd drink together, although right now Benny's not too sure. A lot of the tables have been moved around to accommodate the buffet.

Benny's hands are shaking. He shouldn't have come. He could be at home right now, watching the quiz channel with Mum and Delila, but here he is, exposed before everyone. Sam squeezes his knee under the table. She smiles. Benny tries to smile back, offer some reassurance that he appreciates her being here, that her presence is in some way helping.

'We won't stay long,' he says.

'I know.'

'Just one drink and we'll leave.'

'OK.'

Benny reaches into his front pocket. He's still got that final cigarette tucked away in there, the one he never managed to smoke on the walk. He's been carrying it around all week as a sort of talisman. He hasn't smoked at all since he got back. He doesn't know why. Sam said she thinks it's great, him not smoking – a commitment to a healthier lifestyle – but Benny's not convinced he'll be able to stick to it.

The pub has already begun to fill up. There's now a steady stream of fellow mourners coming through the doors. Benny recognises a few of them from school, some of which are also ex-colleagues from the call centre. Most have avoided him so far and that suits Benny just fine. He came here to pay his respects and leave, no drama.

It was the same at the crematorium. The four of them stuck to the back throughout the service. It was one of Stephen's cousins who did the eulogy and he did a good job, Benny thought, talked a lot about Stephen's childhood, his artwork, his time spent down in London. He didn't once mention Benny or the walk – which was understandable, really. The only time he seemed to struggle was when Stephen's mum erupted in an outburst of wailing on the front row. He stopped speaking then. Everyone spent a few minutes staring at their feet, waiting for it to end.

Cal arrives with a tray, hands out the drinks. There are lemonades for the girls and pints of Guinness for him and Benny, along with a couple of whiskey chasers. Benny thanks Cal and reaches for his pint. Sam raises her eyebrows in a way that suggests she isn't too happy having her choice of drink decided for her, especially since she's ended up with lemonade.

Then she spots the whiskies and frowns.

'They were on the house,' Cal explains.

'They're not on the house,' Sam says. 'Stephen's family are paying the bill.'

Cal shrugs. 'Too late now.'

Sam bites her bottom lip. She's done this a few times during the past hour, usually as a reaction to something Cal has said. She promised Benny that she would stay neutral on the subject of Cal and Christine and so far she's made good on this promise.

Cal and Christine take their seats. Cal knocks back his whiskey, takes a large gulp of Guinness, then lets out a satisfied sigh. Benny follows suit. At first he was thinking he'd take it easy, but he finds himself downing half of his pint in a series of extended chugs. Sam places a hand on his shoulder that either means to reprimand or console him, or both.

There are a few seconds of silence before Cal finally speaks.

'Ah, I don't know what to say. It's just shit, isn't it? I was saying this to you the other day, wasn't I, Chris? How totally *shitty* all this is.'

Christine nods. 'Yep.'

'Not just Ste, either. I mean *fuck*, obviously it's horrendous . . . you know . . . what happened. But it's *you* I feel sorry for, Ben. You're the one having to live with this. The things people are saying . . . I mean, it was an accident! You're as much of a victim as anyone. Isn't he, Chris?'

'Yep.'

'It's fine,' Benny says. 'You don't need to—'

'Nah, but I mean it, Ben. And I'm sorry I haven't been there, y'know? That I haven't been more of a friend. I was saying that the other day too, wasn't I, Chris? About how I should give Benny a call? Be more of a friend?'

'Yep.'

Christine hasn't looked Benny in the eye once since they met outside the crematorium. She'd always been friendly, the few times they'd met in the past, and yet today she could barely even muster a hello. She's slumped back in her seat now, her eyes fixed on her lemonade. All she's said so far is 'Yep', and each time she keeps popping the P, as if she's blowing gum.

'If I were you, I'd have marched right up to the front of the service, Ben. Sat there right beside the family. You got as much of a right as anyone. You and Ste were best mates, for Christ's sake. You've known each other your whole lives.'

Benny takes another swig of his pint. He can make out the buffet table over Christine's shoulder, is keeping an eye out for any of Stephen's cousins. There had been a slight disagreement last week over what should happen with the film from Stephen's camera. Benny had forgotten that he even *had* the camera. He hadn't bothered unpacking since he got home (not even to remove the tub of his father's ashes) and so he was slightly surprised to receive the message from Stephen's cousin, demanding Benny return it. Apparently Stephen's mum had decided she wanted the film developed so she could use some of the photos in a display she was planning, although Benny was certain Stephen wouldn't have wanted this, not if he couldn't select the pictures himself. Stephen most likely would have wanted Benny to *burn* the film, although he knew he'd never be able to do such a thing.

Instead he'd ignored the messages from the cousins, stayed in his room. Until, in the end, a few of them had shown up at the house (including the one that ended up giving the eulogy) and threatened to kick the shit out of Benny if both camera and film weren't handed over immediately. Benny's mum was ready to call the police. Delila could sense something too, began barking from the kitchen. But Benny didn't want any drama. He went out and apologised, let them have the film. They took it and left. There had been no communication since then, and that was something Benny was holding on to – the fact that they'd never explicitly told him *not* to attend the funeral.

'Anyway, like I was saying earlier, there's been a lot of changes, Ben, since . . . you know . . . since we last saw each other. Me and Chris, we're together now. Properly, I mean. We're engaged. We're getting together a deposit for a house. We're even thinking of kids in the next year or two.'

'Congratulations,' Sam says. She's staring at Christine, who is herself staring down at her lemonade, of which she's yet to take a sip. The chatter in the pub is growing around them. Cal raises his voice a bit.

'And Chris has changed too, haven't you? Given up the booze and the drugs.' (No 'yep' this time.) 'And you've probably noticed the nose-job. Cost a fortune like, but it's worth it, isn't it? We were saying so the other day, weren't we, Chris? That it probably even looks *better* than before . . .'

Benny can sense Sam's disgust at this comment. He can feel her eyes on him, willing him to offer some opposition on behalf of the two of them, an argument against the awfulness of what Cal has just said. But Benny doesn't look. Instead he focuses on the buffet table. A few of Stephen's cousins have arrived now, including the one who gave the eulogy, and they're shaking hands, patting the backs of some of the other mourners. It was a bit of a surprise, how many people were at the crematorium, considering how few friends Stephen actually had. Everyone from school had shown up. Benny remembers his father's funeral being a lot quieter. They didn't have enough people to justify hiring out the entire pub, just the function room at the side, and it had annoyed Benny, the sight of regular pub-goers in jeans and T-shirts, drinking and laughing like it was any other afternoon. He's glad that at least Stephen's family aren't having to endure that.

'Oh, and then there's the job,' Cal says. 'You know about the job, right? I thought you might have heard through the grapevine, like . . .'

Benny turns back to Cal. He shakes his head.

'The *call centre*, Ben. I'm starting next week. I'm doing my training with Rick. I'm going to be on the phones with you.'

'He doesn't work there any more,' Sam says.

'Eh?'

'He handed his notice in last week.'

Cal turns back to Benny. 'That true, Ben? You quit?'

Benny nods, takes another swig of Guinness. He's reached the end of his pint. He makes to stand, says he'll go to the bar for another, but Cal says no, not to worry, he'll get them. Sam asks if another drink is a good idea, seems Benny is driving, and Benny says yes, it's a great idea. He wants to keep drinking now, that first pint has decided it for him. They can always get a taxi home, collect the car in the morning.

'That's settled then.' Cal swallows down the rest of his own pint. 'Might have a smoke too, actually. Fancy one, Ben?'

'He's quit that too,' Sam says.

Cal grins. 'OK, boss.' He salutes Sam. Then he turns, heads over to the bar.

A few minutes pass with the three of them sitting there. Christine browses on her phone. Sam glances around the room. Benny watches the cousins over at the buffet table. They're still using it as an outpost to greet their fellow mourners. There are two there that Benny thinks he might recognise – a tall guy with sunglasses and a mullet and a long, black trench coat, and a girl, shorter, with a face pretty enough to offset the fact she appears to be wearing a man's suit and tie. And suddenly it clicks – it's Stephen's mates from uni. Garth and that Russian girl.

'Are you *really* OK?' Sam says.

Her voice takes Benny by surprise. He turns back to face her, only to find she isn't talking to him. She's staring across the table at Christine, who just at that moment looks up and makes eye contact with Benny – as if it was *him* who spoke.

'I know Cal says you're OK,' Sam says, 'but I'm asking *you*. Are you OK?'

Christine snorts, shakes her head. She slumps back in her chair. She makes as if to say something, then stops herself.

Then she shrugs. She sighs. She picks up her lemonade, gulps down the last of it, then places the glass on the table and stands.

'I'll go see if he needs a hand with the drinks.'

Benny and Sam are alone again. Benny rubs his eyes. He can feel the buzz of the alcohol already. He reaches into his jacket pocket, makes sure the cigarette is still there.

He tries to think of something to say. He's found it difficult since Sam came back. It was good of her, to fly over from Ireland just to be there for him, but still, it's been awkward the past few days. The time apart has changed her. It's not just the healthy lifestyle stuff (although she is looking skinnier than ever). It's *everything*. Her new job, her new friends, her clothes. Sam has matured over the last year and a half. Worse than that, it's becoming increasingly obvious that, for some reason, Benny hasn't.

Sam turns to face him.

'I don't want to be here, Ben,' she says. 'I don't want anything to do with him.'

'I know.'

'Did you hear what he said before? About her nose? He's a piece of shit.'

'I know.'

'When are we going to leave?'

Sam waits a few more seconds for an answer, then sighs. She rummages through her handbag, takes out several items of make-up and lines them up on the table. She opens a compact, begins to reapply her lipstick. Without Christine blocking the view, Benny is now in clear sightline of the buffet table, although luckily no one has spotted him yet. Garth and the Russian girl are still there, talking with the cousins. Garth is laughing, twirling his hands to illustrate some point he's making, probably an anecdote from Stephen's university days. Everyone around him is laughing along, including the eulogy-giver, who's now holding a half-eaten sausage roll.

Then suddenly Garth lowers his hands. He stares at the ground. The scene resets into an atmosphere of sombre respect. And then there's Stephen's mum, being led through the crowd. Benny had only been able to make out the back of her head during the service, but now he can see her fully. She's a lot older than he remembers, although whether this has been a gradual ageing or a sudden occurrence brought about by the events of the past couple of weeks, it's impossible to know. Her hair is shorter than it used to be and she looks like she's lost weight, especially in her face and neck. It's strange seeing her all in black – she was always wearing bright colours from what Benny remembers, floral skirts and home-knit jumpers. Even from a distance Benny can see how red her eyes are from crying.

She stops in front of the buffet table. She says something to the cousin who gave the eulogy and he nods in response, disposes of the sausage roll somewhere. He brushes the crumbs from his jacket and embraces her and it's at this point that Benny stands. He can't take any more. He has to get away from here. He has to get out.

Sam shouts after him, something like, 'Oh, so we *are* going?' Benny can hear her scrambling to put the make-up back in her bag. But before she's able to, he's already pushing through the crowd. He can see Cal and Christine over at the bar, another tray being laid out before them – one Guinness ready, the other still settling at the taps. But Benny doesn't want it. He needs to get back to Mum and Delila. The dog has taken a shine to Benny's mum since Benny brought her back with him. The two of them lie together in front of the TV all day and, now that he's not working, Benny usually lies with them on the adjacent couch. He'd been surprised to find Delila was a girl. It was Uncle Ian who'd dropped him back home after the walk, and at first Mum had thought the dog belonged to *him* (although she'd taken to her straight away, once she'd realised she was a stray). Delila's been a big help over the past couple of weeks – something for the two of them to focus on between the phone calls and police visits. Benny's mum had offered to come along to the funeral, but Benny told her not to. He didn't want her to leave Delila on her own. He liked the thought of the two of them being back at the house together. He took comfort knowing they were both there, waiting for him.

It's only as he's about to step out into the car park that Benny sees the door to the function room is propped open. The function room is over on the far side by the toilets and is usually out of bounds to regular pubgoers. At his dad's funeral they'd used it for the buffet, but that clearly isn't the case here.

Benny makes his way over. The room looks different to what he remembers. It appears to have been redecorated in black-and-white wallpaper, with some chaotic pattern. There are two middle-aged women there, neither of whom Benny recognises. Each of the ladies have their backs to each other, and it's only as Benny steps inside that he realises they're looking at the walls at either side. That these walls aren't papered at all, but rather lined with a collection of black-and-white photographs.

Benny approaches the back wall. It's overwhelming at first, the sheer quantity of pictures on display. They're only small – each about the size of a postcard – and they all appear to have a single subject: Frank. It's an image Benny has seen many times before on Stephen's T-shirts. And yet today it feels totally new. Maybe it's the context – a result of where Benny is at this moment, combined with the weight of the events of the past two weeks. Maybe it's the *scope* of it, the fact that there are now hundreds of Franks, all staring back at him. He can see now how each image has subtle variations – the stance, the angle, the way the lighting frames it. Some have props: wigs or items of clothing. One Frank is a businessman, sitting on his morning commute with a briefcase on his lap. Another is a cleaner, bent over with one hand on his back, hoovering the carpet. Another is a policeman; a prostitute; a teenager in a hoodie and a pair of headphones, giving a middle finger to the camera. There are more, so many more. Too many to process.

That's when Benny notices the other photos, tucked away amongst the various skeletal characters. They're landscapes, mostly, countryside scenes – patches of forest, fields and valleys – some of which could be from the walk, although at first Benny can't distinguish one from the other. It's only after a few seconds that he begins to recognise them. There's the beach at Prestatyn; the view of the town from up on the cliffside; the car park at Jubilee Tower, complete with schoolgirls and ice cream van. There's a picture of that statue from the first day, the 'Polo Mint'. There's one of their first campsite, the huge tree with the roots that had kept Benny awake long into the night. There's a picture of the barrage of cow heads they'd encountered, just outside Bodfari, the source of much laughter that afternoon. There's the skull too, he notices now – that grinning ram skull they'd discovered atop the cairn at Moel Arthur – diminished now amongst the sea of other skulls present in the photographs. And sheep. Plenty of sheep. Mothers. Baby lambs.

Suddenly Benny realises he's crying. It takes him by surprise. He hasn't cried at all these past couple of weeks – not when he saw Uncle Ian and told him what had happened; not when he'd got home and had to explain it to his mother, to the police; not even when they'd gone out in the car for the first time and he'd noticed Stephen's forgotten rain mac there on the back seat. And it's not just a few tears now, either – his eyes are *streaming*. His breaths are quickening. He's letting out this deep, tortured sobbing sound. He can't control it. It's like something has given way inside him. It's like his grief is something physical, trying to force its way out.

He gasps in surprise of himself.

One of the women behind mutters something, asks if he's OK.

'I'm sorry,' he says. 'It's just . . . I'm sorry.'

'You don't have to be sorry,' she says. 'It's a funeral. You're allowed to grieve.'

Benny closes his eyes. He can't stop the tears. He can't catch his breath. He stands there for another few minutes, not thinking about anything in particular, just trying to calm himself, bring an end to this outpouring. He's never cried like this in his entire life, as far as he remembers, not even as a child.

He's stooped forwards now, his hands gripping his thighs. His eyes and nose are running. His face is in his hands. He hears one of the women leave. The other (he's assuming it's the one who spoke) sticks around for a few minutes, pats him on the back a few times, before she also shuffles out of the room.

Suddenly he's alone.

It was Delila who had woken Benny that day on the mountainside. At least he thinks so – she was certainly barking when he finally came around, although he had no idea how long he'd been sleeping, or how long she'd been barking. He still remembers it clear as anything, his awakening on the stony ground. He remembers each individual thought that emerged at that moment; the first being that his neck was aching, a result of the position he'd been lying in – his head tipped back over the pack. The second was that the fog had cleared, evident due to the glaring sunlight, the clear blue sky above. The third, that his groin was wet (although in that moment his brain avoided processing any possible reason for this).

The fourth, that it was now just him and the dog. The sheep were gone. Stephen was gone.

The fifth, also that Stephen was gone, although this time the concept felt somewhat more significant. Stephen had disappeared from the mountainside, sure, Benny could see that with a mere turn of his head, but there was more to it than that. Stephen had departed in a much more substantial way and Benny could feel it in the stillness of the valley.

Benny was trembling all over. He tried to stand up, although at first he couldn't manage it – it was almost as if he was strapped to the ground. Then he realised – it was the pack. He was lying back against it, the straps hooked at his elbows, and from that angle he didn't have the power to raise himself. Eventually he untangled his arms from the straps and managed to climb to his feet, and for a few seconds he just stood there, eyes closed, trying to maintain his balance. He felt like he'd been to the bottom of the ocean. He was so weak it was as if his body had been drained of blood. There was a mouldering staleness on the inside of his mouth and the fingers of his right hand were still bloody from the cut on his thumb and it was only once he was standing up that he noticed there was a warmth to the wet patch in his trousers, a stickiness all down the inside of his thighs.

Delila was a way back along the path. She was looking out over the edge of the cliff, still barking at something. Benny tried to call her. Back then she didn't have a name, so all he could shout was 'dog' – to which he received nothing in the way of a response. Now that the fog was clear, Benny could make out the mountains they'd crossed that morning, the road up from the marshes. He could see the forest and the fields beyond and, if he squinted, a thin band of blue that could well have been the sea on the horizon. Still, they'd managed a fair distance, that much was clear. Stephen had done well to make it that far.

There were skid marks on the stones about thirty feet away, indicating the precise distance Stephen had made it to. This was where Delila now stood, barking down the cliffside, and even then Benny knew what she was barking at. He didn't have to go and look. He didn't have to see it for himself. But still, he found himself making his way towards her. He found himself stopping at that precise point on the path. He found himself kneeling there – staring down into the valley below.

The cliffside was rock mostly, only the odd sprouting bushel of yellowed grass or heather. There was a slight ledge just below them, and then a sheer drop, and that's where Stephen's body lay. He'd landed on his front, his arms stretched out at either side. From that height it appeared as if his head was missing, although Benny knew this was impossible, that really it was just the way he'd landed, his chin tucked forward to his chest. His legs were out straight behind him, almost as if he'd made a purposeful dive to the ground, although the longer Benny looked, the more unnatural the positions of his feet seemed (as if one of the legs was on back to front). His track-pants were pulled up, displaying not only his ankles, but his shins too, one of which was cut and bleeding. There wasn't much blood other than that. His pack was open beside him, his collection of soiled T-shirts strewn across the rocks, and there was something about that part of the image that didn't seem real. Almost as if it had been positioned that way. Curated.

Benny turned away. He couldn't look any more. He sat there for a while on the path, curled into a ball, his forehead pressed into his knees. Delila stopped barking and sat down beside him, her head resting on his foot. She let out a deep exhalation, like a sigh. Everything was still and silent except for Benny – his body trembling, his teeth chattering. He held himself like that for a while.

Eventually it occurred to him that he needed to do something. He needed to get help. He reached into his pocket for his phone, switched it on. He only had 1% battery remaining but now there was one bar of signal and suddenly the phone began to buzz. Messages came pouring in, a backlog from the past few days.

Some were from his mum, asking if he was OK, if he was having fun, if he was safe. One from his uncle asking what his schedule was, when and where he wanted to meet up. There was even a message from Sam, a response to his text a few days earlier. She said she'd been trying to call him to talk about things, only she couldn't get through.

Benny didn't read through these texts – not beyond the first few sentences displayed on the home screen. He knew he had to act quickly. His phone would give out any moment. He probably only had enough battery for one call. He had to make it count.

Still, he didn't know who to call. Right then, the only person he wanted was his dad.

Suddenly there's more padding on the carpet. Someone else is entering the room. Benny wipes his eyes with his sleeve, straightens up. He assumes it's Sam or Cal come to find him, bring him back to their table. But when the person finally speaks, he doesn't recognise the voice.

'Stunning, isn't it?'

It's Garth. Benny's a little taken aback at the sight of him – that flowing coat, the little sunglasses, the wavy blond mullet. He's holding a glass of red wine in one hand, a bottle in the other, which he places on the carpet beside him. It's hard to tell where he's looking at first, although soon Benny realises he's staring straight ahead, at the collage on the wall.

'Um, yeah,' Benny answers. 'It's . . . something.'

'His work was always impressive but to see it gathered together like this . . . it really gives it *impact*.'

'Yeah . . .' Benny looks around. He's half expecting that Russian girl to be here too, but she isn't. Just Garth.

'I expect it'd bring him equal parts joy and horror, the fact that it's on display here. He was always quite private about it.'

Benny glances down at his feet. He wants to wipe his face again, but at the same time he doesn't want to draw attention to the fact he's been crying.

'Well,' he says, 'except the T-shirts.'

'Well, yes, of course,' Garth says. 'Apart from those.'

Garth takes a sip of his wine.

'I don't know if you remember,' he says, 'but we've met before . . .'

'Yeah,' Benny says. 'I remember.'

'A few years ago . . .'

'Back in uni.'

'In university, yes. I remember you and Stephen were close.'

'You could say that.'

'I'm told you were with him those last few days?'

'I was, yeah.'

'Well, at least that's something. At least he had you. It's something I've been trying not to dwell on, the fact that I wasn't there. That we hadn't spoken in so long. It just sort of happens after university, doesn't it? You drift apart.'

'I guess.'

'I should have done more, though. Tried harder to keep in touch.'

They stand there for a few seconds, staring straight ahead. Benny avoids looking directly at any of the photos, instead concentrating on a gap near the bottom; a slice of yellow, floral wallpaper amongst a sea of glossy black-and-white grimness. Benny can feel the rising pressure to say something – anything.

'So,' he says, 'you a big, famous artist yet?'

Garth laughs. 'Sort of. I'm teaching now. At the university.'

'Like a lecturer?'

'Like a lecturer, yes.'

'Aren't you a little young to be a lecturer?'

'They don't seem to think so.'

'Right.'

'And how about you?' Garth says. 'What are you up to? Last time I saw you you were studying . . . engineering, was it?'

'I'm between jobs.'

'Oh, right.'

Benny wipes his face, then puts his hand back in his pocket. The only sound is the mummering from the pub behind them. Garth swallows down the rest of his wine and for a moment

Benny thinks that's it, he's going to leave. But then he stoops for the bottle, tops up his glass.

Benny reaches into his jacket pocket. The final cigarette is still there. He runs his fingers along the paper, feeling all the bumps and creases.

'Can I ask you something?' Benny says.

'Of course.'

'Do you ever *hear* him?'

'Who?'

'Stephen. Like, his voice. Do you ever hear him speaking to you?'

'No,' Garth says. He taps his lip with his finger, waits for a moment before adding, 'Why? Do you?'

'Sometimes.'

'*Speaking* to you?'

'Yeah, it's weird. It's almost as if he's right here beside me, you know? Like his voice is as clear as yours is now.'

'Stephen's?'

'I think so.'

Garth turns from the collage to look Benny in the eye. He takes off his sunglasses. 'How often does this happen?'

'Quite regularly, at first. Like, right afterwards. Less so now. It's mostly when I'm thinking about stuff. You know, thinking over everything that happened.'

'What does he say?'

'All kinds, really.'

'Like what?'

'Like all kinds. Sometimes he talks about you.'

'Me?'

'Sometimes.'

'What about me?'

Benny smiles. 'That would be telling.'

Garth frowns, turns back to face the wall.

'Mostly it's good stuff,' Benny says. 'Although, he missed you, I think. Near the end. He wanted to see you again.'

They stand in silence for a few more minutes. Garth sips his wine. Benny puts both hands to his face, rubs at his eyes, then tips his head back to face the ceiling. He takes a deep breath – exhales. He laughs suddenly, out of nowhere. He has no idea why.

Garth doesn't react to any of this. He just keeps on staring at the wall.

Once his glass is empty, Garth reaches for the bottle again. Only this time he knocks it over. Wine glugs onto the carpet.

'Shit.'

Benny takes out the cigarette. It's a sad sight, crooked and crumpled from days of being carried around, passed from pocket to pocket. He straightens it out between his fingers as best he can, places the filter to his lips. It's only then that he realises he doesn't have any matches.

'Do you smoke?' he says, the cigarette bobbing at his mouth.

'I'm all right, thanks.'

'I wasn't offering. I just need a light.'

Garth glances around. 'I don't think you *can* smoke in here . . .'

'You got one, or not?'

Garth removes a lighter from somewhere beneath his coat. Benny takes it from him. He strikes it a few times but there's just the *chkk* sound – no flame.

'It's a dud.'

'Sorry.'

Benny keeps trying. (*Chkk chkk chkk.*)

'This the only one you've got?'

'Sorry.'

Benny shrugs, hands it back. 'I'll find one,' he says.

He turns from Garth and the wall of photos, steps back out into the main body of the pub. The bar is even busier now, the crowd of mourners spilling over into the once empty space between the function room and the booths at the back. Most people are in conversation, although a few glance over. Benny can feel their eyes upon him.

He turns to a woman beside him, an older lady with short grey hair and a black blazer, asks if she has a light. She nods and reaches into her handbag, takes out a box of matches, and

Benny strikes one and lights up. He inhales, breathes deep, releases a cloud of smoke. More people are turning to look at him now, but he pays no attention. He hands back the matchbox and proceeds to the main entrance, out into the car park.

It's late in the day and across the street the sun is low behind the rows of houses. Benny takes another drag, cupping the cigarette to keep it from falling apart. Already he's aware of the effect of the nicotine; a lightness within him; a sense of calm that only comes from the consummation of a long-awaited smoke. The sky is pinkened by the fading of the sun and there are wisps of purple cloud, and it all makes for quite a view. Benny feels that wave of emotion coming again, the same as back in the function room, only this time he manages to control himself, swallow it back down.

'Shit,' he says. 'I'm sorry, Ste. I'm fucking sorry.'

He turns back at the pub. He knows that somewhere Sam will be searching for him. He knows that Cal is there too, waiting to catch up over a fresh pint of watery Guinness. He thinks of Mum and Delila, at home with the quiz channel blurring and the dinner still to be prepared; the inevitability of cooking and eating and washing the dirty dishes. He thinks of the hours that will run into days and weeks and how time will go on now, always from this moment, a marker in his life like a pin on a map. For a moment he almost wishes he could swap with Stephen. Not out of charity, but rather a simple desire to have it all done with.

Then he feels ashamed of thinking such a thing.

'I'm sorry,' he says again, although he can't help but wonder if this is pointless. If he's talking to no one.

# Acknowledgements

To those who walked with me (Schulze, Matty, Josh, Liam); to those who wrote with me (Mike, Matt); to those who taught with me (Robert, Horatio, Jeff, Caroline, Jim); to the libraries that housed me whilst I wrote (Central, LJMU, Liverpool Uni); to those who edited my work (Kate, Josie, Amy, Helen); to my parents, my family, my favourite person (Nat), and everyone who ever asked how the second novel was coming (but even more so, those who knew not to) – thanks.